TEMPLARS RISING

ORDER OF THADDEUS • BOOK 6

J. A. BOUMA

EmmausWay
PRESS

PROLOGUE
PALESTINE. 1340.

The German priest winced as he stretched his back. One hand pressed against the base of his spine as his body contorted forward, the other continued easing his steed along the rocky path along the Dead Sea's shore.

Thunder rumbled in the distance as he settled in for the final leg of a journey that had begun several months before, the wind picking up speed and spraying a misty surf into his face from the sea. The pungent taste of salt and death settled on his lips and tongue as he rode forth. He smiled, nonetheless, for it meant he was that much closer to his destination.

A month into the new year, the man of not-yet-sixty had left his beloved Sudheim parish in the southern wing of the Holy Roman Empire, setting off toward the Holy Land on a once-in-a-lifetime pilgrimage to venerate the holiest sites of his faith. Other than his cassock, his horse, and a leather flask of water, the man bore nothing but a deep, burning passion within his bosom to walk the shores his Lord had walked, to travel the streets his Teacher had taught, to bear witness to the sites of his saving death and glorious resurrection. Faith sparked his journey, the charity of his brethren carried him along, and his Savior sustained him each step of the way.

A rumbling thunder echoed once again across the sea from the far distance as he plodded along the rocky path, the sea beginning to churn with frothy prediction just beyond the shore. As he plodded along, he meditated upon a psalm that had been his anchor of hope for the perilous journey, one of the Songs of Ascent promising assurance of God's protection. He fixed his gaze on the darkening horizon beyond that looked of fierce storms, and began to softly quote Psalm 121 aloud: *"I lift up my eyes to the hills—from where will my help come? My help comes from the Lord, who made heaven and earth."*

"'The Lord will keep you from all evil; he will keep your life,'" he mumbled, his steed jolting at a flash of light and thunder just over the sea. He steadied the beast, then finished the psalm: *"'The Lord will keep your going out and your coming in from this time on and forevermore.'"*

He reached for the leather water flask slung around the front of his saddle, uncorked the cap, and took a long satisfying drink. He corked it and offered a prayer of thanksgiving in response to the psalm.

Thank you, Lord, for keeping my goings and comings thus far. Continue to—

His steed stopped short and whimpered in protest, shuffling away from the shore and backing up into a grassy bank of sand. The priest's heart began galloping forward instead of the horse, disturbed by his faithful friend's sudden response.

The last time this had happened, a trio of Saracens had come out from the shadows just before a highway bridge near Aleppo. They were dark and hooded, brandishing their *kilij* one-handed swords with ill intent, dented and pockmarked with years of use, and demanding payment for access to the way beyond. A bridge tax, they called it. The man tried to reason with the echoes of a menacing terror from centuries past, but it was no use. He was just thankful they were only demanding money. Terrorists of their kind from generations past had put scores of brothers and sisters in the faith under the yoke of slavery—not to mention under the sword for their refusal to recant their beliefs. After negotiating a fee for passage, the priest paid them off and was sent on his way.

And now his four-hoofed companion was indicating a replay of the same dark scenario.

The surf lapped angrily against the shore and a wind whirled along its waters, carrying with it the rain he had seen on the horizon. He slung his flask back around his saddle and pulled hard on the reins to command his steed forward.

The beast took a hesitant step, then stopped and whimpered again—more loudly, more alarmingly.

A dark movement caught his attention. Not one, but two men. They were hustling across the rocky seashore bearing large sacks, a boat left overturned in their wake. They were older than he, their white hair long and unkempt and tied in ropy tails behind them—and moving toward him, swift and sure. They looked Caucasian in origin, their skin a curious weathered tan, not like the Arabs of the region.

One of the men signaled the priest with a raised arm. His horse skittered uneasily in response; he understood the feeling.

The other man waved at him, as well, motioning for him to halt. They were shouting something at him now as they scrambled up the rocky Dead Sea banks, the rain picking up pace. The priest didn't know whether to go or stay, whether they were friend or foe.

He was about to find out.

"Bonjour!" one of them said in a heavy French accent, a short, stocky man with arms bulging through his drenched shirt.

Fluent in French along with the official German of his homeland, he responded in kind. "Bonjour, monsieur."

"Bad time to be traveling along the shore, pilgrim."

"I'm just passing through," the priest said, his horse dancing again as the rain began pounding the men.

"We've got dry clothes and warm food up the road," the other man said, tall and forearms rippling with battle-hardened muscle. "Same for the horse."

"Thank you kindly," the priest said nervously, unsure how to respond. He could sure use a change of clothes. And his belly was already rumbling in protest at the thought of a hot meal. His four-legged companion seemed to be as eager for the rest.

The shorter man said something to the tall man. He nodded, and said, "The Dead Sea will overtake us soon if we keep standing here. Follow us if you will, don't if you don't. But we're heading back to our homestead up the hillside."

The two men darted up the road, bearing their heavy loads with the kind of ease the priest had seen from men returning from battle.

He uselessly wiped his face as the rain continued its assault, glancing behind him and then toward the men ahead who had disappeared around a bend. Worried he would miss the promised relief, he kicked his steed in the ribs and instructed it onward.

He rounded the bend just in time to see the men climbing a narrow trail that rose upward into the mountainous woods. He hesitated, but followed after them. They were running now, but his horse kept up with ease. Several minutes later, they arrived at a clearing of grass and dirt mounted by several dwellings made of rough-hewn logs. People were running in the rain, young women and children and young men, from one dwelling to the next. The two elders ran toward a larger structure of stone, a more established home commanding the center of what seemed like a small village.

The priest urged his companion onward, a few of the other dwellers giving him looks of confusion as he dismounted and followed the men into the comfort beyond the open door.

The warmth from a fire raging inside a large stone fireplace slapped him in the face as he entered. The smells wafting from well-tended stoves was the final blow. He stumbled with joy toward a long wooden table commanding the center of the room, not being able to recall the last time he had either warm lodging or hearty food.

"So then, the promise of dry clothes and warm food was enough to overcome your worries of two elderly men rushing you from the sea?" the short man said with a chuckle.

The priest smiled and chuckled himself. "Let's just say, my belly overruled my brain."

"I should think so!" the tall man said, extending his hand in a greeting of friendship. "Welcome to the Holy Land, friend."

The priest took in a breath of relief, smiled, and shook it. "Thank you. For the welcome as well as the offer."

"Our pleasure," the man said, motioning for the priest to have a seat at a long table set for twelve fashioned from rough-hewn wood, like the dwellings outside. "Sit, my friend, sit!"

The priest nodded and took a seat on the bench stretching the length of the table, sitting next to its head. A woman entered from a room off to the side bearing a large kettle, steaming and smelling of roasted meat and cooked vegetables. Behind her, a younger woman came bearing a good-sized loaf of bread and set it at the center of the table, its heavenly scent filling the space with dizzying memories of his home back in Sudheim.

"My name's Amis," the short man said, sitting across from him and reaching his hand across the table. The priest took it.

"And Ludolph is mine," the priest said, smiling and nodding to each of his hosts.

"This here's Amiles," Amis said, gesturing at the tall man as he took his seat at the head.

The priest couldn't help but grin at their names, Amis and Amiles.

"Is something funny?" Amiles asked.

The priest snapped his head up and shook it. "Not at all. It's just that your names, Amis and Amiles. Like the old French romance *Amis et Amiles*, the one about the legend of friendship and sacrifice."

Both men leaned in close at the mention of the poem, drilling their guest with searching eyes.

Ludolph looked from Amis to Amiles, easing back on the bench under their discomforting gaze.

After a few penetrating seconds, the two men eased back themselves. "Miriam," Amiles said, handing the priest a chunk of bread, "we have ourselves a guest this day. Ludolph of..."

"Sudheim," the priest said, smiling gratefully at the gift and nodding to the woman who was now ladling bowls of the scrumptious stew. Rabbit, if his nose placed it right.

The two men looked at each other. "The Holy Roman Empire," Amis said.

The priest nodded again and thanked Miriam for the fruits of her labor. The woman left the men alone to their bowls and their conversation.

"Let us pray, shall we?" Amiles said.

The three folded their hands and bowed with reverence. Amiles and Amis prayed together, saying:

> *Lord Jesus Christ, Holy Father, eternal God, omnipo-*
> *tent, omniscient Creator, Bestower, kind Ruler*
> *and most tender lover, pious and humble*
> *Redeemer; gentle, merciful Savior, Lord! We*
> *humbly beseech Thee and implore Thee that*
> *Thou may enlighten us, free us and preserve the*
> *brothers of the Temple and all Thy Christian*
> *people, troubled as they are.*
> *Thou, O Lord, Who knowest that we are innocent,*
> *set us free that we may keep our vows and your*

*commandments in humility, and serve Thee and
act according to Thy will. Dispel all those unjust
reproaches, far from the truth, heaped upon us
by the means of tough adversities, great tribula-
tions and temptations, which we have endured,
but can endure no longer.*

"Amen," the two elderly men said, dutifully crossing themselves before attacking their stew.

"Amen," the priest said in agreement. He reached for his
spoon in silence, troubled by the prayer. Not for the contents of
the supplication, but for a single line connected to a distant
memory within the Church.

The brothers of the Temple...

He shoved a spoonful of the still-steaming concoction into
his mouth, considering its words. But then he smiled and
hummed with pleasure; he had died and gone to Paradise! It
had been months since he had chomped into juicy, tender,
scrumptious morsels of any kind of meat. Let alone vegetables
and warm bread. He took another bite of bread Amiles had
handed him earlier. He checked his manners at the door as he
ate with ravenous abandon.

Amiles asked, "So, you're a Christian pilgrim, off to see
sights of the faith?"

The priest startled, unsure how to respond. How could they
have known?

"The cross, around your neck," the tall man said as he
chewed his stew, pointing at the object of gold peeking out
underneath the folds of Ludolph's coat.

Ludolph grinned. "I am." He startled again as something
caught his attention behind Amis, resting against the fireplace.

Two swords, the firelight glinting off their long blades
polished to a reflective sheen.

He traced one of the wondrous weapons with his eyes,

noting a curious pattern etched along its surface and gold accenting the guard, wondering who these men were who bore such—

Then he caught sight of a symbol he hadn't heard word of in a quarter century.

A cross etched in the top of the hilt, its four ends slanting inward toward the center. He furrowed his brow in confusion— and hopeful expectation.

Could it be true?

Suddenly, the priest was falling backward off the back of his bench, and Amiles was upon him, a knife held at his throat.

"Who are you?" the tall man demanded.

The priest gasped for breath as the man held the blade firm, drawing a line of blood.

"Answer me!" the elderly man screamed, his hold far more powerful than his age would suggest.

"A priest," Ludolph managed, "from the town of Sudheim. I've been traveling for months on pilgrimage to the Holy Land." He struggled against the man, but Amiles gritted his teeth and continued holding fast.

The priest glanced at the swords again, then back at the man on top of him. He said lowly, "Is it true? Are you a remnant of the lost Order of the Knights?"

Amiles recoiled, stumbling backward off the priest and twisting his face in confusion. "Remnant? Lost Order? Of what treachery do you speak?"

Ludolph scrambled up from the floor and glared at the two men, Amis matching his companion's disbelief.

"Then it is true? You're members of the Poor Fellow-Soldiers of Christ and of the Temple of Solomon?"

The men nodded and revealed to him they had been Templars, and they recalled for him their last memories of their order, of their fellow knights being slaughtered during the desperate fighting at the fall of Acre in 1291. The two men had been taken captive, and for nearly fifty years they had eked out their lives as woodcutters.

Amiles stood and returned to his seat, apologizing for the attack. He motioned for the priest to join them again. Ludolph nodded and returned to his place at the table.

"Burgundy was the place I called home," explained Amis, ripping another chunk from the bread.

"And I Toulouse," said Amiles, returning to his stew.

The priest nodded in recognition, and said, "So you've been living in these mountains along the Dead Sea ever since, cut off from all communication with Christendom all these years? "

"Ay," Amis said with a food-filled mouth.

Amiles continued, "We survived by working in the Sultan's service, taking for ourselves wives and having children, and then eventually grandchildren."

Ludolph glanced at the door. "The people I saw scurrying about as I rode up?"

"Ay," Amis said again.

The priest thought this was all too remarkable. A forgotten remnant of the powerful Knights Templar holed up in the mountains along the Dead Sea! He set his spoon down and leaned back at the thought that there had been survivors of the most powerful monastic order in Christendom, considering the revelation and its ramifications. The two men continued eating as he stroked his beard in contemplation.

I wonder...

"What do you know of the events in Paris?" Ludolph asked the men.

Amis kept eating, and said, "What events?"

"Surely you know of the suppression of the Order just twenty-eight years ago."

Both men set down their spoons and looked at each other, their faces clearly betraying their ignorance.

"What's this?" Amiles asked.

"King Philip IV instituted a campaign of mass arrests, rounding up every one of the Templars, raiding your compounds and eventually burning your Grand Master at the stake."

Their mouths fell open with the pain of the realization.

"Jaques de Molay is dead?" Amis said with soft disbelief.

The priest crossed himself, bowed his head, and nodded silently. Then he crinkled his brow with wonder and asked, "I wonder, how did you survive the siege?"

Amis answered, "Many of our brothers boarded ships bound for Crete once it was clear the fortress would fall. However, we missed the boat, instead taking refuge in a tunnel that ran the length of Acre, stretching from our compound through the city and to safe harbor."

Ludolph nodded, then sat back and folded his arms. He steeled his face with resolve, and said, "You will return with me back to Christendom, you and your families."

"What?" Amiles exclaimed, looking to Amis with a twinkle of hopeful expectation in his eyes.

"Perhaps, together with your families, despite the scandal of the suppression of your brothers, you will be honorably received at the papal court, allowed to live out the remainder of your lives in peace back in your homelands."

"You can make that happen?" Amiles said, leaning forward.

Ludolph leaned forward himself and smiled. "I can. And, perhaps, you will rise again to new life, with a renewed mission for the sake of the Church."

The men looked at each other, grinning widely and saying with excitement: *"Non nobis, Domine, non nobis, sed Nomini tuo da gloriam."*

The priest nodded with satisfaction.

Indeed. Not unto us, O Lord, not unto us, but unto thy Name give glory.

CHAPTER 1

JERUSALEM, ISRAEL. PALM SUNDAY.
PRESENT DAY.

B*urr, Burr, Burr* the horn sounded clearly with irritated purpose from the street below outside the open window, carried along by the Mediterranean breeze tinged with the heavenly scent of salt and baking challah bread and juniper trees from the surrounding hillside.

Silas Grey rolled his eyes and huffed at his roommate's impatience as he slid his arms into the sleeves of a light blue polo shirt. He grabbed his mug of stale hostel coffee from earlier in the morning that had long gone cold, as well as a packet of Camels and a lighter, then sauntered over to the window.

He took a sip of the nasty brew, the noon sun streaming through a cloudless sky upon his face as he reveled in the view. He set his mug down on his nightstand, then pulled out a cigarette. He lit it, drew in the nicotine-laced air with pleasure, held it, then exhaled the cloud out the window, raking a hand through his thickened hair and pushing his bangs to the side. For nearly twenty years he had kept it close-cropped thanks to Uncle Sam's grooming insistence. The past few months seemed like as good a time as any to take back control of that part of his life. About the only thing he had power over these days.

He stuffed the pack and lighter in his pants pocket and licked his lips, then breathed deeply of the afternoon air still breezing through the window into their modest room, taking in the sight before him: the pale stone walls of Old City Jerusalem, weathered with age and pockmarked with long-held memories stretching to the ancient Kingdom of Israel—ones that still provoked visceral adoration and ecstasy from the faithful. He took another drag on the cigarette and searched for his impatient roommate down below when his phone buzzed with irritation in his pocket.

He brought out the device and saw a text from his roomie, Matt Gapinski. It read: *Silas! Get your butt moving. We're cruising for a bruising as it is from Grandpappy. Another minute longer and he'll whip us good from here to kingdom come!*

Silas smirked. He clenched the cigarette between his lips and texted back: *Hold your horses! I'm on my way.*

He took a final pull of pleasure, then put out the cigarette on a tray sitting on his nightstand. He retrieved his mug and downed the rest of his coffee, grimacing at the combination of burnt cardboard and tobacco as he walked the brown ceramic mug over to the bathroom. Lying next to his sink was his watch, a beat up Seiko with fake gold plating his dad had given him as a high school graduation gift. He'd never left home without it, even through his tours in Iraq and Afghanistan with the Army Rangers. The gift held special memory since his father's passing.

He put it on and walked back to the in-room safe. He punched in the combo then retrieved his trusty Beretta M9, his weapon of choice for his newest gig, a holdover from his days with the Rangers.

Because as Gapinski advised him on Day One of his new career with the Order of Thaddeus: Never leave home without cold, hard steel.

He slid in a magazine, then stuffed another one in his pants pocket. Gapinski sounded forth his irritation for a second time. Silas rolled his eyes again, then stuffed the weapon at his spine underneath his polo.

It's gonna be a long day with this one.

Silas jogged down the stairs and out the front door to the Golden Walls Hostel anchored across the street from the northern front of the massive walls surrounding the Holy City near Herod's Gate. He looked right, then left, searching for Gapinski and their rental.

A man was yelling in Hebrew and waving his arms wildly. He pointed at a silver Peugeot and then at the road, before motioning to a red-paneled delivery truck parked behind the car, clearly worked up about something.

Bingo.

"No hablo Hebrew, amigo," Silas heard through a cracked window on the passenger side as he approached their rental angled and idling in front of the truck.

The man with long twisted locks of hair on either side of his face and a wide-brim black fedora jerked back from the car suddenly as Silas approached.

Silas put his hands up and pointed at the passenger door. He smiled and opened it, then quickly slid inside and rolled the window back up. The man threw his arms up in frustration and mumbled something as he sauntered back to his truck.

"About time, dude!" Gapinski said, throwing the car into gear and pulling out onto Sultan Suleiman Street with a jerk. A chorus of horns protested angrily from behind.

"Right back atcha, pal," he said with a wave. "Haven't a clue what bee was buzzing around in that man's bonnet, but glad you got here when you did or I would have been a skewered shish kebab, for sure."

"I could venture a guess why..." Silas mumbled as they eased north onto Route 60, shoving his hair to the side again.

Gapinski merged with the flow of traffic out of the Holy City and continued with it onto Route 1. So far, it was easy go. Not so much the other way around as the Christian faithful flocked into the city at the start of Holy Week.

"Happy Palm Sunday, by the way," he said, slipping into an easy rhythm as he snaked around through parched, packed earth on the way toward the Sea of Galilee for the day's event.

"Happy Palm Sunday to you, too," Silas said. "And sorry for running late. Sort of a bad habit."

"Not a problem, my man. I'll just blame you when Grand-pappy lays into us for being late. He's one of those punctual types, and he expects everyone else to fall in line. Anyway, ever been to the Holy Land during Holy Week?"

He shook his head. "No, actually, I haven't. Celebrated Mass at St. Peter's Square with Pope Benedict five or six years ago, but never in Jerusalem."

"Oh, yeah? How'd you manage that?"

Silas's smile faded as the memory floated to the surface.

His former academic mentor from Harvard, Henry Gregory, had invited him along for a week of lectures and shoulder-rubbing at the Vatican leading up to the Easter Vigil at sunset. The man had been a sort of second father to Silas after his own father had died tragically in the Pentagon during the 9/11 terrorist attacks. Then a year ago, Silas had witnessed Gregory perish in a terrorist attack during a symposium on the Shroud of Turin, the burial cloth of Christ, at Georgetown University. The ill-fated event nearly ended his own life and radically altered what little was left of it.

Which lead him to sitting in a silver Peugeot traveling along a throughway in Israel as an operative of the Order of Thaddeus and representative of the ancient Church organization during Holy Week festivities in Old City Jerusalem.

He shook away the memory and took a breath, then simply said, "A connection, from a friend."

Gapinski nodded. "Right on. Well, I'll tell you what, you're in for quite a treat! Nothing in the world like walking the streets that Jesus walked before he bled out on the cross to give your faith new energy, new perspective. Sort of a shot of moonshine into the veins of your Christianity, if you hear what I'm saying."

Silas chuckled. "I'm sure it is. It's just too bad our fellow teammates can't enjoy the shot along with us. You sure Radcliffe and Celeste and Naomi were alright with me going in their place?"

The Order Master, Rowen Radcliffe, and his immediate boss of Project SEPIO, Celeste Bourne, had arranged for Gapinski and him to represent the Order at all the major Christian events. Silas was never one to turn down free travel, especially to the Holy Land, but it seemed like a cushy gig for the new guy. He had worried others, like the other newer recruit, Naomi Torres, would resent him for getting to enjoy a perk so soon in his career.

"It's all good, bro. Radcliffe's gone to these outings so often they've almost made him a Grand Marshall of the city's Holy Week events. Celeste and Naomi went last year. My turn was up, and since you're the new guy, I thought the Order needed a solid broly week."

Silas couldn't help but grin at the thought. *Broly week for Holy Week. Nice.*

He rolled down his window a crack to let in some of the warm air breezing by their car. He settled back into his seat for the drive as they left behind civilization and ventured out into the lonely, rugged outback of the Israeli countryside. It was great to get out into the field again after being stuck on desk duty the past few months at the Order's headquarters deep underneath the Washington National Cathedral in Washington, DC. All new recruits got the treatment, he was told, which was fine. Because as a former professor at Princeton University, he lived for research. But as a former Army Ranger, he also lived for adventure. SEPIO satisfied both in spades.

What a year, he thought as they passed a small village nestled in the barren hillside. Never in a million years would he have thought he'd be back traipsing across the Holy Land as an operative of the Order after what went down a year ago.

But as they say, the good Lord works in mysterious ways.

After being dumped by his former employer, Princeton University, he had been officially recruited as an operative of the ecumenical religious order of the Church stretching back to its earliest days and founded by one of Jesus' disciples, Jude Thaddeus. As the patron saint of lost causes, he had already sensed the need to establish a beachhead in the Church's mission to preserve and contend for its central teachings. He exhorted the Body of Christ as much in one of his letters: *"contend for the faith that was once for all entrusted to the saints."*

Ever since its founding, the Order of Thaddeus had been helping the Church guard against threats, both inside and outside the Church. Project SEPIO was formed decades ago to more actively protect the once-for-all faith and teaching tradition, the full acronym being: *Sepio, Erudio, Pugno, Inviglio, Observo.*

Protect, Instruct, Fight For, Watch Over, Heed.

The meaning of the Latin word *sepio* itself captured the project's mission perfectly: "to surround with a hedge." In the case of the Order's project mission, surround the memory markers and teaching tradition of the Christian faith with a hedge of protection—and keep them safe from Nous, the archenemy of the Christian faith and scourge of the Church. Early in the life of the Church, Nous tried to undermine the essence of Christianity by destroying her teachings. The Order had been following the organization for generations, keeping it at bay and stopping it from destroying the Church.

Silas had been their newest recruit after a series of militant incursions by the spiritual menace a year ago threatened to bring about confusion in the Church and the faith's ultimate demise. It was a vocational arrangement that perfectly married his military training and academic background, not to mention his passion for vintage Christianity. Never in a million lifetimes would he have thought of himself as the religious order type. But he was learning it was probably for the best, since his former life in lights as a rising academic superstar had been yanked down in one swift blow, mostly thanks to his personal demons and fatal flaws.

The Lord works in mysterious ways, indeed...

"It's gotta be good to be back here, huh?" Gapinski said, interrupting his contemplation. "Especially since the last two times were a little on the cray-cray side. What with chasing down the hidden Ark of the Covenant and then breaking into the Church of the Holy Sepulcher with your broth—"

The man stopped short. He glanced at Silas, eyes slightly wide and mouth wilting with regret. "Sorry, bro. My bad. Didn't mean to bring him up with everything that's happened and all..."

Silas glanced at him and smiled weakly, the pain of his brother Sebastian's one-two-three punch betrayals clawing its way to the surface after Silas had buried his feelings about it all back in December. He thought he had done a pretty good job of managing the pain of what he had endured throughout the year, even refusing his little blue anti-anxiety meds in the face of it all. But he knew better.

He sighed and reached in his pocket for the Camels and lighter. While he'd kicked the one habit, he'd picked back up an old one from his Army days. Dredging up the memories had made his mind itch for relief.

He held up the pack. "Do you mind?"

Gapinski glanced over and raised a brow. "What, in our rental?"

"Don't worry," he said, rolling down his window farther. "I'll keep it outside."

"OK..."

Silas lit the stick, took a pull, and raked his hand through his hair. He said, "And don't worry about mentioning Sebastian. Not your fault the guy's apostatized from the faith and joined our archenemy." He blew the smoke out the window as the sun-baked brown hills gently rolled past, his gut twisting with the thought of what his brother had become.

An awkward silence settled between the two, the sound of tires on pavement and wind rushing through the open window offering the only soundtrack for their journey.

After the bombshell reveal a few months ago that Sebastian Grey, Silas's twin brother, had been acting as an operative of Nous—as well as the gut-wrenching reasons why—the man had completely gone dark, disappearing without a trace. With Nous's Grand Master locked away in a detention center with the International Criminal Court, Radcliffe had wondered if Sebastian would take the man's place. If not as Grand Master, then at least as a member of the Thirteen, the governing body of Nous. Perhaps even with the upper echelons on the Council of Five, given his intimate connection to the latest SEPIO recruit defending and preserving the Christian faith.

Yet there had been no word, no intel, no nothing about where the man had fled and hidden himself away after Silas let him run off on that frozen pond in Germany. No new plans or incursions against the faith had manifested themselves either, leaving an uncomfortable, if not welcomed, armistice between the two organizations since the ancient threat had launched its latest attacks against the Church the past year. Radcliffe was sure it wouldn't be long until Nous renewed their assault, and he was worried they would be caught flatfooted when they did.

Gapinski cleared his throat. "So, thanks for coming along with me this afternoon. Appreciate the support. And the cover. Love me some Grandpappy, but sometimes he can be a bit...much."

Silas took another pull on his cigarette, then flicked it out the window and blew. He eased his window back up, leaving a crack, and said, "Don't mention it. And thanks for the invite. Never been to the Jordan River before. And what better way to experience it than at a church baptism, or whatever it is he's doing. Something about the Guinness Book of World Records, isn't that right?"

"Yep. Grandpappy's billed it as the largest public baptism in the Jordan River ever. Which is sort of a knuckleheaded distinction, because the largest public baptism ever was apparently a record-breaking 95,000 some odd people during a two-week evangelistic movement in Rwanda."

"Get out of here! 95,000 baptisms?"

"Righto. And a few years ago, a thousand Brazilian pilgrims were baptized where we're headed now, the Yardenit baptismal site near the northern Israeli city of Tiberias. Grandpappy aims to dunk at least double that."

Silas whistled. "Now that's what I call a baptism."

Gapinski chuckled. "It's a Southern Baptist thing."

"Guess so. Us Catholics get the infant pour over treatment."

"That's right. So you've never been baptized as an adult?"

Silas shrugged. "Never saw the need."

"Even after your...I don't know what you'd call it. Conversion experience at that military chapel thingamabob?"

"I don't know if I'd call it a *conversion*. I mean, I was saved as a Catholic when I trusted in Jesus' shed blood for the forgiveness of my sins and believed he rose from the dead. It was more of a rededication of my faith, a deepening of my commitment to Jesus as Lord and Savior."

Gapinski nodded. "Right on. But don't be surprised if Grandpappy tries to get you into the water."

Silas chuckled. "Consider me—"

He stopped short and leaned in closer to his side mirror to look at something that caught his eye. He drew in a measured breath and twisted in his seat for a better look behind them.

He saw thick, black smoke pluming on the horizon. Somewhere near Old City, Jerusalem, by the looks of it. The kind a massive fire would signal. From a burning high-rise, maybe, or a forested hillside.

Or an explosion of terror in the heart of the Holy Land at the start of Holy Week.

CHAPTER 2

Gapinski quickly turned on the radio and began flipping through the channels, searching for answers to the who-what-where-why that continued rising on the distant horizon. All he got was a bunch of top 40s stations with a mixture of Middle Eastern and Euro pop hits.

"No need to panic, Silas," he said steadily as he continued searching for news. "Probably some teenagers being teenagers. Those bone-dry hills catch fire if you look at 'em the wrong way."

"Maybe," Silas said, bringing out his phone and searching for SEPIO command. He found the contact and dialed the number, putting the phone on speaker, then twisted back around for another look. "Or maybe not. That smoke doesn't look right."

The voice of an English-speaking news anchor on the radio suddenly flashed into focus: "—unconfirmed reports of several suicide bombers detonating in sync outside the ancient walls of old Jerusalem."

"There it is!" Silas said.

"Got it."

She continued, "It was like a series of dominos falling one

by one at each of the gates around the Old City, beginning with the Lion's Gate and ending at Herod's Gate. The force from the blast was so great at each of the checkpoints into the religious site claimed by the three Abrahamic faiths, that several surrounding buildings outside the walls have collapsed in addition to several sections of the wall itself and other structures interior to the city."

"Always something," Gapinski cursed, pounding the steering wheel hard and glancing in his rearview mirror as he continued driving.

"We were just there, staying right outside Herod's Gate," Silas said out loud as he contemplated what could have been their own fate.

"Well, thank the good Lord, then, for Grandpappy's little Guinness stunt. Because without that excuse to leave the city…"

Silas looked at him and nodded knowingly. He didn't have to finish the sentence.

"Hello, Silas?"

His breath caught in his chest, his heart seemed to literally skip a beat. It was Celeste Bourne, her perfectly polished British English sending his blood racing with excitement. It was sure nice to hear her voice. Missed her already.

Radcliffe had recruited her out of MI6 as director of operations for SEPIO a few years ago. She had been a sturdy, capable leader for the Order's more kinetic activities against the threat of Nous, the past year especially. And the two had something of a falling in, you could call it, bonding over shared backgrounds with government service and the Church, and developing a closeness through shared near-death experiences. And then when the Order sent the two of them, along with Gapinski, on holiday at a resort in Punta Cana, Dominican Republic, they had begun to explore their sense of a deeper relationship forming. Both agreed there was something there, but their professional relationship complicated things. So they took it slow, attending Sunday services together at an Anglican Church in Falls Church, Virginia, and going on a few dates to test the waters. Still early stages, but he thought there was promise. The first sign of it on that front of his life in a long, long while.

He felt himself flushing and smiling with the joy of hearing her. He glanced at Gapinski and quickly cleared his throat, then nodded and said, "Hey, Celeste. Yeah, it's me. And Gapinski," he said turning to his companion. "We're both here."

"Thank God you're alive! So you're alright, you're not hurt or anything?"

"No, we're both fine."

"Because we've just received word of a horrifying attack in the Holy Land. Near where you were staying, if I reckon correctly. And we all thought the worst of it."

"I know, we're just now listening to the news of it ourselves. We're driving to the Sea of Galilee for a little side trip Gapinski arranged for us, so we weren't anywhere near the explosions. We only got word about it when I saw smoke on the horizon and thought the worst. We've just been listening to the disaster on the radio the past few minutes."

"Disaster is right. Early reports are claiming hundreds dead and thousands more injured."

"Anyone claim responsibility yet?" Gapinski asked.

"Not yet. But you can imagine the Jewish and Christian authorities aren't having too long or tiresome of a think about who might be responsible."

Gapinski and Silas looked at each other and shook their heads. No, they weren't.

"Yeah, but was there any chatter about something of this magnitude among known jihadi terrorist cells and networks?" Silas asked. "Because we sure didn't get any intel giving us the heads-up about active radical Islamists targeting the city when we checked in with the Gendarmerie Corps of Vatican City State yesterday."

"None whatsoever," Celeste said. "From the reports we've received here in DC, and with what we've gathered that is being broadcast live on the BBC and Al Jazeera, this seems to have taken the entire world by surprise. Which is both highly unusual and most alarming, considering the scale of attack and timing of it all."

Gapinski scoffed, "And what perfect timing." He added quickly: "Not that there's any good time for an attack by a bunch of radical Islamic jihadi whack jobs. But during Holy Week? I mean, come on!"

"What would you like us to do, Celeste?" Silas asked.

"I'm not sure there's anything to do. I have to imagine the Vatican gendarmerie and Israeli Defense Force have pretty well locked down the city at this point and are getting things under control. But where are you now?"

Gapinski answered, "Heading north on Route 90 toward the Jordan River, near the mouth of the Sea of Galilee."

"And what is there that's germane to the course of Order business?"

The man widened his eyes and flashed Silas an "uhh oh" look seeking support from the brotherhood. Silas shrugged, offering him none.

Gapinski frowned, and said, "Uhh...well, my grandpappy is performing this mass baptism for...well, the Guinness Book of World Records, you see, and—"

"*The* Guinness Book of World Records? Did I hear that right?" she asked.

He hesitated, then said, "You did. And, yep, that would be the one."

Celeste sighed audibly from the other end of the phone. "Alright, carry on. But be sure to check in with me in a few hours. I may have a change of orders once we're able to process this turn of events on our end."

"Righto, chief."

"Cheers," she said before ending the call.

Gapinski sighed and gripped the steering wheel tighter. "What say you, partner?"

Silas sat quiet for a few seconds, staring out at the barren hills trundling along past them before glancing again in his mirror. The smoke was no longer visible, after the two had veered north. He sighed, and said, "Celeste's right. Nothing for us to do. But...my God, what the heck is going on? An attack on the Old City at the start of Holy Week?" He continued trying to work it all out in his head as they continued driving forward.

"Well, these things do happen in these parts, unfortunately."

"During Hanukkah or Yom Kippur, maybe. Jews have always been the target of these kinds of attacks in Israel, right?"

Gapinski tilted his head and considered this. "I guess so. But what are you getting at?"

Silas shook his head. "Not sure. Just a feeling. But how about we punch it and get to the Jordan River. I'm guessing we're gonna have to jet sooner than your grandfather would like."

Gapinski nodded and pushed the accelerator.

CHAPTER 3

Two hours later, Silas and Gapinski arrived at the most popular baptism site in the Holy Land along the Jordan River.

Located on the southern tip of the Sea of Galilee, Yardenit is one of the world's most important sites of Christian pilgrimage, welcoming half a million of the Church's faithful every year to experience the tranquility and spiritual beauty of the waters in which Jesus was baptized by John the Baptist.

"Jeez Louise, would you look at the circus!" Gapinski exclaimed as he eased their rental into the overcrowded parking lot.

Caravans of large, white tourist buses were packed like soda cans, idling one after another in neat rows. Christians of all stripes—men, women, and many children—were congregating in groups, going into and coming from the site dressed in special cotton baptismal garments of pure white. The garment had been a tradition stretching back centuries, meant as an outward sign signifying the person had been clothed with Christ's new life and his sinless purity.

It was midafternoon, and Gapinski led Silas through the crowds radiating spiritual ecstasy from either anticipating or having just partaken of the ancient spiritual practice modeled by Jesus Christ himself at the start of his ministry.

"'*In those days,*'" Silas quoted aloud as they continued making their way through the parking lot, "'*Jesus came from Nazareth of Galilee and was baptized by John in the Jordan.*'"

"'*And just as he was coming up out of the water,*'" Gapinski said, grinning as he glanced back at Silas, not to be outdone, "'*he saw the heavens torn apart and the Spirit descending like a dove on him. And a voice came from heaven, "You are my Son, the Beloved; with you I am well pleased."*'"

Silas chuckled as they reached the entrance to the modest compound. "Nice work, hot shot."

"Thanks, but it was Grandpappy's doing. He drilled into me Scripture memory through six years on the Bible quiz team. Hated it at the time, but happy to have the Good Book stuffed into every nook and cranny of this here noggin' of mine."

"Bible quiz team?"

Gapinski glanced back at him as they squeezed their way through a pack of white-robed believers waiting for their turn at the Christian rite. "Yeah, Bible quiz team. Sort of like Jeopardy, but without the cash-money prize at the end. Got a few nifty trophies out of it, though. And a few hot dates."

"I bet..." Silas said under his breath as they reached the baptismal site entrance.

On either side of them stretched a wall with the Scripture he and Gapinski had quoted memorializing Jesus' baptism in various languages. A concrete path buttressed by a short stone wall and decorated with trees and flowers wound its way down to the mighty Jordan River below. Flooding that path were hundreds of believers dressed in billowing white robes, dutifully waiting for their turn at being plunged beneath the waters.

Silas's throat grew thick with emotion at the sight of so many people publicly declaring their allegiance to Christ as

Lord and belief in his life, death, and resurrection for the forgiveness of sins and salvation for the life to come. There were people from Africa and others clearly from Europe or America. Asians and Latinos joined the throngs as well, showcasing the wonder and grandeur and diversity of the Body of Christ and God's kingdom.

A passage from the book of Revelation shot into Silas's mind's eye of the great multitude of nations in white robes standing before God's throne at the end of the age:

> *After this I looked, and there was a great multitude*
> *that no one could count, from every nation, from*
> *all tribes and peoples and languages, standing*
> *before the throne and before the Lamb, robed in*
> *white, with palm branches in their hands. They*
> *cried out in a loud voice, saying,*
> *"Salvation belongs to our God who is seated on the*
> *throne, and to the Lamb!"*

"Amen," Silas said softly. He understood the passage was a prophetic image of those who survived monstrous persecution. He thought of those Christians who had just died as martyrs of the faith a few hours ago, presumably at the hands of anti-Christian terrorists back in the Old City. Men and women and even children who were now standing clothed in white before the Lamb. He said a prayer for them and their families.

"Matthew?" a deep voice with a thick Southern drawl bellowed behind the pair.

Gapinski spun round, so did Silas.

"Grandpappy!" Gapinski bellowed back.

A larger man than Gapinski, wearing what looked like a sail and scruffy white beard, bear-hugged the SEPIO operative.

"Nice of you to show up!"

Gapinski glanced at the ground and scratched his head. He went to offer a reply when Silas stepped forward.

He said, "It was my fault, pastor. Sorry to make Matt run late for what looks to be a beautiful occasion marking the public confession of so many believers."

"No worries. I was just razzin' the kid. Now, who might you be?"

"This is the fella I told you about from the agency," Gapinski said, motioning to Silas. "Silas Grey."

Agency?

Silas furrowed his brow slightly before extending his hand.

Grandpappy grabbed it with a firm grip. "Ahh, yes. From that supersecret government-like outfit out of Washington, is that right?"

Supersecret government-like outfit?

Silas smiled and nodded. "That would be the one. Nice to meet you, Pastor Gapinski."

"Aww, fiddle faddle. None of that pastor nonsense. Jim George for me, son. Follow me down to the water, boys. We're about to get back to it."

"Supersecret government-like outfit?" Silas questioned lowly as they followed the man through the crowds. "What's that about?"

"Umm...yeah, I sorta skirted the whole Christian Rambos convo."

"You lied to your grandpappy pastor?"

"I didn't lie," Gapinski said defensively. "I didn't say *government* agency. I said government-*like*. SEPIO is an agency. And it's supersecret. He just didn't need to know what *kind* of supersecret agency." He turned to Silas and grinned. "And, actually, maybe you didn't get the memo, but that's the party line if anyone asks. Ixnay on the whole rojectpay epiosay."

Silas nodded. "Makes sense. Can't imagine your Southern

Baptist grandfather was all that thrilled about his grandson working for a former Catholic order."

"Yeah, probably not. Not that he has anything against the Romans, as he calls 'em. Just different types and stripes and all that. He's only known the Southern Baptist way, so everything else is suspect, if you get my drift."

"Sure. My dad felt the same way about Southern Baptists."

They reached the banks of the mighty Jordan where the concrete met the water. Steps led down into the river, and a series of green metal barriers directed the awaiting baptismal candidates. The two followed Pastor Jim George down the steps, where he told them to wait and watch as the rest of the day unfolded.

The good reverend stepped into the greenish water and waded through it back over to his post, then he called the next person waiting in line to receive the sacrament of baptism.

A blond teenage boy entered the waters and confidently strode to the burly man waiting with a wide grin and outstretched arms. He asked the boy if he confessed that Jesus was Lord and Savior, and believed that God had raised him from the dead; the teenager did. Then the pastor lowered him backward into the water, symbolizing his participation in Christ's death. After a second, he raised him back up, symbolizing the boy's participation in Christ's own resurrection and receipt of his new life.

The crowd cheered and clapped, some hooted and hollered.

"How cool..." Silas said.

"Amen to that!" Gapinski agreed, clapping and adding his own hoot of celebration.

It went like that for hours as one by one, men and women, children and the elderly confirmed their faith. As the afternoon wore on toward evening, a curious desire to enter the waters and experience the ancient Christian ritual began to well up within Silas. Sure, he had been baptized as an infant, received

First Communion at seven, and was confirmed in the faith at fourteen. After reconfirming his faith and rededicating himself to Christ at the chapel service in Iraq, he never felt the need to get re-baptized. Been there, done that.

But now, after witnessing the hundreds of people declaring their faith so publicly, so tangibly—something seemed to beckon him to follow Jesus into the very waters he himself had received the Holy Spirit for ministry and do what those folks were doing.

Silas took a breath and cleared his throat. He whispered to Gapinski, "I think I want in."

Gapinski startled and furrowed his brow. "Want in? You mean, into the waters? To get baptized?"

Silas looked at the mighty Jordan, one end of his mouth reaching upward in anticipation. He took a breath and nodded.

"Alright, my man!" he bellowed, slapping Silas on the back. He shouted down below, "Grandpappy. We've got another candidate!"

The burly man startled after finishing with a young woman. As she waded through the water back toward land, he looked up into the crowds, shielding his eyes from the afternoon sun.

Gapinski was holding up one of Silas's arms, like he had just been declared the winner of a ginormous prize. In a way, he had.

Pastor Jim George grinned widely, and said, "Well, get the man a robe, then come on down!"

A shout of celebration rippled across the crowd as Gapinski fished for a robe. An elderly man handed him an extra one that looked far too large for Silas, but he didn't care.

After Silas had taken off his shoes and socks, and handed his weapon to Gapinski, he slipped the white garment over his polo and jeans. He felt foolish and proud all at once.

Pastor Jim George held open his arms and motioned for Silas to come join him down in the water. Silas hustled through the crowd and dipped into the river, which was cool and felt fresh against his skin warmed from the day. He lifted his arms above the waters rising to his waist and waded over to Grandpappy Gapinski.

The man was smiling broadly as he had throughout the day with each baptismal candidate, clearly reveling in his role confirming the faith of scores of Christians.

After Silas confirmed his confession of faith in Jesus Christ, Jim George placed his hand at the middle of Silas's back, and said, "Silas Grey, I baptize you in the name of the Father, and of the Son, and of the Holy Spirit."

The burly man brought his wet handkerchief to Silas's face, covering his mouth and nose. Silas crossed his arms over his chest and closed his eyes.

The pastor said, "Buried with him by baptism into death..." Silas felt himself being dipped backward before being plunged underneath the mighty Jordan. He held his breath while encased in the dark, chilly waters—much as Jesus had been entombed after the dark hour he had died on the cross.

A second later, he felt himself rising back out of the waters, the sun bright and warm on his face, symbolizing that glorious moment Jesus Christ himself burst forth from the tomb into full, dazzling resurrection glory.

He heard Pastor Gapinski say, "Raised from the dead by the glory of the Father as Christ was raised."

Silas caught his breath and sputtered a bit as the river water dripped down his face from his wet hair into his nose and mouth. He quickly recovered, pushing his soaked hair to the side and smiling widely, proud to publicly take his stand among the billions of people through the ages who had confirmed their own faith in Jesus Christ's life, death, and resurrection, and their confession that he is Lord and Savior.

But where he expected to hear the familiar cheers of his fellow brothers and sisters in the faith celebrating his confession, he only heard high-pitched screams and shouts of fearful protest mixed with an angry, guttural whine of a chainsaw rolling fast down the river.

And then the familiar rapid *pop-pop-pop-pop-pop* of menacing gunfire.

CHAPTER 4

Three narrow boats, hulls shallow and motors whining with ill intent, accompanied by four jet skis raced toward the baptismal site from the south. A black flag marked by white lettering flapped behind each boat, their occupants screaming with bloodlust and letting loose a burst of rapid gunfire from automatic weapons as they reached the sacred space.

From behind the wall in the parking lot, a series of explosions in rapid succession sounded forth with fire and fury, shaking the ground and sending thick, black smoke and debris soaring behind the wall. Bodies flopped like rag dolls high into the air along with the plume as the concussive force sent them flying in wicked dismemberment. More rapid gunfire sounded forth from the lot, distant but encroaching.

And meaning terrifying business.

Women were screaming from the baptismal site, hands high over their heads and waving about in search of safety. Children crouched with terror in the shallow water and against the short stone walls, eyes closed and hands over their heads in search of comfort. Muffled cries and shouts of terror sought salvation from the parking lot as well.

A man's head exploded in front of Gapinski as another round of gunfire exploded from the river boats, blood and gore spraying across the front of his shirt. Another man's chest and neck ripped open next to him with three indiscriminate shots, sending a geyser of blood high before the man crumpled against the stone stairs.

More rapid *pop-pop-pop* gunfire sounded forth, this time at the back. He whipped his head toward the invasion.

A wave of white bodies swelled forward into the baptismal area, followed by a rabid pack of men in desert fatigues with dark masks screaming with intimidation and spraying angry bullets into the air and then into the crowd.

Several bodies dropped hard to the cement, their white robes quickly staining red as their martyr blood pooled out with indifference. Others ran toward the river, but stopped short and spun with uncertainty, realizing they were caught between two terrifying forces.

Confusion took over, sending some into the water and others climbing the wall in escape. Then more menacing gunfire, spitting and swelling and sweeping. More martyrs dropping in death—off the wall and into the river water, its greenish hue turning brown from the floating bodies of Christian martyrs.

It was all happening so fast, yet unfolding for Gapinski in slow motion; he felt paralyzed to respond.

He heard his name above the din of chaos. Then again.

"Gapinski!" Silas yelled, dripping in front of him in soaked polo and jeans, his white rob having been cast aside in the river.

He snapped his head toward his partner, eyes wide with the unexpected incursion and mouth open in a question.

"Snap out of it and hand me my Beretta!" Silas yelled.

Gapinski took a deep, stabilizing breath, then gritted his teeth and slapped his fellow SEPIO operative's cold, hard steel into his open hand. He quickly reached behind his back for his own weapon, a SIG Sauer that had seen plenty of action.

It was go time.

The two quickly hoisted themselves up a short stone wall to a sycamore tree commanding a landing filled with wood chips and wiry shrubs. They wedged themselves between the tree and a second stone wall that buttressed a stairwell, crouching for cover.

"I'd like to visit the Holy Land just once without there being some plot to blow us to kingdom come," Gapinski complained. "Who the heck are these guys?"

"Give you one guess," Silas growled.

"The Old City jihadi whack jobs?"

"Has to be. No way it's a coincidence that a massive baptism is hit like this right after the City of David is blown to shreds."

Another round of gunfire and screams startled the two and sent them farther behind the tree for cover.

Gapinski chambered a round, and said, "No way on our watch these bastards win."

"Agreed."

"You OK?"

Silas frowned. "I'm fine. Why?"

"Because the last thing I need is you to go all PTSD on—"

"I said, I'm fine!"

The two nodded at each other with resolve as the gunfire ceased. The terrorists probably figured they had taken control of the compound.

They couldn't have been more wrong.

Silas opened first, aiming from behind the sycamore toward the boats. It was a good fifty yards away, but his military senses immediately clicked into high gear. Uncle Sam had trained him for such a time as this through his tours in Iraq and Afghanistan. Never imagined that training would come in handy for the Church.

Again, the good Lord works in mysterious ways.

He aimed for the man at the helm of the lead boat and squeezed off *one-two-three-four* rounds.

Two clanged off the console, but one caught him in the chest. The other in his throat.

The man clutched his neck and staggered backward as blood squirted between his fingers and poured from the wound. He slammed against the rubber walls of the vessel and toppled into the River Jordan.

The others in the remaining boats and jet skis reacted as expected: total shock at being fired upon. The response was delayed, but strong and sustained.

Silas spun around behind the tree as round after round after round of lead from the automatic rifles chewed into it with relentless fury, pieces splintering in fearful fits.

"All that firepower for four lousy bullets," Silas complained, but thankful the tree was standing firm against the assault.

"Just wait for this," Gapinski said as he slid against the stairwell wall and eased himself upright, shielded on his left against the river response. He opened up his own front, aiming for the hostiles who were trying to corral the baptismal candidates from above toward the river down below.

Unlike Silas, his targets were well within comfortable range. Not fire-when-you-see-the-whites-of-their-eyes range. But close enough.

He narrowed his eyes and aimed dead-center mass of one hostile taking a cautious step toward their position. He squeezed off three rounds, dropping him in an instant heap of brown fatigues.

He quickly switched targets to the hostile's compadre, who had spun his weapon toward the sycamore after hearing Gapinski's gunfire. The sudden reaction threw off his aim, but Gapinski managed to sink two of the four rounds into his torso.

The man fell back hard, writhing on the concrete as he bled out from two gaping holes in his stomach.

Gapinski smirked as he reloaded. "My bad."

He ducked as a violent protest of return gunfire marched his way.

Two more of the hostiles had broken off from the main group who were still committed to sweeping the Christians into the river. And a smattering of gunfire and screams and undulating *pop-pop-pop* discharges from beyond the rear wall reminded him that the fight was still raging on yet another front with equal terror.

Gapinski cursed at the thought, then turned to Silas and said, "We've got company."

Silas remained behind his tree as the response kept coming in fits and starts. "Have at it, partner," he said, "I sort of have my hands full over here. How many did you see on your end?"

"Ten or eleven, by the looks of it. But I sent two to Davey Jones's Locker, so sliced their advantage by a fifth."

Gapinski glanced above his wall and opened up on the men advancing toward their position, firing wide without aim to let them know who was boss.

The hostiles skipped backward and tried to regain their authority with a sustained irritated response, bullets shattering the stone wall standing between them and Gapinski's head.

"That means we're working with, what, ten-to-one odds here?" Silas said as he sent his own irritated five-round response toward the Jordan.

"Sounds about right."

"I don't like those odds."

Gapinski sent another volley up above, dropping one of the men getting too close for comfort and giving the other pause in his advance.

"Score!" he exclaimed. "Yeah, but I've played those odds in Vegas."

"But did you win big or go home crying?"

The man tilted his head to think.

"On second thought," Silas said, taking aim at the lead operator of the second boat and giving him an early trip to the morgue, "don't answer that. We're getting nowhere, here. There are too—"

"Wait a minute," Gapinski interrupted, standing suddenly in a panic and moving to the edge of the stone wall toward the river. He twisted his head this way and that, searching the area, eyes wide and frantic.

"Get down!" Silas ordered.

"Where's Grandpappy," he said with urgency.

In snapping into instant operative mode, and with the chaos of the moment, the two had forgotten Pastor Jim George.

"Oh, jeez," Silas said, inching out from behind the sycamore and toward the ledge himself. He cautioned a look, and didn't like what he saw.

"There..." he whispered and pointed.

The river was swarming with people dressed in white. On the banks, men in black and others in desert fatigues were pointing their long-barreled automatic rifles at them and firing into the water, missing them by inches and sweeping them into the three boats. The jet skis were playing sheep dogs to Christ's flock as well, corralling them toward the nautical pens as other hostiles were dragging the sobbing men, women, and children on board the rubber vessels.

Including Grandpappy Gapinski!

"No way in hell..." Gapinski growled. He jumped the stairwell wall, then took off with resolve.

"No, wait—" Silas said, twisting after his partner.

But it was too late. The man was moving swiftly up the stone stairs toward the top.

A man in fatigues, face masked in black but for a slit for

dead, dark eyes, raised his weapon as Gapinski ran along the landing.

The SEPIO operative took aim and squeezed off three rounds into the man with ease. His head snapped back, and he crumpled to the ground like a bathrobe, landing on a pile of fallen Christian martyrs.

He went to level another hostile coming up quick, but his SIG clicked empty.

Sonofa—

The hostile, face unmasked with badly scared skin and an inkblot birthmark, began to raise his German-made assault rifle, but Gapinski barreled forward.

He yelled wildly with a sudden surge of adrenaline and plowed into the jihadi whack job like the all-state football defensive lineman he was back in the day, grabbing the man's weapon as he discharged it into the ground and leveling him flat on his back.

He gasped for breath, the wind having been knocked out of him. Gapinski saved him the effort by jamming the butt of the rifle into his head. He went instantly silent.

"That'll leave a mark," he said, grinning and trying to catch his breath.

But his victory didn't last long.

The wall behind him exploded in puffs of anger, sending him to the concrete flat on his stomach behind a wooden bench. An elderly man and woman were lying contorted at ungodly angles on either side of him, their blank eyes staring at him wide with fright and mouths moist with fresh blood.

God Almighty, have mercy upon their souls!

The response was relentless. He worried they were routing him, but he couldn't move. They had him pinned.

"Silas," he yelled, "I could really use some back-up love right about now!"

From his left, a sudden burst of muscular response reassured him his partner still had his back.

"Gotcha covered, big guy," Silas said on his belly behind a short stone wall.

One of the hostiles fell dead in the water, another clutched his leg on shore and crawled along the landing below in search of safety.

Then the air was split by the sound of revving engines. Three outboards grunted to life and four two-stroke inboards whined away like motorbikes.

The two SEPIO agents cautioned a look.

They were horrified by what they saw.

The river was boiling as the boats, loaded heavy with white-robed bodies sitting smashed together like mozzarella cheese sticks, began turning toward the south. They pushed through the flotsam and jetsam of dead brothers and sisters floating in quiet repose, their robes stained pink and gliding along the cauldron of water like ghoulish specters.

Some of the hostiles who had come from the parking lot, acting as herdsmen, had joined the Christian hostages in the boats. Others had mounted the jet skis, bringing up the rear in protection as they left the macabre scene.

"Grandpappy!" Gapinski screamed in a terrifying pitch as he leaped over the bench and down below.

The gunmen reacted on cue, spraying the banks of the River Jordan to cover their escape.

Gapinski sprayed back. His face was fixed with vengeance, arm outstretched like the Terminator, and feet planted with resolve.

By God's providential protection, the bullets all died wide before ceasing altogether as the terrorists faded into the distance, their menacing shouts of "Allahu akbar!" a confirmation of victory.

And SEPIO's defeat.

Gapinski looked on as they sped away with his grandpappy and the scores of other Christians, eyes bulging wildly with agonizing disbelief. He threw his rifle aside and jumped into the mighty River Jordan.

"Grandpappyyy!" he screamed again until his lungs gave out, sinking to his knees in an emotional heap as the celebration and motors faded to nothing.

CHAPTER 5

Gapinski knelt among the floating, bloating bodies of fallen Christian martyrs, paralyzed with disbelief and face buried in his meaty palms, weeping for his kidnapped grandpappy as the day stretched into the evening.

Silas took hesitant steps toward his friend, not sure if he should let him alone with his grief or offer a hand of comfort. He opted for the latter, dipping into the River Jordan and wading knee-deep to his grieving comrade. He placed a hand on the man's shoulder and squeezed it, holding the sign of solidarity as Gapinski continued shuddering with every sob.

He continued standing, not knowing what to say. His throat grew thick with emotion himself as he became overwhelmed at the loss of life and acts of terror perpetrated against the holy site and God's holy Church.

An impression of a memory suddenly came into focus. The day he buried his own father after terrorists had similarly taken him out in a wicked act of violence on that fateful 9/11 day at the Pentagon.

Under a bright, cloudless sky near trees that had begun transforming into autumnal brilliance, he and Sebastian, a handful of extended family and friends, and their parish priest huddled around an open gravesite plot at Arlington National Cemetery a few weeks later. Through the painstaking process of excavating the demolished section of the Pentagon, Thomas Grey's body had been eventually pulled from the rubble, what was left of it anyway. It had been identified through DNA records held by the Department of Defense and given a proper military burial with full military honors.

Attached to that memory was a prayer, offered by their family's priest, Father Rafferty. It was a traditional Catholic prayer for the dead, and he had spent days meditating on it after the burial, trying to burn it into his memory. Didn't know why, but probably had something to do with the final moments of his connection with Dad before saying goodbye. He hadn't touched the memory in well over a decade, until that moment reaching for a comforting word for his friend.

Silas shuddered at the memory of Dad who had similarly died at the hands of terrorists, and felt himself growing weak from its connection to the day's events. But he clung to the memory of that prayer and began whispering it on the banks of the mighty Jordan. He didn't know what else to do.

"Into your hands, O Lord," he prayed, voice strained and shaky, "we humbly entrust our brothers and sisters, these martyrs of the faith. In this life you embraced them with your tender love; deliver them now from every evil and bid them eternal rest. The old order has passed away: welcome them into paradise, where there will be no sorrow, no weeping or pain, but fullness of peace and joy with your Son and the Holy Spirit forever and ever."

"Amen," Silas ended softly. Gapinski echoed him audibly, face still buried in his hands.

The man let them drop into the water with a sudden splash, his face red and eyes puffy and wet with grief. He leaned back and took a deep breath, then pushed it out heavily through his nose before pushing himself up to stand.

Silas offered him his hand. Gapinski smiled weakly and took it.

When he stood, Silas grabbed him in an embrace, and said, "We'll get those bastards, brother. Mark my words, we'll get those bastards."

Gapinski choked back another round of sobs rising to the surface. They stood for several minutes, a gentle, warm breeze offering a balm for their sorrows.

"What's that sound?" he said suddenly, pushing off Silas and looking with fixed concern toward the entrance to the baptismal site.

It was only after his partner had pointed it out that Silas began to hear it too. He lifted his head and looked off toward the parking lot. Thick, acrid smoke was still billowing beyond the pale stone wall. And rising along with it toward the heavens were muffled but audible distressed cries of anguish and agony.

Gapinski narrowed his eyes and clenched his jaw. He climbed back onto the dry land and picked up the rifle he had discarded, an expensive, German-made Heckler & Koch by the looks of it. Which meant major money and major backing. He frowned at the thought, then set off toward the sounds. Silas followed, withdrawing his Beretta as the two quickly ascended the stone stairs toward the chaos, unsure yet also certain what they would find.

It was far more hellish than they could have imagined.

"Dear God…" Silas whispered as they arrived at the parking lot.

It was like something out of a war zone, a scene ripped from countless days he himself had witnessed up close and personal in Iraq and Afghanistan. In the case confronting the SEPIO operatives, however, it wasn't merely a cliché: a war had been waged against the Church.

Crimson and orange flames were still consuming rows of white buses under the darkening sky, the source of the billowing black smoke. A yawning void in a cluster of them indicated the original source where the suicide bombers had detonated their devices, tossing the large vehicles like Tyco play toys and charring tens, even hundreds of baptismal candidates to a wicked crisp.

Bodies littered the black asphalt, piled like rag dolls in mounds and scattered about at ungodly angles, blood pooling underneath and staining their pure, white robes in unholy crimson with bullet holes marking them as claimed scalps for the murderous scum. Others were huddled in groups, praying and comforting and mending open wounds. Still others were seen fleeing into the countryside.

Gapinski stepped forward into the nightmare, but startled when a woman screamed at him from the shadows.

She was half naked, her white robe having been torn on one side and clinging to her thin frame at one shoulder. Her blond hair had turned orange and her face was streaked with blood. Her baptismal robe had received a similar treatment, the signs of human death and misery pockmarking her once white garment with gore. Bodies were piled around her feet, scrunched up and twisted with ghoulish faces—some missing limbs, others barely intact.

No wonder she was distraught at the sight of a giant suddenly appearing from the shadows, bloodied himself and wielding a menacing rifle!

She pointed at him and shrieked again, face contorted with petrified fear and continuing hysterics.

He held his breath and stood still, not knowing what to do. Then he lifted his arm slightly, the one holding his weapon. He nodded knowingly, then swapped it to his other hand and lowered it to his side.

"Don't worry, ma'am," he said calmly. "We're the good guys."

Silas came up beside him and folded his arms, then cupped

one hand over his mouth. "This is unreal," he said, muffled and pained and shaking his head. "Saw the full measure of the wickedness and sheer destructiveness of the human heart poured out in terror during my tours in the Middle East. But this..."

"I'll tell you one thing," Gapinski said, "this ain't what I signed up for, that's for darn tootin'."

They stood taking in the scene in front of them—the burning buses, the scattered bodies, the distraught lady still high on terror—paralyzed with indecision.

Something caught Silas's eye on the far side of the parking lot. He leaned forward slightly, squinting for a better look. Then he turned to Gapinski and pointed in the distance before starting off with purpose and motioning for him to follow.

Gapinski furrowed his brow and looked at the woman, who was still standing and hyperventilating with continued panic. He wanted to pick her up and hold her close, telling her it would be alright.

But he didn't believe it himself.

He offered her a weak smile and took off after Silas.

Trying to sidestep the bodies and avoid the huddled masses recovering from the terror, Silas followed the perimeter of the parking lot to a group of vehicles that had caught his attention in the distance.

He avoided the burning wreckage of the buses, giving them wide berth, and picked up his pace. Then he stopped short with stunned confusion.

It makes no sense...

"Hold up, partner!" Gapinski said breathlessly as he came up to Silas's side. "Where's the four-alarm fire? OK, stupid question."

"Look!" Silas said, sweeping his hand along the back section of the lot.

Gapinski strained forward, not understanding what he was getting at.

Three black pickup trucks, rusting and sagging from age, were parked haphazardly. Must have been how those other hostiles arrived who had swept the Christians into the river from the parking lot. Each roof was anchored by a machine gun, and—

He took a step forward, brow furrowed and jaw dropped in disbelief. "What the..."

Silas put his hands on his hips and nodded in agreement. "Exactly."

Draped over the sides of the truck beds were bodies, dead as doornails and dressed in desert fatigues. Same for the driver's seats in each truck: bodies slumped forward against the steering wheels.

Gapinski moved toward the confusing scene when Silas grabbed his arm. He looked back as Silas raised his Beretta and chambered a round.

He raised his Heckler & Koch rifle with understanding.

The two SEPIO agents stepped forward with caution, weapons raised and ready to shoot first and ask questions later.

As they reached the trucks, they could see bullet holes marred their sides—a lot of them. Some in neat rows, some scattered with abandon. Then there were single-shot holes, execution style, through each of the driver's side windows, a bloody haze of residual blowback left behind on the glass.

They came up to the first truck bed and inspected two terrorists slumped over its side. Their bodies were pockmarked by bullet holes, and they were oozing blood down to the parched ground below. Definitely the same getup as the other jihadi whack jobs who had stormed the baptismal site. And definitely executed with professional precision.

"This doesn't make any sense," Silas mumbled as he scanned the parking lot and surrounding area. "There aren't any military or civilian security forces anywhere to have offered this kind of response."

"Yeah, and I don't hear them coming, either. No sirens, no lights, no nothing."

"Exactly. But clearly there was a show of force here. I mean, just look at these guys. And the vehicles, all shot up like this?"

"But who?"

Silas went to shake his head when something caught his eye several yards away. He barely noticed it with the sun slipping beneath the horizon, but a figure on the ground beyond the blacktop was inching forward through the barren ground in escape.

Silas nodded toward the man and raised his Beretta, then padded forward for a look.

It was one of the terrorists, that much was clear. A dark streak smeared behind him in the dirt as the injured man pushed himself toward safe relief.

"Let me do the honors," Gapinski said, pushing past him. He reached the man and lowered his weapon, then shoved its barrel into the back of his neck.

"No, wait!" Silas yelled, lunging forward and shoving his partner aside as he discharged his weapon into the parched ground.

"Are you crazy?" he yelled again. "He's our only link to whatever the hell happened here."

"The bastard deserves a date with his Maker!" Gapinski shouted as he recovered, taking aim again and moving toward his target.

Silas stepped in front of him and held up his hands.

"Look, I get it. You want revenge. I want vengeance, too. But that's not how we do things in the Order."

"Get out of my way!" Gapinski snapped through gritted teeth, his face red and twisted with fury.

"Stand down, soldier. That's an order!"

The man took a breath and looked at Silas with surprise at the command. Then his face softened. He lowered his weapon and took a step backward.

"Fine," he said before turning his back on Silas and taking a walk.

Silas closed his eyes and sighed, then pivoted toward the terrorist who had continued his slow trek through the desert. He came up to the man and pressed his foot against the side of his ribcage, then pushed him over onto his back.

The man had a wicked hole in his belly that was dark and oozing. He stared blankly into the sky with wide eyes, and his lips were moving with a curious rhythm.

"Who are you? What happened here?" he interrogated the man. But it was no use. He kept staring with those hollow eyes and speaking with a cadence that repeated itself every six or seven seconds. His speech was soft and incoherent and seemingly delusional.

"What the hell are you saying?" Silas dropped to one knee and focused on the man's mouth. He couldn't make it out.

Gapinski came up to his side. "What's going on?"

"He seems to be repeating some sort of mantra. Like his brain is stuck on a cycle. The guy was clearly left for dead, and maybe on purpose. Trying to make out what he's saying. Could be important."

"Whatcha mumbling?" Gapinski taunted. "Can't understand a damn thing you're saying. Slow down and speak up!"

Silas shushed him and bent down lower for a better listen. Gapinski joined him. They both strained to understand the mumbling man, the same phrase still cycling and seeming to grow in importance.

Then all at once, it became clear to them both:

"Non nobis, Domine, non nobis, sed Nomini tuo da gloriam."

He repeated it, the same curious phrase said with the same timbre and cadence. But what the heck did it mean?

Then Silas startled and sat back with understanding. He put his hand over his mouth as he thought about the implications of the ancient motto that hadn't been spoken in over seven hundred years.

"What the heck is he mumbling?" Gapinski questioned as the man continued rattling away his breathy cryptic code.

Silas broke his concentration and glanced at him, but hesitated, as if still disbelieving what he had heard, but quite sure of it. And all of its implications.

"*'Not unto us, O Lord, not unto us, but unto thy Name give glory,'*" he said. "It's Latin. And it changes the game entirely."

"OK...Sounds cuckoo for Cocoa Puffs to me. So why's a terrorist, who by all accounts is an *Islamic* terrorist, mumbling some incoherent Latin in an Israeli desert?"

Silas didn't answer him. Instead, he stood and pulled out his mobile phone, then punched the contact for SEPIO command.

The call rang once, then dropped in three beeps.

He sighed and let a curse slip, then tried again.

Same response.

They needed to phone home and drop the truth-bomb from what had just happened at the River Jordan.

And what they discovered afterward.

CHAPTER 6

WASHINGTON, DC.

A steady hum permeated the dimly-lit, modest chapel of Indiana limestone, filling the sacred space with a sense of sacred significance in the late-morning hour.

Little flames danced on four long candles near the solid white limestone altar in front of an intricate limestone facade of miniature statues of the four Gospel writers behind oak altar rails with kneeling cushions patterned in red and gold. Beautiful stained glass windows depicting biblical scenes in crimson red and leafy green, gold yellow and indigo blue hung with their normal awe-inspiring light muted, the sun's march across the sky shrouded by thick early-spring clouds.

Rowen Radcliffe had retreated to a polished-oak pew in the second row of the Bethlehem Chapel for his prayers, a floor beneath the Washington National Cathedral, America's church and headquarters of the Order of Thaddeus. It was a welcomed respite from the chaos that had begun enveloping the Church during the night.

Aside from the terror that had befallen the Holy Land, there were horrifying reports coming in from Africa of more Palm Sunday terror. Whilst the Church of Africa had witnessed more than its share of persecution in recent years, SEPIO chiefs of station across the continent were sending frantic cables reporting mass kidnappings and rapes and village-wide massacres. One worrying report from the West Coast had just hit Radcliffe's desk before he made his way down to the chapel announcing the wild claim that 6,000 Nigerian Christians had been killed in raids on churches throughout the day while celebrating Christ's entrance into Jerusalem and march to the cross. Another 3,000 had been displaced and half that snatched, only to be taken to Lord knew where.

And all perpetrated by masked assailants wearing desert fatigues and black masks, and flying a black flag with disputed white lettering.

It was all too much for the aged man who had never witnessed as much religious carnage wrought against fellow brothers and sisters in the faith in all his years at the helm of the Order as Master. He feared the early hours were merely an hors d'oeuvre for the horrifying first, second, and third courses that were soon planned.

Which brought him to the chapel seeking fortitude of spirit and clarity of mind for the wicked road ahead.

There was a knock at the door at the rear of the chapel, then it creaked open.

Radcliffe sighed heavily, knowing the interruption meant more terrifying news. He eased his body around for a look.

It was Celeste Bourne, his right hand person as director of operations for SEPIO. She stood at the threshold wearing a look that appeared more grave than usual. She clenched her jaw, then shook her head and nodded for him to follow.

He sighed again, more heavily, as if he were sagging and struggling underneath a great weight. Which seemed about right, given all that had been transpiring in the Church throughout the early hours of the day.

Radcliffe turned back toward the altar and closed his eyes,

praying the Holy Spirit would steel his nerves and empower him with supernatural insight for the day ahead. After offering a determined "Amen," he crossed himself, stood, and sauntered over to the woman who had become something of a daughter to him.

"What have I said, my dear, about bearing news of dread before my morning prayers are finished?"

"Sorry, sir. This couldn't wait."

He frowned and closed the door, then started toward a nondescript walnut entrance with a keypad that would take them down below into the heart of SEPIO command.

He offered her his arm, and said, "The least you could have done was come bearing the gift of tea."

She smiled and took it. "A pot of Darjeeling is awaiting, my liege."

He chuckled as they walked. "That's my girl."

An elevator beyond the door took them several stories beneath the sacred structure built over the span of eighty-three years. The addition to which they were quickly descending was added in the 1980s, when the Order broadened its ecumenical appeal and doubled-down on Project SEPIO. He was installed shortly thereafter and had been stewarding the space and its members ever since, considering them the family his vows to the Church had precluded.

Before revealing the gravity of the day's unfolding events, Celeste brought Radcliffe up to speed on the latest from Jerusalem as they rode downward, courtesy of reports from the Vatican gendarmerie. The two words "mass devastation" pretty well summarized the long and short of it, she explained. The attacks were indeed deliberative and coordinated, maximizing the body count and carnage with four detonations at each of the eight city gates for a total of thirty-two explosive devices at the height of the pilgrim traffic into the Old City. It was reported that all of the terrorists had shouted the same familiar refrain before the attack: "Allahu akbar!" Little doubt was left in the authorities mind that it was the work of Islamic jihadis.

But that wasn't all of it.

Armed gunmen stormed into the sacred Christian sites at Gethsemane, the Garden Tomb, and even the Church of the Holy Sepulcher—ratcheting up the death count hundreds fold. Radcliffe offered the same gasp the authorities had at the mention of the last target, given its understood security within the city walls. And again, the same "Allahu akbar!" calling card of radical Muslim jihadis was shouted before unloading rounds of bullets into the Christian pilgrims.

The two were as surprised by the developments in Israel toward Christians as the authorities. Thanks to a number of increased security measures, it had been a few years since bombs had detonated within Jerusalem. Yet most of those who had been targeted were Jews not Christians, and certainly not pilgrims visiting Christian holy sites. The development was most alarming, especially coinciding with what else had transpired around the same hours.

The elevator slowed to a halt. The doors parted, cool sanitized air and the smell of a thousand thunderstorms flooding the carriage. Radcliffe hustled through the slate-gray hallway lined with doors bearing keypads on his way to his study. When he arrived at its solid walnut doors, he slapped his hand on the palm-reading security measure and waited impatiently for its cycle of blue pulses. It turned green and the door unlocked.

He pushed through into his study, his chest tightening with each step as he resumed his duties. At least he was back in its embracing comfort, a vast space lined with floor-to-ceiling book shelves, familiar tomes lining its shelves stretching back through the centuries, and the center commanded by a grouping of leather couches and over-stuffed chairs where plenty of missions were planned and executed. The smokey warmth of a crackling fire in a generous fireplace anchoring one end was a welcomed relief. As was the pot of tea Celeste had prepared in advance.

He grinned with anticipation and shuffled over to a large worktable that often doubled as a dinner table for working meals. Sitting on it was a silver tray bearing all of the necessities of an English tea sommelier such as himself.

"Alright, my dear," he said as he prepared his cup, "might as well rip the Band-Aid off, as they say. What are the latest developments?"

"Not what," she started. "Where."

He spun around, cup in hand, and took a sip. He closed his eyes and hummed with pleasure, then smacked his lips in delight. "Come again?"

She stepped forward, face falling at the grim news she bore. "Rowen, they've taken out Westminster."

Radcliffe sucked his sip in surprise, sending him into a choking fit. Celeste shuffled over to his side, taking his cup and patting his back.

The man leaned against the table, doubled over and fighting to catch his breath with every wheeze and hack. It took a minute, but he recovered. Everything took longer with age, he often complained.

He slid into a chair from exhaustion, then turned to Celeste and said, "The Collegiate Church of St. Peter at Westminster, you say?"

She sighed and nodded solemnly. "I'm as gobsmacked as you, Rowen. We received word from the London operations center before it hit the wires. But there's more."

The man laughed with disbelief, which sent him into another fit. He held up a hand as he recovered, then said, "I'd ask you to spare an old man the agony of truth, my dear, but my vows to the Church preclude me. As do yours, I'd imagine."

She smiled weakly, trying to appreciate his playfulness but dreading her revelations. "Notre Dame in Paris was also hit. As was Seville Cathedral in Spain and St. Isaac's Cathedral in St. Petersburg, Russia."

"Good heavens…" Radcliffe moaned, closing his eyes and pinching the bridge of his nose as an ache began needling his forehead. "Well, is Vatican City's St. Peter's Basilica still standing?"

"That we know of, yes."

He looked at her with furrowed brow. She added, "It's all so fluid. Reports are still coming in of further attacks. I have to say, I fear there is much more on the horizon. We're still in the thick of it, far from out of the woods."

Radcliffe went to offer a response when the door was suddenly thrown open. In stepped Naomi Torres, another of the SEPIO operatives that had been recruited a year ago by Radcliffe and was typically partnered with Gapinski.

She strode toward them with determination and dread. The two eyed her with concern as she rushed over. It didn't bode well.

"There's been word of another attack in Israel," she said.

"What?" Radcliffe said with shock. "Where?"

"The Sea of Galilee, at the Yardenit baptismal site. A massive, I mean *massive* attack on hundreds, perhaps thousands of civilians. Slaughtered by suicide bombers and mowed down with expensive German-made rifles. There's even reports of boatloads being kidnapped. The hostiles literally came up the Jordan River and carted a whole host of them away!"

"Silas and Gapinski!" Celeste exclaimed.

"What?" Radcliffe echoed with confusion.

She turned to the Order Master, all professional demeanor out the window. "Last we talked, the boys were heading to the Jordan River near the mouth of the Sea of Galilee. Something about Gapinski's grandfather performing a mass baptism for some world record or something or other. At any rate, this report seems like that!"

"Good heavens," he said again with frightened exasperation. He turned to Torres, face urgent and searching. "What about this report of Celeste's? Any word—"

A rumble from above interrupted the man. It was low and guttural and distant, yet seemed to be growing with eagerness in nearness and strength. Confused, he went to raise his head toward the ceiling when he noticed his tea pulsating with rippled, ringed perturbation on the table.

The ceiling began to crack with a menacing tear, and chunks of concrete broke free, crashing to the floor. Books rattled on their shelves next to the fireplace as it crackled in protest.

"Rowen!" Celeste yelled. "Under the table!"

She yanked the Order Master down to the floor and shoved him underneath the sturdy surface as the room continued playing its terrifying game. Naomi followed, joining them underneath with heaving breaths.

Half a minute after the mystery commenced, it ceased. The fireplace's flapping flames and popping wood were the only sounds to be heard. No more cracking, no more falling debris, no more breathing even as the trio held on for dear life.

The three members of the Order of Thaddeus all at once sighed, looking at each other wide-eyed with the same preposterous, yet all-too-germane question on their minds:

Had the Washington National Cathedral, church for America's capital and headquarters for the Order of Thaddeus, just been attacked by terrorists?

CHAPTER 7

A sudden thud against the double doors startled the trio still huddled underneath the worktable in Radcliffe's study. A second later, a click sounded forth. Four security personnel, wearing dark helmets and padding, assault rifles slung around their backs, came rushing in seeking the Master of the Order of Thaddeus and the Director of Operations.

"Ahh, at last the cavalry has arrived," Radcliffe said as he crawled out from underneath the table.

One of the security personnel rushed over to offer him an arm and help hoist him back upright. Two others helped Celeste and Torres.

The Order Master thanked the lad and then surveyed the vast room, sizing up the space before inspecting the ceiling. He took note of a long, deep crack and several good-sized divots where chunks of concrete had broken loose, as well as a lamp that had toppled to the floor in the sudden onset of vibrations.

"Please tell me, officer, that the greater Washington metropolitan area has just been the victim of a freak, sudden release of energy in the Earth's lithosphere, creating the seismic waves we've just endured."

The man looked down at the floor and shook his head. He said gravely, "I wish it were just an earthquake, Master Radcliffe." He took a breath and looked at his compatriots, then said, "We've been attacked."

"Good heavens," Radcliffe exclaimed, leaning against the table and sighing with exasperation. "Not here, too!"

"We'll debrief you in full," the officer continued, "but we need to evacuate you and the others from the compound."

"I should think not!" Radcliffe protested. "We are in the midst of operations of crucial ecclesial import—"

"Sir, you need to come with us, all of you," another officer interrupted, a tall man with shaved head and broad shoulders. Stripes on his arms indicated a degree of rank. "Given the severity of damage on the surface and ongoing nature of the event, this isn't up for debate. The whole command center is at risk of collapsing. We're working out an alternative command center where you and Ms. Bourne can take charge of everything that's ongoing with SEPIO and the Order. But, please..." The man held his arm open as another officer opened the door.

Radcliffe huffed and mumbled something under his breath, but relented and strode forth. Celeste and Torres followed.

"Commander Roberts, isn't it?" Celeste asked the officer who had coaxed Radcliffe into giving up his ground.

"Yes, Ms. Bourne." The man shuffled past Radcliffe, leading the group toward the underground parking garage. Celeste followed and came up to his side. Radcliffe was still mumbling.

"What exactly has transpired up above?"

"An explosion, ma'am. Suicide bomb, by the look of it."

"Blood hell..." Radcliffe sounded from behind.

She took a deep breath and held her face firm. Bloody hell was right.

Frosted glass doors up ahead swooshed open, and the party stepped into a concrete garage with three idling black Mercedes SUVs waiting for their arrival. Heavily armed men were poking automatic rifles out partly rolled-down windows in both the lead and rear vehicles. Commander Roberts guided the trio to the middle vehicle. He opened the rear door, and Radcliffe slid inside, then Celeste and Torres. The commander shuffled around the front to the passenger's side. When he was settled inside, the caravan lurched forward and gathered speed up the winding ramp toward the outside.

No one was prepared for what lay ahead.

Radcliffe instructed the driver to make a left onto Woodley Road and take the group around to the front of the cathedral on Wisconsin Avenue to survey the damage. Commander Roberts protested, insisting they immediately be taken away to safe harbor. But Radcliffe wasn't having anything of it; that was one order he wasn't going to back down from.

Within seconds they had reached the surface and turned onto Woodley, driving west in the early-afternoon hour through sheets of unrelenting rain. Radcliffe, Celeste, and Torres each twisted toward the sacred structure on their left that had held their Order's headquarters, gasping in unison at the scene before them.

The face of America's church had been completely ripped off. Devilish flames were shooting high and clawing up the spires at what little was left of the West facade of the Cathedral Church of Saint Peter and Saint Paul. A deep crater in the patio before the grand entrance smoldered with memory at the explosion that had desecrated the house of worship, smoke billowing upward in puffy plumes and hissing flames struggling against the early-spring deluge.

An explosion from the center of the nave startled the Order passengers and caused the driver to jerk the wheel as they turned onto Wisconsin Avenue. A series of stained glass windows had blown out, and flaming fingers were reaching up the side of the building, hungry to envelop the church with its fiery fury.

"What manner of wickedness has befallen us..." Radcliffe said gravely as the driver pulled up to the curb across from a small park that was smoking from having been enflamed from the initial blast.

Emergency personnel had already arrived and were working triage. Several bodies were being carried to ambulances, others were being bagged. Vehicles announcing the presence of the FBI, ATF, and DC Metropolitan Police were scattered about the grounds, securing the perimeter and rooting out the presence of any further explosive devices or terrorist threats on the premises.

A crack broke through the already taut afternoon air, sounding forth across the street near the front of the sacred structure. All five heads turned toward the cathedral in time to see what remained of its face drooping toward the ground in a slow-motion crumble of Indiana limestone, its spires and gargoyles and stained glass falling into an unholy heaping pile of rubble.

"Dear God, no..." Radcliffe moaned, leaning toward the scene playing itself outside the windshield.

Commander Roberts cleared his throat. "If it's alright, Master Radcliffe, we'd like to take you three to the Basilica of the National Shrine of the Immaculate Conception. There is a smaller base of operations beneath the basilica, as you know, but it should serve as a working HQ until..." The man trailed off and sounded choked with emotion.

Radcliffe sighed and lightly touched the man's shoulder. "Yes, Commander, that would be fine."

The driver made a U-turn on Wisconsin Avenue and pulled back onto Woodley Road to make the thirty-minute drive across town to the nation's largest Roman Catholic church. The drive was solemn and quiet, but for the pounding rain on the roof of the SUV. Upon arriving, the vehicle pulled into a looping driveway off Michigan Avenue and turned into a service entrance on the westside of the basilica behind a stone wall and thick hedgerow.

The occupants exited the vehicle, and Commander Roberts led them to a steel door with a palm-reading keypad. He placed his hand upon its surface. It pulsed blue three times before turning green. The door unlocked, and the commander pushed through into a short, sterile hallway of white that led to an elevator. The group stepped inside, and then traveled three stories beneath the Catholic church to the makeshift nerve center of SEPIO.

After a bell chimed, the elevator doors parted to reveal a red-brick hallway bustling with activity. It seemed the rest of the Order had already been transferred and sent to continue the fight ahead of the Master and Director of Operations.

"This way," Commander Roberts said as he hastened forward through the crowded hallway to a set of double doors at the end. Another palm-reading keypad stood guard, waiting for the commander's hand. When one door unlocked, he opened it to reveal a space that was similar in size to Radcliffe's study, but altogether different.

Dimmed recess lighting around the perimeter shone down upon narrow tables lining the dark walls commanded by workstations manned by agents dutifully executing on SEPIO orders. Where a fireplace stood crackling and popping away at one end of Radcliffe's study, a massive screen tracked critical mission updates and news footage from the world's major outlets reporting on the ongoing mass terrorist event befalling the Church. At the center of the room, where a set of leather couches and chairs anchored Radcliffe's command center, a raised platform with screens and chairs and direct-line phones to operation centers around the world was awaiting the director's control.

Commander Roberts introduced the trio to the other personnel burning the evening hours collating reports of terrorizing persecution coming in from the field, sifting through the data for leads, and reeling from what had been unleashed upon the Church. After the introductions, the commander asked for a status report from the assembled. They spent the next hour detailing the mayhem, bringing Radcliffe and Celeste up to speed with the latest developments around the world.

When they were finished, the commander nodded toward Celeste. "Your lead, Director Bourne."

Celeste nodded back, face steely and ready to take control.

She mounted the platform and scanned the room. She widened her stance and cupped her hands behind her. Then she cleared her throat and said, "Right. Thank you for your attention in the midst of an ongoing operation of utmost urgency. Yes, by all accounts, the Order has just been attacked by terrorists, forcing us to abandon our headquarters and defacing America's church. But it's far graver than our own insecurity. For our brothers and sisters in the faith around the world are enduring the most hideous and heinous of persecution in generations. The great dragon has been unleashed against the Church, operatives, and it is our job to quench its fire and slay the beast in order to save our brethren from no uncertain doom."

She paused and took a breath, scanning the room and feeling proud at the show of force from the Church's only line of defense.

"Now," she continued, "who can tell me what the bloody hell just happened to our headquarters?"

A slight chuckle arose from crowd when a petite olive-skinned woman wearing bright blue glasses stepped forward and raised her hand.

"Ahh, Zoe Corbino," Radcliffe said from the base of the platform. "Always one with answers at the ready."

"What can you tell us, Zoe?" Celeste asked.

The Italian who was responsible for operational support for SEPIO bowed her head slightly and cleared her throat before launching into her report. "As you know, there has been an explosion on the patio at the west front of the Washington National Cathedral, leaving behind a crater the size of a school bus. From what we can tell from the security footage we've obtained so far, it appears the man detonated prematurely."

"How so?"

"Well...see for yourself. Bring up the west facade footage."

A slight man of Indian descent swiveled back to his workstation and entered some keystrokes on his keyboard, then looked toward the main screen at the end of the room. Abraham Patel, if Celeste remembered correctly.

Grainy black-and-white footage began playing, presumably from a security camera mounted on a lamp post. It was facing the entrance to the grand neo-Gothic structure, gleaming under the cloudy sky and doors open for noon service. People had begun arriving for the Palm Sunday event and slowly drifted inside. Suddenly, a figure entered from stage right. He was darkly dressed and bearing a backpack. He walked purposefully forward, then stopped before darting toward the church. Then the screen went bright with blinding, explosive force.

Celeste folded her arms and stepped forward, furrowing her brow and shaking her head. "Play it again, Abraham."

The Indian man obliged. Same grayish footage, same dark figure with black backpack before the screen exploded in a show of fire and fury.

"Go back, right before the explosion." The film rewound and began to play. "Stop! Right there, what is that?"

The room collectively strained forward toward the screen.

Right before the man had taken off toward the entrance and exploded in a furious ball of terror, he had made a curious maneuver.

Torres answered, "It looks like...Well, it looks like he turned around."

There the man was: black and masked and body pivoted back toward the way he came, but with one foot still facing the way he was going.

"Why did you turn around you bloody fool?" she mumbled. She said more loudly, "Why did he turn back toward the way he came? What's he doing?"

The room was silent; no one knew.

"Perhaps the lad was getting cold feet?" Radcliffe offered.

"Then why did he tear off after the entrance a moment later?"

"Good question."

"Maybe he was looking at something," Torres said.

"As if something caught his attention?"

She nodded. "Perhaps...Can we play the rest of the footage leading to the blast, slow motion, inch-by-inch?"

Abraham nodded and pressed another few keystrokes. The image began to move again. One moment, the man was pivoted and staring off back toward the way he came, one foot planted opposite of his direction. The next, he was turning in a blur back toward the cathedral, feet high behind him as he ran to complete his course. And then suddenly—

"Whoa!" Torres said as others echoed her surprise.

"What the..." Celeste wondered as the man fell forward a split second before he exploded.

"Did the man lose his footing?" Radcliffe wondered.

"Back it up again, then replay it frame by frame."

Abraham obliged. One frame, two frames, three frames—

"There!" Celeste said interrupting.

"Good heavens," Radcliffe sounded forth.

"Did his head just explode?" Zoe asked, hand cupped over her mouth with surprise.

"Looks that way," Torres said.

Sure enough, there it was right there in black-and-white. The distinct dark pattern of blood as it sprayed forward from the man's skull as a bullet exited through to the other side.

No one moved; no one said a word.

Celeste finally said, "Do we have more footage of the grounds, any other angles of that scene playing itself out?"

"Working on," the Indian man said as he typed furiously.

"What does this mean?" Radcliffe asked Celeste.

She went to answer when Abraham announced he had two other angles.

"This is from the street cam across from the cathedral, courtesy of DC Metro."

Another grainy black-and-white picture from a lamp post along Wisconsin Avenue showed the park glowing faintly with the clouded, noonday light. A dark figure looked both ways up and down Wisconsin before walking purposefully across the street toward the cathedral. A few seconds later, he was across the street and into the park.

Then another man from the right strode into the frame.

"There!" Celeste said pointing at the screen.

A few gasped at the sight of a light-colored figure walking with long strides along the sidewalk and toward the park as well. She wondered if he was the one they were looking for. It was confirmed when he took a sharp right into the park—seemingly after the man.

"We've lost them. Where's the other angle?" Celeste asked with irritation.

"Coming now," said Abraham as another video appeared. It showed the one black-clad figure hustling through the park and striding toward the steps of the cathedral, then turning just as the mysterious man in white came into view.

Celeste's heart was pounding as she waited for the answer to reveal itself—praying that an answer would reveal itself!

And it did.

Within seconds, the man in black took off running toward the cathedral and the man in white took two long strides forward with his back to the camera. He raised his arm bearing a weapon then fired one soaring shot for the kill, exploding the terrorist's head and sending him stumbling to the ground in a blinding, explosive flash.

The man in white stumbled backward from the blast, but recovered. Standing, he turned slowly and walked off frame, head held high with accomplished pride.

But not before leaving one final piece of revelation.

The room gasped all at once at the sight of a dark cross emblazoned on his front, each end angling toward the middle.

Celeste took in a breath and looked to Radcliffe, and said, "That settles it then."

Radcliffe looked grim and gaunt, his face ashen and astonished from the weight of the revelation.

He turned toward her and nodded. "Indeed. Apparently, the Poor Fellow-Soldiers of Christ and of the Temple of Solomon have risen to fight another day."

"Who?" Torres said with confusion.

"The Knights Templar," Celeste said. "Who else?"

CHAPTER 8

Torres looked from Celeste to Radcliffe and back again as the room looked on as well, the gentle spin of hard drives and low-level HVAC hum filling in for what would have been a forest of crickets filling the void of dumbfounded silence.

"Seriously?" she finally managed, brows raised and mouth staying open with a grin of disbelief. "The Knights Templar. *The* Templars?

"Well, technically not *the* Templars," Radcliffe corrected. "For the Poor Fellow-Soldiers of Christ and of the Temple of Solomon, also known as the Order of Solomon's Temple, disbanded around 1312."

"Obviously, someone didn't get the memo on that one."

"I'm sure what Radcliffe means to suggest," Celeste added, "is that somebody is certainly jolly well impersonating the ancient Catholic military order—"

"*Monastic* order," Radcliffe interrupted, correcting her.

"Right, well, monastic order then. But I'm sure—"

She was interrupted again by a sudden flash of red at the top of the screen above the mysterious figure frozen shortly after the blast, indicating an urgent call from the field.

Celeste said, "Zoe, connect the call. Could be Silas and Gapinski."

She nodded and instructed Abraham to patch through the operatives.

The room stood silently as the call was answered. A wave of static filled the vast space. Everyone recoiled at the sound, while Abraham quickly made a volume adjustment.

Both fingers pressed to her ears and cringing, Celeste said, "Silas, Gapinski? Is that you?"

Only static again.

She looked at Zoe in frustration, who walked over to the Indian man for a word.

Then four beeps sounded, indicating the call had dropped.

"Good heavens..." Celeste complained, planting both hands at her hips. The alternative operations venue was proving to be a shadow of their former headquarters entombed under the National Cathedral. She commanded, "Ring the number again would you please, Zoe?"

Abraham nodded before Zoe could give the order. The dialing call began to sound throughout the hall. A few seconds later, the static was back. But also a voice.

"—is that you?"

"Silas?" the SEPIO director said, taking a step to the platform's railing.

"Yeah, it's me. Gapinski is here, too, on speaker. Sorry about before. We're getting sketchy reception, so we may lose you again."

"Where are you? What's happening?"

"We've been through a sticky wicket over here, as you Brits say," a voice bellowed through another wave of underlying static.

Torres smiled. "Good to hear you're in one piece, Hoss."

"Torres, is that you?" Gapinski asked.

"The one and only."

"You're being patched through on speaker to a makeshift control center in DC," Celeste said.

"Makeshift?" Silas said, registering confusion.

"We've had a bit of a sticky wicket here ourselves, my boy," Radcliffe said.

"Before we get into that," Celeste interjected, "what's your report?"

There was a pause of silence on the other line. Celeste tossed a glare at Zoe, then to Abraham. He shrugged, indicating all was well.

"There's been another terrorist event in Israel, here at the Jordan River. Gapinski and I both witnessed it firsthand."

"We heard, lad," Radcliffe said. "Is it true you were in the thick of it?"

"You could say that," Silas said.

Butterflies exploded in Celeste's stomach. Not only because two of her operatives had been at Death's door. But because Silas had been in harm's way.

"Are you alright?" she said in a panic.

"We're alright, considering."

"But you're safe," she asked with eagerness.

"We managed to find a ride in the town next door," Gapinski said. "Although, I'm sorry to say but SEPIO's gonna be in some hot doo-doo with Hertz for all the damage from—"

"But why the Jordan River?" the Order Master interrupted with irritation. "Celeste said something about some baptism business, but I couldn't make sense of it."

Silas said, "You're right. Gapinski's grandfather was performing a mass baptismal rite for thousands of candidates at the Yardenit baptismal site, a point along the River Jordan just south of the Sea of Galilee. Around dinner time, terrorists stormed the site and..."

Silas trailed off. Celeste thought the call had dropped again, but then understood he was searching for words. She let him before he continued.

"We lost Gapinski's grandfather," Silas finally said.

"No..." Torres said, gasping and placing a hand over her mouth. Others joined her as well.

Celeste knew that she and Gapinski had grown close the past year working together on two separate SEPIO operations. And they had all heard plenty of stories about Gapinski's Southern Baptist preacher grandfather. She folded her arms and looked at the ground in disbelief. Radcliffe did the same.

She went to offer condolences to the SEPIO operative when Silas continued.

"But he wasn't the only one," he said. "At least another fifty, maybe sixty Christians were kidnapped as well."

"So his grandfather wasn't killed, then?" Torres asked.

"Kidnapped, you say?" Celeste asked.

"That's right. Twenty to thirty terrorists rounded them up like sheep to the slaughter. Came in on boats and jet skis up the Jordan River, then several more through the parking lot above."

"Good heavens..." Radcliffe gasped. "Were there any casualties? I have to imagine so, given how large this mass baptismal event sounds."

A wave of static distorted Silas's reply.

"I'm sorry, Silas," Celeste said, "but you were cut off. What did you say?"

"I said, hundreds slaughtered. We did all we could, but it was just the two of us. The parking lot and the River Jordan are littered with the dead. But that wasn't—"

More static intervened in Silas's biggest reveal. And then the four beeps returned, indicating the call had dropped.

"Bloody hell," Celeste cursed again.

This time Radcliffe threw her a look at her indignation.

She blushed and lowered her head, then nodded in understanding. Yes, the hour was fraught with fear and frustration, but that didn't give her a license to bite people's heads off.

Keep it together...

She took a deep breath as Silas and Gapinski rang through again. Abraham connected them.

"Sorry about that," Silas offered.

Celeste replied, "No worries. But you were about to suggest something else happened."

"Yeah, about that..." he trailed off again before saying, "the terrorists themselves were attacked."

She glanced at Radcliffe and Torres, both of whom had glanced her way as well. The three of them both offered each other the same face of confusion.

"What do you mean by attacked, my boy?" Radcliffe asked. "Attacked how?"

"Just like I said. After the hostages were carted away by the terrorists on the boats, we went up top to the main parking lot just outside of the baptismal site. Buses were on fire. Dead bodies littered the lot. Those who were left were—"

"Crying and yelling at us hysterically," Gapinski added.

"Yes, and that. The survivors mostly kept to themselves in small groups trying to comfort themselves and offer first aid. But then I noticed across the lot a grouping of pickup trucks. After we approached them, we realized everyone was dead. Bodies were hanging over the sides of their cargo beds with bullet holes. The drivers were shot through their windows, execution style."

"Good heavens," Radcliffe offered.

"What about the IDF?" Torres asked, having served with them because her mother was Israeli.

"Nope," Gapinski said. "Total no-shows in these parts. Oh, wait. There they are, actually. Wave to Uncle Sam, Silas."

"That's the U.S. military, numbskull," Silas corrected as they passed a caravan of trucks loaded down with military personnel racing up the throughway. And then a number of flashing lights trailing them with more firepower.

"Oh, right. Well, then, wave to Uncle...Samuel?"

"Gapinski..." Celeste complained.

"Then you haven't a clue who perpetuated such vengeance against the terrorists?" Radcliffe asked, bringing the conversation back on course.

Silas said, "Not entirely..."

There was another pause of silence. Celeste glanced at Abraham again. He raised his palms in surrender and shrugged, again indicating all was well.

"Silas," she said, "what aren't you telling us?"

He replied, "There was a man, about ten or twenty yards off. Dressed like the rest of the jihadi whack jobs and crawling through the barren land away from the lot. We came up to him and kicked him over, and we saw he was wounded, real bad. Blood was dark and oozing."

"And he was all One Flew Over the Cuckoo's Nest," Gapinski added, "mumbling on and on about a bunch of malarky. Tell them!"

"I was, until you interrupted....Anyway, the guy was clearly in shock from whatever had happened to his crew of jihadis. Eyes staring off and glazed over. But he was mouthing and mumbling this phrase, like Gapinski said."

"What phrase?" Celeste asked.

"*Non nobis, Domine, non nobis, sed Nomini tuo da gloriam.*"

Radcliffe gasped. Torres turned to him. So did Celeste and everyone else in the room.

The Order Master took a step forward. "*Non nobis, Domine, non nobis, sed Nomini tuo da gloriam*? You're sure, Silas? Absolutely positive?"

"Positive."

"What's he playing at, Rowen?" Celeste said.

Radcliffe turned to answer her just as Silas said, "The Knights Templar. It's their motto."

"Right he is," Radcliffe said. "*Not unto us, O Lord, not unto us, but unto thy Name give glory.*' This rallying cry of the Templars was meant as an explicit rejection of the prevailing knightly attitudes of the time, where the soldiers of the state waged war to magnify their own names and those of their landed families. It reflected their Cistercian monastic influences of piety and self-sacrifice, as well as their patron saint's humility and self-effacement, the Blessed Virgin Mary."

Silas added, "No individual Templar fought for his own glory, or even for the glory of their religious Order, but instead only for the glory of God."

Torres scoffed. "Tell that to the millions of Muslims they slaughtered in the name of that God."

Radcliffe cleared his throat and threw her an irritated look.

Gapinski said, "And some jihadi whack job was crawling through the desert mumbling that motto." Then he gave a chuckle, and added, "Of course, the idea that the Templars have risen all zombielike to avenge martyred Christians is nutso to the max, right?"

He and Silas were met with a roomful of silence, several seconds ticking by as Celeste and Radcliffe pondered their revelation.

"Guys, right?" Silas asked, breaking the silence in search of reassurance.

"Tell him," Radcliffe instructed Celeste.

She said, "Right. So earlier I mentioned we've endured our own sticky wicket across the Atlantic. The Order itself has been terrorized."

"*What?!*" The duo in the Middle East both exclaimed.

"Are you kidding me?" Silas said through a haze of static.

"I wish I were," Radcliffe said gravely.

Celeste explained, "A terrorist detonated an explosive

device just outside the threshold of the Washington National Cathedral. We're still assessing the damage to the SEPIO headquarters, but we're sure the Order wasn't the target itself, but rather the Christian church."

"Why's that?" Gapinski asked.

"Because the same terror befell cathedrals across Europe and elsewhere."

"No..." Silas said.

"Afraid so," Radcliffe added. "Notre Dame, Seville, Saint Isaac's in St. Petersburg, and Westminster all experienced the same persecuting terror and destruction. However, with far graver results." He crossed himself and mumbled something, probably a prayer for the dead.

Celeste said, "And before the attack in Washington, we had been receiving multiple reports of terrorist events across the African continent. Churches being stormed by men bearing automatic rifles and fire-bombed into oblivion. Mass kidnappings and raping of Christian women and children, and also executions."

Silas said, "So clearly what happened in Old City Jerusalem is part of a far larger coordinated attack against the Church."

"Clearly."

"But what does this have to do with the guy crawling through the desert muttering a creepy motto from a long-gone Church order?" Gapinski asked.

"Right. So after the terrorist event, we were promptly whisked away to safer ground by Order security, to the older operations outpost at the Basilica of the National Shrine of the Immaculate Conception. There, we reviewed security footage from a handful of area cameras and made a rather surprising discovery that makes your revelation all the more important."

Gapinski snorted. "Let me guess, some zombie superhero dude sporting thermal whitey tighties emblazoned with a red cross on the front like the Church's ill-forgotten guardians of yore was all Johnny-on-the-spot with a Smith & Wesson revolver blowing the guy's head off to kingdom come?"

The room went quit while a soft wave of static blew through the connection.

"Uhh, guys?"

"That's pretty much the long and short of it, Hoss," Torres finally said.

"Really? I was totally making a funny..."

Celeste said, "The footage shows a man approaching the terrorist subject shortly before he detonated his bomb, shooting him dead in the head and presumably before he wrought far more destruction inside the cathedral. However, we're not at all sure who the bloke was."

"Then how do you know he was our medieval zombie superhero dude?"

Radcliffe cleared his throat, and explained, "Because emblazoned on the front of his long johns, as you put it more pedestrianly, was a red cross, just like the Church's ill-forgotten guardians of yore."

"Always something," Gapinski complained.

Silas said, "And we think that he was a, what? A Templar, come back from the dead to avenge the Church?"

"We don't know what he was?" Celeste reiterated. "We only know that somebody dressed in white bearing a crimson cross managed to intercept a terrorist with all of the markings and bearing the same *modus operandi* as the others who have attacked Christian churches around the world—and presumably in Jerusalem and the Jordan River. And then this bloke took him out before he leveled the National Cathedral and killed hundreds of worshipers inside."

"And combined with what we found at the Jordan River," Silas said, "a man mumbling the Templars motto in some state of shock, presumably brought on by the ass-whooping they got at the hands of a group of dudes in the same superhero getup..."

Celeste took a breath and folded her arms, then said, "There is a bloody-well good chance the Templars, or somebody or *somebodies* playing them, have risen to new life."

"Which means we've got two problems on our hands. The terrorists and the Templars."

Radcliffe nodded. "Indeed."

Once again, the same gentle spin of hard drives and low-level HVAC hum combined with bursts of static filled in the void of dumbfounded silence. The afternoon had stretched into evening, and the room was collectively beginning to feel the fatigue from the day's events.

After several minutes ticked by, Radcliffe announced, "I would like to take a break, to freshen up and gather our wits about us. It has to be near midnight in your neck of the woods, Silas and Matthew, and I'm sure you both could use a breather. Drive to SEPIO's Jerusalem operations center. It is well outside the radius of Old City, so you should gain easy access. And then let us reconvene in a few hours with you two on video conference, along with Celeste, Naomi, and Zoe and myself. It appears that we have lots to discuss, but it would be best to do so under a more secure connection and after having taken a breath or twelve."

There was agreement on the line from the duo traveling along Route 1 now toward the city, as well as from the other SEPIO agents back at HQ. They ended the call as the room cleared with a collective shuffling of chairs and then a shuffling of feet out the door. Zoe and Abraham busied themselves with the continued work of reconnaissance from the day's events.

Radcliffe, Torres, and Celeste took a breath while Silas and Gapinski drove to Jerusalem command. They were going to need every ounce of air for what lay ahead.

CHAPTER 9
LOCATION UNKNOWN.

A sea of stars strewn across the midnight sky sparkled like a billion diamonds over the barren desert just across the border of the Holy Land, the sun having slipped beneath the horizon hours ago. A warm, gentle breeze carried the smell of salt and fish across the beige sand, disturbing a loose flap of canvas to the tent of a man used to the visual and olfactory display from his original homeland of Iran.

Marwan Farhad smoothed his manicured mustache as he sauntered over to fix the offending piece of canvas as it swayed in the breeze, breathing deeply of the pleasurable air. He tied it open, securing the rope to a stake in the still-warm sand. A round of hearty laughs echoed from a group huddled around a campfire several yards away, the warm glow pulsating off of his men who were recharging with food and drink.

Good. They would need it for what lay head.

The man shuffled back into his tent, walking over to a kerosene lamp hanging from wooden cross beams. He reached up to the device and fiddled with a knob, bringing it to life and light. Then he slumped into a pile of red velvet cushions commanding the center of the space, taking advantage of the window of time to rest and recharge himself.

He leaned back and grabbed the long black hose snaking out of a hookah made of blown green glass with a long, elaborate silver stem. Placing its nozzle in his mouth, he sucked contemplatively, taking in a lungful of the mint-tinged tobacco. He let it linger in his body, holding his breath for several seconds before blowing it out in an exhausted sigh, the haze drifting past the orange lamplight and filling his tent.

The day was pure perfection. Executed without a hitch. The Thirteen will be most pleased. Perhaps offer me a promotion to the Council of Five. To Grand Master of Nous, even.

He smiled at the thought of replacing the former Grand Master, Rudolf Borg, who last he heard was rotting away in a cell deep inside The Hague. He took another satisfying drag on the hookah hose and let his mind dance with delight at the thought of the power that was within reach.

A man startled him at the entrance, tall and dressed in black with a German-made rifle slung around his back, hood stuffed in a pocket revealing an angular face with full black hair. He was bearing a silver platter mounted with a bronze Turkish coffee pot steaming with its warm, strong concoction.

"Ahh, Hamid," he said to his second-in-command and motioned for the soldier to step forward. "Come in, come in!"

He did, taking long strides forward and setting the tray on the woven rug blanketing the tent's ground, bowing and then stiffening at attention with respect.

"Your evening coffee, Commander Farhad. I thought you would want it to accompany your evening ritual."

"You thought right."

Farhad closed his eyes as he finished with the hookah, enjoying the combination of the minty tobacco flavor and the earthy, fragrant scent of the Middle Eastern coffee quickly filling his tent. He blew out the smoke and grabbed the pot's long black handle, careful to avoid the scalding metal of the pot itself. Then he tipped it over a small ceramic cup the size of his fist and poured the thick, steaming brew. He carefully set it back on the tray, took the cup, and took a sip, humming with delight.

"I assume you have an operational report for me?" the man said, taking another sip of the strong coffee.

Hamid eased his stance and nodded. "I do. Paris, Saint Petersburg, London went perfectly. Maximum damage and destruction without any issues whatsoever. The Christian churches lay in rubble. Mausoleums for the dead infidels!"

"Excellent," the man said, his mustache wiggling above his mouth with satisfaction. "And what of the others, Nairobi and Abuja, Yardenit and Washington?"

The man took a deep breath, then said, "Nairobi and Abuja netted us thousands of infidels, both in the grave and in our possession."

"Good, good," Farhad said. He took another sip of coffee, then stroked his salt-and-pepper beard.

"But—"

"But?" Farhad snapped, interrupting the man and spilling coffee on his white linen *thawb*. He cursed under his breath before setting down the cup. He held his arms and scanned the tent in search of a towel to wipe away the mistake.

"Over there. Hand me that!" he commanded Hamid, gesturing with an angry finger to a table in the corner.

The man swallowed hard and quickly went to retrieve the towel, dipping it in a basin of water before handing it to his commander.

Farhad cursed again as he labored to erase the stain, then again when he saw he was doing nothing more than smearing the brown stain up and down his garment. He threw the towel back over to the corner, and in one motion, he turned over the silver platter with rage, the coffee flying into the canvas wall and smearing down its side.

"What is this *but* you speak of?" he said angrily.

Hamid stiffened again, looking forward over Farhad's head and clearing his throat. "There were complications."

"Complications?" Farhad growled lowly, easing himself up to stand on the mound of cushions so that he was at eye level with the tall man. "What complications?"

"We slaughtered several hundred infidels at the Christian site along the Jordan River. Five to six hundred by our estimations, as well as captured another sixty."

"*But?*"

"But," the man said, pausing to deliberate over his words. "But several of our men who had arrived by truck were also...slaughtered."

Farhad stepped back, his mustache twisting with surprise at the revelation. "Slaughtered, you say? By whom?"

"Our men from the raid report that there were two armed men accompanying the Christians inside the baptismal site itself. And then, out inside the parking lot, several more of our men were put to death by another set of infidels. However, we are not entirely sure the two episodes are linked."

"Why not?"

"Because of what happened at the Washington National Cathedral."

Farhad clenched his jaw and stepped forward again, mere inches from Hamid, breathing his breath of earthy spices and tobacco into the man's face. "And what happened in Washington?"

"Our man detonated his device," Hamid said quickly, taking another breath, then wincing slightly before recovering.

"*But?*"

"But it was early?"

"Early? What is this word *early*?"

"The plan was to enter the cathedral during the service then detonate the explosive, bringing down the entire structure. Just like the others in Europe and in Russia."

"*But?*" Farhad growled again, growing impatient with the incompetence of his men.

"But from across the street, the guarantor who was standing ready to detonate the device remotely if the primary lost confidence saw another figure come up quickly behind the man. He called out to him and then blew his head off."

Farhad took in a sharp breath. Both in surprise and with concern at the development. He stepped back and bowed his head, contemplating the meaning of it all.

The thought that somebody could have known about such an operation was remarkable. Their people had planned each of the targets with the utmost precision and secrecy, with a tight group consisting of the primaries, guarantors, and then Hamid and Farhad having the only complete knowledge of it all.

Yet somebody had broken through. Or some*bodies*...

Farhad raised his head. "Did the guarantor say anything else, anything that might identify this perpetrator?"

"He said the person had been dressed in white, from head to foot, but for black boots. That is all he saw, for after the explosion the man exited the scene in haste."

A man in white come to save and protect a Christian church. I wonder...

"That is all," Farhad said to the man.

Hamid snapped to attention, turned sharply, and strode out of the tent, returning back to the revelry at the campfire still blazing strong.

Farhad flopped back against the cushions and put his hands behind his head. He took in a deep breath and frowned with concern at how the day had unfolded, worried what it might mean for the rest of all that he had planned for the Christian Holy Week.

When the Council of Five tasked him with taking charge of the operation in Borg's absence, he was hesitant. Not that he disbelieved the infidel followers of Jesus of Nazareth, the *Christ* as they called him, deserved the full measure of their fiery, furious wrath for conning the masses into delusions of eternal grandeur and waging war against his people. He just wondered about the wisdom of poking the beast, especially during its most holiest week. But as the Council unveiled the fullness of its designs, he was convinced that this kind of response was exactly what the world needed. For the Christian religion had royally screwed up the world stretching back to the earliest days of its founding.

Of course, humanity, in all of its curiosity and creativity and compulsion for answers has developed the most magnificent ways to deal with the boring and overwrought and tiresome questions Homo sapiens have asked ever since they stared up into the blankness of the midnight sky and asked the very simple, but inevitable question: *why*? Why is there something rather than nothing? Why are *we*, the collective humanity, something at all instead of a bunch of impulse-driven bipedal animals—able to create and innovate and form societies?

Which led to: *who*? Who is it that set all of this into motion in the first place? Who set *us* into motion, the one we're responsible to when we lie or kill our fellow man? When we cheat on our taxes or cheat on our husband?

And then, of course, this led to the oh-so cumbersome question that has vexed us bipedal animals for 60,000 years: *How?*

Once humanity began to amass a pile of sins stretching to the heavens—both collectively and personally—the question quickly became: how can we wipe the slate clean, how can we attain the all-important do over that will set our hearts and minds free from shame and guilt? And then: how can we appease the wrath of God or the gods or the Universe or whatever? How can we become right with this God or the gods or the Universe or whatever?

Among the religions, Christianity has answered these questions with utmost innovation, devising the most brilliant of schemes: God killing god.

Well, becoming man first before killing himself in an act of suicidal desperation.

But brilliant, nonetheless.

He had heard from Nous counterintelligence that the Order of Thaddeus and their pathetic Project SEPIO took him for a Zoroastrian prophet. He giggled to himself at the thought. Nothing could be further from the truth.

He was a Sunni Muslim who valued Islam's insights for the whole of humanity, believing along with Nous that what the world needed was the will to power in order to rise above our ignorance and a way to lead us there, which he believed Muhammad's life exemplified. Nous didn't always agree, but he was making progress convincing some of its value.

Of course, Islam had nothing close to this Christian innovation of Jesus' atoning sacrifice, believing instead that Allah desires the brute force of the individual will to assuage his wrath—not the bloody sacrifice of a supposed man-god. Farhad believed with every fiber of his being that the way to the utopian existence humanity longed for was found in *sharia*, the code of laws handed down to Muhammad that will please Allah and earn his favor, leading to Paradise.

Not through someone paying the ultimate price of human shame and guilt in our place to make us right with God and repair our human nature. That was utterly absurd!

And in the process of devising this most brilliant scheme of answers to our human problem of sin and death, the Christians, the *Church* as it has called itself, had perpetuated the most heinous acts of terror across the spectrum of humanity the last two millennia. The heresy hunts, the Inquisition, the witch trials. And chief among them: the wholesale slaughtering of his ancestors through those dark centuries of the Crusades.

Which that man in white who showed himself at the cathedral embodied wholesale.

Farhad clenched his jaw and tightened his fists still resting behind his head at the thought.

The hookah sitting next to his throne of red velvet cushions, coal still burning the tender mint-tinged tobacco leaves, caught his attention. He snatched the hose resting next to him and sucked longingly from its tip, the pleasurable smoke filling him with relief. He held it again, then opened his mouth and let it plume out into the tent. He opened his eyes and held the expression, his mind drifting to the unexpected turn.

A man in white, come to save and protect a Christian church.

A shiver walked slowly up his spine as he thought about the unreal, remote possibility of what that meant.

Has an old foe risen, come to exact vengeance once again? No matter. We'll deal with them as we did the last time.

He blew out the rest of the smoke, stood, and began stripping himself of his stained *thawb*. He climbed into the same desert fatigues his fellow brothers were wearing outside. When he finished changing, he grabbed his black hood. He took his rifle that was propped against the tent wall and slung it around his back. Then he retrieved the lantern and walked out into the night.

The men standing around the fire broke out into another round of laughs; they quickly hushed at the sight of Farhad walking toward them. The seven or eight of them, wearing desert fatigues and bearing automatic rifles, stiffened at attention as the man strode past.

Farhad slipped on his black hood and called out to Hamid to join him. The man hustled to his side, grabbing two of the men around the campfire to accompany them.

Several more tents, far more modest and quaint than his palatial dwelling, were scattered about the barren desert, more homely fires burning and ringed by pockets of the same men in black bearing Heckler & Koch automatic rifles. As the head of the alt-spirituality's armory and commander of operations for the organization, he had spent years carefully assembling an arsenal built by the German defense manufacturing company, ensuring his soldiers would be armed with only the best engineering of his adopted homeland. This week they would need it. Nothing could go wrong. The Council wouldn't allow it.

From around each of the fires, the clusters of men scrambled off the ground and stood at attention as Farhad approached and passed. But he paid them no mind. He was only interested in one group of people.

The orange glow from his lantern glinted off a blue metal shipping container as he approached. It was the size of a school bus and planted several yards past the main grounds. A man standing outside the door put out a cigarette and slipped his black hood back over his face, then quickly stiffened to attention and saluted the commander.

"Open it," Farhad growled.

The soldier nodded and hastened to unlatch the metal door. It offered a creaking reply as the man swung it open. There were gasps and moans, then the sound of scurrying, like fleeing rats in a sewer.

The commander swung his lamp out in front and took a step forward, then recoiled at the scent of piss and rancid bodies. Women and children were crouching in fear near the back of the container, stifling distraught sobs. Several older men joined them near the back, but the younger ones stood in front, shielding them with determined looks and firm poses.

Farhad couldn't help but smirk at the scene. He swung the lamp back out in front, then called out, "Who is your leader?"

No one moved. The crowd seemed to shrink farther back inside at the request.

He waited several seconds, then narrowed his eyes and said again, "Your leader, where is he? Show yourself!"

Again, no movement. Except the young men seemed to harden their stance, their arms flexing in front of their bodies and ready for a fight.

Farhad's impatience sent him for his rifle. But a rustling deep inside the belly of the container stayed his hand.

The pond of bodies parted, and a burly man with a sagging, white scruffy face wearing a billowing white robe stained pink and brown stepped forward.

The man stood in front of the masked commander bearing a kerosene lamp and German-made assault rifle, back straight and arms at his side. If he was afraid, he certainly didn't show it.

He said, "I'm Jim George Gapinski, pastor of this flock. I believe you asked for me."

Farhad eyed him from head to toe. A smile crept across his face, mustache wiggling with satisfaction.

"Yes, I did," he replied, grinning with delight. "You'll do nicely."

CHAPTER 10
LOCATION UNKNOWN.

The spark inflamed the tiny sliver of wood, a white burst of light expanding in a sudden blaze before contracting into the quiet yellow flame dancing in the darkened antechamber, its plucky luminescence casting a golden hue on the rough-cut stone blocks that led downward.

The man in white stared at the match he had struck, holding it in front of his face as he contemplated the metaphor.

So many sparks of light that have led me to this moment, standing inside this dark threshold inside the ancient Order's stronghold.

The first of which was November 27, 1095, when Pope Urban II summoned the peasants and nobility alike to a field rallying the Church to his holy cause. The man in white had memorized large portions of His Holiness's sermon years ago as inspiration for his own holy purposes. He recalled portions of it as the tiny yellow flame burned its way down the match:

> *'Many of God's churches have been violated. The*
> *Saracens have ruined the altars with filth and*
> *defilement. They have circumcised Christians*
> *and smeared their blood on the altars or poured it*

*into baptismal fonts. It amused them to kill
Christians by opening up their bellies and
drawing out the end of their intestines, which
they then tied to a stake. Then they flogged their
victims and made them walk around and around
the stake until their intestines had spilled out and
they fell dead on the ground.'*

The match dimmed to an all-consuming nothingness, the darkness laced with the faint, surprisingly comforting scent of burnt wood.

Exactly what the Church herself had endured during those dark, destructive centuries when the Muslim hordes ravaged the Christian lands of Palestine and North Africa on their way toward Europe. Like a locust cloud consuming a summer field of wheat, only to leave it stripped bare and drained of all life.

Exactly what he himself had felt those few years ago when his own life and light was consumed by those same locust hordes...

The man in white stood still, allowing the suffocating void to steal his nerves and his resolve for the vows that he and his renewed Order had pledged. Especially because the rest of Pope Urban's sermon described in graphic detail the extent to which the enemy of the Church would go with their terrorizing persecution.

He took a deep, stabilizing breath, closing his eyes as he further reflected upon the truth of the historical matter that foretold of the violence that would befall the Church a millennium later:

*'Others they bind to a post and pierce with arrows.
Others they compel to extend their necks and
then, attacking them with naked swords, attempt
to cut through the neck with a single blow. What*

shall I say of the abominable rape of the women?
To speak of it is worse than to be silent.'

The memory of that precious young woman drifted to the surface, the one who had died a similar kind of horrifying death in witness to her faith in Jesus Christ at the hand of those locust hordes. Joining the great cloud of witnesses who bore the truth and promise of his life, death, and resurrection.

Emotion caught in his throat at the memory burned into his consciousness of that fateful afternoon, and all that she had endured at the hands of those village terrorists.

"*If you permit them to continue thus for awhile with impunity,*'" the man in white mumbled, once again quoting from Pope Urban's sermon, "'*the faithful of God will be much more widely attacked by them.*'"

He tightened his fist and clenched his jaw at the modern truth of what the medieval Pope had prophesied—the spark that had launched the First Crusade.

The hour for such avenging, protective measures has drawn near once more...

The man struck another match, the wood sliver bursting to life. As the small flame burned, he considered the second spark from history that had led him to that moment.

The slaughtering of 300 Christians and enslavement of sixty more at the River Jordan 900 years ago by the same bloody-thirsty Muslim menace. Of course, Pope Urban II had bewailed the same invasive, murderous species nearly a hundred years prior:

'Let us bewail the most monstrous devastation of the
Holy Land! This land we have deservedly called
holy in which there is not even a footstep that the
body or spirit of the Savior did not render
glorious and blessed which embraced the holy

> *presence of the mother of God, and the meetings*
> *of the apostles, and drank up the blood of the*
> *martyrs shed there. You should shudder at*
> *raising a violent hand against Christians; it is*
> *less wicked to brandish your sword against*
> *Saracens.'*

He considered those events that transpired nearly a millennium ago to the date: the baptismal slaughter that sparked the formation of a monastic order of holy warriors tasked with the express, singular mission to defend the Holy Land and God's holy people.

The monastic order that he himself and those arriving in short order had resurrected from the shadows of history for a new, righteous purpose.

Protecting the Church from the same unholy menace. Avenging those who had been slaughtered, raped, and maimed through cruelty and injustice for their faithful allegiance to Jesus Christ.

The Order had been known by many names across the centuries. The Poor Fellow-Soldiers of Christ and of the Temple of Solomon. The Order of Solomon's Temple. The Knights of Christ.

And more pedestrianly: the Knights Templar.

Or simply, the Templars.

They were Christ's holy warriors who had risen to answer the apocalyptic call that the Pope himself had issued to the original peasants and nobles alike in that field a thousand years ago, echoes of Scripture's own apocalyptic warnings of a beastly dragon that would consume Christ's faithful children in a fiery, furious show of murderous, exterminating force:

> *'With the end of the world already near, it is first*
> *necessary, according to the prophecy, that the*

*Christian way be renewed in those regions either
through you, or others, whom it shall please God
to send before the coming of Antichrist, so that
the head of all evil, who is to occupy there the
throne of the kingdom, shall find some support of
the faith to fight against him.'*

It appeared the Antichrist had girded his loins and armed
for battle once again. And the same call that Pope Urban II
issued back in that day was the same one he and his fellow
Knights of Christ heeded with seriousness of heart in their own
day, joined by a rising tide of fellow knights around the world:

*'Christian warriors, who continually and vainly seek
pretexts for war, rejoice, for you have today
found a truer pretext. If you are conquered, you
will have the glory of dying in the very same
place as Jesus Christ, and God will never forget
that he has found you in the holy battalions.
Soldiers of Hell, become soldiers of the living
God!'*

Soldiers of Hell, become soldiers of the living God!
The man considered this call to arms, understanding the
truth of what His Holiness had issued all too well. For he
himself had been a soldier of hell, an enemy of God.

And the one who was singularly responsible for that
woman's death, the pearl of his eye. The third spark that had
inflamed his own life-course.

The man lit a third match after the second one died to darkness. He went to finally light the torch anchoring the stone wall
when he jolted.

It was the sound of crunching gravel just outside the
massive door to the antechamber he had left propped open.

Someone entered, followed by several more people.

The man in white nodded to each of them, eight in total. His fellow knights had finally arrived.

He lit the torch that had been awaiting his offering of fire. It blazed to life.

He took it and led his fellow knights down below to debrief on their recent exploits, a descent into a refreshing coolness that smelled of staticky thunderstorms and spicy earth, reminding him of his homeland.

Once below, he walked with purpose toward the massive stone fireplace at one end of the vast space the risen Templars had spent months constructing with precision. He dipped the torch inside, and a stack of logs drenched in oil immediately caught fire. It roared to life and offered the blessed light and life the band of resurgent monastic warriors had sorely needed after a harrowing twenty-four hours.

The man in white had given up everything to reconstitute God's battalion—his wealth, his mining business, his status, his standing in his former community—believing with every fiber of his being that he and his fellow knights had been prepared for such a time as this. They were doing the Lord's work, and he was with them every step of the way.

The nine strode to the large rectangular wooden table commanding the center of the space that had served as a great hall for their gatherings. More rooms jutted off from that main one in every direction underground, serving as quarters for the risen Templar Order.

As Order Master, the man assumed his position at the head of the table. He sat down and said, "Praise be to the Lord on high for his magnificent, providential protection during these dark times!"

"*Amen!*" the other eight said as one.

"I return from America, having stayed the great dragon's advance. At least for now. What say you all?"

The rest of the Order members gave reports in pairs and triplets of foiling the menacing plots of the exterminating terror rising to persecute the Church across the world. Each of them had personally experienced in their own way the full weight and measure of that persecution, and so they intimately understood the nature of what Jesus Christ himself had warned against—memories which drove their vows to protect and defend the defenseless brothers and sisters in the faith around the world from the wicked injustice of persecuting violence befalling the Church.

When each of them had completed their reports, the man in white at the head grunted his approval. "Babylon the great, the mother of all prostitutes that John the Seer foretold, has risen to consume the Church, my friends, striking out against her with terrorizing persecution. She is becoming drunk on the blood of God's holy people this week, the blood of those who bear the testimony of Jesus. And it is our holy duty to slay the whore who rides the wicked beast of centuries past with the full might and fury of those holy warriors who went before us!"

Another shout of *"Amen!"* rose from the gathered group.

"But before we fully engage our righteous calling in service of our Lord and his Church, let us pray—for ourselves, for the Church, for our slaughtered brothers and sisters."

The nine pushed back from the table and fell to their knees, propping their folded hands upon the wooden table. Joining with one voice, they prayed a prayer that hadn't been voiced in centuries:

> *Lord Jesus Christ, Holy Father, eternal God, omnipo-*
> *tent, omniscient Creator, Bestower, kind Ruler*
> *and most tender lover, pious and humble*
> *Redeemer; gentle, merciful Savior, Lord! We*
> *humbly beseech Thee and implore Thee that*
> *Thou may enlighten us, free us and preserve the*

> *brothers of the Temple and all Thy Christian*
> *people, troubled as they are.*
>
> *Thou, O Lord, Who knowest that we are innocent,*
> *set us free that we may keep our vows and your*
> *commandments in humility, and serve Thee and*
> *act according to Thy will. Dispel all those unjust*
> *reproaches, far from the truth, heaped upon us*
> *by the means of tough adversities, great tribula-*
> *tions and temptations, which we have endured,*
> *but can endure no longer.*

"*Amen!*" the others echoed with a shout of solidarity.

The man in white stood; the others joined him.

He said, "The hour of action has arrived. We know what we must do." The man paused, taking in a stabilizing breath and surveying those standing around the table. He marveled at those that the Lord had providentially assembled for such a time as this, and he prayed that God would make their paths straight as they resurrected the righteous mission of protection begun nine centuries prior.

He continued, "Our mission is holy, our cause is just. May the beat of our heart fully align with the anthem of our knightly exemplars: '*Non nobis, Domine, non nobis, sed Nomini tuo da gloriam.*'"

"*Amen!*" the others echoed with a shout of solidarity.

The man smiled and nodded, emotion beginning to over-come his eyes at the sight of the group he had assembled over the years and the mission they had mutually pledged them-selves to during these dark times: the protection and defense of Christ's Church in the face of a menacing wickedness stretching back nearly three-quarters of the Church's existence.

Silently, he reaffirmed their anthem, girding himself for the week ahead.

Not unto us, O Lord, not unto us, but unto thy Name give glory.

CHAPTER 11

WASHINGTON.

The revelation that the Templars had seemingly risen back to new life, waging war in full ecclesial vengeance, on top of the terrorizing persecution against the Church had hit SEPIO hard. They had needed time to process, as well as time to take a breath and freshen up from the craziness of it all.

Palm Sunday had crested into Monday, but there was much work to be done in the early-morning hours. The four agents and Order Master reconvened in the operations center a few hours later to get to work unraveling the Gordian Knot both the Templars and terrorists posed—to not only the Order but the Church itself.

Radcliffe and Celeste both bore mugs of steaming, hot tea, settling into the center of a long, horseshoe table facing the darkened screen where they expected the two boys from Jerusalem momentarily. Torres shuffled into the room cradling a mug of stale coffee, making do with what their makeshift operations could offer.

Soon Silas and Gapinski appeared on a massive screen operational support was using to keep apprised of the situation facing the Church. They had just reached the SEPIO outpost just north of the city off Route 1. Instead of coffee, the two sipped on cheap bourbon from plastic cups that Gapinski had picked up at a convenience store along the way. They were both still shaken but functional, and the libation would help.

Because it was go time, and the Church needed every hand on deck.

"First of all," Radcliffe began, "how are you doing, Matthew?"

Gapinski took a breath, then he took a sip of bourbon. He looked toward the ceiling of the cramped space of peeling beige walls and harsh overhead florescent lighting, blinking his eyes rapidly and wiping them and his nose before responding.

"Managing," he said, taking another breath, then another sip. "But eager to kick some serious jihadi ass."

"I'm sure you are," he said smiling. "And I assure you, we will pull out all of the measures at our disposal to appropriately avenge your grandfather's kidnapping and bring the perpetrators of this act of terror to proper justice, not to mention for the sake of the scores of other believers. However, clearly we need to have ourselves a group huddle on these momentous developments and formulate a plan of response before casting ourselves headlong into the void. But before we do, I would like to tell you a story to start things off."

The elderly man cleared his throat and took a sip of tea, then began.

"Nine hundred years ago, during Holy Week in 1119, on Holy Saturday in fact, the miracle of Holy Fire at the Church of the Holy Sepulcher sent seven hundred pilgrims running for the mighty River Jordan in ecstasy."

"Uhh, what miracle?" Gapinski asked, echoing through the operations center.

Radcliffe huffed. "Every year, on the eve of Easter, caretakers would place a lamp of oil beside the remaining slab of rock where Christ had laid buried in death. And, as it was said, it would burst alive with fire through a miraculous intervention of God, flames that would then be used to light the individual —oh, it doesn't matter! The point is that these seven hundred ecstatic pilgrims ran to the River Jordan intending to worship the Lord where Christ had begun his ministry and bathe in its sacred waters. However, they never made it."

"Never made it? Why not? What happened?"

"Goodness me, you're worse than my niece! They were attacked, that's what happened. Much as you yourselves were attacked, Silas and Matthew. As the historian Albert of Aachen recounted, '*there appeared Saracens from Tyre and Ascalon, armed and very fierce.*' These were men from the remaining Muslim strongholds in the region. And they came upon these unarmed civilian Christians who were, in the words of the historian: '*weary after a journey of many days, weakened by fasting in Jesus' name.*' The pilgrims had no chance," Radcliffe said gravely. "Again, as Albert of Aachen reported, '*The wicked butchers pursued them, putting three hundred to the sword and holding sixty captive.*'"

"Three hundred dead and sixty captive?" Silas asked. He had withdrawn a cigarette and lit it, taking a pleasurable pull before adding: "Sounds just like what happened yesterday. So, what, this attack on Yardenit was some sort of reenactment of the past?"

Radcliffe said, "An interesting thought, my boy. One that may not be too far off the mark. That attack back then was one of a series of Muslim acts of terror perpetuated against Christians in the region. So this one at the Jordan River, combined with all of the other acts of terrorism, certainly makes for an interesting historical mirror. But the events are significant for one other very important reason."

"Oh, yeah?" he said, taking another drag. "Why is that?"

"Because at the Mass anchoring the start of the Church's calendar that same year, the Christ-Mass as it was known, a group of nine French knights took vows of poverty, chastity, and obedience to, quote, '*defend pilgrims against brigands and rapists,*' unquote. On Christmas Day, before the Patriarch in the Church of the Holy Sepulcher, these nine men took their monastic pledges, calling themselves the *Pauperes commilitones Christi.*"

"The Poor Fellow-Soldiers of Christ," Silas said, leaning back in his chair, half-spent cigarette dangling from his fingers.

"Indeed."

The SEPIO operatives gave a collective sigh of disbelief that nine hundred years ago Muslims similarly attacked a band of Christian believers at the Jordan River, culminating in the founding of one of the most legendary monastic orders in the history of the Church.

"Now, Naomi," Radcliffe said, turning to Torres who startled at the attention, "earlier you seemed to scoff at the notion that the Templars fought not for their own glory, but instead only for the glory of God. Suggesting they were responsible for millions of slaughtered Muslims in the name of that God."

"I wasn't referring to the Templars, per se," Torres replied, "but to the Crusades that the Templars came to epitomize and the mass slaughter those Europeans perpetuated against the indigenous people. But, yes, I guess that was my implication."

Radcliffe smiled. He mumbled, "The mass slaughter those Europeans perpetuated against the indigenous people." Then he offered a chuckle. "I understand that has been the working narrative of mainstream Western culture for nearly two decades now, but it is an entirely false narrative built on ignorance and revisionism."

"Tell us how you really feel, chief," Gapinski said, throwing back the rest of his caramel liquid and reaching for more.

"But it is the truth of it. Ever since the horrifying terrorist attacks against America in September 2001, a myth has calcified into accepted fact that the Crusades were a bald-faced, expansionistic attempt by Christendom to loot, colonize, and brutalize the tolerant, peace-loving Muslim Arabs who just happened to be occupying swaths of land once held by Christian majorities!"

Radcliffe took a breath and took another sip of his tea. "Forgive my exasperation, but the past days' events of terroristic persecution launched against our brothers and sisters in the faith has shaken me to the core."

He took another breath, and then continued. "Let me spare you the doctoral-level history lesson, but suffice it to say, the Crusades were fundamentally a defensive war, one Christendom had been fighting with Islamic Arabs for nearly 450 years before the First Crusade. It was *Muslims*, originally led by Muhammad himself after he styled himself a prophet and was rejected by Jews and Christians as such and then proclaimed war against Byzantine Christians—it was they who pushed out of Arabia and into largely Christian lands in Israel and North Africa and out through the Christian Ottoman Empire and across the Strait of Gibraltar into southern Spain and on toward Europe at both ends. They slaughtered hundreds of thousands along the way, anyone who refused to bow before Allah and renounce their faith in Jesus Christ. Fully two-thirds of the Christian world had been relentlessly, mercilessly put under the Islamic sword. If anyone were the brutal colonialists, it was the Islamic hordes!"

"Alright, Rowen," Celeste said. "So the Crusades were a defensive measure against the invading Muslims who had decimated once Christian territories. Where do the Knights Templar come into play?"

"Good question," Radcliffe said, crossing his legs and draining his tea. "In response to the terror that befell those Christians that Easter 1119, two veterans of the First Crusade, Hughes of Paynes and Godfrey of Saint-Omer, proposed creating a monastic order with the sole, explicit purpose of protecting the hundreds and thousands of Christian pilgrims that travelled to the Holy Land each year."

"You're speaking about the Knights Templar," Silas said, puffing another cigarette to life.

"Indeed. They were an order of knightly monks who were blessed with the guiding, supporting hand of perhaps the most powerful man in all of Europe: Bernard of Clairvaux, head of the rapidly ascending Cistercian monastic order."

Celeste glanced at Silas at the mention of his name, who seemed to return her gaze. The two had traced a connection between Bernard and the Ark of the Covenant on a mission for SEPIO last fall.

Radcliffe said, "As an early advocate of chivalry, there was perhaps no greater voice in support of the idea of a knightly monk than Bernard. So, he set about writing a Rule for the upstart monastic order, consisting of seventy-two articles that prescribed a schedule for prayers and worship, committed the members to chastity and modesty, outlined more pedantic matters such as menus and dress. He also arranged for a special Church council in 1129 at Troyes, where the Rule was accepted and the Church officially recognized the Order as the Poor Fellow-Soldiers of Christ and of the Temple of Solomon. Unlike existing forms of knighthood, these men did not organize to terrorize the weak and wage war for spoil of treasure. Instead, they were solely dedicated to destroying evil and to *the defense of Jerusalem and the protection of pilgrims,*' in the words of their charter. Their dress emphasized this mission, where their habits and robes of white symbolized their purity, a clearly Cistercian influence, and they abandoned the conventional marks of knighthood, the furs and precious metal ornamentation and such."

"Fascinating," Celeste offered. "In other words, it was the terroristic persecution of Christians and threat of attack upon

Jerusalem by invading Muslims that activated the Templars in the first place?"

"Precisely!"

"Much like what has been happening the past twenty-four hours around the world," Silas added.

"Indeed," Radcliffe said solemnly.

A sigh escaped from Torres, who quickly brought her mug up to her mouth, eyes darting with guilt.

Radcliffe turned toward her. "Is there something you'd like to add, Ms. Torres?"

She set her mug down with a thud, eyes following it to the table. She opened her mouth, but hesitated and closed it. Then she furrowed her brow, and added, "Perhaps I'm sensitive to all of the violence and invasion, given my own heritage and how my people were slaughtered at the hands of the invading European hordes in Central and South America. But surely you don't justify the response by the Church in this way, regardless of how and why the Templars arose?"

Radcliffe nodded slowly and took a deep breath before responding. "I certainly understand where you are coming from, Naomi. And let me be clear: certainly not all Muslims back then were murderous and bloodthirsty, hellbent on Christianity's conversion or destruction—just as those who are aligned with the Islamic faith nowadays are not all jihadis hellbent on terrorizing and persecuting the Church. And we can also be honest about the fact that, yes, Naomi, the European Crusaders were not all righteous and upright in their endeavors. Many did at times devolve into debauchery and dastardly acts of violence not germane to the original imperative to defend Christians and European nations from no uncertain doom.

"Yet Bernard's teachings on the matter emphasized an important difference between *homicide* and *malecide*. Between the sin of killing a man and the act of killing evil itself, which he said God would take as a noble, virtuous act. Now, I understand some may suggest Bernard's distinction was theologically shaky and doctrinally ingenious. However, there was a long line of theological support for the matter of just war and just killing stretching back to the Church doctors Saint Augustine of Hippo and Saint Ambrose of Milan. And, really, even further back to Saint Paul himself, who had framed the Christian life in militant terms."

"*For our struggle is not against enemies of blood and flesh,*" Gapinski quoted from the book of Ephesians, "*but against the rulers, against the authorities, against the cosmic powers of this present darkness, against the spiritual forces of evil in the heavenly places. Therefore take up the whole armor of God...*"

The Order Master flashed the large screen a slight congratulatory grin. "Very good, Matthew. Impressive."

"Bible quiz team," he said proudly. "Thanks to Grandpappy..."

Radcliffe paused and quietly said a prayer of protection and rescue for him and the other Christians. "Yes, well, at any rate, while such language reflected our spiritual rather than *physical* battle, for early believers the truth of the matter was all too real."

"You're speaking of the early martyrs of the Church," Celeste said.

"Indeed. Whether in the amphitheaters of Rome or the throes of death's suffering elsewhere, martyrdom had been the seedbed of the early Church in which the faith grew and spread—"

"And flourished," Silas interrupted. He took a final pull on his cigarette before putting it out. "Tertullian said it best: '*the blood of the martyrs is the seed of the Church.*'"

Radcliffe nodded. "Right you are, my boy. And right he was. The Church flourished and spread like wildfire despite launching into the world with the threat of utter annihilation always hanging over its neck—literally. Pagans came to the faith in droves as the result of Christians being flayed alive and covered with salt, slowly roasted over open spits normally kept for fattened hogs, fed to lions and bears only to be sliced to ribbons and mauled to death. Then, as Christianity gained more tolerance and prominence within the Roman Empire thanks to Emperor Constantine, a theology surrounding war eventually developed. By the time of the First Crusade, the notion that Christians were in an epic struggle wasn't just metaphorical, it was an all-too-real reality."

"But what about Jesus' teachings on turning the other cheek and all that?" Torres wondered. "Didn't that count for anything in their crusading book?"

"Certainly! While our Savior's teachings rang true, the notion of not taking up arms in self-defense in places like Syria and Palestine in the white-hot midst of persecution and battle was increasingly impractical in the face of the militancy of Islamic Arabs who were decimating whole people groups who defied them. And not just Christian ones. Jews and Persians were at their militant mercy as well. Thus, Pope Urban II issued the call to arms in response to Muslim aggression and for the very survival of the Church itself, built on Augustine's own call in *The City of God* to repel the pagan barbarian invasion of Italy, leading to the First Crusade. This was not a land and loot grab, but a noble and holy mission that was defensive and protective in the face of grave injustice. Eventually, Bernard of Clairvaux leveraged this theological case law, if you will, and ecclesial mission to style the Templars as the righteous bodyguards for the Christian pilgrims, not to mention virtuous defenders of the Holy Land, from the terror the Muslim hordes had perpetuated upon the Church stretching back half a millennium.

"During the thirteenth century, the Order may have had as many as 7,000 knights and priests and servants, with other various members many times that figure. By the early fourteenth century, it had built a network of at least 870 castles, strongholds, and houses throughout Western Christendom, and they had amassed enormous wealth in property and gold."

"And then, what, they just disapparated all Harry Potter like?" Gapinski asked.

"Now that is a curious piece to the Templar puzzle," Radcliffe responded. "Around 1340, Ludolph of Sudheim, a German priest who had set off on a pilgrimage to the Holy Land, told a tale of coming upon two elderly men on the shores of the Dead Sea. The priest eventually engaged the men in conversation and discovered something altogether entirely surprising."

"Let me guess," Gapinski said, "some zombie superhero dudes sporting thermal whitey tighties emblazoned with a red cross on the front like the Church's ill-forgotten guardians of yore?"

Radcliffe chuckled. "Not quite, but yes: they were former Templars, captured when the city of Acre fell to the Muslim hordes in May 1291. For nearly fifty years, the two men had been living in the mountains, cut off from all communication with Latin Christendom. Eventually, they settled down and had wives and children, probably even grandchildren. They had survived by working in the Sultan's service and apparently eking out their lives as woodcutters. They had no idea that their former religious Order, the venerable Knights Templar, had been suppressed in a campaign of fire and fury at the behest of King Philip IV decades earlier. Had no clue that their Grand Master, Jaques de Molay, had been burnt at the stake as a heretic during it all. The priest offered to help repatriate them to their homelands of Burgundy and Toulouse, and within a year, despite the scandal of the suppression from earlier, they and their families were received at the papal court, and they were allowed to live out the remainder of their lives in peace. Or, so the story goes."

"So the story goes?" Silas asked.

"In other words," Celeste added, "you think there is more to the story?"

The Order Master fell silent and looked to the floor. "Curiously, these two Templars were the almost-forgotten remnant of what, barely a generation before, was one of the most, if not *the* most, powerful of the monastic orders in all of Christendom. And they vanished, living quaint lives of desperation as woodcutters and in service to the regional governor? Then they were discovered and reinstated back in their homelands, only to slip into quiet retirement, never again to take up the Templar cause? I never fully believed this account, believing instead that the Templars had been concealed within the shadows of history, biding their time in wait, readying to show themselves once more when the time was right."

"Apparently, they thought it was time," she said.

"Indeed."

"But are we OK with that?" Torres said. "I mean, I understand now that originally the Templars and even the Crusades were much more about defense and protection than political expansion and colonialist oppression. But...Well, I can't imagine the Church, or for that matter the Order of Thaddeus, is too high on the idea of a bunch of vigilante superhero dudes sporting thermal whitey tighties emblazoned with a red cross on the front like the Church's ill-forgotten guardians of yore, to continue the colorful picture of our knights in shining armor."

"Shining skivvies," Gapinski corrected.

She rolled her eyes. "Fine, Mr. Smart-aleck. Shining skivvies. But lets be honest about one thing: Jesus never condoned violence, never led an army. He never even bore or brandished a sword! What do we do with that?"

"Yet our brothers and sisters in the faith are being slaughtered!" Silas exclaimed in response. "Gapinski's own grandfather has been kidnapped by those bastards, for Pete's sake! And don't forget about the more than sixty pilgrims from the Jordan that were kidnapped along with him. That's not even counting the thousands more that have been kidnapped and raped and murdered across Africa. What are we going to do about that?"

"I'll tell you what we're going to do," Radcliffe answered, pounding the table with his fist as he stood. "We're going to bloody well go after them is what we're going to do! But we're going after the Templars as well, or whoever they are."

"What do you mean?" Celeste said.

Radcliffe turned toward her and then gestured to Torres. He said, "You and Naomi, your job is to track down the risen Templars. Find them, discover their agenda and motive."

"What then?"

Radcliffe took a breath and furrowed his brow. "I'm not sure. But I cannot imagine their vigilante maneuvers will be good for the Church, as much as the terrorism won't be for the saints."

"Agreed," Silas said, striking up another cigarette. "But what about us?"

"Why, you're going after the terrorizing persecutors of the Church, of course."

"And where on earth could we hope to begin?"

"Connect with Zoe. I believe she and her crackpot team of techno wizards have been working their magic around the clock since the explosion of persecution commenced a day ago. She should be able to give you direction."

The room fell silent as it anticipated the start to another SEPIO mission. This time protecting not just the once-for-all-faith of the Church, but her chosen people as well.

CHAPTER 12

After Radcliffe dispensed his orders, he left it up to Celeste to put them into action. The elderly man shuffled out of the room with his tea, complaining how "this old sack of bones isn't cut out for this cloak-and-dagger business any longer," letting the door close behind him with an echoing thud in the vast makeshift command center.

Leaving Silas and Gapinski, Torres and Celeste to take it from there.

"Right," Celeste began, shifting in her chair and readying herself to take command by pushing a stray lock of hair from her bangs behind an ear. "You heard the Order Master. Tracking down the Templars and the terrorists are both of our priorities. As Radcliffe instructed, it makes the most sense for you two, Silas and Gapinski, to follow the leads that Zoe and her team have collected as to the whereabouts of the terrorists. After we're through, get with her and coordinate your next steps for bringing them to justice."

"Don't worry, chief," Gapinski said. "We'll bring 'em to justice, alright. Signed, sealed, and delivered to your doorstep."

Celeste smiled. "I'm sure you will. But remember, they are clearly part of a larger network bent not only on the persecution of Christians, but the destruction of the Church. So this is bigger than your grandfather and those snatched from the Jordan River, as important as their rescue and retrieval are. Understood?"

Gapinski nodded. "Understood."

"And in the meantime, what are you and Torres going to be doing?" Silas asked, striking up another cigarette.

"Exactly as Radcliffe instructed. Tracking down the whereabouts of the Templars."

Silas blew out the smoke and shook his head. "I'm not one to question the boss on matters like this, but do you think that's a good idea?"

Celeste sat forward and furrowed her brow in confusion. "What do you mean? Why wouldn't it be?"

"I mean, they did slaughter the bastards who terrorized the baptismal site at the Jordan. Could have been way worse had they not intervened. And let's not forget they basically saved our own assess by saving the National Cathedral from being blown to smithereens. That's gotta count for something!"

Gapinski nodded and slammed his fist into his palm. "I'm with Silas. Those dudes deserve medals, as far as I'm concerned. Or dudettes, I guess. Hey, do you think the Templars are still a no-girls-allowed outfit?"

Celeste cleared her throat. "Let's stay on task, shall we? I understand your point, but Radcliffe made his as well. The last thing we need is their vigilante maneuvers stoking sectarian sentiments and further enraging the purported Islamic terrorists, given the history there." She nodded toward Torres, and said, "We'll leave as soon as we're finished here and follow their trail, hopefully finding something useful that could lead us to their whereabouts."

"Then what?" Silas asked.

Celeste shrugged. "Then we ask them what the bloody hell they're playing at."

"I'm with Celeste and Radcliffe," Torres added. "Even if the Templars and the other Crusaders weren't the ones who started the fight, they sure as heck didn't end it! The Church has always prized martyrdom over murder anyway, no matter the cause. They're as much a problem as those damned terrorists, as far as I'm concerned."

There was no further argument from Silas. He threw another butt to the ground and stomped it out. Gapinski nodded as if in agreement.

She settled back into her chair, and said, "With that out of the way, how are you both doing? Can't imagine the past half a day has been easy."

"I'm fine," Silas said quickly, folding his arms and stretching out in his chair.

Celeste noted his curt response, but let it go. She wondered if he really was fine, and would circle around to him again later.

"What about you, Gapinski?" she asked. "I have to imagine you're still reeling from what you've experienced, what with your grandfather's kidnapping and all."

"Yeah, big fella," Torres offered. "I'm numb for you about what happened. I know I'd be devastated if it were my *tio*."

Gapinski took a long breath, then smiled and nodded. "Thanks, guys. Appreciate it. I'm just ready to go all Terminator on those terrorizing the Church. Or, I guess Kyle Reese, since the Terminator was actually the bad guy sent back in time to kill the boy dude who was going to grow up as some sort of savior against the machines in a post-apocalyptic future. Well, that is until his doppelgänger returns a decade later to stop the T-1000 from—"

"Dude," Silas said as he searched his cigarette pack for more relief, "we get the point."

Gapinski shook his head. "Whatever. Anyway, I'm just ready to open a can of whoop-ass on those jihadi whack jobs. You have no idea how much that man means to me." His throat caught with emotion. He took another long breath and sighed.

Celeste nodded and smiled sympathetically. "I'm sure we can all agree that we would all go to the ends of the Earth to rescue any of our loved ones."

She paused, noticing Silas looking off as he took in a slow drag off his cigarette, knowing he had no one left to save. Except his brother, who had betrayed him and his faith.

She continued, "I assure you Zoe and her team have been doing everything to track the whereabouts of those Islamic terrorists in order to bring them to justice and locate your grandfather."

"That's assuming they're Islamic," Silas said, continuing to smoke.

"What do you mean?" Torres asked.

He raked a hand through his hair and sat up in his chair. He took a deep breath and shook his head. "It's just, I'm not so sure they're Islamic terrorists. Or, at least only Islamic. Terrorists I think we can all agree on."

"I don't understand. What are you playing at, Silas?" Celeste asked.

"Yeah, what are you playing at—or, something?" Gapinski added.

"It just doesn't make sense. Radical Islamic terrorists like ISIS and Hamas have traditionally targeted the state of Israel and Jewish sites or major Western cities like Paris and London."

"Traditionally maybe, prof, but they're clearly ISIS whack jobs. You saw the flag."

Celeste added, "Gapinski's right. From what intel we've already gathered, they've displayed the telltale signs. The black flag emblazoned with white Arabic script, dressed in desert fatigues with black hoods and all."

"But doesn't it seem convenient?" Silas pressed. "Sure,

they've attacked major European cities and displaced tens of thousands of Christians in Middle Eastern nations—"

"And beheaded and executed Ethiopian and Egyptian Christians in an online video posted a few years ago. And Abu Bakr al Baghdadi shortly thereafter declared their intention to march *'all the way to Rome'* and promised to *'break the crosses'* of Christians and *'trade and sell their women.'* And guess what, they did. They've forced conversion, slavery, extortion, and execution on the Church wherever ISIS has gone, without a single exception. And now it seems they're marching across the globe."

"All I mean to suggest is that we should tread with caution and do the due diligence here. Could be ISIS, could be something else."

Gapinski looked at his partner, jaw set and eyes narrowed. "Nous. You're thinking it's those other religious whack jobs, aren't you?"

Silas took a drag on his cigarette and nodded. "At least pseudo-religious whack jobs. But, yeah, possibly."

Celeste sat back and shook her head slightly. "I'm not sure I follow. Don't get me wrong. We've certainly had our share of run-ins with the Church's archenemy the past year. But this seems far too...violent to be Nous. Even for Nous."

Gapinski leaned in closer to Silas. "You don't think this is Sebastian, do you?"

Celeste saw Silas flinch at the mention of his brother's name. He stretched out again and took a longer drag than usual, but said nothing. She hated seeing him like this. Had tried to talk to him about it earlier in the year when they got back to America from their overdue vacation in the Caribbean, but it was a nonstarter. He was clearly bottling up his emotions from the past year, especially the betrayal of his brother.

She understood that's what men did. Saw her father do it, which nearly broke her parents' marriage. The man she loved before Silas also stuffed his worries in a sack. But at least Martin slowly opened up to her, which is what she had adored about him.

She shook away the memory and vowed not to give up on Silas. She cared too much about him to let that happen.

Celeste cleared her throat, and said, "I'm sure we'll unravel the mystery in short order and I vow to do everything in our power to retrieve your grandfather. Before you boys head off on mission, would you mind giving us a minute, Matthew? I'm sure you'd like to freshen up before you head out. Perhaps take a shower or grab a spot of tea, or whatever it is you're drinking over there."

Gapinski glanced from Celeste to Silas and tried to suppress a grin. "Uhh, sure. Whatever you say, boss." He stood and walked toward the door off-camera, mumbling as he left: "Take as long as you two lovebirds need..."

Silas rolled his eyes and laughed, taking another drag on his cigarette.

After the door closed, Celeste said, "So how are you, really?"

He blew the smoke out the side of his mouth, furrowing his brow and shaking his head. "What do you mean, how I'm *really* doing? I said I'm—"

"What I'm getting at is the fag sitting between your lips," she interrupted, gesturing toward the screen.

He startled and coughed, reflexively taking the cigarette from his mouth. "The *fag*?" he asked, coughing again.

"Yes, the cancer sticks you've been sucking on this whole time."

"What, you mean this?" He held up the cigarette and rolled his eyes again, then shoved it back into his mouth and pulled in a lungful of smoke. "Old war habit is all."

"That you decided to pick up, what, on the spur of the moment?"

Silas dropped the spent butt to the floor, sighing as he put it out. "What is this, twenty questions?"

"What this is, is your commanding officer making sure you're mission fit."

He opened his mouth to say something but closed it again, seeming to think better of it. He raked a hand through his hair with irritation, pushing his bangs to one side. Then he crossed his arms and waited for more.

"Look," she continued, taking a breath before treading carefully. "I get it, I do. I can't imagine how things have been for you the past few months, with getting sacked from the profession you had built a name for yourself in, getting back into the fray of things after having left all of this sort of work far behind in the American military, and then your brother's betrayal—"

"I said I'm fine, Bourne!" Silas exclaimed, interrupting her this time. His eyes widened and he sat up straighter at the eruption, seeming to know what he had done.

A shot of adrenaline coursed through Celeste at the eruption and the sound of her last name. He had never disrespected her in that way before. The tone and tenor and timbre of it all set her on edge, causing her to flare her nostrils and narrow her eyes. She almost laid into him for the deliberate disrespect, but understood he was barely holding it together and that he had understood what he had done.

"I...I'm sorry," he stuttered. He raked a hand through his hair again, averting his eyes from the video conference camera to the floor and reaching for his cigarette pack but coming up empty. He settled for what remained in his plastic cup, taking a sip before adding, "I shouldn't have spoken to you that way."

Celeste went to say something, but Silas continued.

"To tell you the truth, I'm not fine." He crossed his arms and slouched, staring at the floor.

She silently willed him onward, begging him to open his heart up to her. Not only for his sake, but also for hers.

He sighed heavily and continued, "Haven't been all year. My little blue pills did most of the heavy lifting for the year. Mr. Zoloft dealt with the PTSD still lingering from Iraq and Afghanistan, got me through the drama at Princeton, helped me live with you crazy people."

He smiled wryly and winked. She smiled back.

He shifted in his seat, and said, "I thought I was better. Thought I'd beaten it. Even flushed the last of my prescription down the drain..."

Silas trailed off, lost in his world of memory and misery.

"But then my brother happened. First what he did last summer with trying to con me into verifying that fake gospel, then working to undermine the historic faith during the election. And when he did what he did before Christmas, becoming a full-on operative of Nous and working to undermine the Christian faith and destroy the Church..." He trailed off again, obviously pained to be reliving the memory. "It was too much."

Silence enveloped the space between them across the digital expanse of ones and zeroes through the satellite connecting their video feeds.

"I reckon it would have been too much for anyone," Celeste finally said. "And we're here for you. All of us are." She hesitated, but said softly, "I'm here for you, too."

Silas raised his head, his face softening and a smile managing to form. "Thanks," he said with equal softness.

Another few beats ticked by before there was a tap on the door. Silas jolted upright and glanced off-camera. He motioned for the intruder to enter.

Gapinski came back into view, hair still wet from what Celeste gathered was him taking her advice literally.

She smiled and waved. "I see you took me up on my shower suggestion."

"Boy, did I ever," he said. He rubbed his head with his

meaty palms, sending droplets of water raining down on Silas.

"Hey!" he said, crouching and leaning out of the way. "Get the heck out of here if you're gonna rub your mangy cooties all over me."

Celeste laughed. "Why don't you go back and dry off. Clearly you missed a spot. Besides, we've got a few more minutes here."

"If you say so, chief," Gapinski said, holding up his hands but not before he rained the last bit of water out of his hair back on Silas.

Silas cried out again and slapped the guy on his backside as he scurried out of the room.

Celeste laughed again as the closing door echoed across the speakers. "Ahh, Gapinski. God bless him."

"God bless him my butt. You didn't get a headful of the man's cooties! Anyway, was there anything else you needed to talk about?"

She nodded toward the screen, and said, "One more thing. Your partner over there."

Silas looked off-camera toward the door. "What's the matter with Gapinski?"

"Nothing, per se. I just want you to be ready in case..." She sighed and looked down, not knowing how to state the obvious.

"In case we can't recover Grandpappy Jim George, you mean?"

"Right. I'm not sure yet what intel Zoe has been able to recover, if any. But you should be ready to be there for him in case the outcome isn't what we're hoping for. Given what's transpired around the world, and given the possible involvement of, yes, ISIS, he may not be ready for the inevitable."

Silas clenched his jaw and nodded. "I understand. But mark my words, Celeste: we'll get those bastards. For the Church, for Gapinski."

She nodded herself. "For Gapinski."

CHAPTER 13

PARIS, FRANCE.

Celeste awoke to the smell of fresh-baked bread, frying salted bacon, melting cheese, and strong coffee. Given her sleepless night, she gave serious thought to foregoing her English customs of her mandatory morning pot of tea in favor of the Yank caffeinated alternative.

She parted the simple blue curtains covering the small window of her tiny abbey room, a clear, still-darkened sky greeting her with a full moon and a sea of stars. She groaned and nursed a headache still needling her temple as she slipped into the jeans she had flown halfway across the world in the night before.

Sleep had come in fits and starts throughout the flight and all throughout the night once they had settled into the abbey after hours. She eventually found it, but just barely. She sure had needed it given what they had been through the past few days tracing the multiple terrorist plots unfolding around the world; narrowly escaping their own near-demise after the partial destruction of the National Cathedral; uncovering the staggering revelations of the Knights Templar, seemingly risen back from history's graveyard to avenge the honor of the

Church and guard the lives of her saints. Yet they were no closer to solving the mystery.

Hence the early-morning rise.

The sun was still contemplating whether or not to come out from underneath the covers when Celeste went searching for the hot meal that had rudely awakened her from finally finding deep slumber. As she padded through the aged structure of heavy cut stone and sturdy pine timber that had carried the Church through the so-called Dark Ages of Europe, acting as a bulwark against ignorance and heresy alike, she prayed that the Lord would make their paths straight that day, guiding their search for the Poor Fellow-Soldiers of Christ and of the Temple of Solomon.

All before those blasted Templars did untold damage to the Church and her witness!

The night before, she and Torres had taken an Order-issued Gulfstream jet across the Atlantic to begin executing on Radcliffe's orders to track down the risen Templars and discover their agenda and motives. Because the main SEPIO operations hub was uninhabitable until it was structurally assessed after the devastating terrorist attack, the two were dispatched to the Order's Paris operations that served as a European cornerstone for SEPIO research at the old Port-Royal des Champs Abbey complex.

Southwest of the City of Lights and just outside of Versailles, last fall she and Silas had used the Order's extensive library and research tools housed there to help uncover Nous's plot against the Church. She couldn't help but smile at the memory of the pair working closely together to solve the mysteries surrounding the Ark of the Covenant as she made her way down the cold stone steps—as well as the feelings and connection between them it had stoked.

Originally a Cistercian female monastery built in the heart of the Chevreuse Valley in 1204 in the lineage of the Abbey of

Clairvaux, the abbey launched a number of culturally important institutions, most notably the "Little Schools of Port-Royal," which became famous for the high quality education they offered the community. However, at the start of the eighteenth century, most of the complex was razed after the community was caught up in a controversial Catholic religious reform movement primarily directed at the Jesuits. The Order of Thaddeus later reclaimed the property and rebuilt the abbey for their own intellectual and theological pursuits.

Celeste continued following her nose toward the great hall where she knew breakfast awaited. She rounded a corner and there it was, ceilings vaulted high by solid pine beams with large wrought iron chandeliers affixed by modern light fixtures instead of the candles they had once borne. The center was commanded by rows of heavy wooden tables that were sparsely filled.

Torres sat at the end of a center table, looking like she was halfway through a plate of bacon and cheese eggs. She plopped down across from her, propping her weary head against her arm.

"Good morning," Torres said, taking a sip of black coffee, her long, dark Latin curls wrapped together at the top of her head. "No offense, but you look the worse for wear. How'd you sleep?"

"Fits and starts, thank you very much. And you?"

"Like a rock."

"Lucky you. But that's good, because we have lots of ground to cover today. Our research into the Templars awaits."

"No rest for the weary."

"Unfortunately not. But first things first."

Torres forked a scoop of eggs and held it up. "A plate of cheese eggs?"

"No, a pot of tea."

"Sorry to be the bearer of bad news, but..."

"Good heavens, you're joking!"

"Sorry. But the coffee's not half bad."

Celeste huffed off and grabbed a plate, filled it with the goodness she had smelled from her room, reluctantly filled a large mug of coffee, adding three cubes of sugar and a spot of cream, then sat down to fuel up before the day of research.

It had taken two decades to restore the original abbey complex to its former glory as a working monastery, but the complex was a sight to behold. Through floor-to-ceiling windows, the just-rising sun was beginning to dapple an expanse of rolling green hills outside with burnt orange light. Those hills were punctuated by apple orchards and vineyards that were eventually pressed into apple cider and fermented into wine, then sold to markets in Paris. Three stories of rooms housed the ecumenical coterie of scholars and students dedicated to retrieving and preserving the vintage Christian faith. A large chapel held the daily prayer services, for both the abbey itself as well as the surrounding village community. The largest of the sections was an original one that later served as a national museum: the library, which the women headed out in search for after breakfast.

The familiar smell of old paper and ink was dizzying, sending Celeste back in time to her former life well before the Order, even before her former MI6 group.

After earning a Ph.D. in comparative religion from Oxford, she had nearly taken up with the faculty of theology and religion before she was recruited as an agent. She had always felt torn between matters of the mind and muscle, taking up girls rugby as a teenager, even making team captain, right alongside running herself ragged to earn top grades through her Advanced Level education. While her grandmother would have preferred her staying at home and settling down with a nice British lad, her mother encouraged her to keep pursuing her twin loves of brain and brawn. It was only after she met

Radcliffe, and became part of SEPIO, that she finally felt at peace with who she was, being able to marry the two for the good of the Church.

She breathed in deep as she and Torres wandered the vast estate trying to recall where she and Silas had conducted their research into the Ark. The mixture of paper and ink was a drug-addict high that only bibliophiles like her and Torres and Silas could appreciate. The dark walnut-lined walls, bookcases, and affixed burnished bronze light fixtures primed the senses even further.

"Just think about all that these walls have witnessed over the years," Torres marveled, running a hand across a shelf sagging with ancient tomes. As a former archaeologist and treasure hunter who held dual master's degrees in Mesoamerican and pre-Columbian studies at UCLA, she was salivating along with Celeste at the dizzying array of books and ancient manuscripts stretching to the earliest centuries of the Church. "I bet you they've got untold secrets stuffed away in these shelves. And treasure."

"Ms. Bourne, is that you?" a gravelly voice called out from behind the ladies.

Celeste turned and spied an aged, hunchbacked man with a kind smile and even kinder eyes slowly approaching the pair.

"Brother Rémy?" she asked, recalling the name of the dear soul who had assisted Silas and her last year on their hunt for the Ark.

"Sharp memory, young lady. Welcome back!"

"A pleasure being back. We arrived late last night on another temporary research assignment with the Order of Thaddeus."

"Ahh, yes. Rowen Radcliffe sent word about some urgent something or other to protect the Church and all it holds dear from no uncertain doom. And you are?" Brother Rémy said, turning to Torres.

"Naomi Torres, Brother," she said, extending her hand. The man took it.

"Brother Rémy is the caretaker of this wonderful literary establishment," Celeste explained.

"And quite the establishment it is," Torres offered. "How many books do you have in this library?"

"Half a million housed inside, with nearly as many more in climate-controlled vaults beneath."

She whistled and craned her head down one of the hallways trying to get a glimpse of the literary wonderland.

The man chuckled, then started hobbling forward with a cane, leading them through a passage narrowed by bookcases on either side. "I assume you'll need the same arrangements as before, Ms. Bourne, the use of one of our research spaces with access to all the privacy and resources you need to accomplish your work?"

Celeste nodded. "That would be much appreciated, yes."

They rounded a corner into a large, spacious room with high ceilings that took up the three floors of the building. At one end, a fire crackled and popped in a stone fireplace the size of a person, tendrils of spicy smoke escaping and mingling with the musty scent of old tomes. The elderly man took them up a set of stairs to a modest room with large windows overlooking the vineyard. The sun was proving to be bright and cheery as it continued climbing high in the cloudless sky, which would serve them well as they poured over texts for the next several hours in search of answers.

"Here you are. I'll leave you to it. Again, tea and coffee and some fuel for the research race ahead are yours to enjoy—"

"There's tea?" Celeste interrupted, grabbing Brother Rémy's arm. "Thank the Lord! I thought the Order had devolved into barbarism."

The man offered a chuckle. "Yes, over on the cart. Earl Grey, if I recall correctly. At any rate, the workstation terminal gives you access to a catalog of everything we have housed in our facility. The e-readers give you access to an expanded billion-book catalog at the Order's disposal. You can even send articles from the terminal to the e-reader tablets. And then notebooks and pens are provided for your analogue convenience. Oh, and the television mounted on the wall is one of those new smart televisions all of the youngsters are talking about these days. Apparently you speak to it using the command 'Alexa' and it should do your bidding, though I'm not sure who or what that is."

"I'm Alexa," the television announced from across the room, "talking to you through your smart television. To learn more about me just ask, 'What can you do?'"

"Oh bother," the elderly man huffed before leaving and telling them to shout if they needed anything more.

They thanked him as he left, then they got to work.

"Where do we even begin?" Torres said, grabbing an e-reading device as Celeste walked over to the cart of goodies.

"Right," Celeste said. She plopped a tea bag in her mug and filled it with steaming water, savoring the heavenly scent of bergamot. "So what do we know so far?"

"That the Templars were a bunch of rogue Islamophobic Europhiles bent on the colonial conquest of Arabs and eradication of a rival religion?"

Celeste threw her a look as she plunked two lumps of sugar in her tea. "Cheeky, but not appropriate."

"Sorry," she said, offering a short grin before sinking into a chair and playing with her e-reader.

"And as Radcliffe said, dead wrong."

"Yeah, yeah."

Celeste took her tea and walked over to the computer terminal. "Let's see what this thing can do."

She logged onto the powerful Boolean search engine to cross-search databases from hundreds of research institutions around the world, including the Vatican's own secure digital records. She typed in the first obvious search string: *history of the Knights Templar.*

Within seconds, an array of search results filtered across the screen.

The first entry was a copy of the original *Regula commilitonum Christi,* the Rule of the Knights of Christ, developed by Bernard of Clairvaux. It looked like a one Johannes Michael offered a preface to the Rule, acting as a scribe for the original Church council that gave the Templars their charter. His opening words were an important, clarifying revelation of the order's foundation.

"Listen to this," Celeste said. She read from the screen:

Our message is especially directed to all who oppose following their own will and in the purity of their soul desire to fight for the highest and true king, so that they may hope to obtain the armor of obedience and a distinguished life by fulfilling the rule with most attentive care, and that they may fulfill this rule through perseverance. Therefore, we exhort you, who until now have embraced the secular army, in which Christ was not the reason, but by human favor alone you were drawn, to constantly strive to join the body of those whom God has chosen from the mass of the damned and has brought together for the defense of the holy church through His kind devotion. Moreover, above all, whoever you are, o soldier of Christ, it is proper that in choosing so holy a life you show pure devotion and steadfast resolve concerning your profession, which is distinguished by God as so holy and so high that, if you keep this rule purely and steadfastly, you will deserve to possess your lot among soldiers who have given their souls for Christ.

> For in this profession the military order has now emerged and so revived, which, when the desire for justice had been despised, strove not to protect the poor or the churches (which was its duty), but instead to rape, pillage, and kill.

"Seems like maybe the Templars were founded for good reasons after all," she said. "Being *'chosen from the mass of the damned'* and *'brought together for the defense of the holy church through His kind devotion.'*"

"To rape and pillage and kill Muslims, maybe," Torres mumbled.

Celeste smirked. "No, silly. Those were the other Crusader blokes."

"See! Told you."

"I was being cheeky. Listen to the first rule of the Templar monastic order. A spiritual call to arms, if there ever was one:

> Surely may you, who renounce your own will and others with you who fight temporarily with horse and armor for the highest king and for their souls, strive unfailingly to hear with devout and pure affection matins and every complete service according to the canonical tradition and the custom of regular clerics of the Holy City.
>
> Therefore, reverend brothers, it is your obligation most of all because having despised the light of the present life and having ignored the suffering of your bodies you have promised to count as vile the raging world for the love of God, nourished and filled by divine food, and learned and strengthened by the teachings of the Lord after the consummation of the divine mystery.

Let no one fear battle, and let him be ready for the crown.

"God's holy warriors," Torres said.

"Indeed."

Celeste continued reading through the Rule, not finding anything more helpful. She sighed and returned to the search results. An article caught her attention, titled "The Fall of the Knights Templars: Their Last Stand and Final Demise." She clicked on the link and scanned it, expecting some insight that would give them something to go on.

The author recounted the events leading up to what could arguably be called the Templars last stand in 1291, at the city of Acre in the kingdom of Jerusalem.

Apparently, this fall began in Tripoli, where the Muslim hordes slaughtered all the men and enslaved the women and children. The Muslim commander razed the city to the ground and headed to Acre, vowing not to leave a single Christian alive. After weeks of fighting, the main city of Acre fell and the men, women, and children were slaughtered, leaving the Templar fortress all that remained. Finally, on May 25, the Templar marshal agreed to surrender with the understanding that those inside would be granted safe passage. However, when the Muslims entered they began to molest women and boys, provoking the Templars to fight back. Their commander retreated with the Order's treasure and sailed to their sea castle just off the coast at Sidon. Three days later, the Acre Templar fortress fell, and those still alive were led outside the walls and beheaded. The city was smashed to pieces until almost nothing was left standing.

The events ended forty years after that when a German priest on pilgrimage came upon the spot and found only a remnant living amidst the desolation of what had once been the splendid capital of territory rescued by the Crusaders from the hands of the Muslims, and handed back to the Church.

A summarizing conclusion came from Michael Haag's book *The Templars*:

> Though not unexpected, the fall of Acre came as a shock in the West....But it was the Templars who felt the loss most intensely. The defense of the Holy Land and the protection of pilgrims was their raison d'être. For the Hospitallers [monastic order] the ethos of their charitable work took precedence; they had never abandoned their original function of caring for the sick. But the Templars were founded as a knighthood, their role to fight against the infidel, and in that cause to service crusades and direct the finances of Popes and kings. Now cast out from the Holy Land, the Templars found themselves in limbo. (p. 207)

"So the trail grows cold at Acre..." Celeste sighed and folded her arms. "Then where does that leave us?"

"Hold on," Torres said, pointing at her e-reader. "They may not have been entirely disbanded."

Celeste shuffled over to a chair next to Torres and took a seat. "What did you find?"

She traced what she had read with her finger, and said, "An entry from a book on the history and myth of the Templars explains how the Templars seemed to have continued in various iterations. It begins with the same story Radcliffe told us and you just read: a German priest visiting the Holy Land came upon two elderly men in the mountains overlooking the shores of the Dead Sea, a remnant of their fellow knights who had been slaughtered during the desperate fighting at the fall of Acre."

"What does it say happened from there?"

"Some of the history of it all is totally speculative and conspiratorial. Like them morphing into the Freemasons, where a Scotsman by the name of Andrew Ramsay suggested the collapse of Crusaders states with the fall of Acre forced them to return to their homelands in Europe and establish Freemason lodges there. He even suggested that *'every Mason is a Knights Templar.'* Then of course there's been the whole Holy Grail business, first suggested by the romance writers of the thirteenth century and later revived by the likes of Dan Brown's *The Da Vinci Code.*"

Celeste scoffed. "Stuff and nonsense, that is. So what's the fact of the matter? Is there any truth to Templar survival claims?"

Torres continued scanning the e-reader, tracing it with her index finger and flipping to the next page. "Says here that when Philip IV of France ordered the suppression of the Templars in 1307 and eventually burned their leaders at the stake in 1314, Edward II of England dismissed the charges of heresy as implausible, resisting the Inquisition and permitting each Templar to make a public statement that they were *'gravely defamed'* by the accusations. Apparently, each of these English Templars was granted reconciliation with the Church and sent to live peaceably at some monastery. The fate of the Templars in Scotland was similar to that of England. They were unpunished, but the Order was dissolved and their land was for the most part handed over to the Hospitallers religious order. The original ownership of the land has not been forgotten, however, for even today such properties are designated in transactions as 'Templarland'."

Celeste considered this. "So Scotland is a strong contender for a reincarnated Knights Templar. And much of the Templar past seems to survive in England, too. If not as the Freemasons, then as former Templar property after they were integrated back into society, isn't that right?"

"Appears that way. Then there's the version that survived in Portugal, but under a new name. It says here that in 1319, King Diniz reconstituted them with Papal permission as the *Ordem dos Cavaleiros de Nosso Senhor Jesus Cristo*."

"The Order of Christ," Celeste said.

"Exactly. The only difference between the two seems to be explicit obedience to the king, in addition to their traditional vows of poverty and chastity. Apparently, they were eventually awarded all of their property. Then in 1357, the entire religious Order was transferred to the former headquarters northeast of Lisbon at Tomar, a magnificent rotunda patterned after the domed Church of the Holy Sepulcher in Jerusalem, where it made its base of operations."

"So England, Scotland, Portugal. Anywhere else?"

Torres nodded. "Spain. The Templars had always been enthusiastically welcomed in Spain because of their invaluable assistance in the struggle against the Arab-Muslim occupation of the Iberian Peninsula. King Jaime II of Aragon, a northern province, declared the innocence of those Templars who were put on trial, despite the verdict of heresy and guilt of other crimes in France. With the permission of the Papacy, he formed the new Order of Montesa with old Templar assets. They were pretty much the Templars, risen back to life and charged with the defense of the peninsula."

"So the Templars essentially continued in Spain under another name," Celeste said.

"Exactly. For the next 175 years, the descendants of the Templars played a vital role in driving out the last Muslim invaders when Granada fell to them in 1492. However, it looks like the Order declined after that, and Philip II joined the office of Grand Master with that of the crown. But still. The Templars clearly continued on. And given that Spain was far more sympathetic than France to former Templars, perhaps the remnant found in Palestine by the German priest found greater kinship with the Order of Montesa."

Celeste sat back and folded her arms. "But whether or not these lunatics playing dress up are holed up there is anyone's guess. Or England, or Scotland, or Portugal, for that matter."

Before Torres could respond, a *purring* ringtone interrupted their deliberations, coming from the television mounted at the one end of the room, accompanied by a flashing red bar at the top of the screen. The same kind of notification from the makeshift command center at the basilica in DC indicating an urgent call.

"Alexa," Celeste said hesitantly, "Answer the call." The screen came to life. On it was Radcliffe, looking pained and panicked in a darkened room with monitors scrolling behind him and out-of-focused bodies shuffling about—presumably at the command center in the basilica in DC.

"Rowen, is everything—?"

"Do you have access to the Internet?" he spat out with interruption.

"Yes, we do. Why?"

He paused and took a worried breath. "Then you're going to want to see what has just commenced streaming across the globe."

CHAPTER 14

Torres commanded the television to bring up a web browser and go to YouTube; Alexa did as she was told.

It was immediately obvious the site had been hijacked: the normally white-washed webpage was bathed in black; the red logo had been replaced by a black flag bearing white Arabic script; a live-feed video was streaming dead center, all other clips having been removed.

A man dressed in desert fatigues, face masked in black with a salt-and-pepper beard peeking out below was speaking into the camera, his voice measured and deliberative, and enunciating the English words with hardly any of the harshness typical of Arab English speakers. Behind him, a light blue cloth hung, rippling with disturbance from off-camera. Affixed to it was the telltale signs of ISIS: a black flag with white Arabic scripting and a white logo was emblazoned across the sheet.

Celeste grabbed a remote in the center of the table and turned up the volume.

"All praise be to Allah, the lord and cherisher of the world," the man intoned, "and may peace and blessings be upon the prophet Muhammad. To the nation of the cross, we are back again in the sands where the companions of the prophet, peace be upon him, have stepped upon before, telling you that Muslim blood that was shed under the hands of your religion is not cheap. We will exact a penalty."

"The nation of the cross?" Torres asked, turning toward Celeste.

She took a breath and stepped closer to the television. "He's speaking of the Church."

The mystery man continued. "In fact, their shed blood is the purest blood because there is a nation behind them which inherits revenge. And we swear to Allah that the ones who have disgraced you, dear brothers in the faith—by our hands you will not have safety, you infidels, even in your dreams, until you embrace Islam. We will continue to go from country to country, city to city, village to village, church to church, and family to family until every one of you have confessed the *shahada*."

"The shahada?" Torres asked again. "What's that? I'm not all too familiar with Islam, I'm afraid."

Celeste continued staring at the television. Without turning to her companion, she explained, "It's the Islamic creedal confession, one of the Five Pillars of Islam that declares belief in *tawhid*, the oneness of God, and the acceptance of Muhammad as God's prophet. You've probably heard it before but were unfamiliar with its origins. In its shortest form, it can be roughly translated: *'There is no god but God. Muhammad is the messenger of God.'*"

She nodded. "I've heard of it. And it sounds like these jihadi whack jobs, as Gapinski so eloquently described them, are on a mission to force the worldwide Church to submit to it."

The man continued droning on, staring blankly into the camera behind a thick, black mask of menace and dark intent. "Those who perform prayer and pay alms," he growled, "will have their blood and property protected by the Prophet unless Islam dictates otherwise. You pay the *zakat* tax with willing submission, feeling yourselves subdued. Our battle is a battle between faith and blasphemy, between truth and falsehood, until there is no more polytheism—and obedience by all the world becomes Allah's in its entirety."

"How positively medieval..." Celeste whispered.

"What's that?" Torres said.

She startled, entranced by the television and forgetting herself. "Just that I can't help comparing the demands of these...these jihadi whack jobs, as you said Gapinski framed it, to the early Muslims who ravaged the medieval Church, forcing conversions and requiring a tax, the *zakat*, and enslaving thousands of believers of Jesus Christ. It was either that or death. It's what launched what we know as the Crusades in the first place. In fact, the tax and enslavement and persecution is what also led to the rise of the original Templars."

The man continued, "The Islamic state has offered the Christian community this many times and set a deadline for this, but the Christians never submitted to Allah's commands. That changes today!" he shouted, raising a clenched fist.

Torres eased up next to Celeste and said, "What are the chances these are the same terrorists who've been wreaking havoc on the Church this week?"

Celeste looked at her, lips pursed and eyes wide with agreement. "I'd bet my bottom dollar they're the same blokes. Bears all the same markings, and their demands for conversion or payment could point to an ultimate aim for their terrorism."

Suddenly, the masked man stood straight and stiff, as if girding his loins for the climax of his monologue.

"All Crusaders, hear this," he growled, bending toward the camera, arms stiff at his side and eyes transfixing the audience beyond through slitted cloth. "Safety for you will be only wishes, especially if you are fighting us all together. Therefore we will fight you all together. The sea you have hidden Sheikh

Usama Bin Laden's body in, we swear to Allah we will mix it with your blood!"

Celeste noted the clear reference to the raid by the Obama administration on Bin Laden's compound on May 2, 2011, and the subsequent dumping of his body in the Arabian Sea. Which this spokesperson for Islamic terror had just vowed to mix with the blood of Christian martyrs!

"And yet," the man said, his posture softening and voice growing less menacing, pastoral even, "there is hope for the infidel. For our great prophet wrote in the Holy Quran, *'And when the forbidden months have passed, kill the idolaters wherever you find them and take them prisoners, and beleaguer them, and lie in wait for them at every place of ambush. But if they repent and observe prayer and pay the Zakat, then leave their way free. Surely, Allah is most forgiving and merciful.'* We will extend the same mercy during the next twenty-four hours if the infidel Christians around the world repent of their ways and leave behind their religion of lies."

Torres grunted a laughter. "Fat chance."

The man stiffened again, bending toward the camera and raising an authoritative finger toward the lens, as if offering her a reply. "If not, blood will soon flow down the aisles of your churches like the great Tigris and Euphrates rivers of ancient times. Beginning with these infidels."

The camera widened to a square, squat space, then panned stage right. The scene before the women made them both gasp and recoil backward in shock.

Arrayed in two neat rows, shrouded in darkness under dim incandescent bulbs in what looked like an underground bunker, were arrayed a number of individuals dressed in white, their robes stained and dirty. Black hoods darkened their faces, tied tight around their necks. Sitting on chairs, their arms were tied behind them and feet looked to be bound.

All sound had been cut off, or at least that's how it

appeared. Only a hazy, fuzzy silence permeated the space beyond the connection, filling the room with dread. No fearful cries, no agonizing moans, no nothing.

Celeste stood still. One hand covering her agape mouth, the other clenching her aching stomach.

The man returned, his feet echoing across the cement floor until he stood at stage left of the group, hands behind his back, his darkly masked face giving him the appearance of an Inquisitor of yore come to lop off the heads of the heretically accused.

In more ways than one, that's exactly what he was.

"We have already given these nineteen followers of that wretched religion of Christianity the opportunity to repent. But they have declined."

The hooded man walked across the front of the group, then stopped at the end and nodded off-camera. Another person, taller and bulkier, entered the feed wearing the same desert fatigues and dark mask, hulking behind the nineteen people with menacing purpose.

"Praise be to Allah," the first man intoned. "By the mercy of Allah towards this *ummah*, he has opened the gate of repentance to it, the whole community of blessed Muslims bound together by ties of religion and his mercy, and it will not cease until the soul reaches the throat at death or the sun rises from the west.

"By His Mercy to this *ummah*, he has prescribed for them an act of worship which is one of the best acts of worship, by means of which the sinner can draw close to his Lord with the hope of his repentance being accepted. All that is needed to come into the good graces of Allah is to voice the following testimony with conviction and understand its meaning: *'Ash Shadoo an La ilaha illa Allah, Wa Ash Shadoo ana Muhammadan rasoolu Allah.'* Which is translated, *'I bear witness that there is no true god except Allah, and I bear witness that Muhammad is the Final Messenger of God.*"

He walked over to the first of the Christians arrayed in front of the camera at the back row. The bulky man behind the group joined him, edging to just behind the person. The first masked man bent down in front of the person who was hunched over. Man or woman, it wasn't clear. He growled, "Do you confess that there is no god but Allah, and that Muhammad is his messenger?"

A convulsive wave shook through the Christian captive centered in the picture. Then the person sat upright, rigid and defiant. The hooded head shook side to side with deliberation, then stood still.

"'Lord Jesus!" the figure cried out, its pitch and tenor high and heady, like that of a woman's.

Then all at once, the front of the hood exploded forward, a spray of blood and clumps of gore and pieces of the black hood pluming off-camera before the body slumped forward and was shoved sideways to the ground.

The image pulled back as the bulky man withdrew a pistol and moved to the second hooded figure.

The other man walked over to the next of the Christian martyrs-in-wait, who was in the middle of reciting the Lord's Prayer in a deep, breathy, halting tone.

The same scene replayed itself: the masked man bent down, and he asked, "Do you confess that there is no god but Allah, and Muhammad is his messenger?"

"...and forgive us our debts, as we also have forgiven our debtors," the Christian man stuttered through the line, refusing to answer the question and continuing on through the prayer his Savior had taught his disciples to pray.

Again, the bulky man in black stepped behind the martyr. But where the viewer expected his head to be blown off, a large, pale hand reached around the forehead and snapped it back.

Then in one motion, a long blade came around the front and slit the man's throat.

Blood gushed from the wound. Choking, gurgling sounds could be heard through the live-feed video before the body slumped to the side, head lolled the other way and barely attached.

"I can't take anymore of this," Torres said, leaving Celeste's side and walking to the window overlooking the gently rolling, very-alive hills of green grass and fruit trees and ripened vines, back turned to the mayhem and death.

Celeste stood still, forcing herself to honor the memory and courage of the martyrs who, one by one, refused to disown the name of Christ and his cross of shame to follow Islam. The words of the loud voice in heaven proclaiming the magisterial words in Revelation 12 came to her mind: *"But they have conquered him by the blood of the Lamb and by the word of their testimony, for they did not cling to life even in the face of death."*

The drama continued for another agonizing fifteen minutes until every single one of the Christians dressed in white had been martyred for their faith—their brains blown out or throats slit for refusing to recant their testimony of faith in Jesus Christ as Lord and Savior.

When the terrorists were finished, when the last of the bodies had slumped to the floor in a pool of blood and gore, heads detached with vacant eyes and opened mouths searching for answers, the masked man of death walked back to his previous perch in front of the light blue cloth. The camera followed him, panning to the right and centering the frame upon the man once again.

He said, "There are forty-one infidels just like them who will be dealt with in the same manner for their heretical unbelief tomorrow, Holy Wednesday, if the leaders of the Church and worldwide Christian community refuse to collectively repent of their ways and voice the *shahada*. First among them will be the pastor of this flock that we captured in the Jordan River."

Celeste gasped, so did Torres. She whispered, "Jim George..."

"No..." Torres groaned.

"Allahu Akbar!" the masked man exclaimed, echoed by several more voices from off-camera. "God is great! And the Christian Church has twenty-four hours to repent before your churches flow with more blood."

He bowed, and said, "Ma' al-salāmah. Goodbye."

Then the feed cut to black.

CHAPTER 15

Celeste was numb. And after turning to Torres, mouth agape with nothing to say, it was clear the sentiment was equally shared.

The two walked to the center of the room and immediately knelt. Celeste lead them in a prayer for the fallen martyrs. Inside she was raging at the injustice of it all, and she wanted to do something. But in that moment, there wasn't anything else to do but pray.

"Almighty God," she intoned, "who gave your servants boldness to confess the Name of our Savior Jesus Christ before these captors, as well as the courage to die for their faith, by whose grace and power these holy martyrs triumphed over suffering and were faithful even unto death, who kindled the flame of your life in their hearts: Grant us to be so faithful in our witness to you in this world, that we may always be ready to give a reason for the hope that is in us, and to suffer gladly for the sake of our Lord Jesus Christ, receiving with them the crown of life after rejoicing in their triumph provided by their example; and may you draw those who died with your name on their lips quickly to your side, where they may know eternal peace and life; through Jesus Christ our Lord, who lives and reigns with you and the Holy Spirit, one God, for ever and ever. Amen."

"Amen," Torres said softly, crossing herself and wiping her moistened eyes with her hands.

The same *purring* ringtone from earlier sounded from the television, accompanied by a flashing red bar at the top of the screen.

"Alexa, answer," Celeste managed, still shocked from the latest revelations to move, still shaken to contemplate next steps.

Radcliffe appeared on the screen. The two stood.

He said, "I presume by your mutual countenance that you watched the latest attack in its entirety?"

Celeste wiped her eyes and nodded.

"We believe these are the same terrorists who attacked the mass baptism at the Jordan River a few days ago," he continued, "and absconded with Matthew's grandfather, based on his and Silas's story of the sixty or so Christians being abducted along with the pastor. No other attacks have occurred in the region matching such a description."

She stepped forward toward the television and folded her arms. She narrowed her eyes, widened her stance, and said, "Then what the bloody hell are we going to do about it?"

Radcliffe went to answer when a shuffling sound startled him. Zoe came up fast to his side and showed him a tablet, then pointed to the wall behind him.

His eyes widened even more than they already were. He covered his mouth as a curse slipped through his lips. He stood, holding the tablet with his backside turned toward the ladies in plain view, clearly ignorant of his immodesty.

Celeste glanced at Torres, who shook her head in confusion. She cleared her throat, and said, "Rowen? Are you still there? Please don't tell me there has been another attack. I can't bear to watch another—"

"There has been. But it's different than the one we've all just witnessed." He sat down quickly, then leaned toward the conference camera and said, "Zoe has just now brought it to my attention. I'll let her explain."

Radcliffe motioned for the petite Italian to come to the camera. "Explain," he simply said.

She adjusted her baby-blue glasses and looked down at her tablet. "One of our European outposts in Marburg, Germany, intercepted a video that has just been posted to an alternative sharing platform in the Dark Net."

"Dark Net? Sounds ominous," Torres said.

"It is," Celeste replied. "It's the hidden web of the World Wide Web, the contents of which are not indexed by standard web search engines. It's the super dodgy part of the Internet where bad stuff happens. Wicked bad stuff."

"Not only bad stuff," Zoe corrected. "It's also where the alternative Internet goes to congregate. And someone, somewhere found or shot a video that deepens the stakes for sure."

"More than they already are?" Torres wondered.

"What could be deeper than Gapinski's grandfather waiting no uncertain doom?" Celeste asked.

Zoe took a breath, and said, "I'm sending a video file to your screen. Just wait and see for yourself."

Celeste huffed and rolled her eyes with impatience. "Can you at least give us the 411?"

"Let's just say the video title says it all." She wrote it down on a piece of paper and held it up to the camera. It read: *'Those F#@%ING Terrorists Got PWNED by F#@%ING TEMPLARS!!!'*

Celeste closed her eyes and groaned.

Not again...

As Zoe typed on a keyboard, she said, "I have to warn you that you're in for more gratuitous violence. Not the gore from earlier, but...well, you'll see."

. . .

WITHIN SECONDS, the television *tinged* after having received the file. Then the screen faded to black and an image faded into view before starting to play a herky-jerky clip clearly taken with a smartphone camera.

The first few frames glimpsed the inside of a modest cathedral, ceilings vaulted high by marble columns of intertwined brown and white chocolate colors. A high altar anchored the front, all golden and regal. The next few frames slid beneath a wooden bench, presumably the owner of the smartphone hiding. There were anonymous screams of confusion and shouts of protest.

Then rapid gunfire and guttural commands in what sounded like French.

"No está bien," Torres said.

Celeste said nothing, remaining planted with eyes squinted as the camera jerked around behind the wooden bench before rising for a peek, heavy breathing and whispered cries of fear punctuating every dip and dance of the picture.

Then it adjusted again, showing eight or nine figures wearing desert fatigues and black masks. Gunfire burst from a few of them as they strode through the nave. A pair of them were at the back of the sacred space waving the parishioners forward with long-barreled weapons.

People took hesitant steps forward, and the cameraman backed up ever so carefully, the drama being kept in frame as he shuffled along the ground and back along the benches to one of the brown-white columns for protection. The picture went out of focus as the operator adjusted and pivoted behind his newfound hiding place, then came back into focus as more of the hostiles came into view, firing their weapons and shouting commands to the worshipers inside.

"You're telling me this already happened, that this isn't live?" Celeste asked.

"Correct. It isn't live," Zoe replied. "We've confirmed the act of terror happened a few hours ago in a border town in France near Spain."

Suddenly, there was a scuffle off-camera. The picture jerkily swung toward the disturbance, capturing a few of the male parishioners trying to take on the terrorists.

Rapid gunfire echoed angrily throughout the cathedral and the men were blown back, slumping dead to the ground.

Cries of agony and loss replaced the gunfire before it all returned again, leveling several of the worshipers and sending others to the ground for protection.

The man with the camera whispered with fear, and appeared to be praying as an apparent leader approached the priest.

There was an exchange before he shoved the elderly man and a loud clattering rang out. The picture showed the priest's garments stained crimson and several white chips scattered about the floor.

The Eucharistic elements had been overturned. The memory markers of Christ's Body and Blood had been desecrated.

Celeste cringed. Torres crossed herself and mumbled something.

The leader grabbed the priest and shoved him down in front on all fours before withdrawing something from behind his back.

Where Celeste expected another pistol, something long and silver shimmered instead.

Torres gasped. "Dios mío..."

"My God..." Celeste echoed in disbelief.

A sword.

There was a loud exchange between the leader and the priest in French. With the echo and the distance it was hard to make out. But the final word on the matter from the priest was unmistakable.

Non.

The man with the sword raised it, readying his act of martyrdom. But before he let it swing, the priest got off one final reply that surprisingly rang strong and true:

"Je crois que Jésus-Christ est à la fois Seigneur et Sauveur!" the man of God shouted before the sword came down upon his neck and his head popped off his body, bouncing down the stairs and rolling to a stop out of sight, trailed by a stream of crimson.

The meaning of the man's final declaration was clear: *I believe Jesus Christ is both Lord and Savior!*

Another martyr of the faith had refused to recant his confession in the face of death. A passage from the book of Hebrews, chapter 11, struck Celeste as describing the truth of what that dear man of God had faced—what the worldwide Church was facing:

> *Others were tortured, refusing to accept release, in order to obtain a better resurrection. Others suffered mocking and flogging, and even chains and imprisonment. They were stoned to death, they were sawn in two, they were killed by the sword; they went about in skins of sheep and goats, destitute, persecuted, tormented—of whom the world was not worthy.*

The world was not worthy indeed...

"Allahu akbar!" the masked men erupted in shouts, hopping up and down in a celebratory dance, adding spats of gunfire for added measure as they praised the death of another member of the nation of the cross.

Screams of horror from around the nave punctuated their cheers as the men continued dancing, corralling the remaining

Christians toward the front. No doubt readying them for a similar fate.

Lord Jesus Christ, Son of God, how much longer must the dead wait for relief?

"Allahu—"

As if offering an immediate reply to her prayer, the jihadi expression was cut short by rapid-fire *pop-pop-pop-pop-pop* from the back of the nave off-camera.

The smartphone swung in a herky-jerky motion from behind the column toward the surprise response, catching the perpetrators as they strode into view.

There was a band of them, at least eight or nine and similarly dressed. Just like the one glimpsed on the grounds of the Washington National Cathedral, a snug white garb with faces concealed.

The firing ceased, from both ends of the nave. The terrorists seemed dazed by the intrusion and unsure of what to do next; the Templars seemed to be biding their time to finish what they started.

The camera swung toward the high altar as the one darkly masked man who murdered the priest strode forward, shouting something in French.

It swung back, jerky and uncertain, just as one of the men in white met his stride and shouted something in reply. This time in Latin, which Celeste had immediately remembered from the debrief with Silas and Gapinski.

Non nobis, Domine, non nobis, sed Nomini tuo da gloriam!

The Knights Templar had come to save yet another day.

All at once, the Templars ran forward in one giant swell of white, cresting toward the fatigue-clad men in black hoods, holding some sort of shield out in front of them, seemingly without a care for the reply of lead that awaited them from up ahead.

And what a reply it was.

The smartphone swung back around the column to catch glimpse of the terrorists banding together near the high altar, kneeling as one, and opening fire with abandon.

Still the Templars rushed forward.

And not a single one of them dropped dead.

"What the blazes?" Celeste wondered at the magical display of resilience and resistance.

"That's gotta be some wicked armor to resist all that fire-power," Torres said, matching her wonder.

"I imagine Gapinski's going to want to get his hands on that."

The terrorists continued firing, but began standing and backing up when the men in white continued forward without injury.

Yells of passion exploded from deep within the Templars as they reached the Muslim horde. And then swords of vengeance glinted bright and proud as they came out from their backs, swinging with purpose toward their intended targets.

The sound of expertly sharpened metal slicing through flesh was heard clearly across the nave, like a chef's knife chopping through juicy cantaloupe in the heat of summer without a care in the world.

Some of those swords were met with equally loud clangs as they connected with assault rifles, a final desperate defense by the terrorists. Others connected clear through the chest, sucking in and out until the bodies slumped over in death.

The lead Templar sought the lead terrorist. Soon, they were in a fierce fight, matching sword for sword with clanging blows and grunts of strength.

But with a single wrong move on the part of the darkly masked figure, the Templar connected with the man's neck, sending his head flying through the air in a fit of poetic vengeance for the martyrdom of the priest.

When the final terrorist had been vanquished, one by one

the figures in white strode with purpose through the nave and back out the entrance through which they came. They greeted not the horrified parishioners who had watched the drama unfold, nor offered a word of explanation. They simply left as quickly as they arrived.

The man with the smartphone whispered something in French, then crept slowly out from around his column. He took a hesitant step into the nave before jogging past the last row of wooden benches after the group for more footage.

When he reached the entrance, a brightness flashed before the camera adjusted to the lighting differential. Then it caught sight of one of the masked men climbing into the back seat of a white vehicle.

And there it was. Clear as day.

A crimson cross, stained into the pure white garb of Christ's knight.

Confirmation that the Templars had indeed struck again.

THE VIDEO CONTINUED PLAYING as a caravan of three white vehicles sped past and through cramped, dusty streets before they disappeared around a corner market.

Sirens began screaming in the distance as the camera man talked excitedly in French, then the picture faded to black.

Celeste and Torres stood still, too numb from yet another horrific video surfacing during the bloodiest Holy Week in recent memory to have any opinion about what they had just witnessed.

The television chimed with an arrival announcement before Radcliffe and Zoe faded back into view.

"What the bloody hell was that, Rowen?" Celeste said with exasperation.

"Clearly the Poor Fellow-Soldiers of Christ and of the

Temple of Solomon have a few more tricks up their ancient sleeves."

"And it won't take long before the world sees yet another example of Western wackos terrorizing Muslims," Torres said.

Celeste turned to Torres, face twisted with a mixture of confusion and disgust. "All due respect, but who was terrorizing whom there? What I saw were a band of Good Samaritans saving a church full of worshipers from no uncertain death at the hands of Islamic terrorists."

Torres took a breath and bowed her head. She sighed, and said, "For sure. I didn't mean to imply they were without fault. Of course! All I meant was that once this is out on the Internet, outside the deep-web wing of the World Wide Web, there will be an interesting narrative at work of Westerners slaughtering Muslims, playing into past grievances. I can only imagine how the clip will be sliced and spliced to show the Templars and Muslims engaged in a death match."

"There is a bit of truth to what Ms. Torres is suggesting, Celeste," Radcliffe said. "Which is why you two need to get moving. Have you discovered anything in your research of benefit? Anything at all that could be useful to determining where these vigilantes might be hiding?"

Celeste went to answer when she was struck by something on the footage.

She said, "Zoe, could you bring up the frame from the video when the...I can't believe I'm saying this," she mumbled, "but when the Templars escaped?"

"Sure thing. Hold on a second."

She and Radcliffe remained on the screen in the upper corner as the footage was brought back.

"What is it?" Torres asked.

Celeste shook her head. "Not sure it's anything of significance, but the cars struck me as out of place."

"The cars? What about them?" Radcliffe questioned.

"There were three of them, and not like any I've ever seen in Europe before."

Torres said, "Didn't take you as a car gal, Celeste."

She offered a smile and turned to her as Zoe scrolled through the video to find the frames in question. "Daddy was into all manner of wheels. He brought me along to vintage car shows once a year, so I had my fill."

"Here we go," Zoe announced. She let the video play through from when the smartphone operator stepped outside until the cars vanished behind the market.

"Wind it back to the beginning," Celeste said. Zoe did. "There, stop."

One of the men was halfway in the back seat of the rear vehicle, the crimson cross clear and clearly of Templar origin.

"What's the make and model of that thing?" Celeste wondered aloud.

"Looks like a vintage Beamer to me," Torres said.

"Vintage, I'll give you. But not the German variety."

"Far from a Mercedes, as well," Radcliffe added. "A Peugeot perhaps? The picture is too bloody blurry to be of any use. Zoe, can you work your techno magic, please?"

"On it," Zoe said. "I've captured several frames of the vehicles leaving and running them now through an—"

"No need for the techno travelogue, my dear," Radcliffe complained.

She huffed as the clacking of a keyboard sounded through the television speaker as she worked. "Now this is interesting..."

The techie fell silent. Celeste grew irritated.

She said, "Zoe, dear. Care to fill us in on what has you so intrigued over there in Washington?"

Zoe looked up sharply, then smiled and began to redden. "Sorry. The model is indeed vintage. Something called an Alter III, from some outfit called União Metalo-Mecânica in Portugal."

"Portugal you say?" Celeste said with surprise.

She nodded. "Why? Does that mean anything to you?"

"In our research, we discovered that the Knights Templar continued living onward, reincarnated as the so-called Order of Christ in Portugal."

"Goodness me," Radcliffe said.

Torres added, "Guess that means we're heading to Lisbon after all."

"I'll ready the Order Gulfstream."

CHAPTER 16
LOCATION UNKNOWN.

Marwan Farhad jolted upright from deep within the inner recesses of the night. He was panting hot, heavy, worrisome breaths. His *thawb* was clinging to his back and chest, soaked through with perspiration.

He spun around on all fours on top the mound of cushions that were his bed inside the darkened chamber, its walls undulating in and out in sync with a wicked wind that had picked up pace outside.

He closed his eyes and swallowed hard, remembrance hitting him.

His ancestral tent, patterned after the Bedouins of generations past, used as a mobil command center; mounted on the barren desert floor, on the border with Israel; the prisoners in the safe house.

Farhad sighed and slumped back down, nestling in the cushions on his back and wrapping himself in a thick blanket dyed crimson. He labored his breathing, recalling the nightmare that had awoken him.

Wondering what in Allah's and his holy prophet's name it had all meant.

Sometime, in the dead of night, it felt as if he had been

instantly transported to his homeland, Iran. He was fifteen, the traditional age of maturity in Islam, and his Sunni family hadn't yet been driven from his hometown by the masked Shia villains who had persecuted his people for generations. It was dinner, and he was enjoying a traditional Persian meal with *Bademjan*, an eggplant and tomato stew; *Baghali Polo*, of rice and fava beans; and kabobs of juicy lamb that had been slaughtered earlier that day and marinated with lemon and herbs, then pressed in against minced onions and wedges of lemon on thin, steel rods and roasted over an open wood fire.

Around the table was his *pedar* and *madar*, his two younger brothers, Arman and Omar, and his sister, Jasmine. There were stories from when father had courted his mother, bouts of laughter from his brothers' silliness, more stories from when both father and mother were children themselves.

And then there was a knock at the door.

He looked up, and his father motioned for him to answer it. His mother was staring at him, as were his brothers and sister. No one said a word. They just looked at him and smiled, as if urging him to go forth and open.

So he did.

He arose from his chair and walked to the door with careful, hesitant steps. He looked back toward his family for reassurance, but they were gone. Nowhere to be found. This troubled young Marwan, but he continued toward the entrance and grasped the door handle anyway, twisting it and slowly opening the heavy wooden door. The high-noon sun was blindingly bright, so much that he had to squint his eyes and shield his face to look outside.

And there he was.

A man was standing several steps from the doorway in the barren desert, dressed in white with a raised hand. Then he inched forward, his own *thawb* a brilliant white and hands outstretched with curious markings, as if reaching in for an embrace.

Young Marwan's heart raced forward, and he immediately fell to the floor. His faith had taught him about such messengers, to take heed of such prophets sent from Allah himself bearing tidings of joy or sorrow.

He didn't know which, but he figured he should prostrate himself in either case.

"Stand up and follow me." The Persian man said. Or, at least he seemed Persian at first glance. But now that Marwan reflected on the vision after the fact, his skin was darker.

Jewish even.

"Who are you?" Marwan stammered, face still deflected away toward the ground, heart thumping wildly in his chest and nose touching the stone tiles of his family's home.

The man in white replied, "I am the Alpha and the Omega. I'm the way to Heaven. No one can go to the Father, except through me."

This startled young Marwan, and confused him. He slowly raised his head to see what man would say such a thing.

But he was gone.

And the blindingly bright afternoon had turned into the darkest of nights. The barren desert had been replaced by a horrific scene of blackened sand and mountains, shrouded in darkened clouds and lightning, spewing fire and molten lava. Then a ball of fire raced across the midnight sky and crashed into the Earth with thunderous menace.

Sending Marwan scrambling backward across the stone floor back into his family's home and jolting upright from his deep slumber in the desert borderlands.

Farhad took in a deep, measured breath and ran his hand through his hair to calm his frayed nerves, still startled from the encounter with the man in white.

And his words...

*"I am the Alpha and the Omega. I'm the way to Heaven. No one
can go to the Father, except through me."*

What sorcery it was that provoked such an encounter, he
wasn't entirely sure.

But he had an idea.

The nation of the cross.

Had to be. Ever since his men had captured and then
dragged the sixty-one men and women Christian infidels across
the Israeli border to the temporary desert compound, things
had been happening that only *Shaytan* could conjure, those
evil spirits working to defy the will of Allah.

A gust of wind blew hard against the canvas sides of his
temporary dwelling, causing the entrance to flap wildly and
shake the kerosene lantern hanging above with a violent clang.
The air was chilled and smelled of sulfur.

Eblis...

He launched himself up from his mound of cushions and
moved quickly to secure the wayward canvas flap. As he pulled
it back toward his dwelling, the compound holding the infidels
caught his attention. The square, squat building was black
against the clear sky showing the first signs of next-day life.

He crouched, holding the canvas and remaining still,
holding his breath even as he eyed the structure.

Nothing stirred, nothing sounded forth.

And yet, an uneasy dread wound its way up his spine,
causing him to shiver and recoil back into his tent.

Farhad went to draw the flap closed, when a different
thought entered his mind.

He looked back at the structure of stone and wood and
corrugated metal when a new breeze, hot and heavy and laden
with the filthy smell of the infidels, gusted across the barren
desert, hitting him in the face and recoiling him backward.

He coughed, pulling his *thawb* tight across his mouth and
nose. Then the same chilled, sulfuric wind returned, loosening

the canvas from his hand like a renegade sail and sending the kerosene lamp crashing to the floor behind him.

That's it...

Farhad stood and grabbed the lantern, lighting it and hustling to a campfire at the center of several more smaller canvas tents housing his men. A few of them were huddled around the small, warm campsite, flames flapping in protest when their commander approached.

"Commander," the four men said as they stiffened their arms to their sides before offering a salute.

"Come with me," Farhad growled, passing them and making for the safe house they had outfitted as a prison for the captured infidels.

The day's dawn began to offer its light when he arrived at the door, locked and guarded by two more men. The hour was fast approaching, and he might as well prepare for the inevitable.

He knew good and well when he made the unequivocal appeal to the nation of the cross for immediate and complete submission to Allah's rule and confession of the *shahada*, Islam's primary profession of faith, that they wouldn't budge. Which was no matter at all. It gave the pretext for what he and his men, and the rest of them around the world, would continue to unfold during the Christian Holy Week.

"Open it," he growled again, drawing his *thawb* tight across his face as the stench of bodies and rot and waste returned in force.

A soldier nodded and shuffled to unlock the steel door securing the treasure beyond.

The Christian men and women and that wretched pastor from the Jordan River.

A deafening clang rang throughout the space as the door was thrown open, leading into a dim, open room with warped wood floorboards and a single incandescent bulb swinging from the unfinished ceiling, covered with buzzing flies seeking the source of the stench.

Underneath was another entrance, a pair of steel double doors leading down into the makeshift prison. It was far more secure than the shipping container from before at their temporary site just after the raid on the River Jordan.

The soldier hustled forward to unlock the prison doors, then opened them with a harsh, high-pitched, weary creak, the doors bouncing off the floor with a deafening clang.

Farhad moved close to the entrance, swinging his lantern to the stairs descending into the maw of darkness below.

The space stirred with sleepy surprise, the bodies below still dressed in soiled white robes rising from the floor with resigned dread at what the intrusion meant.

"Where is the pastor?" Farhad called into the darkened void. "A man by the name of Jim George, if I remember correctly."

From the midst of the pool of bodies rose the burly man with the sagging, white scruffy face he had faced a few nights before, his billowing white robe stained pink and brown.

"Come with me."

The Christian minister stepped forward, and the crowd parted for his departure. He thudded loudly up the stairs with heavy, weary steps. The soldier yanked him forward by the arm, then threw the doors closed with another harsh clang.

Farhad stepped close to the man, drawing the lantern to his face and coming to within inches of him, barely able to stand the stench but wanting to look the man in the eyes for what was to come.

He also wanted to ask him a question.

"The Alpha and the Omega..." he announced with hesitation, trailing off without context or explanation.

Jim George startled, his eyes growing wide and face going limp. "Wha–What did you say?"

"The Alpha and the Omega," Farhad said more confidently. "What does that mean to you?"

The pastor took a step back and cocked his head, furrowing his brow with confusion. "Where did you hear that?"

"I only want to know what it means!" the man roared, rising to his tip toes with spittle flying from his mouth.

Jim George recoiled, raising his hands in fear to shield his face.

Farhad closed his eyes and took a breath, lowering the lantern to his side. He said, calmly, "Please, tell me what it means."

"The words are from the last book in the Christian Scriptures," the pastor quickly said. "From a passage in the book of Revelation. It says, *'And the one who was seated on the throne said, "See, I am making all things new." Also he said, "Write this, for these words are trustworthy and true." Then he said to me, "It is done! I am the Alpha and the Omega, the beginning and the end."'*"

"I see," Farhad said slowly. He brought his free hand to his chin and stroked his long salt-and-pepper beard. "And where are these words spoken?"

"From Heaven."

"And who is this who is doing the speaking? The man, in this Christian book of yours, who is he that is seated on the throne?"

"Why, it's Jesus Christ himself."

Farhad's eyes widened with surprise; the color drained from his face.

Isa...

"Why do you ask?" the pastor said softly.

Farhad shook his head and took a breath. "That is none of your concern. That is all. Take him away."

The guard nodded and roughly grabbed Jim George's arm.

"The passage continues, you know," the pastor said with purpose as Farhad turned to leave.

He turned slowly back around to face the man. "Go on."

Jim George swallowed and took a breath. "'*To the thirsty I will give water as a gift from the spring of the water of life,*' Jesus says. '*Those who conquer will inherit these things, and I will be their God and they will be my children. But as for the cowardly, the faithless, the polluted, the murderers, the fornicators, the sorcerers, the idolaters, and all liars, their place will be in the lake that burns with fire and sulfur, which is the second death.*'"

"Enough! I've heard enough. Take him away."

"Jesus said elsewhere," Jim George yelled as he was dragged away, "*I am the way, and the truth, and the life. No one comes to the Father except through me. If you know me, you will know my Father also. From now on you do know him and have seen him.*'"

Recognition instantly hit Farhad. That was the other line the man in white from his vision had said. *No one can go to the Father, except through me.*

He ran to the pastor and grabbed him by his neck. "What did you say?" he roared again as he squeezed, his eyes bulging and teeth bared with fury.

Jim George made hideous choking sounds as he gasped for breath and struggled against the man, face turning red and knees growing weak from the struggle. He tried reaching for Farhad, but the guards held him at bay.

Then all at once, Farhad let him go, panting and grunting from the exchange.

Jim George collapsed against the guards' arms, and they let him flop to the floor on his knees.

The pastor reached for his neck, still gasping for air and struggling to recover.

"You..." Jim George croaked. He swallowed and winced and rubbed his neck again. "You've seen him...haven't you?"

Farhad snapped his head toward the man at the suggestion.

"Get him out of here!" he screamed. "All of them! Time to do what we should have done three days ago."

CHAPTER 17

JORDAN.

S ilas drove their Order-issued gunmetal-gray Mercedes G500 4x4 in silence through the barren wilderness as Gapinski sat staring out his window, the sun stretching ever upward in the clear, blue sky above and beating down without mercy. He pushed it as fast as he felt comfortable across the border from Israel without finding themselves with a military tail wondering who was racing through their desert.

Silas wiped his forehead beading with sweat, even though the air was cranked. He cracked his window and retrieved the pack of Camels he had picked up before the drive.

"You don't mind, do you?" he said, holding up the pack.

Gapinski glanced over at him, startled from his contemplation. "Naw, it's fine."

Silas nodded, then smacked the pack against his leg and pulled out a cigarette with his teeth, driving with one hand and lighting it with the other. He puffed it to life and inhaled a nice, long lungful of nicotine-laced air. He held it, then blew it out the window as a car passed on the other side, a random dark-blue clunker caked with dirt from roof to windshield to body to tires, passing them in the borderlands of Jordan at a faster clip than even they were driving.

He looked back as he took another drag, making sure the vehicle kept going. Couldn't be too careful given what they were up against.

The stakes were far, far too high.

Once the Islamic terrorists had broadcast their ultimatum to the Church to basically convert or die, Silas and Gapinski connected with Zoe. She had been leading a small team of crackpot analysts ever since the abduction of Jim George and the rest of the Christians from the baptismal site in the Jordan River. The live-feed broadcast the day before had given them extra techno-ammo for the fight. So they scoured the Internet through the night for residual clues left behind as they back-tracked the signal, seeking its original source.

They caught a break the next morning when a string of code was traced to a cell tower along a road in the middle of nowhere several miles across the Israeli border in Jordan. Zoe had confirmed and reconfirmed the code and coordinates, veri-fying it had indeed been left behind from the broadcast.

That's all it took for Gapinski to commandeer a suitcase-full of automatic rifles, ammo, and grenades; suit up in Kevlar battle gear; and then commandeer a vehicle from the SEPIO outpost in Jerusalem. Within an hour, the pair were heading for Jordan for the fight of their lives.

The Hashemite Kingdom of Jordan is a majority Muslim country that has mostly been a moderating force in the region, particularly in the face of Islamic terror organizations oper-ating out of Lebanon and Palestine in the west, and the rise of the jihadi militancy of ISIS to the east in Iraq. Although many believe Jordan may be next in ISIS's sights. From the emerging intel, it seemed clear they were already operating cells out of the kingdom.

Given its proximity to Israel and its shared border with the Jordan River, it made sense the terrorists had fled there. Silas hoped they stayed put long enough for them to extract Jim George and the others before...

He didn't even want to think about the alternative.

He continued smoking as he drove, gearing up for what he expected was going to be a hornet nest of fighting. He wished they had waited for backup. But given the timing of it all and the continued attacks against the Church, they were all pastor Gapinski and the others had.

He finished his cigarette and flicked the butt out the window, then closed it. He wiped his forehead again with his sleeve and stole a glance at Gapinski. He was still quiet, sullen, distant.

Silas cleared his throat, and said, "You never told me why your grandfather means so much to you."

"Huh?" Gapinski grunted, stirred from his thoughts.

"Earlier you said that I had no idea how much that man, your grandfather, meant to you. I mean, I understand he's your grandpappy and all. Just seemed like there was a bigger story, that's all. Wondered if you wanted to share it. Take your mind off what's been going on and give you something to focus on as we gear up to open a serious can of whoop-ass on those jihadi whack jobs."

Gapinski offered a weak smile before his face quickly faded to the same weary, stoic stare. He sighed, and said, "Well, for starters, Grandpappy was more like a dad than Pops ever was. And actually, he played the part of Momma pretty dang well, too."

Silas frowned. "How so? Unless you don't want to talk about it. Don't want to open up old wounds."

"Naw, it's fine. Short of the long of it: Pops was a drunk and Momma was hooked on opioids before that was a thing. As you can imagine, the two never earned Parent of the Year awards."

"I guess not."

Gapinski breathed in deeply and sighed again. "Grandpappy had always looked out for me. But when things..." he stopped, staring out his passenger's side window.

Silas let him, not pushing anything he didn't want to talk about.

"OK, can I be honest with you? And can you not go all SEPIO high command on me?"

"Sure, alright..."

"Because I've never told anyone this part of my story. And, well, I'm not sure how the Order might take it, knowing that there are certain parts of my past that scream red flags."

Now Silas was worried. He tried not to show it, but wondered what on earth could be hiding in his partner's past.

But the man needed to share. And he'd be damned if he was going to let protocol stand in the way of whatever it was that was weighing him down.

Especially considering the circumstances.

He said, "It's just me and you right now, bro. Silas and Gapinski. Two friends. SEPIO ain't got nothing to do with it."

Gapinski stared forward. After a long several seconds, he finally said, "Well, as you can imagine, life pretty well sucked to high heaven with the kinds of parents I had. Which pretty much made every other part of life suck. One thing led to another...Well, several things led to another, and before I knew it, I was a high school dropout who wanted nothing to do with the world. Nothing to do with life. So much so, one afternoon while Momma and Pops were both passed out, I strung myself up from the neck and kicked a bucket out from underneath me."

Silas's heart sank to the floorboards.

Had he heard him right? Gapinski tried to kill himself, and failed?

He braked hard, sliding across gravel to a stop along the shoulder of the road. He put the truck in *Park* and turned off the engine. He took a breath and pivoted in his seat, leaning against his door as Gapinski stared blankly forward through the windshield.

"That's the part SEPIO doesn't know about," he said flatly. "And I'm not sure Nurse Ratched would be too keen on one of their lead operatives going all cuckoo for Cocoa Puffs back in the day."

"Don't worry about it," Silas said softly. "But Matt, I had no idea..." Emotion caught in his throat at the thought of it all. He didn't know what to say, so he went with: "What happened?"

Gapinski shrugged. "Did it wrong, is what happened. Too much slack in the rope, and when the bucket went one way, I went down. Except the rope tightened around my neck just so, so that I was standing on my tiptoes but couldn't do jack with the rope above."

He paused, silence filling the emptiness as gusts of wind blew sand across the road outside and another dirt-caked car whizzed by from behind.

"So there I was, twistin' and turnin' on the rope, gripping it with both hands above and trying to escape all Houdini style while pretty much choking to death. But not so much that I was actually dying. It was purely by the grace of God that Grand-pappy walked through the door and found me the way I was. That day, literally after he carried me out of that house with a cotton pickin' rope burn ringing my neck, he filed for custody with the court and got me the hell out of dodge. Raised me up to be the man that I am."

Silas put his hand up to his mouth and looked outside, understanding more why Gapinski's grandfather meant so much to him.

His partner snapped his head toward him, face etched with pain and agony, eyes red-rimmed and swelling with emotion.

Gapinski said softly, his voice strained, "We got to save him, Silas. We just got to..."

Silas clenched his jaw with resolve and nodded. "We will, partner. By God, we'll get those bastards."

He squeezed Gapinski's knee, then patted it before turning the engine over; it roared to life. He threw the truck into *Drive* and floored it, kicking up gravel as he lunged back for the road and sped toward the coordinates Zoe had given them.

In under an hour, the deep ruts of well-worn tire tracks jutting off from the main road and lined on either side by brambles and weeds gave the telltale signs of a well-used, makeshift road that would take them to their destination. Silas confirmed it matched the coordinates Zoe had given them, then he threw the wheel to the left. The pair jumped onto the trail leading to a long building in the distance, the sun beginning to rise higher as the Church's deadline drew to a close.

Silas eased the truck down into a dry riverbed he had spotted that ran along the road a half mile away and threw it into *Park*. The SEPIO agents would hoof it to the hostile's camp from there.

Gapinski was out of the car first, more than ready to exact his pound of flesh. He popped the trunk and started unloading their hardware.

"I'm warning you, Silas," he said as he grabbed a beige SIG716 G2—a weapon that meant serious business, featuring a short-stroke pushrod gas system that slung bullets with easy precision in any harsh environment. He handed Silas his own rifle, and continued, "If those jihadi whack jobs laid a pinkie fingernail on Grandpappy, I swear I'm gonna rip them apart from here to kingdom come."

Silas grabbed the weapon and nodded. "Understood. Just be careful, alright? The last thing we need is for the civilians to get caught up in any crossfire."

Gapinski shoved a magazine into the rifle and slung it around his back. "Don't worry. Those jihadi whack jobs ain't gonna know what hit 'em."

After they loaded up with extra magazines and backup handguns, the pair moved out.

The sun was cresting back toward Earth, and the sand was rippling with heat. They started jogging toward the coordinates when Silas's phone started vibrating with an incoming call. He answered it.

"Silas, it's Zoe."

He nodded toward Gapinski as they continued forward. "Hey, Zoe. We're about half a mile outside the coordinates you gave us. Should be there soon. Everything good?"

Hesitation on the other end almost caused him to falter his steps, but he kept at it, waiting for the Italian techie to get to the reason for the call.

"It's started," she simply said.

Silas looked at his partner, who had slowed his pace waiting for word. He said, "What do you mean by started?"

"Started? What's started?" Gapinski said with irritation.

"The twenty-four hours are up, and the terrorists are broadcasting again."

Silas slowed to a stop and lowered his arm holding the phone. He closed his eyes.

Dammit...

He realized his error before it was too late. Gapinski grabbed the phone from Silas's hand and started interrogating Zoe with panicked questions.

"What the hell's going on? What's started? What's happening to Grandpappy?"

"Gapinski!" Silas said, wrenching the phone back from his partner's ear. "Sorry about that, Zoe. Go ahead. What's going on?"

"Like I said, the Church's ultimatum to convert to Islam has passed. The terrorists opened up another socket on the Internet and are live-streaming another broadcast."

"Which means we're out of time."

"I'm afraid so."

"Please tell me the coordinates you gave us are still good."

"They're good. We've been monitoring the traffic on the node and it's clear the video is being routed through the same ISP channel."

"Thank God."

"What's she saying?" Gapinski said, his face twisted with agony.

Silas took a breath. "That we're out of time."

"Sonofa—" his partner cursed before taking off toward the compound rising up in the near distance.

Silas started running to keep pace. He said to Zoe, "Text me the link to the video and keep monitoring that channel. Call me the minute you know anything else or anything changes."

"Got it. Sending the URL now."

Silas ended the call and continued after his partner.

Lord Jesus Christ, Son of God, according to your lovingkindness have mercy on us and your servant Jim George. And help us kick some major jihadi butts!

CHAPTER 18

From Facebook to YouTube, Snapchat to Instagram, the Internet was again hijacked by the terrorists and engulfed in another live-stream feed. The same menacing image broadcast worldwide:

A sheet drawn behind a figure wearing the familiar desert fatigues and dark mask, a black flag with white Arabic writing mounted proudly on the sheet.

But where before the masked man stood alone, another person joined him.

He was seated on a chair, face wrinkled and baggy, with a bushy white beard and wisps of whitened hairs struggling for attention on the top of a balding head ringed by more white hair. The man was large, and he wore a familiar white robe, dirtied and soiled from days of neglect.

Pastor Jim George Gapinski.

His hands were bound in front of him and tied to his bound feet. He was facing the camera, head held high and eyes bright with defiance.

So far, anyway.

"As-salamu alaikum. Peace be with you," the masked man said, his voice strong and commanding and in polished

English. Just as the man had sounded from a day ago. "All praise be to Allah, the lord and cherisher of the world, and may peace and blessings be upon the prophet Muhammad. Twenty-four hours ago, I issued an ultimatum to the nation of the cross, swearing to Allah that they who have disgraced him through generations of countless acts of provocation and through heretical teachings denying Allah's way and the blessed teachings of his prophet Muhammad—your men and women, even your children, will not have safety, even in your dreams, until you embrace Islam.

"Until every one of the infidels have confessed the *shahada*," the man continued, voice rising high, "we will not rest until they are vanquished from the face of Earth unless they confess their allegiance to the one true God, Allah, and his only messenger Muhammad. Your time is up, nation of the cross. We will show you the kind of punishment we will render from heretofore starting with the criminals we apprehended from the Jordan River a few days ago."

The camera panned to a group of people, dressed in white and hooded in black, kneeling on a cement floor with hands bound behind their backs. Had to be thirty or forty of them together, bunched and awaiting their collective fate.

"Twenty-four hours ago," the masked man continued as the camera refocused back upon him, "I told Christians of the world to recant their beliefs and for the Church to declare its allegiance to Allah and Muhammad. Yet we have heard nothing. Christendom has been burning for three days, your men and women have been slaughtered and taken captive as our rightful slaves, your buildings have collapsed...and still nothing?"

The man sounded mystified, disbelieving that his commands for confession had gone unanswered.

He spat to the side, then said, "No matter. The nation of the cross will continue to feel the might of Allah's warnings against the infidels, with all of their corruption and misguided heresy. Starting with those forty-one remaining Christians from the River Jordan."

The group came into view again, the camera having widened its shot and panned back over to the kneeling men and women in dirty white robes. This time they were singing, clear and with conviction, their voices rising in muffled defiance through the black hoods.

"When peace, like a river, attendeth my way, when sorrows like sea billows roll," the voices rang out, "whatever my lot, Thou hast taught me to say. It is well, it is well with my soul."

Before they could continue on to the chorus, there was a loud cry from off-camera: "Allahu Akbar!"

Then the dim light glinted off from a steel sword swinging through the air before it connected with the neck of one of the Christians.

The believer's head sailed off-screen, their body left behind spouting blood and slumping to the ground as the group of Christians continued singing, harmonies and all, their voices rising in supplication and in witness to the Lord before his throne: "It is well with my soul. It is well, it is well with my soul."

They continued on to another verse with defiant confession as the terrorists continued with their horrific beheadings.

"Though Satan should buffet, though trials should come," they sang as more brothers and sisters in the faith gave up their souls. "Let this blest assurance control, that Christ hath regarded my helpless estate, and hath shed his own blood for my soul."

The chorus was marked by a continued blood bath, as the old and young, men and women alike lost their heads and slumped over in pools of rising blood until one lone voice remained.

Shaky yet defiant, an elderly man gave one last gasping

testimony to faith in Jesus Christ as a fatigue-clad Muslim fighter readied his blade dripping with the blood of the martyrs.

"And Lord, haste the day when my faith shall be sight," he said, breathy and off key. "The clouds be rolled back as a scroll..."

The hooded man stepped to the Christian's side and swung his sword high.

The elderly child of God sang, "The trump shall resound, and the Lord shall descend..."

"Allahu Akbar!" the terrorist screamed with bloodlust before letting his sword swing.

"Even so, it is well with—"

THE TWO SEPIO agents came up fast along an outer fence of the compound near what looked to be a heavily used shipping container. Sand had blown against its faded blue side in knee-high drifts, its girth offering cover for their covert invasion.

Gapinski withdrew a set of cutters from his belt, the high-noon sun beating down on their necks, and he began cutting the fencing to offer them an opening inside. He wiped his brow as he worked, making quick work of the chain links.

Silas had pulled out his smartphone and clicked the link Zoe had texted him through to the live-stream video, witnessing the beginning slaughter of the Christian martyrs while his partner continued working. He stuffed the phone back into his pocket as Gapinski finished, his stomach churning with anger and dread at the persecuting injustice.

He cursed. They were almost out of time.

They pushed through the opening and shuffled along the backside of the container.

Gapinski stopped short at its edge for a lay of the land. Dead center was the structure Zoe had pegged as ground zero for the terrorists' operations, a building of stone and roofed with corrugated metal sunk deep into the desert. A car and a truck lay moored out front, along with three abandoned tents, their canvas flapping in protest as a hot breath of air gusted across the barren wilderness.

And not a soul in sight.

He took a shaky breath and wiped his brow again.

"I don't get it," he mumbled.

"What's that?" Silas said, inching around for a look himself.

"It's like *The Walking Dead* out there. Two cars, a few tents, and no one keeping guard. Way less accommodations than the jihadi whack jobs we saw kidnap those Christians and Grandpappy.

"My guess is they're in there," Silas said, nodding toward the structure. "Zoe hasn't given any word that the signal geotagging has changed. Gotta still be in there."

"Let's get to it then," Gapinski said, taking off toward the building.

The pair hustled along the structure of corrugated metal sunk into the desert. They came up to a set of stairs leading down to a heavy metal door, crouching in the sand and looking around before descending. It was like a cellar, which would give the hostiles the advantage, even with the element of surprise.

"The place sure does look abandoned," Silas admitted, taking in their surroundings again, voice betraying worry.

Gapinski was breathing hard and glancing around the compound as well.

"Oh, they're definitely getting their jollies on inside," he said, his voice trying to fake confidence. "No way are they missing a good Christian martyrdom."

"Then we better do this," Silas said lowly, descending the stairs and getting into position next to the door.

Gapinski joined him. He took a breath, then silently ticked

off the count with his fist, counting with his fingers down *three, two, one, go time.*

Closing his fist, he nodded to Silas. His partner nodded back.

Time to roll.

In one motion, Gapinski threw the full, solid mass of his six-foot-four weight against the door.

Once, twice.

It gave on three.

He launched into the room with maximum surprise and was met by a space the size of a small urban basement, with all of the look and feel and smell of one, too.

A chill permeated the dank, darkened space lit only by a few incandescent bulbs hanging by their wires at odd angles, casting ghoulish shadows around the space. The faint *drip-drip-drip* of water echoed in one corner, with a winding stream of water searching for an escape at one end. Musk and mold underlaid the dizzying scent of death clinging to the walls and hovering with purpose.

Gapinski slung his rifle around toward the expected hostiles, ready to let it rip with abandon.

But where he expected resistance by the wickedness that had taken up residence deep in the desert, he was met with a different kind of resident evil.

The sound of buzzing flies and the putrid stench of rotting flesh and stale blood left for hours in the suffocating heat, even days.

And bodies.

A dozen littered the ground. Men and women. Several more were tied to old metal chairs, their arms bound behind them.

All had met one of two unholy fates.

Either they had been shot in the head, their brains blown out the front; many were like this, their bodies slumped forward in a pool of blood that had drained from their head wounds.

Or their throats had been slit wide open—some just above the collar bone, right through their thyroid and on into the trachea and the carotid artery; others from ear to ear. Every one of their heads had been wrenched back at ungodly angles, echoes of their fierce screams still lodged in the void of their open necks.

Every single one of the bodies littering the floor or still mounted on chairs were martyrs of Christ and standing before his throne as witnesses to his truth.

Silas came up fast and continued forward, sweeping the room with his Beretta outstretched as Gapinski sank to his knees in disbelief.

"I don't understand..." he said breathlessly. His rifle clattered to the cement floor as he fell forward to all fours, panting with confusion and on the verge of retching. "These bodies look like they've been here for hours. Maybe a day."

"What the hell is this," Silas marveled as he continued searching, forearm covering his nose and mouth to mask the stench.

"We had...coordinates," Gapinski said, heaving great breaths as he stared at the floor, making deep guttural sounds of someone about to lose their stomach. "Zoe said they checked out."

"They checked out alright," Silas growled, continuing to sweep the space. He opened a final closet, discovering nothing but wires and blinking nodes, confirming what they both immediately understood.

The coordinates were right. Just the wrong ones.

They got it all wrong.

Dead wrong.

CHAPTER 19

The masked man was panting hot, heavy breaths, dizzy with the thrill of the kill. He was drenched with blood, from mask to boots, the crimson liquid all at once slick and sticky against his hands, the taste of copper heavy in his mouth and sending him into an ecstatic high.

He took deep breaths to calm himself, wiping his sword gleaming with the fruits of his labor against his pants and sheathing it for the grand finale. He licked his lips dry, that taste sending his heart rate climbing again before he took another deep, calming breath to steel himself for the final act.

The infidels had been slain.

All except for one.

The man slowly strode back toward the main stage, the sheet billowing in protest as he arrived. One of his men came up to him and whispered something into his ear.

So, the ruse had worked...

Over the years, Nous had perfected the art of techno deception, amassing a coterie of highly skilled techies to advance their mission of eradicating the Church and establishing an alternative spirituality. That same group had successfully masked the origin of their live feed, routing it through their safe house in Jordan. Not only was the protective measure meant to mask the feed and shield it from any brute-force interference. It was also meant to sidetrack anyone who might try to discover its origin and disrupt his plans.

He had just been told agents of the Order of Thaddeus had discovered the fruits of their previous labor. They were still inside now.

The man grinned at the thought, knowing that one of those agents was the grandson of the final remaining infidel. And soon, it all would be concealed anyway.

"I know my end is near," Jim George said suddenly. "But I have a gift for you."

The man reached down toward his feet with this bound hands and pulled the robe up toward his waist. A guard appeared in the frame, but the masked man raised a hand to stay him.

He angled his arms toward his face then reached underneath his robe into his front pocket to retrieve something.

Farhad furrowed his brow, curious what the man was doing while the camera was still rolling for all the world to see.

When he was through fishing, Jim George pushed his robe back down to this feet, and he simply announced, "Here."

The masked man stifled a grin underneath his mask, amused at the effort to win over his captor this late in the game.

He took a hesitant step toward the side of the man, and asked, "What is this? What do you have?"

"I give to you my Bible."

"Your...Your Bible?"

The pastor held the small book up to his enemy between his bound hands, an offering to the man who would behead him, its pages stained a dim gold and dirty with age and bound by a tattered green cover that had seen decades of wear.

Farhad said nothing. He stood still, not expecting such a response to his final victim.

Jim George turned his head toward the masked man and smiled, his eyes searching and face tender. "I want you to know that I love you, Mister. So does Jesus. And when you take my life, read this book. Like those men and women before me, I am not ashamed of what it contains. The gospel of Jesus Christ, God's good news of his crazy love for you, Mister." He paused and raised the little green book higher, then said, "For that good news, right here in this itty-bitty book, is the power of God for salvation to everyone who has faith. First to the nation descended from Isaac, but also to those who descended from Ishmael."

The masked man was taken aback by the infidel's brazenness, understanding he was speaking about the Jews and the Gentiles, especially those who claim Ishmael as their patriarch.

His people. Those who submit to Allah and claim Muhammad as his prophet.

"For in this good news," Jim George continued, "the righteousness of God is revealed through faith for faith; as it is written, 'The one who is righteous will live by—'"

Farhad smacked the man clear across his face with the back of his hand before he could finish the sentence, sending the pastor flying backward to the ground in his chair.

"No more talk!" he screamed, motioning for the guard to raise the infidel back upright.

As his final victim was raised back to sitting position, he let out a bloodthirsty cry with all of the fury and satisfaction of the original Muslim persecutors of the nation of the cross.

"Allahu Akbar!"

SILAS RETRIEVED his phone and swiped it to life, returning back to the live-feed video. His gut twisted with recognition as the face of the man who had baptized him just a few days ago stared back at him, having been uprighted after the outburst from the masked man before his final death. His face was marked with calm indifference.

Or was it peaceful resignation?

He couldn't be sure. All he knew, and what he couldn't bear to tell his partner who was still doubled-over on the floor, was that something had gone horrifyingly wrong.

There he was, Grandpappy Jim George, on the live-streaming video in a similarly darkened cement structure with the jihadi whack job they had seen before.

Yet there they were, standing in an entirely different darkened cement structure littered with bodies that had been dead for hours. Days even.

And no Grandpappy.

Gapinski's grandfather was about to go home to meet his Savior.

And in the most horrendous way imaginable.

When it became clear what was what, realization dawning with horrifying recognition, Gapinski recovered and scrambled up from the concrete floor.

"Give me your phone!" he said, stalking over to Silas, face stricken and pained with the full understanding of what was about to go down in some other godforsaken desert.

Silas held the phone above his head and took a step backward.

"I don't think that's a good idea..."

"Give it to me!" his partner roared.

"You don't want to do this! You don't want the final memories of your grandpappy to be...to be whatever the hell is about to go down."

Gapinski got up in Silas's face, standing toe-to-toe with him, reaching high for the only lifeline left to the man who was the only true family he had.

Silas took a step back and bent backward to keep the phone from his friend's reach.

The man reached forward and swatted for it, but Silas pressed a hand against his chest and gently pushed him away.

Gapinski stepped backward and caught his heel on a patch of slick blood that had been oozing from the neck of a headless man, sending him scrambling to stay upright.

His foot slid into the body, and he fell forward. But thankfully he caught himself before landing in the pile of Christian martyrs.

That's when all hell broke loose within him.

"You sonofa—"

Gapinski launched himself at Silas. Head down, square in his solar plexus.

Silas recoiled in pain and lost his breath. But he still held onto the phone.

The beast catapulted his unsuspecting partner against the cold cement wall, and roared, "Give me the friggin' phone!"

Silas recovered a breath and managed to lift his legs up. He shoved them hard into the man and pushed off the wall, regretting the use of force against his partner. But with the raging bull completely unleashed, he was left with few options.

Gapinski fell back hard against the cement floor. Thankfully, he missed the gore that sat stewing just behind his right shoulder.

"Don't do this..." Silas coughed and bent over, continuing to catch his breath and gripping the phone with purposeful protection.

His partner was panting now, too. But recovering far quicker than Silas.

Gapinski slowly stood, head bent low but eyes fixed on Silas with menacing resolve. He narrowed his eyes and grunted. In one motion he lunged forward and swiped the phone from him with his meaty palm.

"No, wait..." Silas said, stumbling backward from the force of it all.

His partner spun around and brought the phone to life, then tapped in the SEPIO passcode. Staring back at him was a man in desert fatigues with a long beard looking like Zoro.

And he was standing behind his grandpappy.

He threw his other hand across his open mouth and let out a whimper.

Giving Silas the chance to come from behind and swipe the phone back.

Gapinski spun around to face Silas, his nostrils flaring, lungs heaving. "Give. Me. The. Friggin'. PHONE!" he yelled with misdirected rage.

Silas stood straight and swallowed hard. He held the phone in front of him, its face casting soft light upon Gapinski's own face from the gyroscope auto-on feature.

"You don't want to do this," he pleaded.

"Yes I do!"

"No way, brother."

"GIVE IT TO ME!"

Silas startled from the force of his rage. He had seen his partner angry before, like any man. But not like that.

He sighed, finally resigning himself to his partner's demand. "Fine. You want the phone? You really want to do this to yourself?"

Gapinski swallowed hard himself and grunted his affirmative reply.

"Fine." Silas threw the phone to the floor with force.

It landed face down, its face shattering into tiny spider-web fragments. Totally obscuring its face and rendering it useless.

"NO!!!" Gapinski yelled, throwing himself on top of the device and cradling it like a broken bird.

Silas closed his eyes and tried to catch his breath. He was breathing hard from the fight, from the emotion of it all, but didn't regret a thing. The last thing his partner needed was to see his grandpappy's head get torn off.

He lumbered over to his partner, still on the ground cradling the phone and muttering something indistinguishable over the piece of shattered technology. Silas bent low and put his hand on the man.

Gapinski tensed at the touch, but didn't move. He kept muttering, then slowly started rocking back and forth.

Silas bent lower, getting on his knees and wrapping an arm around Gapinski's shoulders. Finally, the man stopped all at once—the muttering, the rocking. Then he melted, curling in on himself and wrapping the phone up within his thick arms, reduced to a heaping pile of agonizing sobs.

"I know, buddy. I know," Silas whispered as he held his friend.

Sounds like nothing he had heard since his time in Iraq and Afghanistan emanated from the broken grandson, ricocheting off the cold, concrete walls, and joining the cries of injustice from the faithfully departed.

Lord Jesus Christ, Son of God, Silas silently prayed, *run to your beloved son, Jim George Gapinski, with arms wide open as he enters into Paradise this day.*

"*THE LORD IS MY SHEPHERD, I shall not want,*" Pastor Jim George Gapinski prayed as he was slowly brought upright, his face on fire from the whack across his mouth. "*He makes me lie down in green pastures; he leads me beside still waters; he restores my soul. He leads me in right paths for his name's sake.*"

He clenched the small green Bible between his bound hands, holding it to his thundering chest as he muttered the words to Psalm 23, the one he'd had since he was a teenager. The one given to him when he decided to follow Jesus. About the only thing he thought to do as he prepared to go home and meet his Lord, his Savior.

"Even though I walk through the darkest valley, I fear no evil; for you are with me; your rod and your staff—they comfort me."

"Allahu Akbar!" he heard the man scream who had martyred his dear brothers and sisters mere minutes ago.

A surge of fight-or-flight adrenaline shot into his bloodstream, causing his heart to lurch forward. His chest began to constrict in on itself through the stress. Breathing became difficult even as he gulped down more fiery breaths, straining to bring air inside and remain faithful until the very end.

He continued quoting the psalm in halting mutters. *"You prepare a table before me in the presence of my enemies; you anoint my head with oil; my cup overflows. Surely goodness and mercy shall follow me all the days of my life, and I shall dwell in the house of the Lord my whole life long."*

The sound of the masked man's boots scraping against the cement sounded forth as he moved into position.

Jim George felt his presence hot on his back as he waited for the end.

His mind instantly jumped to the first time he heard about Jesus. A traveling preacher had strolled into his small town and set up shop in a field near Main Street. It was one of those tent revival meetings. Momma and Papa had dragged him and his siblings kicking and screaming to get religion, even though the two of them weren't all that religious themselves.

He remembered two things from that evening of song and preaching. Something that the preacher said that laid him out cold.

"Jesus is who you've been waitin' for your whole life, whether you know it or not."

Jim George thought the man was off his rocker. When he turned sixteen, he discovered booze and girls were what he'd been missin' his whole life! But then the preacher quoted some guy he'd forgotten the name to, which made a bit of sense: "There is a God-shaped vacuum in the heart of every man which cannot be filled by any created thing, but only by God the Creator, made known through Jesus Christ."

He had to admit it, the man had a point.

But he was floored by item number two: "God loves you and wants to be your friend."

He had never heard those words before. He'd always reckoned God was pissed off at him for all his boozin' and swearin' and messin' around with girls. But the preacher backed up his words with Scripture.

First, he quoted John 3:16, *"For God so loved the world that he gave his only Son, so that everyone who believes in him may not perish but may have eternal life."*

Then he added one more to the mix from John 15:1, *"'No one has greater love than this, to lay down one's life for one's friends. You are my friends if you do what I command you. I do not call you servants any longer, because the servant does not know what the master is doing; but I have called you friends."*

The preacher said Jesus came to die for us so that we could be called children of God, his friends. And right then and there, seventeen-year-old Jim George Gapinski shuffled down the aisle of browned grass in that tent to the one he'd been waiting his whole life to fill what the world promised to do itself, but couldn't.

Tears began to wind their way down both of Jim George's cheeks at the thought that through a random traveling preacher, the good Lord had chosen a red-neck hillbilly from a small town in Georgia to be his friend, his family. And then called him to share that same message with the world.

The masked man suddenly wrapped his hand around Jim George's forehead and wrenched his head back, his neck popping in protest.

Father, forgive them; for they do not know what they are doing...

Suddenly, there was a sharp pain at his throat, like a paper cut magnified and exploding a million fold. Then he could feel his blood squirting and then bubbling out of the wound like a drinking fountain—down his chest and down his throat and into his lungs. He tried to cough, but it was no use. The warm liquid was filling his lungs and spilling down his chest.

He wasn't dead yet, for he felt his body moving back and forth, and his head was wrenched back and to the side as his captor continued sawing through his throat, and then through his neck muscles until he could sense the steel blade hitting squarely against the bone of his spine.

Through it all, he could feel a power hovering close to his body. Like a thousand suns pulsating all at once, full of light and life and comforting warmth.

And love. A purity of self-giving, self-sacrificing, self-denying love had swarmed every atom of his being so that all fear had completely evaporated away.

Lord Jesus Christ, Son of God, into your hands I commend—

All at once, the light of this world was extinguished, and Jim George Gapinski was ushered into the awaiting, rescuing arms of his Savior, tears streaming down his face with unimaginable delight as he heard the words he'd been waiting ever since that tent revival when he was a teenager:

"Well done, good and faithful servant! You have been faithful until the very end. Enter into the joy of your Lord!"

It took a few minutes until Farhad had finished the job. He was out of breath from working the knife. They normally went quicker than that one. But he also wanted to give the world a show.

He threw aside the blade and grabbed the head of yet another fallen Christian martyr, the man he had gotten to know as Pastor Jim George Gapinski. His eyes were bulging and tongue was slung over his gapping mouth, as if he were surprised by what had happened.

The body of the pathetic martyr crumpled to the floor like a used bathrobe, hands still clutching his worthless little book.

Farhad scoffed, but reached down for the small green object. He set the head on the floor, then wrenched back the man's fingers and pulled it from his clutches.

It was small, with a gold foil line running around the edge and the words *Holy Bible* stamped on the front. Its pages were edged with gold as well. He stained them red from the blood of the martyr as he flipped through its worthless pages.

He went to toss it next to the man's head, when he thought better of it.

He had never actually ready the Christian Scriptures. And yet he had spent his entire life waging war against the wretched group of infidels. Now that he was on the verge of becoming Grand Master of the Thirteen, of Nous, he might as well become more familiar with the scourge of humanity.

The masked man stuffed the small book inside the folds of his *thawb*. *"'Those Christians and Jews are they whom God hath cursed,'"* Farhad mumbled, quoting the Quran. *"'And those whom God hath cursed, thou wilt find, have no one to help.'"*

He sneered at the infidel and sent a glob of spittle sailing toward the dead man, landing just shy of his severed head. He stepped over it and ordered the feed cut, then continued walking out of the secondary safe house and into the sunshine.

Smiling and basking in the favor of Allah.

CHAPTER 20

I t was as if time itself had stopped. All feeling, all sensing, all concept of forward motion ceasing in the vortex of agonizing ignorance, while still being left with the awareness of what was happening somewhere out there.

Of what had *already happened* somewhere out there.

To Grandpappy Jim George.

Gapinski was thankful Silas had done what he did, withholding the phone from him and smashing the display. In the moment, he was pissed about it. Wanted to rip the man's head off because of it. All he had wanted to do was to bear witness to his grandpappy's martyrdom, to his faithfulness to Christ and his perseverance in his faith right up to the end.

But, as they say, hindsight is twenty-twenty. There was no way he wanted the fields of his cherished childhood memories to be salted with...with his beheading.

The man sat still on the cold concrete floor, slumped over with legs crossed, letting those memories wash over him like a warm bath. All of those school football, basketball, and baseball games his grandpappy cheered him on in the stands before he dropped out. The Saturday movie nights with all the pizza and candy he could stomach. Help with doing his homework and fixing his car. Advice with girls and how to navigate every other minefield of life.

All of that was gone now. Destroyed in one fell slice of the blade by jihadi whack jobs hellbent on destroying the Church.

And they would pay for it. Dearly.

Especially one in particular.

The coward-ass man with a long salt-and-pepper beard looking like Zoro.

One way or another, he'd find out who he was and hunt him down.

Then he'd get his revenge.

"Vengeance is mine," the good Lord says in the Good Book.

Vengeance my ass! Zoro won't even know what hit him when I'm—

A sound from behind startled him out of his vengeful stupor.

He turned toward it, seeing Silas leaned over inside some sort of closet. His partner had left him alone with his thoughts, contenting himself with examining the building for anything they could use to help them sort out the mess from the past few days. Not to mention the mess scattered about in the safe house.

Gapinski sighed, leaning back to—

"Argh!" the man screamed, scrambling off the floor and scurrying toward Silas.

"What the heck?" Silas yelled, jolting from the closet.

The two smashed into each other, yelling again and cursing at the collision.

"What happened? You alright?" he asked.

Gapinski dropped to one knee, taking in heavy, heaving breaths.

He swatted at a fly that had landed on his shoulder. It moved to his other shoulder; he swatted it there. Then it moved to his nose. In exasperation, he smacked at it there, too. Then he cried out again.

"Dude—"

"Head!" was all Gapinski said, still doubled-over and waving an arm toward the center of the room.

He caught sight of a severed head from one of the martyred Christians a few yards away settling after having been disturbed by Gapinski's stretch.

"I think I'm gonna be sick, man."

Silas patted his partner's back, then returned to the closet.

As the man fiddled with whatever it was he was fiddling with, Gapinski took in several deep breaths of rotten air made all the worse by the heavy heat. He scanned the room, taking in the revolting air through his mouth, having forgotten what they had stumbled into during the confusion of it all when they had expected to find his grandpappy. They had propped the door open to air the place out, but it still reeked to high heaven.

It was like something out of the Saw franchise of horror movies he had made the mistake of seeing fifteen years ago after one of his buddies conned him into joining the guy for the first one. Ran from the theater after screaming like a little school girl once it dawned on one of the characters that a pair of hacksaws were meant to be used on their feet, not their chains. No way, no how was he going to sit through that gore and—

Another clang to his right snapped him out of the mesmerizing scene.

He stood and sauntered over to Silas, who was head-deep in the closet again.

"What the heck is all of this racket about?"

"Investigating," Silas mumbled.

Gapinski sighed. "I see that, Sherlock. What are you investigating?"

"This," he said, leaning out of the closet and pointing to a bundle of wires and a plastic box lit up like a Christmas tree.

"What is it?"

"Reminds me of the gear I got when I ditched my cable box back home after I cut the cord and went Netflix-only."

"So they were watching re-runs of *Homeland* or something way out here?"

"This looks way more powerful than your run-of-the-mill Internet router." Silas walked over to his abandoned smartphone still lying on the floor, screen smashed beyond use.

"What are you doing?"

"Seeing if I can still phone home. Get HQ up to speed on what happened here and see if Zoe can help untangle the hardware."

Silas held the base of the device to his mouth, hoping it would still function on voice command without the operation of the screen.

"Hey Siri," he said.

Took a second, but the device went to a black screen and registered a *ping*, the familiar rainbow wave sparking near the bottom behind spiderwebbed glass.

She said, "I'm listening..."

He sighed and nodded at Gapinski, then told her to dial SEPIO on speaker. He held the phone between them as it rang twice before being answered.

"Praise God from whom all blessings flow!" Radcliffe answered. "When we hadn't heard anything, we became worried. And when we couldn't reach you, we assumed the worst after..." The man trailed off before adding: "How are you, Matthew? Did you...Surely you didn't—"

"I'm fine," he said, cutting in. "And, no, I didn't watch it all go down. Silas took care of that for me." He offered his partner a weak smile of thanks.

Silas squeezed his partner's shoulder, affirming the gesture of support.

There was another awkward silence. "I have to ask," Radcliffe finally said, "what happened? All of us were praying for the success of your mission, knowing you were heading to storm the ramparts of the terrorists' nest and retrieve the captured Christians. Most of all, Pastor Jim George."

"That's just the thing, we weren't."

"Come again?"

"The coordinates we were given were not the ones for the terrorists' compound. At least, not the one where Gapinski's grandfather and the others were being held."

"Sit tight, would you please. I'm bringing in Zoe." Within seconds, the Italian director of operational support was on the line. "Be a good lad and explain to our resident techie what you're playing at, would you please, Silas?"

"Sure thing. I was sharing with Radcliffe, Zoe, that we never made it to the compound to rescue Gapinski's grandfather."

"What? Why, what happened?"

"They were the wrong coordinates. Or at least the right coordinates to the wrong place."

"No way!" Zoe exclaimed. "That intel was solid."

"I don't know what to tell you, but they ain't here. Or..." he trailed off, taking in the scene around them of littered bodies and pooling blood. "Well, most of them aren't. By the looks of it, the nineteen Christians who were martyred as a warning to the Church when the lead terrorist gave his ultimatum are here. Just not the rest. And not Pastor Jim George."

"That's nutso to the maxo!"

"You're telling me. Near as I can figure it, they left soon after the first broadcast. There's a closet down in the safe house with a mess of wires and some heavy hardware lit up like a Christmas tree. So it looks to me like they routed the live-feed signal through a highly sophisticated network node modulator, disguising the signal as originating from the coordinates you gave us while they were nowhere near here."

"Now *that's* nutso to the maxo. And some pretty sophisticated technological wizardry. Takes more than your Best Buy Geek Squad rep to pull something like that off. Not only the know-how but the moolah, too. More than I would expect from some backwoods terrorists."

Silas nodded. "I hear that. I'm beginning to think this is more than ISIS. "

A sudden surge of *clickety-clacking* sounded from the phone. "I'm going to backtrace the code we found the other day that led us to those coordinates and infiltrate that system. See if I can brute-force it in and have a look around."

"Good idea."

"Now, Silas, what do you mean that it's more than ISIS?" Radcliffe asked.

"It's what I said a few days ago when I wondered what business ISIS had targeting the Church in such an overt, aggressive way. Most of those recent jihadi attacks have been against the state of Israel and against Western targets generally, like the Paris nightclub bombing and London Bridge attack mowing down pedestrians. Nothing ever specifically Christian."

"Until now, duh!" Gapinski said, his voice raised and ready for a fight.

Silas took a breath and nodded. "Yes, until now. Or so we thought. But what if it's not ISIS, or just ISIS?"

"What if it's Nous, isn't that right?" Radcliffe questioned.

"Can't rule them out."

Gapinski himself had wondered whether or not the Church's archenemy stretching back to the early centuries of the Church had been behind the attacks. Whether Nous had been behind what happened to his grandpappy.

"I must admit," Radcliffe continued, "I had my doubts when you brought up the theory earlier. But, given the sophistication of the recent broadcasts and the sweeping, coordinated nature of the attacks, I have to admit there must be a more powerful force at work than simply a band of Islamic miscreants."

Silas said, "And what larger force could be at work against the Church than her darkest, most vicious enemy?"

"Sweetness!" Zoe sounded through the speaker before Radcliffe could respond.

"I'm guessing you found something?" Gapinski asked.

"Boy, did I ever. I was able to backtrace—"

"Zoe..." Silas moaned in protest.

"Oh alright! Jeez, can't a girl gloat when she's brought home the bacon?"

Gapinski's stomach growled at the mention of the word, a siren song of salted pork for his rumbly tummy that hadn't seen a meal since the morning.

Silas raised a brow and glanced at his partner's oversized gut as it rumbled with recognition.

Gapinski blushed, and complained, "Now why'd you have to go and mention a thing like bacon. It's been hours since we've eaten, and I could really use a Wendy's Baconator Double right about now."

"What'd you find, Zoe?" Silas said, stifling a laugh.

"The real coordinates to where those jihadi terrorists ran off to."

Gapinski sulked away, his stomach rumbling again. Had to take his mind off the bacon, and standing still wasn't helping.

"You're certain, my dear?" Radcliffe asked.

"Positive. The backtrace...err, I'm sure. Well, at least the location of the originating signal is right. Now, whether the hostiles are still there is another question."

Silas smiled and raised his hand in victory at the precious bit of good news that had been a long time coming. Gapinski gave a thumbs up and wandered back toward the closet.

"Nice work, Zoe," Silas said. "I'd ask you to text the location to me but my phone is a little under the weather at the moment. The face of it is totally busted and useless. I'll need to get another one when we get on the road again."

"Bummer. Do you have a piece of paper?"

"Umm..." He shoved a hand in his pocket but came up empty. He searched the room, looking for something that might have been left behind. "Going to have to wait until we get back to our car."

Gapinski bent low to the ground to inspect something that had caught his eye near the door to the closet. He ran a thick finger along the base of the frame, scratching at parts. Then he blew.

"What the heck is this?" he mumbled.

Silas furrowed his brow and walked over to his partner. "Hold on a second," he said to the phone, kneeling beside him. "What do you got?"

Gapinski sighed and shook his head. "Looks like some sort of wire coming out of the closet and running out to God knows where. Look."

He pointed to a curious wire snaking out from underneath the door and covered with grime. Looked like the thing ran along the base of the wall and around the room.

"There's another one over here," Silas said, shuffling to the other side of the door frame and pointing to its base. He ran his fingers along an exposed part, then started picking at similar dirt and grime caked on it. He managed to rub it down to black plastic sheathing, then started tracing the rest of it along the wall.

Gapinski was already ahead of him, having run alongside the wire to several junctures along the outer wall's base, disappearing into crates and barrels left behind. Silas discovered the same scene on the other side of the room. A few more wires led into the walls.

Which didn't bode well.

They hadn't noticed it all when they arrived. Too focused on saving Grandpappy Gapinski. And then they were caught up in the moment and distracted by all of the dead Christian martyrs.

"I've got a bad feeling about this," Gapinski announced. "Bad, bad mojo in this place."

Before Silas could reply, Zoe sounded through the speaker.

"Wait a minute..." she said, voice low and trailing off.

"Found something?" he said, shuffling back over to Gapinski.

The only reply was the clacking of a keyboard. Then a gasp.

"You both need to get the heck out of dodge!"

The two SEPIO agents looked at each other, eyes wide and ready to bolt by her tone.

Gapinski said, "What are you talking—"

"A line of code has been running a countdown sequence since, oh, about the time that video feed cut to color bars."

"Crapola!" Gapinski cursed.

They didn't even have to wait for Zoe to tell them how much time they had left.

Had to be seconds.

"Run!" Silas yelled.

"Always something!" Gapinski replied as they took off toward the open entrance, dodging a macabre obstacle course of bloody slick spots, fallen heads, and rotting corpses.

Silas launched over a body face down with the back of its head blown off, white robe dirty and stained crimson. He managed to dodge a puddle of blood, reaching the threshold of the door first.

Gapinski wasn't so lucky.

His first step through the darkened cellar caught the leg of a large man, nearly sending him tumbling forward. He jolted and screamed at the incident, sending him backward and tumbling into the crates, popping the lid off of one of them.

Which exposed a massive cache of explosives.

"C-4!" he yelled, scrambling off from the splintered wood and sloshing through pooled blood toward the exit.

"Then let's get the hell out of here!" Silas yelled back as he ran through the open door.

A fierce wind ran wild above, whipping up sand into his face as he ascended. He shielded his eyes as he hustled up the stairs, taking them by twos and cresting the threshold to the ground above as Gapinski came up close—

A guttural moan deep within the belly of the mausoleum to the Church's fallen, faithful saints sounded.

Then a belching explosion of fire and fury spit the pair out through the stairwell the rest of the way, sending them flying through the air and tumbling across the barren compound as the safe house shot high up into the air, the desert acting as a cannon for the remains of the compound buried halfway into the Earth.

They scrambled for cover under the truck that lay a few yards away as chunks of concrete and mangled corrugated metal and body parts rained around them.

"That'll leave a mark," Gapinski complained, heaving heavy breaths.

Silas swallowed and gasped for air. "I just hope to the good Lord above that Celeste and Torres are faring better."

CHAPTER 21
LOCATION UNKNOWN.

Marwan Farhad woke up in a panic in the late evening, eyes wide and frantic, mouth open and heaving desperate breaths.

He spun around on the mound of cushions inside his family's ancestral tent on all fours, searching the darkened space for signs of intrusion. A sound, a smell, a glimmer.

He found none.

But he swore he heard the flap of his tent open and the distinct sound of footfalls padding toward him. He had trained his ear for such things as an operative with Nous before his rise to power. It was why he had succeeded where others had failed, given the way he had honed his senses as an expert assassin.

A breeze carried the scent of burning wood and frying meat into his tent, the opening canvas to his dwelling flapping from the infiltration. Perhaps that was all, just the gentle desert breeze and his own carelessness before retiring for the night after such a monumental day.

The man closed his eyes and huffed a heavy breath out of his nostrils, exhausted from it all and frustrated at being awakened from his slumber to attend to the opening flap of his dwelling for a second night.

He pushed himself off from the bed of cushions, his muscles aching in protest, his mind still hungover from the elated high he had been riding from the day's events stamping down those wretched infidels. Sticking it to the Church and showing the world that the nation of the cross would bow before the might of Allah and eventually succumb to Nous and its new spirituality was what he had been craving for decades.

And he was finally in the position to do something about it.

He sauntered over to the opening of his tent, a stronger wind picking up and sending the flap of his entrance whipping around like a wayward sail. Laughter from his men huddled around the campfire beyond echoed across the barren sand, memories from his days in the military before being recruited to Nous flooding him when he enjoyed similar gayety.

Good, let them laugh and enjoy themselves. They deserved it after the success they had enjoyed. It would do them good for what yet awaited.

He grabbed hold of the canvas and wrestled with it briefly as the wind continued its assault. Then he pulled it tight against the threshold and tied it down, shutting out the world beyond in order to gain a small measure of peace and rest after what he had accomplished hours earlier.

He more than deserved it, given his success at all levels.

After he had slit the throat of the final captive from the nation of the cross, the minister of that wretched flock, he had received word that the technological ruse his men had set for any inquiring minds had worked. And apparently, the security warning system had detected the incursion of two operatives, who they were certain had expired in the detonation rigged to trigger after the final broadcast of the live-streaming execution.

Farhad had no way of being certain, but he had hoped it was those wretched men in white he had heard rumor of the past few days, the remnant of those bloodthirsty Crusader operatives who had been the scourge of his people stretching back nine hundred years.

The Knights Templar.

No small amount of terror had kneaded itself into his consciousness the past few days after getting word of the plots that menace had foiled. First the Washington National Cathedral, then another in Spain. There were further unconfirmed reports in Africa and Eastern Europe as well, and it was making him nervous—given the high-stakes game he was playing and the impending triumph he awaited.

It could also have been SEPIO, the scourge of Nous stretching back two millennia. They were always a nuisance that group, foiling his carefully laid plans the past year.

Either way, his enemy had been blown to bits in a show of fire and fury, and their position had been concealed through the careful work of his loyal soldiers.

Yet there was one more act, one final stroke of terrifying genius to unleash against the nation of the cross before the week was out. And he needed every ounce of energy—mental, physical, spiritual—to pull it off.

When he did, he would have full reign over Nous and the Church would bow before his might.

He pulled the last of the straps securing the canvas entrance flap tight, gritting his teeth for extra measure. Satisfied, he stood and turned back toward his mound of cushions to—

A crack like lighting striking a tree sounded forth, its terrifying timbre sending Farhad falling backward against the canvas he had just tied. It held, and he tumbled awkwardly to the floor.

It sounded again, inside his dwelling, lingering with terrifying intent. He covered his ears from the sound that seemed to hover in the room, a vibration that rattled the gold fillings in his teeth and continued through his entire body until every one of his nerves were humming with resonance like a tuning fork.

Then a blinding light exploded from the center of the space. It started small, an orb of brilliance like the edge of the moon after a retreating eclipse before growing in strength, bursting with blossoming force, the fabric of reality itself tearing within Farhad's tent at its center just above his mound of cushions.

He covered his eyes but it was useless. The force of the luminescence penetrated his entire being.

But the light wasn't the end of it.

Voices launched forth in windy whispers, tongues unknown. They lingered in the shadows, ricocheting from one side to the other before growing and crescendoing into a chorus that was all at once breathtaking and terrifying. They seemed to be calling Farhad's name, beckoning him to consume the experience laid before him in all of its visual and aural sensory intensity.

But he was scared stiff by a dread that was all at once melting him into oblivion and paralyzing him into inaction. He remained still, eyelids clenched closed and hands pressed against his ears with intent. His mouth opened in a maw of soundless horror, his lungs straining and throat aching from a scream he could not muster.

Then he felt it. A presence in the room that was warm and heavy and sweet, pressing in against him yet leaving him standing in frozen inaction.

The crack of lightning returned. And splitting from top to bottom, the curtain separating Farhad's reality from an entirely different one was pulled back.

He managed to wrench an eye open to steal a glance, unable to bear the ignorance any longer. What he saw made his bowels grow weak, his heart seize with fear, and his eyes weep with amazement.

He saw a throne, high and lofty and golden-hued, surrounded by all of the brilliance of a rainbow after a midafternoon rainstorm. Trailing down from it and filling his tent was the hem of a robe from the One who was seated upon it. Seraphs were in attendance above this One, each bearing six wings. With two they covered their faces, with two they covered their feet, and with two they flew. Voices erupted from each of them, one called to another and on to the next in a mighty chorus, saying:

'Holy, holy, holy is the Lord of hosts; the whole earth is full of his glory.'

The tent reverberated from the force of the chant, its canvas vibrating with perturbation under the holy words, its wooden supports shaking as if they might splinter from the glorious weight of heavenly voices.

Farhad trembled at the sound, every fiber of his being shaking in response to words no man dare hear. He thought he should shield his eyes from the glory of it all, but he could not help but look upon the One who was seated high, entranced with wide-eyed disbelief and holy awe at the sight laid bare before him.

The One seated upon the throne looked like jasper and carnelian, those precious stones covering the full spectrum of the universe's palette of pigmentation. Around the throne, the brilliance continued to shine with undulating waves across a sea of glass, like the finest crystal Farhad had ever seen. Then the curtain expanded to reveal twenty-four other thrones surrounding the One in the center of his dwelling. Seated upon them were twenty-four beings, humans by the looks of it. They were dressed in white robes, crowned with a golden brilliance that sparkled with alternating colors of blue and red and green.

Lightning cracked again, its light and sound splitting through the tent and laying Farhad flat on his stomach trembling for relief. Rumblings peals of thunder reverberated throughout.

He raised his head and caught a glimpse of four creatures on each side of the throne that held the One seated there, full of eyes in front and behind: the first living creature like a lion, the second living creature like an ox, the third living creature with a face like a human, and the fourth living creature like a flying eagle. These four living creatures, each of them with six wings and full of eyes all around and inside, sang a song that melted Farhad like wax:

> *'Holy, holy, holy, the Lord God the Almighty, who*
> *was and is and is to come.'*

In reply to this anthem of glory and honor and thanksgiving to the One seated on the throne, the twenty-four other beings fell before the One in worship, casting down their golden crowns upon the glassy sea surrounding his throne and singing a song of their own:

> *"You are worthy, our Lord and God,*
> *to receive glory and honor and power,*
> *for you created all things,*
> *and by your will they existed and were created."*

Farhad was weeping now, streams of tears flowing freely. Not in fear, but with childlike giddiness and wonder at the power of the experience gripping him. Deep within his inner man, something else began to churn, a force he had not felt before that needed to find release.

A confession.

"Woe is me!" he cried in an ecstatic utterance. "I am lost, for I am an unclean man who has committed acts unworthy of the King, the Lord of hosts!"

The lighting cracked again, and the entirety of the experience repeated itself—from the One who was seated on the throne to the twenty-four elders and their song of worship, from the four living creatures and their anthem back to the One who was seated on the throne—with all of its terrifying brilliance.

But then a hush descended upon the expanse of both realities: a silence filled the one through the veil and the one inside Farhad's tent with a deafening void. And the faintest of faintest sounds began searching for a hearing, a different voice slicing through the void of silence arose that cut Farhad to the quick.

"Marrrwaaan..." the Voice said, silky yet sturdy.

It penetrated through every joint and marrow in his body, through every complex layer of his very soul. It was the voice of One who knew the depths of his being; the voice of One who was the *ground* of his being.

Farhad could not help but snap his head toward the sound. What he saw was wholly unexpected.

The One, the Source, the Voice who had been seated on the throne had stepped down into his own reality. This Voice was standing inches from Farhad, with feet of white gold and legs of iron. Craning his head high, he saw the face like that of a man, but that was not all. It was shapeshifting—from a lion to a calf, and then from an eagle to a lamb, and then back again to a man.

"Marrrwaaan..." the Voice said once more, laying Farhad out flat upon the ground again, the force of it like a heavy bass against his body, but not low or growling. There was a tenderness to it, an intimacy that laced his name. There was no menace or malice to it. There was a purity to its call.

Like the way a lover might cry out to his beloved.

"Marwan, you are killing my people. Why are you persecuting me?" the Voice wondered, a sadness extending across every word, every syllable, every letter—across the very question mark itself.

Farhad remained prostrated against the ground, eyes clenched but emotion leaking through, mouth open with a question he dared not ask.

And then he did, his voice mousey and trembling: "Who are you, Lord?"

At first, there was no answer. Everything had ceased again in one timeless, soundless void. The room darkened into nothingness. Farhad thought he had died, consumed by Allah and banished into *a'raf*, the borderland between Heaven and Hell.

Then there was a high-pitched noise, faint at first but growing in intensity. It was that of a human, a young boy. It continued sounding forth unabated. One note and tone, one pitch and timbre.

The Voice shifted, high and higher yet. Like it was reaching for something unseen. Then it plummeted before splitting into three tones. Harmony and dissonance all colliding in a song that had yet to be sung since the founding of the universe. It was a searching song, floating around Farhad.

Searching for him.

When it laid hold of him, the Voice offered an answer to his question with penetrating insight and clarity.

'Who are you, Lord?' you asked. 'I AM will tell you.'

And the Voice did. Everything.

He told him everything he ever wanted to know. About himself, his life, his world. Who he was, who he was not. What he ever did, why he ever did it.

When it was over, Farhad had his answer. To everything.

He wept at what he had heard, a man broken by his depths, the truth of what it contained laid bare, yet held in the palm of the One who knew him better than he knew himself.

And loved him despite it all.

Suddenly, one of the seraphs flew to the repentant man,

holding a live coal that he had taken from the altar with a pair of tongs. The seraph touched Farhad's mouth with it and said: "Now that this has touched your lips, your guilt has departed and your sin is blotted out."

The Voice—the I AM of the lion and calf, the eagle and lamb, the man—had blown everything to pieces. And when Farhad saw where the pieces landed, he knew he was free.

CHAPTER 22

LISBON, PORTUGAL.

The small villages and barren fields scattered about the welcoming springtime countryside dappled under the still-waking sun reminded Celeste of home, with all of its history and quaintness and rugged practicality. As the Portuguese world flashed past in a blur of greens and browns and grays outside her window, she longed for those days again, when life was simpler, safer, serene.

"Thanks for driving, love. I'm positively knackered," she said to Torres, who was commanding their Mercedes G-Class SUV northeast of Lisbon toward Tomar. Torres thought the rental was overkill, but Celeste knew better after one too many encounters on the road with hostiles. Couldn't be too careful, even on mission for the Church.

Especially on mission for the Church.

Torres shrugged. "Don't mention it. Besides, you've got the return trip."

"Deal." She nestled against her window, settling in for the drive and staring out into a world that a part of her wished she could join again.

After over a decade tracking down terrorists of all stripes, first for Her Majesty and then for the Church, and her non-stop, dogged commitment to her work, she was beginning to feel like life was passing her by like the landscape outside her window. Like marriage, like motherhood. A change of heart Granny would sure be pleased to hear about, but one her mother would be disappointed with equal measure.

In recent months, she began to wonder whether she would ever be able to settle down, whether she would ever be *ready* to settle down.

She'd never been one to worry about such pedestrian longings, preferring a life of solitude and throwing herself full bore into her work than getting worked up about finding a mate, bearing the burden of changing diapers and wiping running noses, and taking on all the other trappings of domesticity.

And yet, a longing had begun to kindle inside her for something more than catching the latest villain. Not that she minded being at the forefront of saving the world. She quite fancied the satisfaction of seeing justice served and bringing the good-versus-evil balance back into proper alignment. It was especially satisfying to be doing so in service of Christ and his Church. Besides, giving her life in this way to Jesus and his mission of rescue seemed to be a sort of proper penance, a making up for lost time after spending most of her life refusing to follow his way and believe in him for salvation—both existential and ultimate.

But she wondered if there was more in life, more for her to get out of life. It was a question that had been needling her in recent months, poking her for a response.

Until she found one, she was all-in to protecting and preserving the Church and the memory of her faith. At the top of the week's agenda: preserving and protecting the reputation of the Church by tracking down those bloody Templars!

Celeste and Torres had already been in the air flying to Lisbon when the ultimatum had reached the end of its fuse, sending the remaining forty-one Christians to their martyrs reception at the feet of Christ—including Gapinski's grandfather.

From the plush comfort of their Gulfstream G650, surrounded by polished mahogany and creamy leather, the two had watched along with the rest of the world as the heads of those faithful saints were lopped off, one by one. Torres couldn't stomach it and busied herself with plotting their course. Celeste refused to look away, desiring as before to bear witness to what she wondered if she could do herself.

When push came to shove, at the end of blade or noose or barrel, could she die for her faith, like those brave, courageous men and women from the River Jordan?

The question still haunted her as they continued driving through the Portuguese countryside in search of those who were ready to lay down their lives to protect others in the face of terrifying persecution.

When she was in active service for Her Majesty, there wasn't a doubt about the lengths she would go while running operations deep in the heart of Pakistan, coming head-to-head with some of the vilest of humanity for the good of her fellow citizens. Of course she would lay down her life. "For Queen and Country!" had been bred into her from birth. However, an equal allegiance to the cross had been something of a struggle after coming to faith later in life.

Daddy and Mummy had their own faith in bits and bobs, and they shared it with their children. But the family hadn't been involved in a local Church of England parish. Her parents preferred to freelance their Christianity rather than institutionalize it. So while she had been exposed to Christianity in its essence, she had never grown up in the Church. Her granny was always worried with fright for her four siblings' spiritual neglect. Celeste was a different matter.

She had always been curious about spiritual things, and she began searching for answers as she grew older. Like many of her maturing adolescent peers, she wondered about the meaning of it all—whether there was a God or gods; whether she could know this God; whether he himself knew of her, and what he thought of who she was and how she lived; why there was something rather than nothing; if God was so good, why life was so bad; where she could find rescue from herself, her guilt and her shame; where it all was heading, whether there was any hope for a future life of bliss and restoration.

It wasn't until she was at Oxford that things finally clicked for her. She had attended a religious rally put on by a local church, and for the first time in her life it all made sense. The Spirit of God had opened her eyes and ears and eventually brought her to put her faith in Jesus to save her from her rebellion against God and trust him as Lord over her life.

She still remembered the moment vividly, and she smiled at the memory as they passed a small village, the steeple of a church rising high toward the heavens, a beacon of hope and invitation to come and taste and see the Lord's goodness.

The Oxford parish had brought in a speaker to share about why the Christian faith was believable and invited the students to ask questions. She had gone with a friend, and didn't remember much of the presentation except for one thing: the preacher made the point that it was women who first found the tomb of Jesus empty, signifying the resurrection. He mentioned in passing the fact that testimony of women are included in the Gospel accounts of Jesus' resurrection is remarkable. In those days, women weren't allowed to give testimony in legal proceedings. So the fact the Gospel writers included the women's eyewitness accounts in a story about the resurrection of a dead man is an important point of proof that makes the story believable. If the disciples made up the story, then why let women tell it? That was the quickest route to being discredited in those days, allowing women to give evidence to validate a claim.

Of course it would be strong, dogged women who brought her to faith, given her own Mum and Granny. The testimony of those women and the inclusion of that testimony in the Gospel accounts spoke to her, enflaming the first spark of curiosity into the man Jesus and his teachings and the broader story of God in the Bible. Those women were the reason she had believed, why she had pursued a PhD in comparative religion and considered joining the faculty.

They were also the reason she was in a Mercedes rental driving toward Tomar to investigate whether the Templars had truly risen from the graveyard of history. Like those women, she wanted nothing more than to help preserve the memory of her risen Lord and Savior, Jesus Christ, and get to the bottom of the mystery surrounding those who could sully that memory.

After landing, Torres and Celeste had spent the evening researching more into the possibilities surrounding the Order of Christ of Portugal and their connection with the original Knights Templar from Jerusalem.

In the cache of research Zoe had prepared, they learned how the kingdom of Portugal had formed during the centuries of Christian resistance against the Muslim forces that had occupied the Iberian Peninsula, a resistance in which the Templars played a vital role. As with the Spanish monarchy, the Portuguese refused King Philip IV's encouragement to turn against the Templars, disbelieving the king's motivations were anything but political and financial, rather than theological and biblical as he purported. That's when the new Order of Christ was founded.

Both Celeste and Torres read with interest as two academics how after the Christian reconquest of central Portugal from the Muslims, a vast part of the frontier region was given to the Knights Templar by the Portuguese king. Tomar, northeast of present-day Lisbon, was founded in the mid-twelfth century on the site of an ancient Roman colony when then Templar Grand

Master of Portugal, Gualdim Pais, chose the site and constructed the castle and monastery that would become the Order's Portugal headquarters.

Twelve miles south of Tomar sat another possible location for the seemingly reconstituted Templar order, the castle of Almourol mounted on a small, rocky island in the middle of the Tagus river. The site had passed into the hands of the Knights Templar during the *Reconquista*, and by 1171 they had built an impressive fortress, incorporating their innovations and lessons learned in the Kingdom of Jerusalem. Similar to Tomar, it included ten round towers set along the outer walls and a three-story keep. It was another location the two SEPIO agents would have to scout out as well.

Celeste just wished Silas Grey was at her side instead of Naomi Torres.

She was surprised as anyone that a connection had been sparked over a year ago when they first worked together to secure the Shroud of Turin and prove the authenticity of Jesus' resurrection. And then when they worked closely to uncover the plot surrounding the Ark of the Covenant, fighting and researching and traveling together as two equal partners in service of the Church and Christian faith, that's when the spark ignited. It was fanned further during Christmas when the two helped uncover Nous's interests and intentions surrounding the purported Holy Grail. But the months since had been a frustrating endeavor, like pulling teeth from a mule!

The man all at once intrigued her and confused her; sent her heart sailing and sent her mind reeling. The past few months hadn't helped matters, what with growing out his hair and starting up the nasty habit of smoking. She recoiled at the thought. Although the longer hair was a nice, sexy touch.

Oh Silas...

"Oh, Silas?" Torres questioned from her left.

Celeste jolted upright, her eyes widening and breath catching in her chest as she glanced at her companion.

"And, yes, in case you were wondering that was out loud."

She reddened and felt herself sinking deeper into her seat. "I said nothing of the sort..." she mumbled, trying to quickly deflect the embarrassing reveal.

"Oh, come on! Yes, you did. I heard you drop his name. Now, what I want to know is, why? Especially since you're trying to play all coy about it."

"It's nothing," Celeste quickly said.

Torres laughed. "Yeah, right. I know that look. Spill it, sister."

She sighed, propping a foot up on her seat and running a hand through her hair. "Silas and I, we've sort of had a thing."

"A thing?"

"Well, not a legitimate thing. Like not official and all. But we've gone out on a few dates—"

"Spare me the gory details, please!" Torres interrupted.

Celeste giggled and smacked her partner's leg. "Stop. Our dates have been nothing but holy."

"Mmm-hmm."

"They have!"

"Alright, so you've gone on holy dates. What's the problem?"

"The problem is that he's changed. Grown his hair out, started up with the cancer sticks."

"I sort of liked the change." Torres looked at Celeste, and said, "The hair, not the cancer sticks."

"I gathered. And I understand it's some sort of external way he's dealing with all of the change he's internalized—with the loss of his former profession, the loss of his brother, and all. So I get it, I completely empathize with what he is going through. I just wish he would open up about it."

Torres scoffed. "Men! Can't live with them, can't live without them. But you can sure damn try."

"Oh, really?" she said turning in her seat, a wry grin spreading across her mouth. "I seem to remember some bloke from Cali during our mission to get to the bottom of the American presidential election. What was his name?"

Torres shifted in her seat and stared forward. She mumbled, "Grant Chrysostom."

"Ahh, yes. Grant! Cheeky fellow. Whatever happened to him?"

She sighed and shrugged. "What happened is what happened the first time, when we were engaged to be married. He got bored and left."

Celeste frowned. "Sorry, love. Well, then what about you and Matthew?"

Torres whipped her head toward Celeste and scoffed. "Gapinski? Are you even kidding me right now?"

"Come on, yourself. I've seen the way you two banter back and forth."

Torres scoffed again.

"You're telling me you've never even been remotely attracted to the guy? Never dreamt about snuggling up to—"

"Celeste...I'm warning you, sister. I've got control over the wheel."

She giggled and broke off the assault. "How about a truce for a while when it comes to the men in our lives?"

"Deal."

Celeste returned to staring out the window as Torres continued driving, the countryside slowly suburbanizing into a larger village of white buildings with orange roofs.

She considered again Silas's shift. Martin had been the same way after his first series of tours with MI6, distancing himself from her and closing up. Even took up the same nasty habit again, which was probably what unnerved her the most about Silas's smoking. Reminded her too much of the other man she had ever loved. The one who had been killed.

"Looks like we're almost there," Torres announced, breaking Celeste's concentration and snapping her back to the mission at hand.

She navigated their vehicle through tidy streets lined with flower stands, clothing shops, pubs, and other eateries before arriving at the entrance to the former Templar castle fortress.

She eased their rental into the property, and asked, "What are the odds the Templars really have risen from the grave and are holed up in there?"

Celeste shrugged. "Honestly, who knows. One way or another, we're about the find out."

CHAPTER 23

A large structure of pale stone commanding a hill rose through the trees ahead, the *Convento do Cristo.*

Its impressive outer walls still stood after centuries. The main architectural features had been introduced to the country by the Templars, particularly the use of round towers in the outer walls, which improved the defensive lines of fire. Even the main citadel and keep inside, one of the oldest in Portugal, was still erect and proud, greeting visitors as they came to check off the visit on their Travelocity bucket list, or perhaps see for themselves if the rumors of remnant Templars were true.

"So what do we know about this joint, anyway?" Torres said as she navigated the winding road through leafy trees spread around the base of the hill toward the visitor center parking.

"Right," Celeste said, taking a breath and pushing a lock of her bangs behind her ear. "I had been reading about it earlier—"

"Before dreaming about Lover Boy?" Torres interrupted.

Celeste playfully smacked her leg. "Stop, not fair. Truce, remember?"

She giggled, and said, "Alright, alright. So what's with

Tomar and the Templars, anyway? Any truth to the idea that a remnant is holed up in there someplace?"

"Don't know about that," Celeste said, retrieving the tablet filled with notes that Zoe had sent through to the SEPIO operations platform, a sort of Evernote on steroids. "What I do know is that the history of it all is fascinating, filled with all the military barbarism and underdog heroism you'd expect from a fanciful tale about the Templars."

"Sounds about right."

"Apparently, the presence of the Templars at Tomar protected Christian settlers from the north against Arab incursions, and in 1190 they saved the entire country from being overrun by the Muslim hordes operating out of Morocco. Calif Abu Yusef al-Mansur had already ravaged southern Portugal by the time he laid siege to Tomar where he faced a vastly outnumbered garrison of Templars in the castle fortress commanding the city. Yet the motley crew of Christ's soldiers succeeded in repelling the calif's attack and driving him and the Muslim army back to Morocco."

"That is interesting. And I guess it's one more nail in the coffin of my Westernized vision of the Templars Radcliffe was razzing me about."

"Spoken like one who has been properly chastened. Radcliffe has that effect on people."

"Yeah, yeah, yeah. What else?"

Consulting her tablet, Celeste said, "Says here, it was because of this long history defending the kingdom that King Diniz resisted French and Papal pressure to suppress the Templars and hand them and their possessions over to the Church. Instead, in 1319 the king transferred Templar property and personnel to the newly created Order of Christ, which returned to Tomar in 1356. Prince Henry the Navigator, who had been made Grand Master of the Order in 1418, later renovated and enlarged the Templars' castle, known as *Convento do Cristo*, with its round church."

"The Convent of Christ," Torres added.

"Right. And the Grand Master used Templar resources to send his ships on bold voyages into the Atlantic and down the coast of Africa, his caravels powered by sails painted with the Templar cross."

"So that's where those famous red-cross sails came from. But what about this castle fortress itself?"

"Apparently, the Templars built it as one of a handful of their strongholds in 1160 on the hill there overlooking the river Nabão and the town. It's one of Portugal's most important historical monuments and a UNESCO World Heritage Site. Now, on the eastern side of Tomar is the Templar church of Santa Maria do Olival. Twenty-two Portuguese Templar masters were buried in the church, among them Gauldim Pais."

"Isn't he the guy who founded the Order of Christ?" Torres asked as she circled the lot for a parking spot.

"He is. His bravery and tireless struggle against the Islamic invaders made him something of a Templar exemplar, and his memory continues to be cherished in Portugal. The church passed into the hands of the successor to the Templars, the Order of Christ, and during the age when Portugal was building up a great empire overseas. It served as the mother church of the Portuguese missionary efforts planting churches in Africa, Asia, and the Americas."

"Ever the colonialists..." Torres lamented, parking the rental and turning off the car.

Celeste smirked at her partner's cynicism, reaching for her trusted SIG Sauer in her passenger's side door compartment.

She withdrew the magazine and inspected it, then shoved it back inside and placed the weapon at the small of her back. "Sad commentary on the state of things when we need to pack heat to a visit a famous convent."

"Yeah, but come on. It's the Templars," Torres replied, checking her own SIG and stuffing it at her spine. "And as Gapinski said to me first day on the job—"

"Never leave home without cold, hard steel," Celeste finished.

Torres nodded and got out of their rental. "Exactly."

"Silas learned his lesson the hard way last mission," Celeste mumbled, the two hustling across the blacktop toward the entrance.

Her homesickness returned again as they passed the impressive keep and tower to the right, reminding her of a childhood long past when Daddy and Mummy took her and her siblings on outings to the famous castles strewn across her beloved England. They passed a group of tourists with one of those European travel companies on their way into the main compound, bright green well-manicured, knee-high bushes and mature oak and cypress trees punctuated by bushes of red aloe vera flowers greeting them. Ahead was the famous round church within the castle that was built in the second half of the twelfth century.

Like several other Templar churches across Europe, it was modeled after the Rotunda of the Church of the Holy Sepulcher in Jerusalem. A sixteen-sided structure, its stone was a mishmash of pale and beige that was grayed and pockmarked with age. Strong buttresses across the nave that was later added along with the round windows reminded Celeste of Notre Dame Cathedral and Westminster Abbey. After Prince Henry the Navigator became Grand Master of the Order of Christ, he added the Gothic-style nave to the original round church, so that the rotunda that Celeste and Torres were about to enter became the apse of the enlarged sacred structure. A sizable bell tower soaring high into the sky with two massive green patina-covered iron bells greeted the pair as they walked up to the double oak doors.

"Here we go," Celeste said, pushing the heavy wood. It creaked in protest on tired hinges. When they entered, their collective breaths were taken away.

Nearly every inch of the circular octagonal interior was covered with a marvelous palette of colors, from crimsons to blues, and oranges to greens. Gilt columns supported equally gilt archways, its gold covering offering visitors a taste of the heavenly. Walls soaring high were decorated by several panels of late Gothic paintings and frescos depicting mainly biblical scenes.

"Blimey," was all Celeste could muster.

"Agree," Torres said, nodding and craning her neck as the two continued farther into the sacred space.

From SEPIO's mission a year ago saving the Shroud of Turin and contending for Christ's resurrection in Jerusalem, Celeste could see the resemblance between the round structure and the Church of the Holy Sepulcher. At the center sat an octagonal structure nestled within the rotunda itself. A massive crucifix hung from inside and was visible through an archway. The two walked toward it on instinct, mutually drawn to the sacred icon depicting the central event of their faith, the reason so many were now dying for it.

The death of Jesus, the Lamb of God come to take away the sins of the world through his sacrificial ransom payment on those wretched Roman boards of execution.

Angelic frescos greeted them from above as they walked inside the small chapel-like structure, standing directly beneath the massive Christ in crucifixion.

Torres crossed herself as they stood beneath the sculpture. Celeste joined her.

Her partner gasped, then pointed toward the ceiling. Staring upward, they both began to twirl and smile as they took in the magnificence of the space. The entirety of it was overlaid with gold and patterned with blue-bordered circles around the arches. Another crimson-bordered butterfly-shape pattern stretched across the height of the columns all the way to the top. A sea of sky blue bathed the apex of the rotunda, where seven crimson arches bowed toward the center, and what looked like golden puffs of clouds seemed to float in the blue sky above.

After taking in the heavenly vision, Celeste walked out from the central portion of the rotunda; Torres followed. She folded her arms and took in the surroundings, eyeing a few tourists who were noting the frescos on the outer walls. A brown shadow came into view, hulking and slumped over slightly.

A monk caretaker of the storied ecclesial property, was her guess, the brown wool habit swishing with each step at his feet. Another, shorter duplicate crossed paths and offered to snap the picture of a family.

"The Templars sure knew how to build a church," Torres said in wonder.

"I'd say."

"But where do we go from here? Nothing is screaming Templars, to me anyway. And there certainly ain't any of those old-crusty Anglos running around in whitey tighties emblazoned with crimson crosses."

Celeste smirked. "No, unfortunately not."

"Can I help you?" a low, accented voice thundered behind her.

She nearly whipped out her SIG Sauer at the surprise, but a decade of training and experience stayed her hand.

The man, skin bronzed and weathered with a bald head, and wearing the same brown monastic garb as the other men she had spotted, stepped back and raised his hands.

"Forgive me, young lady. I meant no harm," he offered, wearing an embarrassed smile, eyes heavy and sunk within his skull.

"It's alright. You just gave me a fright is all."

"I've been told I have that effect on people." He chuckled, then stuffed his hands in his sleeves and propped them at his belly. "They pay us to be of help to the guests who come seeking spiritual solace. You understand."

Celeste folded her arms and widened her stance. "Yes, well, we're here for different reasons than solace."

"Oh?" the man said perking up, a jagged scar running from ear to mouth catching in the dim light.

She nodded toward Torres, and said, "We're actually here on assignment from the Vatican."

In rare circumstances she flashed SEPIO's loose association with the Catholic Church. It often opened doors that would otherwise remain shut. Namedropping the city-state of the Holy See also sped things along considerably.

The man smiled, his eyes betraying something she couldn't place.

She continued, "We're making inquiries into the Knights Templar. We understand they had originally occupied this castle fortress and built this church."

"Yes, they were the original occupants. But that name has been long dead from this place, the property having been given over to a different Order, and then assumed by the State."

"We understand that, but we thought..." She lowered her head and smiled, thinking it foolish now that she was voicing it all to a perfect stranger. "Well, the fact of the matter is, we thought there may yet be a connection between this place and the Templars. That a remnant might yet be operating from the premises, as a sort of reconstituted Order."

The man leaned back, one end of his mouth curling upward with recognition. Then he thrust forward toward the pair, and whispered, "I will show you something of interest."

He walked off toward an exit from the rotunda into a larger space beyond, the Gothic nave.

Celeste turned toward her partner and offered a grin of

victory. Torres shrugged, but nodded toward the man with approval. The SEPIO operatives followed after him.

The dimly lit nave of beige walls, ceiling vaulted high and empty, was a far cry from the rotunda, with all of its gold gilding and colorful fresco panels. The ceiling was lined with curious ribbing, and the space itself was constructed of unassuming, unadorned limestone bricks. The room was also empty, tourists too caught up with the main attraction in the rotunda to pay much attention to it.

The man motioned for the pair to follow him through a low wall dividing the space into a larger one, light streaming through a massive round window above. What looked like wooden high-back chairs could be seen peeking above the stone barrier. Celeste recalled this section of the church from Zoe's research, the Manueline Chapter House.

The two followed after the monk, wondering what they would find about the Templars. They joined him past a velvet rope apparently erected to ward off wayward tourists. A short, darkened entrance through the brick wall brought the SEPIO agents to the other side.

Greeting them was the monk, wielding a pistol and wearing a menacing grin.

"Move, over there. Away from the entrance."

"Now, is that any way for a servant of Christ to act?" Torres said, obeying the man and walking toward the walnut choir stalls.

Celeste remained where she was, arms at her side and legs planted firm and wide and ready to strike.

The man lowered his head, his grin falling and eyes seeming to sink further into his skull with darkened intent.

"I. Said. Move..." he said lowly, stretching the arm wielding the weapon toward her, the cuff of his habit opening to reveal something unexpected.

Wait a minute...

A tattoo of dark lines stood against the paler skin of the man's under arm.

A very specific tattoo that Celeste had seen far too many times before, a calling card that meant no uncertain danger.

The familiar stick bird, its two intersecting lines bent at each end signifying the mythical phoenix rising to new life.

It also signified the archenemy of the Church, the power that was hellbent on destroying the Bride of Christ and the teaching tradition at its center.

Nous.

Celeste narrowed her eyes and clenched her jaw.

This isn't over. Not by a long shot.

She sauntered over to the choir stalls and took a seat next to Torres. The man followed from a distance.

"What do you aim to do with us?" she asked.

"First things first," he growled. "What do you know of the Templars?"

So that's why you're here.

"Did you say Templars?" Torres asked with mocking tones, her face twisted with feigned surprise. "As in the Knights Templar? You a Monte Python fan, amigo?"

"Something like that."

"You go first," Celeste said, folding her arms and crossing her legs.

"Yeah, why do you care, anyway?" Torres asked.

"Because we've gotten word that a certain band of men in white have been, shall we say, creating a disturbance recently. They've become real trouble, those ones. And we aim to do something about it."

"What, they've messed up your genocidal plans to erase Christianity from the face of the Earth?"

The man said nothing, holding his weapon and scowl fast.

So it is true...

Not only was this guy Nous, Nous was behind the latest

wave of worldwide Christian persecution. And the videos showing men in white stopping attacks against the Church, Nous thought they were the Knights Templar—risen to protect Christians and avenge their deaths at the hands of their persecutors.

"I know who you both are," the man continued. "Celeste Bourne and Naomi Torres, operatives with SEPIO, of the Order of Thaddeus. So let's cut the crap and—"

The man gasped and doubled over instantly after Celeste thrust her crossed leg into the man's groin. He coughed, trying to catch his breath as he waddled forward on useless legs.

Celeste had always maintained that the genitofemoral nerve was useful in times like that. Even though she admitted it was a low blow. Literally.

The two agents darted to the right and left as the man popped off a shot, then another in pain and irritation and anger at the assault on his manhood—both shots sinking into the vacant wooden stalls.

Nervous cries and confused shouts echoed toward them from the rotunda. The man staggered to recover, but the agents had already whipped out their weapons, Celeste finishing what she started by swiping the barrel of her SIG across the man's head. He went down like a bag of dog food, hitting his chin with a loud clacking sound on the wooden choir stall before slumping to the stone floor.

"That was easy," Torres said.

But it wasn't over.

One of the men Celeste had spotted in the rotunda wearing the same getup appeared in the short entrance, a large man with an even larger gun who was taking aim after spotting his partner lying on the floor—and ready for vengeance.

But Torres wouldn't give him the satisfaction.

She sent four rounds sailing toward the man, three of them

lodging in the limestone brickwork, but one connecting with the man's upper arm.

He yelled and fired on reflex, the weapon discharging three bullets high into the air before he scrambled back through the entrance toward safer ground.

"Nice shot," Celeste said. "But one out of four isn't what I'd call SEPIO worthy, love."

"What can I say? The sun was in my eyes."

Celeste turned around at the large, round window high above at their back. She smirked, then bent down beside the body of the fallen hostile to verify the man's identity. She took in a deep breath and threw her hair back. The heavy firepower was definitely not expected, and she wondered how they were going to get out of it all.

She pushed the man's fallen cuff back up, verifying what she had seen earlier. There it was.

"Nous?" Torres said breathlessly, coming up to her side.

"Looks that way."

"Always something," Torres said.

Celeste threw he partner a grin. "That's Gapinski's line. I thought you weren't keen on the fella."

She shrugged. "What can I say. The man's grown on me."

A loud thud echoed toward the pair, causing them to rise with weapons outstretched. The doors to the entrance of the rotunda thudded heavily against the aged limestone walls, shaking the SEPIO operatives back into the moment.

Screams echoed throughout the sacred space, followed by gunfire. An angry *pop-pop-pop* sliced through the old church.

Security perhaps?

"I've got a bad feeling about this," Torres complained.

Celeste said nothing. Instead, she nodded toward the short entrance, inching forward with weapon ready to respond.

CHAPTER 24

Another volley of *rat-a-tat-tats* sounded forth as Celeste and Torres ducked through to the other side of the dividing wall, eliciting another volley of screams and shouts for relief from the onslaught.

Not again...

The Church had seen enough bloodshed the past four days. Why add a handful of tourists scoping out a former Templar holy site to the pile of the dead?

Families and couples and single tourists streamed past a barrier of carved darkly-stained spindles erected between the Gothic nave add-on and the original rotunda, dragging children and purses and elderly loved-ones. A barrage of gunfire behind them sent the escapees ducking for cover and shouting in mixed tongues for relief, their fear palpable to the SEPIO agents who were trying to assess what the heck was going on.

The fleeing crowd pushed past Celeste and Torres toward a massive set of wooden doors to the right that led back outside. A burly man sweating through a charcoal sweater struggled against a stubborn iron latch that hadn't seen much recent use. Pounding the thing with his meaty palms, he worked it loose and released it, then swung one of the doors open, ushering the frightened men, women, and children outside to safe harbor.

More gunfire erupted from the rotunda. Its source seemed completely oblivious to the civilian targets escaping.

Perhaps they weren't the actual targets in the first place.

Then what the bloody hell was going on? Who was targeting whom?

Celeste had half a mind to join them in their escape, but knew she and Torres needed to finish their mission.

Now more than ever, given Nous's clear involvement.

"Come on," she said, motioning to Torres as she shuffled toward a marble baptismal font.

The sacred vessel was nestled in a corner against the beige stone wall, butting up against an archway that stretched high and around the entrance to the rotunda, relief sculptures of vines and cherubs and demons etched into its narrow stone surface. She hefted the sacramental object out from the corner and out of her way, toppling it to the ground behind her, its holy water spilling across the square stone tiles.

She crossed herself at the misdeed, then directed Torres to the other side. The spaces were tight, but they would offer them enough protection from the gunfire, as well as angles of attack of their own.

Past the wooden-spindle barrier she could see one of the faux monks she had spotted earlier. A long black barrel of an automatic rifle stuck out with purpose from the billowy cuffs of his brown habit. Must have hid the weapon-of-war inside, waiting for the moment to strike.

The man let it rip toward the oak entrance doors, bullets chewing the centuries-old frescos and fragmenting plaster statues of saints long gone.

And then all at once, the man went down, his head blown back in a geyser of blood and brain matter against the stone wall from a single shot that cracked through the holy place.

An expert marksman, Celeste reckoned.

One you certainly wouldn't find on a Rent-a-Cop security task force stationed at a UNESCO World Heritage Site.

Was it the local Tomar police, or the military, perhaps? Surely she and her partner would have heard sirens or the heavy rumble of vehicles. And the timing of it all was way off. Far too soon for the show-of-force response in the rotunda.

Pop-pop-pop gunfire from her left caught her off guard. She pressed herself against the cold stone wall only to realize it was Torres.

Her weapon sounded forth again in angry fits before she dropped her arm wielding the weapon and pumped her other arm next to her side in victory.

Score one for SEPIO!

But who else had scored?

That worried Celeste as much as the fact Nous was apparently intimately involved in the recent attacks. Their prime architects, even.

All at once, the gunfire stopped. All sounds of leaden violence and unholy desecration came to a dramatic halt, as quick as it all had started.

Celeste threw Torres a furrowed look of confusion.

Torres matched her, but took a hesitant step out from her narrow shelter and forward underneath the archway.

She joined her partner, fingers tightening around the butt of her weapon, muscles taut for action.

They both padded forward, weapons outstretched and ready for business. They met in the middle, coming to the threshold of the rotunda anchored by two short marble columns stabilizing the wooden-spindle barrier.

Standing before them was the octagonal structure, its columns covered in intricate gold gilding and pastel pink-and-blue patterns. Angelic frescos high above looked down on them with disapproval, bearing witness to the wickedness below.

And there was Christ in crucifixion, mounted high above beyond within the structure, his penetrating, convicting gaze upon the world below of desecrating violence that had transpired just beneath his feet.

Celeste held her breath, every one of her senses tingling with high-alert strain. She glanced at Torres who was heaving breaths of anticipation.

She went to cross the threshold into the rotunda when a figure dashed across the void beyond Christ near the entrance, his footfalls making nary a sound in the echoey place.

Celeste raised her weapon to fire, but it was too late.

She went to step forward to give chase when more movement caught her eyes at both ends of the structure. Two other figures peered around the inner columns just below the feet of Christ, heads masked in grey and hands raising black weapons for the kill.

The two agents quickly raised their own weapons and fired. Five shots each, without mercy. Enough to throw the hostiles off their game and give them leverage to move in and engage.

But not enough.

Two more figures, heads veiled in what looked like grey meshing and bodies wrapped in white leaned out from around the outer columns and opened fire themselves.

Catching the SEPIO operatives completely off guard and sending them stumbling backward for protection.

The shots went high and wide, ricocheting off of the limestone beyond.

The pair were pushed back into the nave toward the choir loft from where they came, their footfalls of retreat echoing loudly high above in the ribbed vaulted ceiling as the gunfire ceased.

Brown stained doors anchoring both sides of the sacred space thudded loudly behind them. Two more hostiles entered from both doors, catching the SEPIO agents by surprise.

Checkmate.

The pair backed up against one another and took aim. Celeste forward at the original four hostiles, Torres backward at the two new ones.

But they quickly assessed the obvious.

Game over.

There was nowhere to go. They were completely surrounded by six men, weapons black and sophisticated pointing at them and ready to take them down.

The four from the rotunda stepped forward, weapons drawn with protective intent.

The Knights Templar.

They looked like modern incarnations of the ancient religious order, their bodies fitted tight by a scaly white mesh material in place of their original monastic robes, muscles bulging through the skin-tight garments with crimson crosses emblazoned on their chests that the world had come to know as their calling card; their heads shielded by what looked like a polymer-based chainmail-like hood, masking their faces in place of the original steel helmet that had shielded the Templars' heads, but for a slit giving them visibility; their weapons of choice, polished steel swords, shaped and sharpened in the style of the Vikings, had been replaced by the cold, hard steel of modern-day assassins, Italian-made Berettas, by the looks of it.

Silas would be proud.

"Hold your fire! We're on your side," Celeste shouted, releasing the trigger of her SIG Sauer and holding it by its grip. She put up both hands and outstretched her arms, making sure it was clear she was surrendering.

But the lead Templar apparition didn't seem to care.

The man took aim just as Torres began speaking.

"Non nobis, Domine, non nobis, sed Nomini tuo da gloriam," she shouted, echoing the original motto of the Poor Fellow-Soldiers

of Christ and of the Temple of Solomon throughout the former sacred space of the storied religious order.

The man recoiled slightly, clearly taken aback by the invocation of the Templar motto. He narrowed his eyes and eased back off his aim, then glanced to his brothers.

"Who are you?" the man spat his question, voice rumbly and lilting in a way that betrayed an obvious non-English accent, though Celeste couldn't pinpoint it.

Celeste shouted, "We're operatives with a religious order, like your own, stretching back centuries. The Order of Thaddeus, defenders of the Church and the central teachings of her faith."

This gave the man even more pause. He lowered his weapon, and she imagined him furrowing his brow in either confusion or recognition underneath that bloody mask of his.

The SEPIO agents lowered their arms as well, still holding their weapons by their grips to indicate continued surrender.

"The Order of Thaddeus..." a man behind the frontrunner said with raspy, aged weakness, the same lilting accent undergirding the tone and timbre of his comment. "I have heard inklings of this Order, rumors passed through the ages in records preserved by our brotherhood. Tales of safe harbor and assistance when the knights of Christ needed it most."

Safe harbor and assistance?

That was news to Celeste. But perhaps not entirely unlikely and not unexpected, given how both ecclesial orders had pledged themselves to Christ and preserving his Church, but in different ways.

"If you won't answer my *who* question," she continued, "then what business did you have coming here?"

The raspy man replied, "Those bloodthirsty evildoers, enemies of the Church and persecuting terrorizers of our brothers and sisters—"

"You're speaking of Nous," Celeste interrupted.

The lead man blanched in recognition at the name. He eased his head back and lowered his weapon. "They were seeking a shadow from another era."

"The Templars..." she whispered. "They were seeking you, evidence of your resurrection, after foiling their plots."

"So you're Templars then?" Torres added. "Members of the Poor Fellow-Soldiers of Christ and of the Temple of Solomon?"

The lead man said nothing, eying them with continued suspicion, the other hostiles' weapons still drawn and pointing with intent.

The purported leader strode toward the women, who had turned to face the man. He stopped short of them, his arms at his side and saying nothing.

The eyes beneath the grey hood were dark and searching, and Celeste noticed they were shrouded in black, further hiding the identities of the man.

He raised an arm, and the other five men in white all at once backed up, weapons still drawn. He said, "Leave this alone. This is your first and final warning."

He backed up, joined by the other two brothers who had come through the side entrances, the two of them padding backwards with weapons trained on the women as the man turned and walked back through the rotunda and underneath the feet of Christ. The others joined him as he strode out through the wooden entrance doors from which they had arrived. The last of the mystery men thudded the doors loudly behind them, disappearing as quickly as they had arrived.

Celeste closed her eyes and sighed, her throat dry and a shaky breath escaping from the adrenaline rush of the moment.

Torres doubled over and steadied her breaths herself.

Then Celeste narrowed her eyes and took off after the men. She tore through the sacred space and came up short to the door, stealing a glance through the glass slats and catching glimpse of the last of the men in white leaving through the entrance in the stone wall beyond.

"Not on my watch..."

She threw open the door and took off running down the brick walkway, Torres shouting at her to wait up as sirens began to scream in the distance. She pumped her arms to give her momentum, grabbing her phone from her pocket as she rounded the wall entrance and sprinted toward the parking lot.

A rumble of heavily horse-powered engines sounded forth as she reached the lot, a caravan of white SUV-like vehicles snaking out in haste.

She swallowed hard then snapped with abandon as she stood catching her breath, hoping she got at least one crucial shot that they could use to verify who had just shown up at their party.

Torres caught up to her just as the vehicles left, their engines fading into the distance as the angry authorities wailed even closer.

"Come on," Celeste said, panting. "We shouldn't tarry. The last thing we need is to get caught up with the authorities."

Torres nodded, and the two took off for their car. Within minutes, they had circled back down around the hill and out of the compound, the mysterious hostiles nowhere in sight.

Torres made a hard right and floored it, which was a good move. Because several yards back, white and blue lights streamed back into the compound toward the former Templar convent, the two narrowly avoiding the authorities and a series of very uncomfortable questions.

Celeste looked behind them. "Who the bloody hell was that?"

"Umm, the Templars?"

She turned back around and threw her partner a look. "Thanks, Sherlock. What I mean is, *who* are they? These men—"

"Or women," Torres corrected.

"Alright, *people*. Who are these people who are prancing around in white, heads hooded and all, brandishing pistols like those bloody Templars of yore brandished those polished, pounded shafts of metal way back when?"

"All I know is, they sure saved our asses back there from the Nousati."

"And it was clear they were saving their own asses as well, keeping the archenemy of the Church from discovering evidence of their resurrection."

"That's assuming those Anglos really have risen back again."

"Oh, I think at this point it's safe to assume they bloody well have. We arrive to scope out a former Templar headquarters that had been transferred to a reincarnated version of the monastic order, and Nous shows up. Then the mysterious men in white intercept them to seemingly cover their tracks. It's the Templars, alright. Or some version of them. But Anglos, that's another thing altogether..." She trailed off, turning toward the window as the world outside rushed by, the urban slowly turning pastoral.

Torres glanced at her partner as she continued driving south of Tomar. "What are you thinking?"

Celeste continued to consider something that had needled her from the exchange with the purported Templars.

She shook her head, and said, "I'm not entirely sure. But the two men who spoke, they sounded almost...almost African."

"African?" Torres exclaimed, her face twisting with doubt. "That doesn't make any sense. From what I understand, there's zero connection between the Templars and Africa, all of the men having been of Anglo-Saxon descent."

Celeste went to respond when her phone vibrated in her pocket. She pulled it out. It was Radcliffe. She answered it, putting it on speaker.

"Radcliffe, good to hear from you."

"You as well, but you sound out of breath. Have you been having it out over there?"

"You could say that..."

Rather than digging deeper, he said, "I'm eager to hear your report, but I've come bearing some rather horrifying developments."

Celeste's breath seized in her chest. *Silas?*

"Please don't tell me something has happened to our boys in the Middle East."

"No, nothing of that sort." He paused, taking a long breath, then said, "It's Rudolf Borg..."

Celeste sighed and put her hand on her head with relief. She checked the phone for its connection after Radcliffe trailed off.

Still four bars, still connected.

"Radcliffe, are you there? What about Borg?"

"He's escaped."

"Escaped? Bloody hell..."

"Indeed."

"I thought he was in The Hague," Torres exclaimed. "How does that even happen?"

Celeste said, "I agree, Radcliffe. What happened? I thought the place was like an American Supermax prison."

Radcliffe said, "That's the idea, that those convicted by the International Criminal Court for crimes against the international community would endure unencumbered, secure recompense for their misdeeds. Like Borg. But it seems Nous had other ideas."

"Is the Order getting involved in the situation? Is SEPIO at the ready?"

"It's all too early and more drama than anyone is able to endure at the moment, given the crisis the Church is facing this week."

"Understood. We've had our own fair share of drama in Lisbon."

"Oh? Found yourselves some Templars, did you?"

"Yes and No." Celeste took a breath, then said, "We were attacked. Nous showed up."

Now it was Radcliffe's turn: "Bloody hell..."

"Indeed. We arrived at the former Templar compound to investigate the Portugal angle when they showed their faces. One nearly sent Torres and myself to early retirement."

"And I assume some sort of rising phoenix stick tattoo confirmed it for you?"

"You're right. Telltale signs on the back of the wrist. But that's not all." She took a breath, disbelieving what had transpired herself, then said, "The Templars, they also showed themselves."

"There, at the old Templar headquarters?"

"It appears they have indeed risen back again. In fact, they saved our lives from the Nousati who had come to scope out the place themselves. Or, at least the mysterious men in white we've come to know as the Templars saved us."

"But how can you be sure, my dear," he said, skepticism lacing his words. "This would be highly significant if it were true, given their storied history. Not to mention that none have heard nary a word from them for centuries. Even the Order of Christ seems to be largely defunct."

Celeste nodded. "I understand the skepticism. I have been, too. However, they looked exactly like the blokes we saw from the video Zoe discovered on the Dark Net. And, hold on—"

She jumped over to the camera app on her phone and brought up the pictures she had snapped just as the men in white were leaving. She sucked in a breath and held her jaw tight, knowing what that picture meant.

"That confirms it," she said.

"What does?" Torres asked. Radcliffe echoed her.

"I was able to snap several pictures of the caravan carting away our mystery men. And their vehicles clearly match the ones we saw in Zoe's video. The ones that were a Portuguese make and model that led us here to begin with."

"Which means there's a good bet they're local," Torres said.

"Right. And if they weren't holed up at the *Convento do Christo*—"

"Then there's only one other place they could have made their secret lair."

Celeste nodded. The castle fortress on the river island in Almourol.

Torres smiled and nodded with recognition, then shifted their rental into higher gear and floored it south toward the Tagus river location, the sun beginning to crest toward evening on the distant horizon.

"Radcliffe, we're following a lead on the Templars," Celeste said, pulling her weapon out of her waist. "We'll get back to you with what we find."

"Godspeed, you two. And be careful. No telling what the Templars will do when cornered."

She ended the call and settled into her seat for the hour drive. She told Torres that once in the area, they would grab a quick meal and load up on any necessary supplies, explaining they were in for a long night staking out the former Templar castle fortress.

Because it was time SEPIO got some answers from the former monastic military order.

CHAPTER 25

NAZARETH, ISRAEL.

It had been a dark twenty-four hours for Silas and Gapinski. Their failure at rescuing the Christian hostages pressed in against the two SEPIO operatives. Their failure at rescuing Gapinski's grandpappy from martyrdom, compounded by the other numbered dead, was a devastating blow almost too surreal to accept.

Which called for a bro's night at a local burger joint in Nazareth.

After hobbling away from the burning husk of the terrorist safe house in Jordan, the pair had spent hours roaming the border region in search of the jihadi whack jobs who had ended Jim George's life and martyred the other forty-one Christians, waiting for any sort of guidance from Zoe and her crackpot team of operational support techies.

Yet all they had from the frantic searching was bupkis.

It didn't help matters that the server they had been combing through was blown to smithereens. What little they had scooped up in their forensic investigation had yielded no useful intel. The code she thought would lead to the real coordinates of the terrorist's compound was gone.

After hours roaming the barren Jordanian wilderness, the

sun slipping into a dark, starless sky, Radcliffe had ordered Silas and Gapinski to abandon the search. The two had loudly protested the command—Silas more that Gapinski, the weight of the lost mission saving his partner's grandfather sitting heavy on his shoulders. The Order Master was having none of it, given the dangers of two American citizens, let alone Christians with a clandestine ecclesial agency, roaming the largely Muslim countryside being overrun by ISIS super fighters coming in from Syria.

It took a good bit of convincing on the Order Master's part and not a little rank-pulling to get the men to take a breath and a break and leave the hunt to the support staff for the evening. Finally, the SEPIO operatives relented.

They returned back to Israel and stayed in a safe house in Nazareth to recuperate and regroup, getting new phones before showering and then getting a good night's sleep before heading back into the fray. Radcliffe had promised them that everyone back in DC at the makeshift command center was burning the wick at both ends trying to locate the terrorists. Not only to avenge Jim George's death, but also to get to the bottom of the menacing persecution that was continuing to ravage the Church worldwide.

He shared SEPIO intel reports from the majority world that showed a clear ratcheting up of Christian persecution. From China and India, to Iran and Egypt, to Sub-Saharan Africa and even parts of South America, men, women, and children were being snatched by state actors or the familiar jihadi ones. Thousands more were being uncovered in mass graves with the familiar headshot wounds or severed heads. And church buildings by the hundreds were being set ablaze.

He also updated them on the status of Celeste and Torres in Portugal, explaining what had happened to the pair of SEPIO operatives at the *Convento do Cristo*, the surprise Nous attack indicating their involvement, and even more surprising coun-terattack by a band of purported Templars.

Everything within Silas wanted to jet to Lisbon to stand by Celeste's side. Not only to protect her and keep her safe, though he knew she was far from needing such chivalrous maneuvers, given her background with MI6 and physical prowess. He also just flat missed the thrill of working together and researching side-by-side; missed the softness of her skin, the mix of lavender and vanilla she wore with ease, the sound of her voice; and longed for the calm-ness he felt around her, as if the world itself could be crumbling into oblivion, but she would prop him up and hold him steady. She was largely the reason he had been able to climb back out of the PSTD-induced panic attacks still lingering from his time fighting for Uncle Sam. And he needed her help now more than ever.

While Gapinski was waiting to get their food, he reached inside his pants pocket for his pack of cigarettes, an impulse that had calcified in recent weeks into a far more regular occur-rence than he had intended when he started smoking again.

He sighed as he pulled one out, longing to be by her side, yet all at once confused about their relationship and where they stood together. He went to light it, when the other thing Radcliffe had told them needled for his attention.

Borg.

Silas held the tobacco stick between two fingers, tapping it against the table and considering the implications that Rudolph Borg had escaped The Hague.

How the heck does that happen?

A word caught in his throat. The truth and gravity of it too painful and possible to utter.

Sebastian...

He took a steadying breath then swallowed a mouthful of beer as he contemplated the idea that his brother had been instrumental in Borg's release.

The thoughts continued: had Sebastian assumed control of Nous, standing at the head of the Council of Five in Borg's stead? Had he personally organized the effort to extract the former Grand Master? And did that mean his brother had also orchestrated the menacing assault against the Church, the bloodiest week of Christian slaughter in recent memory?

His stomach churned at the thought. Especially since he wouldn't put it past him, given the thermonuclear revelations of what happened to Sebastian as a teenager at the hands of that priest. As well as all of the fallout it had meant for his faith in Christ and relationship to his Church.

When Silas last saw them both just before Christmas after Nous attempted to exploit a purported Holy Grail for its unholy purposes, Borg and Sebastian had seemed close. As Silas continued tapping his cigarette against the table, waiting for his food and contemplating the bombshell revelation of Borg's release, he wondered what his return to the helm of Nous would mean for Sebastian, as much as for the Order of Thaddeus and the Church of Jesus Christ.

He took in a wearied breath, then he finally lit his cigarette.

Gapinski sauntered over with their meal, a tray of thick burgers stacked with all the fixings and his own pint of beer. He set the tray on their table and plopped down in a seat across from his partner. The Richard Burger Bar was a highly rated joint on Google, and the pair had figured a taste of home would do their bodies good, let alone their psyche, after another long day of searching. The smell of the grilled beef and fried potatoes sure offered a convincing promise.

Silas puffed the stick to life and stuffed his pack back in his pocket, noting it was running on near-empty. He'd have to remedy that soon.

After picking back up the bad habit he dropped a decade ago, he had made it a point to stagger his smoking sessions, and only when needed. They were never absent minded or to simply pass the time. The boundaries around his ritual made him feel better about himself after becoming dependent upon yet another fix after flushing his pills down the toilet last year. But after the past few days, and especially the past twenty-four hours, he'd blown through the same number of cigarettes that would normally take a week to smoke.

He hated how weak it made him, that he still depended on a stick of shredded dried leaves packing a chemical punch to get him through the day. He wondered what the good Lord thought of it all, resting in the comfort of nicotine rather than in the power of his Spirit.

He recalled a passage of Scripture as he sucked in another lungful of pleasure: *'For we do not have a high priest who is unable to sympathize with our weaknesses, but we have one who in every respect has been tested as we are, yet without sin.'*

Silas scoffed at the verse from the book of Hebrews, chapter 4, lodged in the back of his brain, disbelieving Jesus had ever been tempted to toke on whatever grass they had back in the day. Although perhaps the point from the Word of God wasn't that he sympathized with his weakness to smoke, but rather his need for it in the first place. His need to medicate his anxiety and bolster his confidence, to take away his fears and numb his pain.

The next part of the passage offered some passing comfort: *'Let us therefore approach the throne of grace with boldness, so that we may receive mercy and find grace to help in time of need.'*

He shook his head and sighed, taking another drag while praying that the good Lord above would make good on his promise, sending mercy and grace to help in his time of need —*both* of their times of need.

Because there surely was more testing on the near distant horizon.

"Cheers," Gapinski grunted, raising his glass weakly and

looking like he'd just walked off a red-eye from London, his hair a mess and large bags anchoring his eyes.

Silas nodded and put out his cigarette in the ashtray sitting in the middle of the table. He raised his glass. "Cheers."

They clinked glasses then ate in silence, a theme that had permeated their work since abandoning their search.

Several minutes ticked by like that, until Gapinski said, "So what's up with you and Celeste?"

Silas snorted beer up his nose in surprise, the burn launching a coughing fit.

"What do you mean?" he finally managed after drinking some water to recover.

"Come on, dude. None of that middle school bull. We've been through too much."

He cleared his throat and shifted in his chair, wondering what to say to his partner—to himself, even. He went with: "It's...complicated."

Gapinski scoffed. "Complicated my ass." He chomped through his burger, and said with full mouth, "Spill it, dude."

Silas raked a hand through his hair and went to reach for his pack of Camels, but opted for a mouthful of beer instead.

He shrugged. "We're sort of dating, I guess."

His partner stared at him in silence. Not chewing, not moving. "You're *sort of* dating? You *guess* you're dating? How the heck can you not know whether you're dating or not?"

"It's—"

"Complicated. That's right, got it."

"No. That's not what I was going to say." Silas sighed and took another swig, then said, "It's just that I've been a mess the past few months, what with losing my job at Princeton and diving back into the fray and losing my brother to God only knows what."

Gapinski snorted. "Yeah, I've noticed. The whole cancer stick thing..." He shuddered, then bit back into his burger. "And, sorry to break it you, but that whole shaggy-hair thing died out with disco, dude."

Silas threw him a wry grin and took another bite himself. "Thanks. I appreciate the advice from someone who's bald. Anyway, I don't think I've been in my right mind enough to know what's up with me let alone between me and her."

"So that's your only excuse? You haven't got your stuff together?"

Silas rolled his eyes. "That, and we haven't had the whole DTR convo yet."

"DTR?"

"Yeah. Define the relationship."

His partner stared at him in silence again. Then a giggle started, a deep and guttural noise that churned somewhere in his belly and reached up and out, crescendoing in cascading guffaws until Gapinski's head was thrown back and he was nearly falling out of his chair with laughter.

Silas looked around as the man continued making light of his self-confession, embarrassed at the spectacle as much as irritated at his response.

"What the heck's so funny?" he asked.

"Dude," Gapinski said, winding down with one final hurrah before smiling wide and saying: "Grow a pair and ask her to date you or court you or, heck, marry you! Because if these past few days have taught us anything, it's that you never know when a bunch of terrorist whack jobs are gonna show up at your baptism and send you to an early death. The fuse on life burns too damn quick to worry about whether or not you've got your stuff together to make a move."

The man returned back to his meal, snorting and shaking his head in laughter again before taking in a mouthful of grilled beef.

Silas chomped into his burger as well, munching on it with a mixture of irritation and appreciation and understanding at the talking to—realizing his partner's response was the cork of a bottle of emotions finally letting loose in the only way the man knew how. He didn't fault him for it. Sort of appreciated the ass-kicking. Lord knew he needed one.

He continued munching, staring out into the world outside and considering Gapinski's advice when the door opened and a group walked in.

Gapinski went to take another bit when he stopped short, mouth open and burger mid-flight. He gasped, dropping it with a messy splatter across his tray.

"Holy. Friggin'. Bamoly, Batman…" he whispered, glancing at the group before sitting stiffly. His eyes had gone big. He shifted in his seat, then bent low behind Silas and gathered up the remains of his meal.

Silas eyed the man with confusion, then turned around to catch a glimpse of what had shocked his partner so dramatically.

"No, no, no…" Gapinski hissed.

He ignored him, spotting a trio of men standing at the counter, tall and muscular, wearing desert fatigues caked with dirt and grime from a day well-done.

Why did IDF soldiers send Gapinski fumbling?

Silas turned back around and leaned in toward his partner, twisting his face in a mixture of confusion and amusement. "Anything I should know about, partner?"

Gapinski leaned toward him, and said lowly, "That dude over there at the counter, the one in the middle wearing the darker fatigues with gnarly skin and that inkblot birthmark thingy across his face."

"Didn't catch the man's Facebook details. But yeah, what of it?"

He stole a glance across Silas again, then took a shaky breath. "Can't be sure, but…No, I'm pretty sure."

"Sure of what?"

The man leaned in closer, and whispered, "He was one of the jihadi whack jobs who stormed Grandpappy's baptism fiesta."

Now Silas's eyes went wide. He started to turn, but thought the better of it.

"At the Jordan River?"

Gapinski tilted his head, as if saying '*Where else, moron?*'

"You sure, bro?" Silas said.

"Dead certain. I went toe-to-toe with the guy and caught a mighty good look at his nasty mug. The dude almost sent me packing to Saint Pete's pearly gates before I leveled him to the ground. Thought I did him in. Apparently not."

"And then he shows up at a burger joint across the border in Israel?"

Gapinski shrugged. "Even jihadi whack jobs need to eat, I guess."

"But this just seems too good to be true. Like one of those badly done *deus ex machina* moments in a cheap airport paperback thriller."

"The Lord works in mysterious ways, bro. You'll learn that the more you work with us. This happens all the time. Last year, Torres and I were scoping out Mr. Mustache—"

"Mr. Mustache?" Silas asked.

"Yeah. Marwan Farhad. Member of Nous's Thirteen. Doesn't matter. So there we were, grabbing some grub at a KFC in Rome—"

"KFC?" he interrupted again. "You ate from Colonel Sanders's greasy trough, in Rome of all places?"

"Hey, don't judge! And how is munching on greasy burgers in Israel any different?" He huffed, then said, "As I was saying...There we were, pickin' up some grub and—"

"They're on the move. Coming this way," Silas said lowly, looking down at his plate and hunching over his meal, shoving some fries into his mouth.

"Just act normal," Gapinski said, doing the same.

"What do you think I'm doing?"

The men sauntered by, smelling of sweat and body odor, having clearly not showered in weeks. Silas glanced up at the man with the birthmark.

The man scowled, slowing as he returned the gaze, but then broke off and returned to his saunter.

Had he recognized him on his return pass?

If he had, he didn't show it. The trio left the restaurant with haste, and rounded past the front windows out of sight.

The two SEPIO agents wiped their mouths in sync and stood. They downed the rest of their beer, then left their half-finished burgers for a much bigger prize.

Vengeance.

CHAPTER 26

PORTUGAL.

S itting atop a hill a hundred yards away from the former Templar island stronghold of Almourol since just after dinner reminded Celeste why she hated stakeouts so much.

The boredom was only outmatched by the bugs.

In this case, the grape-sized mosquitoes relentlessly strafed her ears with their high-pitched violin-like twang, assaulting her sanity as much as her skin.

Smack!

She threw one against her shoulder with an open palm, squashing it into oblivion.

One down. A thousand more to go.

The sun had settled beneath the horizon a few hours ago, the night quickly advancing toward the next day, Good Friday. Cicadas were strumming their evening songs, joined by croaking frogs and singing birds settling into their riverside beds for the evening.

After they left Tomar in haste, Celeste and Torres raced toward Almourol, thinking they could catch the mysterious men in white, the purported Templars, as they escaped back to their stronghold—if, in fact, it was the island castle compound built in the twelfth century. But they saw no sign of them along the route winding them through the Portuguese countryside.

They arrived at a ferry dock on the mainland a quarter mile east of the island that gave riverboat tours. Again, no sign of the men in white. Torres was able to communicate with the ferry operators, explaining she and her friend had wanted a private ride to the famous former Templar stronghold, but it was no use. The man who styled himself the next Captain Kirk offered a firm, stern negative reply, eying them suspiciously when he explained the island hadn't received tourists in awhile. Apparently, it had become private property months ago with a hard no-trespassing rule since its purchase.

They gave up and went searching for food and supplies, the day already quickly retiring toward sunset. Given the presence of the men dressed as former Templars in a former Templar compound, there to exact revenge on the Nousati and stem the organization's incursion into Templar business; given the fact the mystery men fled in vehicles resembling the ones visible in the online video of purported Templars protecting Christians and punishing their terrorist persecutors, all vintage Portuguese makes and models; and given the fact a former Templar compound had recently been purchased, the tourists kept away—all of it offered signs pointing to the only other former Templar compound as a possible ground zero for the risen monastic-military order.

Which led to the two SEPIO agents perched on a cliff overlooking the river below, nestled amongst laurel trees and aloe vera bushes on rocky soil taking turns peering through binoculars at the Tagus river below.

Inky, purple shadows were cast upon the roaming water as the sun began slipping beneath the horizon. The moon was out in force, complemented by lazy clouds moving across the sky without rhyme or reason, offering them ideal conditions for their stakeout.

Smack! Another successful deflection of the natives.

"Stakeouts are the death of me," Celeste complained as she flicked the dead nuisance off her hand.

Torres scoffed, setting down her binoculars. "I thought you were bred for this sort of thing, given your service to Her Majesty with MI6."

"That was then. And I paid my dues, thank you very much."

"Oh, yeah? So you saw action?"

A memory flashed to the surface. She and Martin, alone on a hill much like the one she and Torres were crouched on, were on a similar stakeout. It was the dead of night, and they were monitoring a meeting between two tribal leaders in Pakistan and a group of known al-Qaeda operatives, including a pair of British sympathizers who had defected. There was concern at the highest levels of the British government that they were planning a second wave of attacks after the horrifying July 7, 2005, London Bombing.

They were spies sent by Her Majesty's government to monitor and record the meeting amongst terrorists in the dead of night with all of the sophisticated technology afforded them. It was made bearable by the company, by the one whom she had pledged herself to in marriage. She knew it broke protocol, the marriage proposal itself, but more so the secret, platonic liaisons with the man she had fallen in love with and who was her junior officer under her command. But she didn't care, it was blissful.

Until it wasn't.

The two had been sitting for hours watching and listening across from the meeting location, weariness settling in deep in their bones and the thrill of the chase stoking the fires between them. They knew they shouldn't let their guard down; *she* knew they shouldn't—neither their guard nor their observation of the compound itself. But they had.

And with drastic consequences.

Whether it was him or her, she couldn't recall; probably her. But a kiss had been stolen, and then another. Before they knew it, there was a soft crack behind them before black sacks were thrown over their heads. It was that moment of weakness that would eventually lead to Martin's head being blown off under intense interrogation.

It was why, to this day, Celeste Bourne hated stakeouts.

Another mosquito landed on her exposed hand, searching for sustenance. Celeste didn't notice, too lost in her memory.

She took a breath, and replied to Torres's original question, "You could say I've seen action, yes."

Torres nodded silently, not pushing for more. She brought the binoculars back up to her eyes, then startled.

"Hold on..." She pressed them against her eyes, as if it would help discern what she was seeing, and adjusted the lenses. "I think it's them. Look."

She pointed toward the stronghold, handing the ocular device to Celeste for her own look.

Celeste grabbed them, a caravan of clouds moving rudely across the moon's path, darkening her view. She scanned the river below, straining for signs of—

There it was.

A luminescence shining upon the water, followed by several white objects taking great care in their crossing of the Tagus, trailed by faint wakes.

The mystery men in white. The Templars.

She sucked in a victorious breath and nodded to Torres. "Let's go."

They descended from their perch with deliberate steps and carefully hustled through the undergrowth and fallen limbs from aged trees that littered the rocky hillside.

Several minutes later, they reached a sandbar that made up the shoreline across from their target. They crouched in the sand, looking off toward the island, searching for signs of the Templar's advance.

"Where'd they disappear to?" Torres whispered with tired strain.

"Dunno. There's a reason why the Templars have remained hidden after all these years. Come on."

Celeste took a hesitant step toward the river, her boot sinking through the sandy water. She stepped forward and waded into the river, its icy coolness catching her by surprise as it rose to her knees, and then to her waist. Torres joined her, and soon they were floating toward the towering walls that held the secrets of the Knights Templar.

But for their eyes and nose, they were submerged beneath the dark current just as the Templars before them, slowly making their way across the river Tagus under the providential cover of a cloudy, moonless sky in search of answers. They reached the other side just as the clouds parted and the full moon returned.

The Templars were nowhere to be found.

The SEPIO agents hustled out of the water as the moonlight shone brightly down upon them in force, a series of massive, unforgiving boulders strewn about the shoreline standing in their way. They climbed up and over them, then scrambled up the slope toward the castle fortress, crouching low and taking careful steps as fallen branches and limbs tore at their clothes for their intrusion.

The base of the stronghold appeared almost suddenly, rising from the island like a mystical, fantastical fairytale castle, as though conjured by some magician in the dead of night. It was made of gray stones quarried from the land beyond the Tagus, and beige mortar held them together proudly and surely through centuries of abandonment. Having been erected to service the growing military and financial needs of the

Templars, it was surely a testament to the power and ingenuity of the monastic-military Christian order.

The two stood against the wall, the sound of the river rolling by without a care in the world. A gentle breeze blew against their chilled bodies, disturbing the sycamore trees farther up the hill, their haggard arms bending stiffly and scratching for attention.

"Where to now, chief?" Torres said, breathless and rubbing her arms against her chilled, wet body. "Don't suppose we can ask Alexa where those blasted Templars wandered off to, can we?"

"Shh!" Celeste said, "Listen."

They strained close to the walls of the castle fortress for signs of life.

Torres wrinkled her forehead. "I don't hear anything..."

"Come. This way."

Celeste scrambled farther up the stone-strewn hill toward a grouping of trees that butted up against the stone structure. Voices floated up overhead and down toward the pair as they continued making their way around its base. They were indiscernible, but they were there.

She pressed herself against the wall, uselessly trying to discern the conversation. Then she started craning around toward the trees, searching for something in the moonlight that could give them leverage.

And she found it.

She smiled at the Lord's providence, pulling Torres toward a sturdy-looking tree that rose high against the walls.

They both started clambering up the ancient trunk, reaching higher even as its roughness scrapped up their hands.

"Do you think we should risk it?" Torres whispered, nodding toward a limb that was stretching toward the stronghold walls. It looked like it would give them just enough reach to pull themselves up the old, rugged battlements, giving them access inside.

Or it could be a very bad idea.

Celeste sighed, clinging to the trunk and rubbing her head. "Looks sturdy enough. I'm giving it a go. Wait here."

She said a prayer as she ventured out on the limb, the clouds returning to offer a darkened cover for their incursion. It creaked under her weight but held steady.

Step by step, she inched across the goodly bough toward the stronghold. When she reached it, she stood and stretched for the battlements above—toward the open slot where archers would have once stood, raining down arrows upon unsuspecting invaders. She was thankful they stood empty that night.

Good heavens...

Her fingers barely crested over the stone gap. She willed herself to stretch farther, scratching after the opening with all of her will and might, trying to wiggle her palms above.

But it was no use. Time for more drastic measures.

She held her stance, but carefully bent her knees, easing herself down for a one-shot jump that would hopefully launch her high enough to grab hold of the battlement and hoist herself up to safety.

All without breaking the bloody limb and sending her crashing to near-certain death below.

Leaning against the stone wall, hands up and ready for her gymnastics, she crouched, then launched upward with a spring to her legs that sent her sailing for the stone gap.

There was enough blessed oomph that her forearm slipped inside, grabbing the other end of the wall with one hand and the top stone with the other.

She strained against the stone, its surface all at once slippery from weathered wear and scratchy from centuries of pockmarked age. But she managed to pull herself inside, the void beyond the walls silent and faintly lit from the moon above.

The space was generous enough for her to sit upright and pivot around back toward Torres. She hesitated to turn her back on the inside, but she needed to help her partner.

Torres was already scrambling across the limb when Celeste gave two thumbs up. It creaked with protest as she got into position, worrying Celeste that they may be pressing their luck. Her partner was shorter than she, so it would take an extra bit of oomph to send her sailing high enough to reach the battlement.

Celeste got on her belly and reached for Torres. She offered one arm to her partner, while she reached for the stone battlement with the other for support, her legs dangling off the edge inside.

Her partner braced herself against the wall and reached—

A sickening *crack!* sounded forth.

Sending Torres leaping for Celeste's arm as the limb broke, crashing to the rocky ground below.

Celeste was pulled forward as Torres grabbed on with both arms. Her legs opened like scissors to keep her from falling overboard.

The two struggled to keep it together, but years of training kicked into gear as Celeste gripped her partner with firm hands and pulled her in, even as Torres worked her upper body as if her life depended on it.

Within seconds, they were both sitting and panting inside the battlement, recovering before they advanced farther inside.

"Thanks. I owe you one," Torres said, swallowing hard as she caught her breath.

"No worries. But we're far from the end of it, I'm afraid."

"I don't hear anything. No voices, no sounds, no nothing. Except for the trees and river down below."

"Must have ventured farther into the compound. But where is anyone's guess. The place looks like it's been nothing more than a tourist shop for decades. At least until it was apparently bought up months ago."

They were facing the inner castle of the medieval fortress, offering them providential privacy for their infiltration, with a thick wall dividing them from the rest of the interior. To the right of their position stood a tall, commanding square tower, a steel stairway having been added to the side for inquiring minds. A small walkway ran the length of the battlements where archers would have taken up positions, with a narrow set of stairs leading down below to a doorway out into the main castle portion.

Celeste nodded toward those stairs, then hopped down onto the walkway, closely followed by Torres. They carefully padded across the aged stone and down the narrow stairs, the clouds above parting again to aid their infiltration.

They came up short to the doorway and hesitated before entering, standing still and leveraging all of their senses to discern any danger beyond.

Sensing none, Celeste took a hesitant step forward. The moon showed soundly above, casting soft white light into the interior compound ruins, its insides showing like a dried up carcass, its flesh long gone and bare bones remaining. She turned back toward Torres who encouraged her forward with a nod.

She quickly made her way down a stone path that hugged the massive wall of the interior castle, rounding the square tower and coming up to the main entrance. Its solid, sturdy wooden doors were closed tight. Next to it sat a square tent and table with boxed-up Templar t-shirts and tchotchkes leftover from its days as a tourist destination. A stairwell led down into the darkness, where a faint golden glow and voices, low and growly, struggled toward the surface from below.

The SEPIO agents crouched at the threshold and peered over the edge, catching a glimpse of a barely-open hidden vault door in the wall below. They eased back from the edge, then looked at each other for confirmation as much as reassurance.

Celeste took a breath and began descending down into the ribcage of the former Templar beast, followed closely by Torres. The glow and voices from around the corner guided them ever downward.

They reached the bottom and stood still, hearts pounding and lungs heaving from the intrigue. Then they crunched carefully across the gravel floor bed toward the vault, a sliver of light clearly accentuating the door that led into the heart of the hidden Templar lair.

Standing slightly open like a jigsaw puzzle piece that fit perfectly into the side of the ancient structure was the gateway into the mystery the SEPIO agents had sought for days. Celeste stretched her fingers into the gap, even as her heart pounded in her head, wrapping them around the stone while taking a shaky breath before slowly pulling with intent.

The door groaned under the weight of her tug, but it relented and swung open, revealing a torch-lit stairwell that descended deep beneath the former Templar stronghold.

Laughter down below caused her to falter her step forward, but she recovered and began the slow plunge into the answer to the question that had haunted her from the start of the week:

Who were the men in white, what was their intent?

The temperature quickly dropped as they descended farther, the musty smell of a damp basement and pungent mildew drifting upward upon a cool updraft with each step downward.

When they reached the bottom, the stairs opened into a chamber the size of a basketball court. Light from a strong, sturdy fire out of view cast dark shadows across the room. A table commanded the center of the space, and seated at its head was a man. To his right and to his left were two more figures.

Celeste's face fell and brow furrowed with confusion when she caught sight of them.

All three were unmasked, their appearances true and clear.

She snapped her head to Torres who wore the same look of surprise. Her partner said to her, "I don't think this is at all what we thought it was."

Celeste went to agree when the world exploded in stars before fading into darkness.

CHAPTER 27

ISRAEL.

"Stakeouts bite," Silas moaned, stretching his back and adjusting his binoculars for a better view of the camp down below, the rising morning sun beginning to offer enough light for the SEPIO operatives to finalize their assault on the grouping of tents splayed before them on the barren Israeli desert.

"You're telling me!" Gapinski grumbled. "My innards are about to eat themselves out of house and home if I don't eat something soon."

"Even after the burgers and fries?"

"*Half* of burger and *half* the fries," his partner corrected.

Silas couldn't help but smile as he adjusted the binoculars again, training them on a pack of men in desert fatigues huddled around a dying fire in the middle of the camp. He couldn't recall a single mission where Gapinski wasn't complaining about his stomach, God love him. Perhaps it was a sign the man was slowly getting back to his normal self.

Which was a good thing, considering what they were up against several hundred yards below after catching the providential break of a lifetime.

He counted no less than five men huddled around the fire. Another four had been wandering around the camp, lazily scoping out the perimeter and keeping guard. So at least nine armed men, which didn't even count whoever else were still fast asleep in the four tents splayed around the desert, especially the larger one that commanded the center. Could be another few, could be another ten or twelve. Only time would tell.

Which would arrive in T minus ten if Silas had anything to say about it.

Enough sitting. Time for action.

The pair of SEPIO operatives had spent the evening hours carefully, silently scoping the camp after they had followed the trio from the restaurant to a hideout deep in the Israeli countryside buried between a collection of hills far north of Nazareth.

After the men had disappeared around the corner from the restaurant, Silas and Gapinski rushed out into the street in search of the hostiles. Silas went one way, Gapinski the other, their ears glued to their new phones to keep each other apprised of what they came across.

It was Silas who first spotted them, two riding in a military truck that was a day shy of retirement with faded black 'IDF' lettering printed across the side, one of them the guy with a gnarly face and inky birthmark. Another was riding in the back of the truck armed with a mega-calibre gun mounted to the bed.

"That's nutso to the max," Gapinski said into his handset, rushing to rendezvous with his partner at their vehicle a few blocks away, "because I know Inkblot Dude was the guy I tussled with at the Jordan River. No doubt about it. So what's the deal with the IDF wheels?"

"They obviously somehow got ahold of an Israeli Defense Force vehicle and set of fatigues and are playing the world for fools. The damn thing looked like it was on its last leg, so I doubt Israel's military has missed it much."

The two rounded their separate corners all at once, ended their calls, and took off running for their own truck.

Neither could explain the subterfuge. All that mattered was catching up to the bastards and following them to their lair.

Silas eased out of their parallel-parked space, then floored a U-turn in front of an irate Toyota sedan that had seen better days. Gapinski waved out his window as his partner threw their own vehicle into high gear and sped off toward their target.

A red light snagged them at the intersection where Silas had last seen the terrorists. But a red light never stopped the man before. He looked both ways then floored it, praying to the good Lord above that the blues-and-whites were holed up at a falafel stand.

He sped forward along the main thoroughfare, thinking it would make the most sense to just continue on the main drag in hopes they hadn't missed their chance at interception.

Gapinski directed him with frustrated, frantic arms to divert their chase down side streets, because any jihadi whack jobs worth their salt wouldn't just take the easy roads. They'd try and throw off anyone who might be following them and slink away in the shadows like a cockroach, rather than in the daylight of the main roads.

Except Silas knew they weren't just any jihadi whack jobs. He figured if they had gone through the trouble of securing an IDF vehicle and costumes to blend into their surroundings, then it wouldn't matter where they were driving. The main roads would make the most sense.

He figured right.

He smiled and pointed ahead.

There they were, the beige truck with the fatigue-clad man chilling in the bed, slumped back and mega-caliber gun at ease.

"Would you look at that..." Gapinski said. "Guess you know

a thing or two about this supersecret Church agency stuff after all. Now we've got 'em!"

"Gee, thanks. But it definitely ain't over. Because following them back to their lair ain't gonna be no walk on the National Mall back home in DC."

So they kept their distance as the truck drove east outside Nazareth and toward the Sea of Galilee, always staying five or six car-lengths behind until the vehicle drove farther outside the city through several small towns. Then they extended the target's lead by several more car-lengths when they turned north until the sun started slipping behind the horizon and following them became difficult.

After several miles more of this, the truck veered off to the left without warning, trundling through the open landscape toward a set of hills far north of Nazareth.

Silas slid their truck to a halt and watched them flee, apprehensive to follow so obviously.

"Watchya waiting for?" Gapinski complained, arms gesturing again with irritation toward the cloud of dust pluming in their wake.

Silas said nothing, holding steady along the side of the road as the cloud continued rising from the speeding IDF truck.

Gapinski huffed and folded his arms. "So, what, we just let them get away?"

"They're not getting away. They're going back to their lair. And anyone veering off after them would only draw suspicion. And besides, you said it yourself: I know a thing or two about this supersecret Church agency stuff."

He glanced at Gapinski with a wry grin. His partner rolled his eyes, but nodded and relaxed his arms.

Silas gave it another minute before he eased their truck off the thoroughfare and followed after the jihadi whack jobs Gapinski and he were ready to take down.

Only problem was, they'd lost them.

"Doesn't give me any pleasure in saying this, but I told you so," Gapinski said through his downed window.

Silas had rushed out of the truck after realizing the mistake and began the frantic hunt, flashlight in hand as the sun slipped farther down the horizon.

An unknown town twinkled to their left, a few miles south of their position. A river of clouds dappled in reds and purples streamed up from where the sun had retired, offering a helping hand of evening light down below, but not nearly enough.

He searched the ground frantically for tracks, but it was too dark, and the ground was too obscured by shrubs and rocks.

Are you kidding me?

He hit the hood of the truck in frustration then threw up his hands behind his head. He paced back and forth across the length of their vehicle, Gapinski silently looking on through his open window.

"Hey what's that sound, off in the distance?"

Silas whipped his head toward his partner, then followed the direction of his pointing arm. He turned around and squinted toward a set of hills set against the sky of purples and reds, then strained his ears toward them.

It was faint, but it was there.

A grunting motor and vehicle on a grouchy suspension echoing off the landscape and back toward them, almost with providential purpose. Then, from the west, the faint but unmistakable thwapping of airborne blades fluttered across the horizon toward the same set of hills.

He chanced a hopeful grin as he hustled back to the truck.

"What are the chances that helicopter and hijacked IDF truck are heading toward the same rendezvous point?" Silas said, climbing back into their vehicle.

"Looks like Vegas odds to me," Gapinski said, mirroring his hopeful smile.

Silas nodded and threw their vehicle into *Drive*. He turned toward the hills, tires spitting dirt and gravel in excitement. Their truck's headlights eventually spotted the faint traces of a barely-used access road that wound its way toward the rising mounds now shrouded in darkness.

He took it, his heart beginning to pick up pace along with their truck.

Soon, the faint smell of burning wood drifted into their cabin through opened windows, and a faint orange glow danced in the distance. Silas cut the lights and the engine, and ambled off the path next to a grouping of boulders that served as a threshold to the first of several rising mounds.

It was game on.

From there, Silas and Gapinski hoofed two packs laden with weapons and explosives up a hill overlooking the camp. They crested the top just as the helicopter ascended back into the sky from the camp below. They settled into a ridge where they waited out the night, biding their time until the daylight hour to avenge Grandpappy Gapinski and the other Christian martyrs, and hopefully get some concrete answers to the mayhem that had been ravaging the Church all week.

That hour had arrived.

Gapinski shoved a magazine into his SIG Sauer 516 assault rifle, then stuffed four more into his belt before grabbing two hand grenades and a backup SIG Sauer handgun.

Silas did the same, trading the SIG for his trusty Beretta but packing as much heat. About the only thing they had going for them, given the odds below.

"Ready?" he said to his partner, slinging his own assault rifle around his back, a Beretta equivalent. The AEX160 that he grew a liking to after suffering with Colt's M-16 while working for Uncle Sam.

"Locked and loaded," Gapinski said, starting toward the camp.

He grabbed his partner's shoulder. "For Jim George."

The man took a breath and nodded, then set off down the face of the hill, Silas close behind.

Earlier, they had scoped out a series of embankments capped by aged trees and shrubs nestled up against the camp. The spot looked as good as any for their assault.

They continued making their way toward their launch site under the cover of the early-morning darkness, crouching low and using the surrounding foliage to navigate unannounced as the camp began to awaken more fully. At one point, Gapinski slid down a steep section, falling badly on his backside and sending rocks and gravel cascading down the face of the hill.

They held steady and held their breaths, searching for recognition down below. Blessedly, not one of the men flinched, seemingly too caught up with waking up and preparing their morning meal.

Several minutes later, they reached the staging point, catching their breaths and checking their firepower before commencing their assault.

Silas brought out the binoculars for one final glance, scoping the perimeter and the tents, then the interior where a group of ten or twelve men were congregating, bowls held with one hand and utensils with the other, guns propped against the side of the canvas tents or slung around their shoulders.

But then they stirred, setting their meals down on the ground and standing stiffly.

He scrunched up his brow and scanned the area, finding the source of their shift.

A man wearing the same fatigues and a long salt-and-pepper beard strode toward them. Silas was sure it was the same man from the videos that had taken over the Internet.

Which meant there was a good chance Salt-and-pepper Beard Guy was the same man who had slit Grandpappy Gapinski's throat and martyred the other sixty Christians from the Jordan River. He was trailed by someone who confirmed it.

Inkblot Dude.

Silas sucked in a lungful of air, then handed the binoculars to Gapinski for a look.

He took them, then startled. He looked at his partner and grimaced. "Inkblot Dude."

Silas nodded. He took the binoculars back for one final look.

When he did, he got an even bigger surprise.

"Are you kidding me?" he whispered.

"What is it?"

He lowered the field glasses in disbelief, and said, "Borg."

"What?" Gapinski exclaimed.

"Quiet!" Silas hissed, shoving his partner to the ground and doing the same.

"Always something," he growled, the pair chancing a glance back at the camp. No one seemed to have noticed the outburst.

And there they were, the three of them huddled out in front of the larger tent and making their way toward the center baker's dozen of jihadi whack jobs.

"I'm guessing the man was on that in-bound bird earlier in the night," Silas said, checking his gear.

"Which will make our mission double the fun." Gapinski held up his rifle and grinned.

"And double the trouble. Borg changes things. The goal was to apprehend the man who orchestrated the attacks on the Church and the kidnappings and...well, the deaths of the Jordan River Christians. Preferably alive to stand trial at the International Criminal Court."

Gapinski scoffed. "Look how that turned out. The mastermind behind the Church's archnemesis got sprung from the ICC clink and is chilling in the middle of an Israeli desert, for Pete's sake!"

"I understand, but the goal is to take the man alive, whoever he is. And now we can add Borg to the list."

"Whatever. It's now or never, partner. Shall we?"

He gestured to a path running along the ridge down the embankment to behind the camp.

Silas took a steadying breath and nodded, then set off toward the larger tent below.

The pair hustled along unsteady steps, the soil rocky and loose with diminishing shrub coverage. Thankfully, the tent blocked their view.

They rounded past a large sycamore leaning on unsteady, parched legs and started coming up to the backside of the beige canvas structure moored on the east flank of the camp.

When they did, one of the four soldiers patrolling the perimeter had the same idea, coming around the rope anchoring it to the desert sand.

In the split second he saw him, Silas popped off a single shot that landed hard into the man's chest.

The jihadi fell back, but not before letting out an angry, wild reply from his rifle.

"There goes all element of surprise," Silas complained, coming up fast to the canvas wall and edging toward the corner, the man bleeding out on the desert sand and falling still.

"Well, you know what I always say."

Gripping his ARX160, he glanced at his partner. "And what's that?"

Gapinski backed up from the tent, then withdrew something from his belt. "When in doubt. Throw a grenade."

He gripped the pin in his teeth and yanked at the black, bulbous ordnance, then pulled back his arm and let it swing like he was back in his days as a college football all-star.

Voices of confusion echoed around both sides of the big top before a deafening explosion of fire and fury echoed through the valley, sending a geyser of sand and soot high into the clear, blue morning sky.

"Bullseye," Gapinski said with pride, hustling against the

tent with his back up against his partner's. However, all feelings of success would be short lived.

A pair of hostiles rounded both sides of the canvas structure, bearing those same blasted black Heckler & Koch rifles that greeted the SEPIO agents at the mighty Jordan.

The SEPIO agents let their own rifles rip, leveling the four in surprise. But not before they recoiled their weapons in defeat, spraying the sand and nearly sending the pair to their own early deaths.

Four down. A dozen more to go.

Not good odds.

"Come on!" Silas said, inching forward and chancing a glance around the canvas corner.

All clear, but for a hole in the center of camp belching black smoke and angry red flames. Two tents were also on fire, and cries of confusion in Arabic tongues echoed all around.

A man dressed in dark clothing, white and tall with broad shoulders draped by greasy black hair, darted past the maw of fiery chaos, followed closely by three of the jihadis masked by desert fatigues and black.

Borg.

Bingo.

Silas opened up on the group, even as the hostiles returned the volley with equal force. He side-stepped to a white Jeep butting up against one of the two remaining smaller tents and dropped to the ground.

Gapinski offered a solid reply as he joined his partner.

One of the men fell to the ground with a scream.

"Sissy," he said sliding down to the ground next to Silas. "Did you see Borg scurrying away?"

Silas swallowed and nodded as he reloaded his rifle. "Affirmative."

The vehicle tinged under assault by the two others, sending the pair pressing back against the canvas and low next to the

Jeep. More rounds skipped off the sand in powdery puffs, others sliced through the canvas above.

Another weapon rattled on the other side, then another was added to the mix. It seemed the whole camp wanted in on the action.

They were pinned.

"Gapinski..."

"Already on it, chief."

Gapinski was pulling the pin on his last grenade. He sent it sailing toward the angry hive.

It detonated without mercy, sending bodies flying and ceasing the relentless hornets of lead.

The sound of flames and the dying were the only reply.

The SEPIO agents eased themselves off the ground, weapons ready for business.

Silas went to take a step forward when rounds started skipping off the back of the Jeep, one of them catching his arm and sending him stumbling backward against the canvas and hard to the ground.

He yelled in surprise at being caught flat footed as much as by the pain.

Gapinski opened up on two hostiles who had flanked them from behind.

They went down quickly.

Silas cursed through gritted teeth as he clenched his bleeding arm. It throbbed with pain, the hot metal having sliced through skin and muscle.

"Let me look at it," Gapinski commanded.

He eased back against the tent wall and let go of his arm, clenching his weapon with his other one in pain as much as in guarding the two as his partner assessed his wound.

"You're one lucky sonuvagun," Gapinski said. "Bullet went clear through, and looks like it missed all the good stuff. But we need to stop the bleeding."

Silas winced, cursing his luck. But in the next breath, he thanked the good Lord above that it wasn't worse.

The two jolted as more rounds tinged off the Jeep from the front again, sending Gapinski to the ground.

But it was short lived.

Gapinski opened up on the hostiles and drove them back. Just enough so he could rip off a part of his undershirt with his blade and staunch his partner's bleeding arm.

"Won't take care of the wound. But at least we've got the bleeding under control."

Silas moaned at the maneuver, but swallowed hard and stood. A quickened pulse throbbed just inside the wrapping.

But he could deal with it. He'd have to. They still had a job to do.

The sound of revving engines caught both of their attentions. They glanced at each other, then eased out from their hiding.

No one greeted them, except for the bodies strewn about from the melee.

They hustled forward toward the original yawning hole that had died down to a backyard campfire. Then stopped short when they saw what they had heard.

Two vehicles. One with the IDF lettering they had seen before, the other a black Mercedes SUV.

"Always something!" Gapinski exclaimed.

"Come on. Back to the Jeep."

Borg and Salt-and-pepper Beard Guy each climbed into the two separate vehicles.

Silas and Gapinski ran back to the only vehicle left, hoping it still worked after the bruising it took from all that lead.

"You think that thing's still gonna run?" Gapinski asked, the two climbing into the vehicle.

"With a dose of God's good graces..."

Silas reached underneath the steering wheel and yanked

out a mess of wires. His arm ached with pain, but he pushed through it. He reached toward two of them with his blade, slicing them in half. He stripped the ends off, then got to work, striking them together to bring the car to life.

The engine coughed once, sounding like it had laryngitis from all the lead it ate. Then again before turning over.

Silas floored it, confidence rising as the Jeep did its thing.

"Thank you, Lord!" Gapinski exclaimed.

He agreed, and didn't waste any time taking the good Lord's helping hand for granted.

He threw the Jeep into gear and tore off after the two trucks that had at least a klick or more head start.

The pair had taken off down the service road Silas and Gapinski had followed Inkblot Dude down the night before, then on toward the barren wilderness, dual plumes of dust trailing them as they sped away, likely unsure who or what was responsible for the sudden assault.

A dip and then a bump sent the SEPIO agents sailing in their seats and heads thudding against the roof.

"Sonofa—"

"Sorry!" Silas said, holding their speed but keeping a better eye out on the road.

Inch by inch, the two were gaining on the jihadi whack jobs, their passion for revenge and answers outpacing the hostiles' desire for escape.

There was a grimy sheen on each of the back windows, but two men could be seen sitting in each of the cabins; the driver and a companion. There was also a man in each bed.

Both stood up and opened up on the SEPIO agents' approach.

A bullet hole shattered through their windshield, the intrusion spiderwebbing as the pair cried out and ducked out of the way from the sudden blast. Several more rounds sparked off the Jeep's hood and cabin roof. Others fell away into the sand.

Silas jerked the wheel to evade more lead hornets.

"No way, no how, Paco!" Gapinski bellowed. He grabbed his assault rifle, then leaned out the window.

"Hold her steady, partner," he said before letting it rip, spraying both escaping vehicles without discrimination.

An angry reply sent him ducking back into the Jeep.

When it died down, Gapinski popped out again and answered with more lead until he clicked empty.

He cursed, grabbing a magazine to reload.

When he did, an ashy face framed by black could be seen staring at them through the dirty window from the SUV on the right.

Borg. No doubt about it. Which meant the main target of their operation was in the truck.

Then all at once, the two vehicles split off in two separate directions. The SUV went west, the truck went east.

Borg one way. Salt-and-pepper Beard guy, the one who very well killed Grandpappy Jim George, the other.

It wasn't even a question which way the SEPIO operatives would go.

CHAPTER 28

"**H**old on!"

Silas jerked the wheel west. The car went with it, slamming Gapinski's head against the frame of his door.

The man cursed. "That'll leave a mark."

He glanced over at his partner. "Sorry about that. But you better get ready. I'm guessing we're gonna have more—"

Another bullet smashed through their windshield and shattered out the back.

"Sonofa—" Gapinski said, reaching back out his window.

He propped his six-foot-four frame on the window ledge and brought his SIG Sauer out along with him. He stretched out his massive arm and took aim for the man in the truck bed.

The man had the same idea, letting loose another barrage of gunfire, sending Gapinski ducking but with little recourse.

Silas veered right to shield his partner from the brunt of the attack, bullets strafing the roof with malice and causing Gapinski to sing with surprise.

He pulled back toward the truck as the gunfire eased, giving his partner a window to act.

Pop-pop-pop-pop-pop the rifle sounded from his right. Then again, longer and far more exacting.

The man in the truck bed stood up and shook, arms outstretched like a good John Wayne western and pockets of red blossoming from his chest. Then he crumpled, clearly dead.

The SIG Sauer assault rifle clicked empty when he did. The last of the magazines.

"Always something," Gapinski growled, shoving it back into the Jeep and grabbing his pistol. He yelled to Silas, "Get me closer!"

"I'm trying!" Silas yelled back.

"Well, try a little harder!"

He huffed, but chanced throwing the Jeep into sixth gear. He was worried about pushing it too much in the open, rugged terrain. But the truck ahead was pulling away.

And they had a date with the man responsible for the Church's terrorizing persecution.

Possibly even Grandpappy Gapinski's execution.

The extra oomph from the highest gear slowly collapsed the distance between the two vehicles.

Silas continued pushing it, while Gapinski lined up the shot.

Just a few more yards...

The truck veered left just as Gapinski chambered off three shots. The man cursed at the sudden change.

But Silas was on him, turning with it and sharpening his angle so that he was able to sidle up closer to the driver's side.

And that's when it happened.

There was another *pop-pop-pop* crack from his partner.

The bullets shattered the driver's side window, as well as the driver's head, misting the inside cabin with a mixture of crimson and pink matter.

The man slumped against the steering wheel, the horn

sounding while the truck spun wildly until the corner of it slammed into a misplaced boulder, flipping it onto its side and rendering it dead in the desert.

Steam was hissing from the front of the beast when Silas swerved to a stop a few yards from its rear.

The passenger's door suddenly opened. A man with a dark chest-length beard and masked face, wearing a white *thawb*, climbed up and stumbled out. He was unarmed, so he did the only thing he could do.

The man took off across the barren wilderness toward a town in the distance.

Gapinski threw open his door and yelled after the man. Then tore after him with holy intent, bent on bringing the man who had ravaged the Church to justice.

And the one who had probably martyred his Grandpappy.

White billowed behind the terrorist as he hustled through the desert, his arms pumping and head glancing back to check his progress.

But it wasn't even a contest.

Yards away, Gapinski steamrolled up to the man with ease and barreled into him, tackling the jihadi to the ground.

They skidded across the barren wilderness in a heaping pile until both men were crumpled on the ground. Then they returned to their feet again, ready to battle one another.

All at once, the two forces collided under the high-noon sun beating down against them without mercy. They strained with equal power, the two caught in a bear hug as they struggled against one another.

"Are you the whack job who murdered my grandpappy?" Gapinski roared.

The man broke free to reassess, thrown by the question.

Which was the wrong move.

Gapinski's massive paw smashed into his face, sending him

stumbling backward to the ground and erupting his nose in a geyser of crimson.

When the man fell, an object tumbled out from his cloak, skittering across the ground and catching Gapinski's attention.

A small green book. Gold-edged pages glinting in the sunlight above, and the words *Holy Bible* etched onto its surface bordered with a thin, gold line.

The man was hunched over and holding his broken nose. The SEPIO agent shoved the man to the side and gently picked it up, cradling it with care and marveling at it, as if it were some sort of object from a distant planet.

"Grandpappy?" he said breathlessly as he opened the cover flap to confirm what his gut had already known.

There it was. Scrawled in faded blue ink was *'Jim George'* in a young hand from decades ago.

He gasped, eyes widening with recognition. Then they narrowed with rage. He huffed a hot, angry breath out of his nostrils. A lion, ready to pounce on his prey.

With a primal, ancestral scream that exploded from generations past buried deep within his DNA, Gapinski tossed the small book to the side and launched upon the man.

The jihadi balled himself up in defense, holding his hands over his face as his nose continued to bleed and trying to shield himself from the blows.

But it was no use. Gapinski pummeled the man's head with righteous vengeance.

One, two, three punches. Then: *four, five, six, seven* more.

"Who the hell are you, you bastard?!"

Silas came up behind him and grabbed his arms, trying to wrestle him off the man. But it was no use. Gapinski shoved him to the ground with ease.

He snatched for the hood still clinging to the man's head. Gapinski grabbed one of the man's arms as he struggled against the man, trying to wrench it back and rip his mask off.

276 | J. A. BOUMA

When he finally succeeded, what he discovered was not at all what he had expected.

In one motion, he twisted the man's wrist and pulled back on his arm. The man screamed in agony. Then he yanked the mask off and sat back with wide-eyed disbelief.

"Mr. Mustache?" he said breathlessly, sitting upright with surprise. He blinked in rapid succession, as if confirming the revelation in all of its crazy truthiness.

Silas scrambled up next to him, cradling his arm. "Who is this?"

"Mr. Friggin' Mustache?!" Gapinski roared.

"Marwan Farhad? The Nous operative?"

"Not just any Nous operative. He's part of the Thirteen. Torres and I chased his ass last summer trying to recover the apostle relics. Then he nearly killed Torres with a friggin' drill!"

Gapinski was huffing and puffing, his disbelief transforming into anger and then rage as he realized who it was who had done the darkest deed of them all against the only person in his life who had truly been family to him.

"He was also the bastard who killed my grandpappy," he growled, head low and eyes narrowed.

"You know that for sure?"

He grabbed the small green New Testament from the ground and shoved it in Silas's chest. "This! Grandpappy's Bible from when he was a teenager. Never left home without it. Which can only mean one thing."

Silas took it, recalling the masked man with a long salt-and-pepper beard standing over the good pastor in the live-stream video. He turned the object over in his hand, then groaned as he opened the cover flap, seeing the faded name that confirmed what Gapinski had already said to be true.

In one motion, Gapinski withdrew his SIG Sauer pistol and pointed it at Farhad. "Time to meet your Maker you—"

"Wait!" Farhad yelled, holding up both hands in front of

him, his face a bloody mess and pleading for mercy. "Don't shoot! Don't shoot!"

He chambered a round with deliberating purpose, then shoved the barrel into the man's forehead, the force of it smacking him hard against his skull and sending him toppling backward.

"I've...I've met him!" the man stammered incoherently as he scrambled backward.

Met him?

"What the hell are you mumbling about?"

"Isa!" the man yelled, the words trembling on his tongue. "I've met Yasu!"

Silas stepped forward, gasping and face falling at the mention of the name. He put a hand on Gapinski's shoulder, then slid it down his outstretched arm bearing the SIG Sauer, forcing it to retreat.

Anger flashed across the man's face as he looked back at his partner, drilling him with narrowed, hateful eyes.

"What are you doing?" he spat at Silas, teeth clenched and lips trembling with rage.

"I'm calling for you to stand down, Matthew," Silas said softly.

He went to raise his weapon again when Silas yanked his arm back down and spun him around to face him.

"Stand down?" Gapinski said with disbelief. "What the—"

"Stand down, Gapinski. That's an order!" Silas commanded.

The bulky man took a step back, and screamed, "Like hell I am. This guy murdered my grandpappy! He slit his throat, man. Tore his friggin' head right off his body!"

Silas lowered his head slightly, but then positioned himself between his partner and Farhad. He said, "I understand that. But things have changed."

"What's changed? The man offers some Arabic mumbo-jumbo and we turn tail?"

"It's not just some Arabic mumbo-jumbo!"

"Oh yeah? Then what the hell did he say?"

Silas turned toward Farhad, who was cowering on the ground, face bloodied and caked with sand, hands still raised above his head in surrender.

"Jesus," Silas mumbled. "Farhad said he met Jesus."

Gapinski stepped back again, face twisted with a mixture of confusion and revulsion and agony. Then his face fell with recognition, and he stuffed his SIG in the front of his pants.

"Always something!" he yelled, throwing his head back with frustration.

He turned around and started pacing in the desert, dirty and drenched with sweat and clearly struggling to come to grips with the turn of events.

Then he stopped, huffing with frustrated breath and putting his hands on his hips.

The man who had murdered his grandpappy was about to become his brother in Christ.

CHAPTER 29

With his one good arm, Silas dragged Farhad toward their Jeep. When they reached it, he opened the back hatch, yanked the man up from the ground, and shoved him into the back.

Time to get some answers...

And he didn't waste any time or mince any words.

"Did you kill Jim George Gapinski?" Silas growled, nodding toward Gapinski. "His grandfather?"

The man swallowed hard and looked at the ground outside. He said flatly, "Yes, I killed your grandfather."

Gapinski scrunched up his face and took a breath, then roared with another primal scream and launched after the man.

Farhad shrank back inside the Jeep at the sight of the hulking beast wanting to exact revenge.

Silas stood between them, hands on Gapinski's chest trying his best to hold him off.

"What the hell are we doing?" Gapinski hissed at Silas before he walked away toward the front of the Jeep with hands on his head.

Silas was panting from the exchange. He took several deep breaths, then returned to Farhad.

"Talk!" he commanded the man.

Farhad held a trembling hand up to his mustache and smoothed it down to his beard before launching into his tale.

He took a deep breath, then said, "I am part of what you call Nous. The archenemy of the Church of Jesus Christ stretching back millennia."

"No. Friggin'. Duh, Mr. Mustache!" Gapinski yelled.

Silas reached out a hand to silence his partner, then continued the interrogation. "What is your role with Nous?"

"I'm a member of the Thirteen, and was the soon-to-be Grand Master."

"Fat chance, Paco," Gapinski said from the front. "What with your little jailbird Rudolf Borg busting out of the clink."

Farhad sighed. "Yes, well, that wasn't my call. The Council of Five arranged for the extraction without my knowing it."

"I don't give a damn about your political aspirations," Silas continued. "What I want to know is Nous's plans. Explain the past few days. Seems awfully violent, even for Nous."

The man shrugged. "The Council and Thirteen thought the time was ripe for a revolution, setting the world on fire and flushing out the Christians like vermin out of a sinking ship. So we planned and plotted, believing the Church's Holy Week would serve as the best stage for our pyrotechnics."

"Did a good job of hiding the true source of terror," Silas said, "what with all the black flags and white Arabic script and all. A perfect ISIS mask for your plot."

"It was a marriage of convenience for Nous, and the radical Islamists were all too willing to participate. It was also a personal victory for me, to finally see my people exact its pound of revenge for centuries of Christian colonialist oppression, looting, and conversion stretching back to the Crusades."

He scoffed. "Oppression? If my memory serves me right,

history has a very different take on the subject. It was Muhammad and his Arab followers who launched murderous attacks against the Christians of Arabia who refused to bow a knee to him and embrace him as a prophet equal with Jesus, sweeping through North Africa and the Middle East, through the Iberian Peninsula and on their way to Europe. A violent and relentless Muslim campaign of extermination and forced conversions obliterated the Church. But that's neither here nor there, and not important."

Farhad opened his mouth to respond, but stayed silent.

Silas glanced at his partner. He was standing still, feet planted firmly apart and arms folded like a bodyguard ready to come back and pounce. He said, "The Jordan River. Whose idea was that?"

The man turned toward the front and stole a glance at Gapinski as well. He sighed, and said, "Rudolph Borg."

"Borg? He was helping direct the operation from prison?"

"He was."

"But why the baptism?"

Farhad shrugged again. "As pagan and anti-Christian as he is, Borg is a student of the Church, especially of Church history. After reading about the record-setting Christian ceremony on the Internet from his prison at The Hague, he thought the 900-year anniversary of the Muslim attack on the Christian pilgrims was too convenient. And then we all thought it would make for a dramatic addition to our show of force."

The man stopped and let his head dip. His eyes grew moist with emotion and his lower lip started trembling. He whispered, "And then he visited me..."

Silas looked at Gapinski, then back to Farhad. "You're speaking of Isa, of Jesus?"

The man raised his head at the mention of the word, his face and eyes seeming to brighten. He offered a smile and nodded.

"Tell me about that."

"Yeah, tell us," Gapinski yelled, his back turned to the man and still leaning against the driver's side door. "Talk!"

Farhad smoothed his mustache and sighed. He stroked his beard and said, "You wouldn't happen to have a cigarette, would you?"

Silas sighed and reached into his jacket for his pack.

"No way, Jose," Gapinski complained. "The guy doesn't deserve a pot to piss in, let alone a cancer stick!"

"Come on, there's no harm." Then he said to Farhad, "But then you better talk. Get to the point."

He nodded, then took the cigarette Silas offered him.

Silas lit it, and Farhad puffed it to life. He took a long drag, closed his eyes, and sighed.

Silas put away his lighter and pack of Camels, and said, "Now talk."

Farhad took another drag, holding the tobacco-laced smoke before blowing it out.

"I've killed lots of people in my lifetime," he began slowly, almost at a whisper, his eyes unblinking as if staring down the barrel of a memory. "Willingly, without care. All Christians. Well, mostly Christians. We were bred that way, you know. From an early age, we were told that Allah despises the infidels, and it was our duty to convert them or eradicate them from the face of Earth."

He paused to take another long drag before continuing. "I've not only killed Christians, but I've actually enjoyed doing so. My whole life. And in the past few days, I've been the one responsible for the terror that has swept the globe. Orchestrating all of the various operations with painstaking precision that have wrought violence and bloodshed and terror upon the Church around the world. Reveling in the misery and praying to Allah that my people would finally see the day when the infidels were either brought to his feet as converts or as sacrifices."

Silas added, "Not to mention finally finishing what Nous has been working at the past two thousand years. The destruction of the Church."

Farhad looked up at him and nodded. A trembling hand brought the cigarette back to his mouth. He went to take it, but gulped back a rise of emotion instead. He lowered it, and stayed the tremble with his other hand.

The man said, "But in the past few days, I had begun having dreams of this man in white. He came to me and said..." He trailed off, as if disbelieving what he himself had been experiencing.

"He came to you and said what?" Silas questioned.

Farhad looked at the man, and said, *"You are killing my people."*

"That's what the man in white said? That you were killing his people?"

He nodded and looked back to the floor.

Silas raked a hand through his hair. This was unreal. His mind immediately went to the story in the book of Acts when the most famous persecutor of the very first Christians had a similar encounter with a man in white.

Saul of Tarsus, a young Pharisee who would later become the apostle Paul. He had presided over the stoning death of Stephen and *'was ravaging the church by entering house after house; dragging off both men and women, he committed them to prison.'*

As the story goes, while he was *'still breathing threats and murder against the disciples of the Lord,'* Paul appealed to the high priest of Jerusalem for letters to the synagogues at Damascus, *'so that if he found any who belonged to the Way, men or women, he might bring them bound to Jerusalem.'* When he set out to travel on that Damascus road, *'suddenly a light from heaven flashed around him. He fell to the ground and heard a voice saying to him, "Saul, Saul, why do you persecute me?"'* Paul responded, *'Who are you, Lord?'* He received a similar reply from a similar man in white: *'I am Jesus, whom you are persecuting. But get up and enter the city, and you will be told what you are to do.'*

The experience left the man blind, and eventually he found a disciple named Ananias in Damascus. The Lord Jesus appeared to the disciples and sent him to find Saul so he could see again. When he did, *'immediately something like scales fell from his eyes, and his sight was restored. Then he got up and was baptized, and after taking some food, he regained his strength.'*

The former persecutor of the Church became its most important apostle. The apostle Paul.

Is that who this man is before me now?

Silas couldn't help but think it was. He knew that in Muslim cultures, dreams and visions play a strong role in people's lives. He had heard similar stories as Farhad's told by Muslims around the globe who had had visions of Jesus, personal encounters with a man in white who had confronted them about their unbelief, leading them to place their faith in him as Lord and Savior. One missionary magazine reported that 25 percent of Muslims who converted to the Christian faith did so through dreams and visions. The prophet Joel from the Hebrew Scriptures foretold such encounters: *'I will pour out my spirit on all flesh; your sons and your daughters shall prophesy, your old men shall dream dreams, and your young men shall see visions.'*

Silas believed that Jesus reveals himself to people in different ways that are relevant to their culture, so they can understand him and his heart for them. In fact, he had heard similar stories as Farhad's of ISIS soldiers who had gone on murderous sprees throughout Iraq and Syria having visions of Isa and being confronted in the same way Farhad was: *"You are killing my people."* And then the man in white invited the ISIS soldiers to follow him as Lord and Savior, finding forgiveness from their sins for persecuting his people and salvation from death and condemnation.

Farhad cleared his throat, interrupting Silas's thoughts. The man took a final drag on the cigarette before tossing the butt to the ground below the Jeep. He started sharing again.

"After I...After the death of Jim George, I started to feel really sick and uneasy about what I was doing. Before I killed any more Christian for Nous, for Islam itself, Isa asked me to follow him in my dream. And then before—" The man paused, looking down to the ground and sighing. He continued, "Before Jim George died, he gave me his little green Bible as a gift. I've been reading it ever since, enraptured by Isa's story—his life and teachings, his death and resurrection."

The man raised his head, his eyes watering with regret and hoping for redemption. With trembling voice, and barely above a whisper, he said, "Now I am asking to become his follower. I want to be a Christian. I want to be a disciple of Isa; I want to join his Church."

Gapinski spun around, then walked to the back of the Jeep to face the man once more. He was breathing hard. His face was scrunched up in a mixture of pain and disbelief.

Silas instinctively took a protective step forward, readying to step between the two. But where he expected his partner to erupt with rage again, the man's face softened, eyes welling with emotion and overflowing down his face.

"Isa forgives you, Farhad," he said resolutely, the words of power and redemption echoing around the barren wilderness with hope. He paused and swallowed, then whispered through trembling lips, "And so do I."

Farhad raised his head and gasped. One corner of his mouth struggled upward, reaching for a grin of relief, yet seemingly struggling to believe it to be true.

Gapinski took a step forward, then another until he was standing before the man. He slumped to his knees, Farhad recoiling back into the Jeep at the sudden change of circumstances. Even Silas took another hesitant step forward, wondering what his partner was doing.

The man placed both of his meaty palms on the slight man's kneecaps.

Farhad flinched. He was clenching his eyes now, and starting to shudder with terror at the weight of the moment.

"Marwan Farhad," Gapinski said, staring up into the man's eyes dead center.

Farhad opened them, and with trembling lips uttered, "Yes?"

"Do you confess with your mouth that Jesus is Lord and Savior, and believe in your heart that God raised him from the dead?"

He swallowed and nodded his head. "I do." He swallowed again, and whispered, "I do, one hundred percent. I have seen him. I have read about him in the book your grandfather gave to me. And I believe."

A grin struggled to break through Gapinski's pain and agony and disbelief at the turn of events. Everything within him wanted to rip the man's head off.

But the grin won out, if only for a moment. It flashed across his face, then he sighed and stood.

"Silas, let's get Mr. Mustache baptized before I change my mind and do something I'll regret."

Farhad eased himself out of the Jeep, but grabbed Gapinski's arm, desperate to unload a burden.

The man tensed, but withheld his hand, waiting for the man who had become his brother through a mystical act of confession to spill it.

He hesitated, letting go and smoothing out his mustache. Then he said, "There is something you must know."

Gapinski widened his stance and folded his arms.

Silas did the same, and said, "Go on."

"The devastation has not run dry."

Silas glanced at his partner, then nodded for the man to continue. When he did, he told them of the final plans Nous had carefully laid.

The ones that Borg was all too eager to unleash upon the Church.

CHAPTER 30

PORTUGAL.

frican. Asian. Arabian.

The words begged for attention, reaching for the surface of Celeste's consciousness even as she slumbered in a darkened void after having been struck over the head. It throbbed with pain and confusion, even as her body ached with stiffness and chill.

A faint popping needled for her to awaken, along with the soft, undulating glow of oranges and yellows and reds that gently slapped against her closed eyelids. The smell of blackened meat and freshly baked bread finally brought her back to the land of the living.

Celeste startled awake, jerking to right herself even as her head exploded with pain. She quickly realized her situation was not as expected.

She was curled up on her side, with bound hands behind her back and feet together in a bundle. At least there wasn't a bag over her head. Her vision adjusted, and she began eyeing her surroundings.

She was in a vast room vaulted high, made of exposed cut stone and rough-hewn logs—all bearing the marks of age, centuries even. A walk-in stone fireplace stood across from her at one end through a modest wooden table, a generous fire crackling in the hearth and hissing from a spit resting above its hungry flames, cooking a carcass of some sort. Giant wrought iron chandeliers hung low, bearing candles with flickering flames. A low hum permeated the place, and she thought she caught whispers from the shadows.

She ventured to crane her neck, catching sight of Torres, who was lying to her right, back turned to her. Still and similarly bound. Had to have been hours since she was clobbered over her head.

Clomping footstep moving with purpose interrupted her. Then powerful arms reached for her from behind. She yelled and jerked her body in protest, bucking her legs and gnashing her teeth in assault, but it was no use.

The arms dragged her over to a bench at the table. They hefted her up and around and plopped her down, back to the fire. She admitted its warmth was welcomed, even though the circumstances were not.

"What the hell is going on?" stirred Torres from across the room in the shadows, groggy and disoriented.

"It's me, Naomi," Celeste shouted. "We've been taken hostage!"

Before her partner could answer a voice offered a reply, the same non-English lilting timbre and tone from the *Convento do Cristo* in Tomar.

"You've experienced no such hostility," the voice announced. "In fact, I would say it was the other way around, given that it was you and that there partner of yours who committed the real crimes against this household."

The person attached to the voice stepped into the firelight, several more joining him, the memory of the surprising sight she and her partner had witnessed before they were knocked unconscious returning. Along with the words that scratched for attention minutes ago.

African. Asian. Arabian.

The figures before her were all dressed in the same scaly, tight-fitting white garb the SEPIO agents had seen before, from the convent and the Internet video, muscles bulging as if they were Marvel superheroes come to save the universe from no uncertain doom.

The man's mask had been removed, revealing someone of African descent with a shaved head, skin dark and stubble darker around a mouth gleaming ivory.

He wasn't the only one showing his face; every one of them had been unmasked.

The lead man was flanked by two more Africans, both big and bulging with heads of short black and grey hair. From around their sides stepped two Asian men, hair long and pulled into tails behind their heads, faces angular and set, stances wide and ready. They were joined by an Arab man, skin bronzed and body similarly fit for battle.

But the biggest surprise was the three women who joined the ranks: another African, hair braided and spun up into a hive that meant business; an Asian with fair skin and piercing blue eyes that could level any threat; and an Arab woman, skin olive green with shaved head and full, parted lips. But there was something different about her...

The left socket of her eye was a void of nothingness, an eyeball missing and socket scarred.

Celeste's breath caught in her chest. Not only at the sight of the maimed woman, but from the picture that began to slowly unfold about the rest of her companions.

The African woman bore a stump at her elbow, the rest of her arm long gone. Light caught the Asian woman's face, a pattern of bubbles and ripples betraying a story of badly burned skin. Three of the men were missing their entire arms at the shoulders. Some right, some left. The Arab man was also missing an eye, same left socket. A prosthetic leg seemed to bear up one of the Asian men, its slender design not as full within the tight-fighting outfit he wore.

The only one who didn't seem to have any sort of deformity was the African man with shaved head glaring at Celeste with searching, probing eyes.

Aside from the presence of the three women and missing appendages, the big surprise was obvious: there wasn't an Anglo to be found among the nine purported Templars.

Where Torres and Celeste had expected a reenactment of the original crusading monastic order from Europe, the reconstituted Knights Templar was the antithesis.

It was a representation of the persecuted majority world.

"You look surprised, woman."

Celeste closed her mouth, aware that she had let it drop in astonishment. She fixed her gaze on the bald African, her mind a vortex of questions. She went with one.

"What the bloody hell is the meaning of this?"

The man chuckled, tossing back his head and smiling widely. He widened his stance and put his arms behind him. "I could ask you the same thing, Celeste Bourne. Or maybe I should ask your partner, Naomi Torres?" He motioned toward the woman, still lying in the shadows.

Her eyes widened; she couldn't help it. Before she could respond, there was a scream from the other side of the room and the sound of a struggle.

"Get your grubby hands off of me if you know what's good for you!" Torres yelled.

One of the Asian men had grabbed her by the arms and was dragging her over to the table.

Torres continued fighting; the man strained against her might. He bent down and withdrew something from his backside. With the flick of his wrist, he cut the bindings clinging to her feet and hands. Before she could protest, the man hoisted her up to the table and set her down with a thud.

"Oww!" she complained. "What a way to treat a lady."

The man snorted as he walked away, retreating to the safety of his fellow brothers and sisters.

The lead African man came up behind Celeste, withdrawing a similar blade. He bent down and reached underneath her bench, then sliced the plastic zip ties on her feet. He did the same with the ones binding her wrists, then rejoined his group.

"Thanks," Celeste offered, rubbing her wrists. She looked around the vast room, taking in the space again, wondering how long the men and women had made it a base of operations, undetected by the world outside.

Wondering what it was they were playing at in the first place, and what it was they were planning for the future.

Time for answers.

She pushed her bench back and stood, startling the man and his companions. She walked toward him with purpose, stopping short a foot from his own two feet. She folded her arms and widened her stance, and she made a show of inspecting each of the nine people in front of her.

Then she demanded to know: "Who are you?"

The African tossed his head back and laughed again; the others joined in.

"I should ask you the same thing," the man replied, folding his own arms and widening his stance. It was clear he wouldn't be outmatched.

"Apparently, you already know our identities."

"Yes, we do."

"How?"

The man shrugged. "We know people in high places within the Church."

Celeste smirked and looked away.

"What I want to know is, what are you doing here?"

"First things first," she said shaking her head and taking

back control of the conversation. "Seriously, who are you people? If you know who we are, you know who we're with. The Order of Thaddeus, as I mentioned the first time we met just yesterday. Which means we're on the same side, working for the same good. So how about a proper introduction before we get down to business, shall we?"

The man eyed her, then chuckled again. "I like you, woman. Reminds me of an African proverb: '*There are three friends in this world: courage, sense, and insight.*' I'd wager you have all three in plentiful measure."

Celeste smiled. "I'll take that as a compliment."

"As well you should. And I agree: we are due for a proper introduction. Before we get down to business, as you say. Although, given all we've been through together the past day, we should be old friends by now."

The man offered another chuckle before stepping aside and motioning toward his eight companions, who had remained mum.

Torres joined Celeste at her side as each of the persons began stepping forward for a brief introduction.

The first was one of the other African men, tall and brawny and broad shouldered. He was missing his right arm, and he wore a wicked slash from his ear to his mouth. "I am Abednego of Nigeria," he said, his voice deep and silky. He stepped back with nothing more.

Celeste and Torres nodded toward the man before the other African stepped forward, his left arm cut several inches below the shoulder. He had kind eyes and an even kinder smile, wide and missing several ivory-white teeth. His skin was weathered and wrinkled with age, and grey crowned his head. Perhaps the other man who had spoken at the *Convento do Cristo*.

He said with a rasp, "I am Gonzaga of Uganda." The two women nodded.

He stepped back, and the Arab man stepped forward, a

gaping hole anchoring the left side of his face along with a gaping smile. He opened his arms, as if embracing the women visitors, and said, "I am Malak of Iran."

The two Asian men stepped forward. "I am Yi from China," one man offered in halting English, bending his tall, well-built frame in a bow of respect. The other man, older by at least a decade announced that he was Daegon from Korea.

Joining him at his side was the Asian woman. "I am Cidu, of Korea as well," she said softly.

The Arab woman missing an eye from the same socket as Malak stepped forward, head shaved and held high. "I am Esther of Pakistan," she said before stepping back again.

"I am Sufia of Somalia," the African woman said stepping forward, head similarly shaved and neck long, with broad shoulders and a toned left arm, the other missing at the elbow.

"What a beautiful name," Celeste said. The woman bowed her head and stepped back.

"And I am Mukasa, from the land of Guinea," the lead African man announced, stepping back in front of the group and returning his toe-to-toe stance with Celeste. "So there you have it, our introduction." He motioned toward the table, and said, "So if we could sit and—"

"Appreciate the personal introductions, and all," Celeste interrupted. "However, when I asked my original question at the start, I was thinking more along the lines of who you *all* are. As a collective."

"Yeah," Torres said. "Are you the Templars or what?"

The men and women said nothing. No smirk, no sound, no shifting poses. No nothing.

Finally, Mukasa cleared his throat and crossed his hands in front of him.

He smiled at her, ivory-white teeth gleaming through his dark skin. He said, "Let me tell you a story."

CHAPTER 31

Mukasa again motioned toward the table and invited the women to sit.

Celeste glanced at Torres before wandering without a word over to the wooden benches flanking the long wooden table. Torres joined her.

The SEPIO agents took a seat on opposite sides, and Mukasa joined them at the head where they had first glimpsed him the previous evening.

The man took a deep breath, smiled, then said, "As I was saying, let me tell you a story. There was once a married mother from my African continent, a kind, gentle woman of twenty-two years old. She had a father who continuously hurled insults at her for being a Christian. However, the woman pointed out to her father that, just as a pitcher of water could be called nothing else by any other name, nor could she be called by any other name than that of *Christian*."

He paused, as if chasing a memory; his face fell as if he'd caught it.

He continued, "The man raged at her insolence, lunging for her and grabbing at her eyes to rip them out for being so obstinate. She managed to fight her father off, but the attacks against this Christian woman didn't end there. You see," he said, his voice lower now, quieter, "the father was a man of influence with the local authorities, a powerful and wealthy man who had her put into a local prison, a place of darkness and suffering."

The man closed his eyes and swallowed hard. He offered a weak smile again, and said, "You have to understand, it wasn't that the man objected to her Christianity, per se. He was only looking out for her safety. For a wave of persecution had broken out against the religion in recent years, and so he had her locked up as much to keep her safe as to break her of her devotion to the religion of the cross. Yet, she did not break. In fact, she asked for her infant, and he was brought to her. The young mother nursed the child in prison, keeping him with her at all times."

What a horrible story, Celeste thought. She wondered why the man was taking the time to recount it now.

"A few days later, the woman and her father learned that the local authorities would try her for her Christianity. Horrified, the father raced to plead with his daughter to recant, promising to never again mock or ridicule her for her faith if she would only deny her allegiance to the Christ. Sadly, he was as much concerned for his own social image and business dealings, as he was for her life, not wanting to be humiliated for having a Christian daughter in a land that was not Christian—much less put his own life at risk for having one. However, she would not recant. The next day, she was brought before the tribunal, where she was instructed to recant her belief in Jesus Christ and confess her allegiance to another."

He paused again, taking a breath, weak and shallow. "Instead, she said, *'I am a Christian,'*" he bellowed the four words, the anthem echoing throughout the hall of stone. "Her father begged her in front of the tribunal to reconsider, to offer the required confession, but she refused. The man was taken outside and beaten by the authorities, and the young woman was taken away, without her infant, to be executed in three days' time.

"As you can imagine, the man was beside himself. So the father reappeared at his daughter's prison with the same plea, ripping out the hairs of his beard to emphasize the need for her to wizen up and give the authorities what they demanded. But she would not deny Jesus, and all that he had done for her. All that he had meant to her as her Savior and Lord."

Celeste thought she could see moisture seeping from the man's eyes. He wiped them before continuing.

"Afterward, she experienced a vision, an ecstatic revelation from Heaven above that she would confront not only wild beasts in short order, but the devil himself. Still, she said she knew that victory was hers, no matter the outcome—because Christ had died for her and rose again from the grave. When the day arrived, the captives were led into the public square of the local village. They showed no fear. In fact, if they trembled at all it was for joy, not fear. The joy of witnessing to their confession in Jesus Christ and being counted worthy of martyrdom. Others before the young mother were slaughtered first, their heads chopped off with long swords of polished steel by masked cowards. There was so much blood that some called the event a second baptism, bathing those martyrs in the unholy runoff of the convicted. However, the presiding judge over the women he had condemned to die for their faith, including the young mother, decided to offer them something else. A bull."

"A bull?" Torres said, face scrunched up with revulsion.

The man nodded slowly, eyes solemn and jaw set. "Yes, a bull. A raging, wild bull was unleashed upon the women. It bucked and bludgeoned them. And as they were dying from their wounds, they were arranged in a row to have their throats cut and heads severed like the rest. One by one, each of the women were killed and passed quickly from this life to the next. However, the young mother was held for a different purpose. Believing that she had a taste for pain, the executioner pierced her side with the sword. She shrieked out, and when the swordsman, a novice, couldn't find the right place to strike, she plunged into the sword herself, where it sliced through her neck."

The man took a breath, then put his hands flat on the table, leaning back and looking down, finished with his tale.

"How horrid..." Celeste mumbled. "But why are you telling us this story?"

"Because, agent Bourne, that young mother was my daughter," he said flatly. He swallowed, then roared, "I was the father!" His nostrils flared in shame, spittle flying with regret as he heaved heavy lungfuls of pained breath. "I was the one who was ashamed in a country of radical Islam that I had a daughter who claimed the name of Christ. I sent my sweet Penina, the pearl of my eye, to her death. And she willingly took it! She refused to deny her Savior in the face of persecution, even unto death."

Celeste said nothing; neither did Torres.

"Her death, the death of all of those Christian martyrs, affected me in more ways than simple paternal regret. It also spoke to me spiritually. I could not believe that one would willingly march to the grave for the sake of one's faith. Not exploding oneself like those jihadi Arabs in the belief that their god has instructed them to do so, killing the infidels if they will not convert. But rather, willingly marching to one's death with head held high, especially a march so gruesome, so violent, with only the singular care of faithful devotion."

The man swallowed again, his face sweaty and sallow from his confession. He continued, "Eventually, I took the small, battered New Testament Bible she had been given by a group of traveling missionaries from America, written in our own language. I started reading it for myself, beginning with the story of Jesus and continuing on to the letters of Saint Paul the apostle and the others who explained the significance of Jesus' life, death, and resurrection for me and my own life." He paused and sighed. "For the life of my sweet Penina. Eventually I, too, became a follower of Jesus, the one whom my daughter refused to deny in the face of death. I sold all I had for Christ— sacrificing my mining business that made me very wealthy, my homes and cars, my social standing. And I used that wealth to build all you see here, purchasing this island of the lost order of Christ's knights and outfitting it for new life. And I vowed that one day, I would put a stop to it all. "

"So then you're out for vengeance?" Torres asked, her face registering confusion.

"No, not vengeance," the man said, shaking his head and scowling. "Protection! For all of the other women and children, for the men across the majority world—across Africa and Asia and the Arab world—for those who are under the iron-grip of sheer wickedness, spawned from the loins of Satan himself, who are one raid away from being dragged out of their beds and from their homes and slaughtered in the streets, or burned alive in their churches for worshiping Jesus Christ and refusing to deny his name, their Lord—for refusing to offer the mandated *shahada* and confess Allah to be the one true God and Muhammad his one true prophet! Or for refusing to bow before the State in all of its worldly might and power."

This gave Celeste pause. What the man touched on was true.

The majority, non-Western world had begun to find itself under immense pressure over the last several years. From Asian house churches being burned in China and the communist government cracking down on Christian freedoms, to videos popping up on YouTube showcasing Arab men in orange jump-suits kneeling in the sands along the Mediterranean getting their heads lopped off, to thousands of women and children being raped and kidnapped by Muslim jihadi terrorists across the African continent in a bid to purge the lands of the nation of the cross, as the recent live-stream video had said.

Whereas in centuries past, the Muslim hordes had swept through the Middle East and North Africa and on through Central Asia and the Iberian Peninsula toward Western Europe in a bid to eradicate Christianity, persecuting and even killing all who confessed the name of Christ along the way—now it was a completely different situation. Now, men and women were persecuted and threatened with death for claiming the name of Jesus in Africa, Asia, and Arabia. True threat of persecution wasn't a Western phenomenon; it was a non-Western, majority-world crisis.

Months ago, Celeste remembered reading reports about a sharp rise in persecution throughout these regions. A spokesperson for an international persecution watch group described a potent cocktail ravaging the worldwide Church: the militant Islam in Nigeria; the statism of China's communism; the militant Hinduism in India; the North Korean combination of communism and emperor worship. In all of these countries and more, intolerance toward Christian worship and even personal confession has ratcheted up remarkably, played out in violence and oppression being reported by SEPIO operatives and other partners on the ground almost weekly. Just a few weeks ago, jihadi militants in Nigeria slaughtered 120 Christians, and reports in India have pegged an increase of persecution at 57 percent. She had particularly noted a pleading from the archbishop of Canterbury, who described the plight of hundreds of thousands of Christians in the Middle East having been forced from their homes, and warning that Christian communities that were the foundation of the universal Church now face the threat of "imminent extinction," as he put it.

So she understood the grave modern dangers facing Christians around the world. But still...was the Templar response the way to go about answering the threat? The same one that answered the original persecution 900 years ago, the one answering it now?

Mukasa grinned. "I can see it in your eyes, the two of you. Western disbelief and skepticism at our response."

Celeste glanced at Torres, but the woman said nothing.

The man shifted in his seat, and said, "A few years ago, twenty-one Egyptian Christian brothers were killed in Libya by Islamic terrorists, martyred for their belief that Jesus Christ is Lord of all and for their faith in him as Savior of the world. Their execution was broadcast around the world in an unholy, vile video. When I saw the execution, bearing witness to their death in martyrdom, I was encouraged. I was encouraged because I knew that what my people have been taught in history books about early African Christians being martyred for their faith is not just history, but that there are Christians today who are brave enough to face death rather than deny their Lord! When I saw those young men praying as they were being prepared for execution and then many of them shouting '*O Lord Jesus!*' as their throats were being slit, I realized that the Gospel message can still help us to hold on to the promises of God even when facing death! I also remembered a rumor of warriors stretching back to the colonies of the Portuguese empire in my home country of Guinea, a rumor that has been passed down through my people going on generations."

"You're speaking of the Order of Christ," Torres said.

The man nodded. "You are correct. In Portugal around 1319, after the death of the final Grand Master Jacque de Molay under the false pretenses of heresy and ecclesial insurrection, a new order was founded that assumed ownership of the Templar's assets, their land and castle properties, but also their mission of driving the persecutors out from their remaining strongholds in Europe. They took the same vows of poverty and chastity as other monastic orders, and soon they were joined by two others, special men in the faith who bore the memories of the brotherhood."

"The remnant," Celeste whispered, sitting straighter at the revelation.

Mukasa smiled and nodded. "You are as learned as you are beautiful, my dear."

The corner of her mouth turned upward at the compliment, even as she blushed. "Go on. You were saying?"

"You are right that a remnant of the Templars had survived the final stand of the Order when Acre fell to the Muslim hordes in 1291. Everything was lost, one Templar wrote, so that Christians no longer even held a palm of land in Syria. Those men survived by the grace and good providence of the Lord on high, saved for such a time as this when the fires of persecution's furnace were stoked to burn bright and strong and hot again against Christ's Church. Eventually, these two surviving Templars were discovered by a passing German priest on pilgrimage, another providential act of God. He convinced them to return to France, where they continued serving the Lord with the new Order of Christ, passing along their wisdom and their mission to the brothers and forming an unbroken chain of continuity to the original religious order. Through the centuries, even after the reconstituted Knights Templar was secularized and forced to bow and kiss the ring of the secular king, secretly the Order of Christ carried forth the heart and soul of the Poor Fellow-Soldiers of Christ and of the Temple of Solomon, taking upon themselves the same mission that imbued their original founding charter: to defend the city of God and protect his people."

"Jerusalem and pilgrims, maybe," Torres said, snorting with derision. "But what does that have anything to do with what is happening in the world today?"

The African twisted up his face with a mixture of appall

and confusion. "What does it have to do with anything, you ask?"

"And how is it remotely Christian to use violence for the sake of self-preservation, considering Jesus instructed his disciples to turn the other cheek, and all?"

The man scoffed and tsk-tsked her, joined by mumbles of protest from his brothers and sisters.

Mukasa propped his elbows on the table and brought his hands together like a tent, as if preparing for a defense. He said, "First of all, the great humanist Erasmus of Rotterdam, writing during the height of the Reformation on the question of waging war against the Muslim Turks, heaped scorn upon those who consider the right to wage war to be totally forbidden to Christians, believing it to be so absurd to not even need to be rebutted and teaching that war should never be undertaken except as a last resort when all else had failed. That is what we have on our hands, my dear. War!"

Celeste nodded, but put out her hand to offer a rebuttal. "Yes, that is true. However, while he acknowledged the danger of the Ottomans and went on to consider a philosophical justification for war, he believed the best route to peace between Islam and European Christianity was converting unbelieving Muslims to the way of Jesus Christ through faith in him as Lord and salvation through his shed blood."

"Yeah, and I believe Saint Peter put it best," Torres added, "'Conduct yourselves honorably among the Gentiles, so that, though they malign you as evildoers, they may see your honorable deeds and glorify God when he comes to judge.' He went so far as to even instruct the Church to honor the emperor, the same one who had put them under the yoke of harsh persecution and suffering, reiterating his original point: 'For it is God's will that by doing right you should silence the ignorance of the foolish.'"

Mukasa scrunched up his face and waved his hand. "And yet, Erasmus mentions the lost ideal of the Christian warrior, the man who armed himself for battle for the sake of defending the defenseless and offering justice where only injustice reigns! This ideal warrior, the one the Templars themselves embodied, was sorely missed during those times of trouble and confusion during the Reformation and the threats of hostile Muslims, and the Renaissance scholar was reminiscing upon those soldiers whom Saint Bernard of Clairvaux described as monks and knights, extolling their great moral probity and their warrior courage."

"And you represent that lost ideal?" Celeste asked, her voice laced with skepticism. She noticed he had sidestepped an engagement with what the Bible had to say about the subject.

"The original monastic order of the Knights Templar was founded by nine men committed to a life of poverty, chastity, and self-sacrifice for the sake of protecting Christian pilgrims who were being slaughtered without mercy. And it has continued with another core of nine, men and women who have all experienced the sting of persecution first hand, whether those hands were government or radical religions from across the African, Arab, and Asian worlds. We and others stationed across the world have continued the original mission of the monastic order, pledging ourselves to protect and preserve the Bride of Christ, knowing that whether we live or die, we are the Lord's."

A silence settled amongst the vast hall of stone, the gentle snapping of flames and popping of logs the only sound to be heard.

Celeste glanced at her partner then eyed the other men and women still standing around the table, their heads nodding in agreement. There was a part of her that admired them for their convictions and for their willingness to put their lives on the line for the sake of others. After all, Jesus said it himself: *'No one has greater love than this, to lay down one's life for one's friends.'*

And yet, Jesus had other words that mattered just as much...

Finally, Celeste broke the silence. Clearing her throat, she said, "I appreciate the sentiments. I really do. There's a part of me that even sees your point—"

"But..." Mukasa interrupted.

"But...how do you square your response with Jesus' commands to love your enemy? In his most famous set of teachings, he instructed his followers, *'Love your enemies, do good to those who hate you, bless those who curse you, pray for those who abuse you. If anyone strikes you on the cheek, offer the other also; and from anyone who takes away your coat do not withhold even your shirt.'*"

"And don't forget the Beatitudes," Torres added. "Jesus said, *'Blessed are those who are persecuted for righteousness' sake, for theirs is the kingdom of heaven.'* And then he added, *'Blessed are you when people revile you and persecute you and utter all kinds of evil against you falsely on my account.'*"

Celeste nodded. "And consider when Jesus Christ himself was persecuted, beaten and flogged, and crucified by the Empire and religious authorities. He didn't strike back. He didn't utter a single word of condemnation!"

Torres added, "He prayed to the Father to forgive them, didn't he? Isn't that our model of response to persecution? Jesus, not the Templars?"

"Spoken like a true white, Western woman," someone sneered from the back of the hall. It was Sufia, the African woman if Celeste remembered her name right.

"Easy for you to say," another added. It was Malak from Iran. "You're not the ones being slaughtered!"

"Your women and children aren't being raped and killed," Abednego said, "nor are your houses being set ablaze!"

"And your churches aren't being burned to the ground and parishioners dragged to prison," Yi said, the man from China.

The SEPIO agents looked at each other as more of the resurgent Templars grumbled a similar response, unsure how to respond.

"What my brothers and sisters mean," Mukasa explained, "is that you are not living with the threat of persecution hanging over your heads. The biggest threat any Westerner faces is losing tenure for speaking publicly about their faith, or a friend ostracizing you for converting, or perhaps a mean op-ed piece in the national newspaper. Better yet, Facebook and Twitter banning you for an errant post."

"I'm not sure that's fair," Celeste said. "There was some nonsense in the news recently about a Catholic woman in my homeland of the UK being harassed by the police for misgendering some transactivist."

Sufia giggled. "Oh, yes, that's right. Police threatened her with lock up for a tweet. Isn't that right? Poor thing, a fine and some prison time for defending her faith. Try losing an arm!" She waved her stub in the air and walked away in exasperation.

Mukasa added, "Or how about a leg or an eyeball. Or try losing..." he trailed off, closing his eyes and swallowing before saying: "or how about a daughter. Persecution in the West isn't persecution. It's an inconvenience."

The room fell silent. So did Celeste and Torres; they had nothing to say to that.

The Templar leader sighed, then stood. "We hear your theological concerns. We ourselves have wrestled with the dilemma between pacifism and defending the oppressed. And we have not chosen our path lightly, bearing the weight of defensive violence while also reckoning with it as a moral abomination! However, I am not at all interested in a debate, but rather action. I understand your own religious order carries with it a mission to contend and fight for the once-for-all faith entrusted to God's holy people, as Jude Thaddeus instructed the Church. Isn't that right?"

Celeste nodded. "It is."

"Well, then fight!" he said, pounding the table. "Because this isn't over."

Torres looked at Celeste, and said, "What do you mean?"

"There is one final target that is meant to bring maximum damage and destruction to the Church."

Celeste asked, "Where? When?"

Mukasa shook his head. "*When* is Holy Saturday. However, *where* we do not yet know."

"The night of the Easter Vigil," Torres said, "memorializing the vigil that Christ's followers held for him outside of his tomb, waiting for his resurrection."

"Indeed."

Celeste stood, then said, "We may know someone who can fill in the blanks."

CHAPTER 32

SOMEWHERE OVER THE
MEDITERRANEAN.

Another plane, another flight toward destiny.

And no uncertain doom and destruction if memory served Silas right, given the last five operations he had undertaken for the Order of Thaddeus.

A ripple of turbulence shuddered the well-appointed Gulfstream jet of creamy leather and polished mahogany, as if adding an exclamation point to the observation.

He gripped the soft armrest of privilege with one hand, his bandaged arm aching in protest from his bullet wound; he gripped his tumbler of Scotch with the other, downing some of the two-fingers neat caramel liquid to stay his nerves.

He hated flying, always had. His father might have had something to do with it. Always going on about how the good Lord didn't give people gills for swimming the ocean blue, and he sure as hell didn't give 'em wings for flapping in the heavens above. It was why Dad had joined the Army, and why Silas followed in his footsteps.

The watch his father had gifted him scratched for his attention, probably brought on by his father's memory. He adjusted it around his wrist just as the jet skipped over another air pocket, his hand once again returning to the tumbler for relief.

Silas sighed and smacked his lips together, the spicy, oaky liquid a balm for his anxiety—all of it, from the plane ride to the desert romp and to the mission staring them down the barrel at the other end of their flight plan. The FAA had banned smoking decades ago, God love 'em. So Scotch would have to do.

He took another swig then stretched out his legs, settling into the soft leather recliner for the final leg of their journey streaming toward the Eternal City.

Toward Rome.

More specifically, the massive Italian Renaissance church at the heart of the Vatican City, the papal enclave inside Rome.

The Papal Basilica of St. Peter in the Vatican.

Or better known as St. Peter's Basilica.

When Farhad dropped the revelation bomb on him and Gapinski back at the Jeep in the Israeli desert detailing a plan to detonate coordinated explosives at the Easter Vigil held in the Eternal City on Holy Saturday, Silas immediately phoned Radcliffe to share the intel. He walked through the events at the campsite north of Nazareth, the unbelievable tale of the high-ranking Nous operative's conversion, and finally Farhad's detailing of the plan to level the basilica and everyone inside— just as they had done to Notre Dame, Westminster, and part of the National Cathedral.

The Order Master was positively gobsmacked. Not just that Nous would be so brazen as to attack perhaps the central structural icon in all of Christendom. But he could hardly believe in the possibility, no matter how resourceful Nous had been the past week in bringing similar attacks against key symbolic Christian churches, let alone the non-symbolic mass slaughtering of men, women, and children throughout the Christian world—he thought the idea that jihadis could get past the Swiss Guards was the height of nonsense.

And yet, as preposterous as it all sounded, Silas knew it

wasn't entirely farfetched. Recent comments made by the Pope extolling the similarities and minimizing the differences between Christianity and Islam and other world religions revealed a lax attitude toward the very real threat the religion posed to the Church. Or at least the radicalized, jihadi whack job variety that had always existed within Islam, finding surer footing and a broader hearing in recent years.

Silas recalled one particular vivid quote from the Pope, still confused by the assertion as he recited it now in his head as when he first heard the Holy Father's comments in a recent visit to an Arab nation seeking to bolster Catholic-Muslim relations:

> I do not believe it is right to identify Islam with
> violence. This is not right or true. They seek a
> peaceful encounter. This fundamentalist group
> which is called ISIS is not Islam. I do not believe
> it is true or right that Islam is terrorist.

Except that Silas knew better.

Certainly not all Muslims were violent, bloodthirsty, murderous people. Most lived quiet lives who wanted what everyone else wanted: a free life in which they could raise a family and find meaningful work, and live in devotion to their god. He had fought alongside several such Muslims in Iraq, men of courage and fine character doing right by their country. Sure there were right-wing outliers in every social community. New Zealand bore witness to that very fact when a right-wing whack job murdered nearly fifty innocent Muslims in a mosque. That was as horrendous as the jihadi whack jobs who attacked the Paris nightclub a few years ago.

But for those who have studied Islam's holy book, there is an obvious increasing proclivity toward violence and warfare in the Quran. The last major chapter to be revealed, the Disavowal, is its most violent chapter. 'Kill the polytheists wher-

ever you find them,' it reads in one verse, which included Christians and Jews, *'lay siege to them, take them captive and sit in ambush for them everywhere. If they convert to Islam leave their way.'*

The book instructs Muslims to *'Fight those who do not believe in Islam, from among the people of the book,'* a euphemism used of Jews and Christians, *'until they pay the jizya and feel their subjugation.'* The *jizya* was a ransom tax required for non-converts. The Quran instructs that Allah sent Muhammad with guidance from the Quran and the true religion of Islam *'in order to prevail over all religion.'* It curses and condemns Jews for their belief in Ezra as the son of God and Christians for believing the Messiah, Jesus, is the son of God with these undeniable words: *'May Allah destroy them.'*

This was the last major chapter of the Quran revealed to Muhammad chronologically containing the final instructions for Muslims—in many ways, the Quran's final marching orders. And they are the most violent teachings found in its pages. Not only does it advocate *jihad*, the violent physical struggle and aggression toward non-Muslims, it commands it. *'March, whether heavy or light, and carry out jihad with your wealth and your lives in the way of Allah,'* chapter 9 instructs. *'That is good for you, if you only knew.'*

Muhammad himself lived these commands, as did the caliphs who rose to power after him, commanding and directing Muslim men to persecute and slaughter Jews but especially Christians on their way toward dominating Arabia and on to the rest of the world. Were it not for the brave men who answered the call of Pope Urban II to resist the incursion of the Muslim hordes and launch the defensive war known as the Crusades, Europe itself could have met the same fate as the Middle East and North Africa.

The Western Church had forgotten all of this, forgotten what believers used to endure on an almost daily basis for tens of centuries: violent persecution and suffering at the hands of not only Muslims but State actors as well, like the Roman Empire. And that forgetfulness would not serve the Church this week. Especially not the Vatican, even in the face of the overwhelming evidence writ large across the world.

Yes, security would be tight around the basilica, as always. Yet the notion that Islamic jihadis hellbent on destroying the central edifice of Christianity, stretching back to the 1500s and well beyond to the original fourth-century church begun by the Emperor Constantine the Great, would never cross the minds of the pontificate and his administration. And apparently would be wholly disbelieved by the Pope himself.

Which meant it wasn't entirely out of the realm of possibility that Nous, with the help of ISIS, could bring down the Catholic icon and center of Christianity for many stretching back to the apostles' original mission—offering a powerful symbol of the destructive might and power waging war against the Church worldwide.

And given that St. Peter's Basilica can hold 15,000 people, it would also mean the single greatest event of persecution and terror Christianity has ever seen.

Though skeptical, Radcliffe certainly believed Farhad's self-confession and had ordered Silas and Gapinski to apprehend him in order to bring the member of Nous's upper echelon to justice for his crimes and utilize him to stop the final act of terror the Church's archenemy had planned. Silas had to give it to the man. Farhad went willingly, desiring to do everything possible to stop the killing of Jesus' followers and atone for his sins—whatever the cost.

Before boarding their Order-issued jet at Ben Gurion Airport a few hours ago, they had raced back to the SEPIO Jerusalem operations center in the dilapidated Jeep to get Silas's arm patched up before heading out. Gapinski's t-shirt had held steady, but the arm was in need of care. His partner had seen a thing or two on the field, so he offered steady medical help. It took some work to clean the wound and dress it properly, but he had worked his magic. Silas should mend just fine.

A snort from up front startled Silas. He snapped his eyes open from his concentration, glimpsing Gapinski with mouth open, snoring to his heart's content. He grumbled at the interruption and adjusted in his seat, catching Farhad napping across from him, dead to the world as well.

Good thing he was resting up. The man was on point for the final leg of the operation that began when he instructed his jihadi whack jobs to blow up the world. And then kidnap and kill Grandpappy Gapinski and all of those other innocent men and women at the Jordan River.

His heart stirred with anger at the man for all that he had unleashed on the world, finding it difficult to forgive what he had perpetuated against his brothers and sisters in the faith. Gapinski was a shining example of such forgiveness given his immense loss. So he drew strength from his partner's example and asked the good Lord to soften his heart toward Farhad, his new brother in the faith.

But that wasn't the end of it. There was another major piece of the puzzle that was connected to it all.

The Knights Templar.

Radcliffe had filled them in on everything Celeste and Torres had discovered in Portugal: the resurgent monastic-military Order's secret headquarters, the mysterious identities of the masked men in white, which lead to their motivation— protecting the majority world from militant persecution ravaging the African, Arab, and Asian world.

Silas was as surprised as the Order Master was, not to mention Celeste and Torres, with learning the identities of the risen Templars. Like the rest of SEPIO, he had expected them to be a bunch of Anglos playing dress up to exact vengeance for the Islamic terror being waged against the West. But it made sense; he understood why non-Westerners would want to take matters into their own hands, considering the persecution they had been suffering the last several decades.

The big question remaining, however, was how the Templars would play now that SEPIO was leading the mission to thwart Nous, accompanied by one of the Thirteen who had been responsible for the mayhem and had become a fellow brother in the faith.

They would soon find out.

The plane began to dip toward the blue waters below. It banked right, veering in descent toward the Eternal City where Celeste, Torres, and the nine Templars were waiting at SEPIO's Rome operations center to coordinate with Silas, Gapinski, and Farhad a response to stop Nous dead in its tracks.

CHAPTER 33

WEWELSBURG, GERMANY.

The blood dripped in heavy crimson drops down the side of Rudolf Borg's right forearm, pulsing in tiny rivulets after removing the ceremonial tubing he used to offer his blood to the universe. It was a token gesture, but one he felt aligned the stars and strings vibrating with divine purpose in the quantum world according to his own designs.

He pressed his fingers together and ran them down the length of the tube, extracting the last vestiges of his life force from the rubber into the ceramic bowl.

Later, he would carry the offering deep beneath the castle of stone and iron that had served similar primal intentions just eight decades ago, when Heinrich Himmler had made it the central headquarters for the Third Reich. There, he groomed a new generation to discern the holy patterns and purposes of the universe, bringing science and religion together in a unique marriage—one which he was gladly carrying forward.

When he finished, he lay the tubing back inside its wooden box, padded by red velvet cloth. He closed it, pushed his hair back behind his ears, then opened his mouth and let his tongue wander across the length of his arm, mopping up what remained of his offering, the coppery taste sending him to dizzying flights of ecstasy.

Borg slouched back in his large leather chair resting securely in his study in the castle fortress he had called home for years, very much a free man after having been extracted from the cursed confines of the international community in the Netherlands. A fire crackled and popped a few feet from him, his elixir still running down the length of his tongue and into his belly as he reveled in the comforts of his life: the wood shelving lining the study; the array of books containing knowledge, both accepted and arcane, from all corners of the globe; the tribal artifacts used for sacrifices from lands that died out far too soon; the athame ceremonial blade still dripping with his blood.

Wet snow slapped against the window panes in the early morning light, continuing its assault from the evening and blanketing the quaint northern German town below, summoned by an unusual cold front that had collided with the normally warmer pockets of air by that time of the year. A childhood verse came to mind—they always came to mind at the most inopportune times, having been beaten into his brain by that pathetic little church that sat half a mile outside those castle walls, the one with the spire that stretched toward the heavens.

"*Though your sins are like scarlet,*'" Borg mumbled through the words to the first chapter in the book of Isaiah, "*they shall be like snow; though they are red like crimson, they shall become like wool.*'"

He sputtered his lips and let loose a laugh, the world outside continuing its ode to those words from the Word of God.

He once believed as those mousey parishioners from his childhood church believed. That he had to be expunged of all of the many ills that had come to define him, that he had to be purged of all that was natural to man—the impulses and desires, the wanton acts and reactions that came to define the human condition.

"No, no, no!" he said aloud, continuing to meditate upon the Christian belief that a man-god had cleaned the slate of those who bent the knee in submission, scrubbing out the scarlet, crimson sins that soiled a person and making them as pure wool.

As white as snow.

Clean, undefiled, sinless.

But that was poppycock bull. Because Borg knew that what Christianity defined as human sin was really just another word for human consciousness—what made us *us* to begin with, with all of our abilities to choose a myriad of courses and persuasions and identities and predilections that the Church wanted to rip from our hands.

But no more. The world was so close to ridding itself of the scourge of humanity.

Just a few more hours and it will all be ours. The will to power. The permission to decide for ourselves what is right and what is wrong without those meddlesome Christians telling us what to do and how to behave and who to be!

As he came off from the sanguineous high, he considered all that had gone into the planning of the attacks, particularly the partnership with the like-minded, yet less-than-trustworthy fellows the world had come to know as ISIS. That was his idea, knowing the hatred Islam had for Christians stretching back to its near founding—making the partnership a natural fit, if not an inevitable one, given the religion's own desire to eradicate the Church from the planet.

A verse from the Quran floated to the surface as a reminder about the attitudes of the prophet toward unbelievers, especially Christians who dominated the region:

> *When ye encounter the unbelievers, strike off their heads, until ye have made a great slaughtering among them; and bind them in bonds. O true believers, if ye assist God by fighting for his religion, he will assist you against your enemies...as for infidels, let them perish--catastrophe awaiteth the unbelievers.*

He giggled at the blatant hostility, as well as the brutality early Church bishops chronicled—the Muslims having no respect for the old and orphans alike; for the poor, pregnant, or priests, whose holy altars they defiled with abandon.

But of course, slaughtering Christians had been something of a sport stretching back centuries, to the very founding of the wretched religion. The Roman empire had perfected the art, nearly drowning the upstart sect in blood before it ever got off the ground.

Many Christians were crucified just like that dead god of theirs. Others were burned alive or boiled in vats of oil. Still other were sawed in two, skinned and covered with salt, slowly roasted on spits before cheering crowds, torn apart by lions and tigers and bears!

Oh my!

Borg tingled with excitement at the thought of those fools dying for the god who would take pleasure in his beloved children being slaughtered for his name. He also relished the idea of blowing a goodly lot of them up in the square of Saint Peter to kingdom come, joining the ranks of the strongmen who stood up to the silly notion of living and dying for the Kingdom of Heaven.

The Republic of Heaven was all there was!

And soon, very soon, the world would wake up to that reality, crowning him *optimus princeps* for his genius and moral fortitude to do what countless others had tried but failed.

Eradicate the nation of the cross, the Church of Jesus, off the face of the Earth!

He purred at the thought, taking another pleasurable lick from his wound, the taste of pennies sending his head spinning with delight. As he came off from the high, his mind considered that title again, *The Best Ruler.* It was one assumed by a weak-willed Roman emperor who didn't have the cajonas to finish what his precursor had started.

Trajan...

Pliny the Younger, governor of Bithynia, had written the emperor to let him know he was making quick work of stamping down the rise of Christianity, asking those wretched members of the Church if they were Christians, up to three times if they continued to admit it as a warning of the punishment that awaited them and their wretched brethren and sistren. Yet, he called them out in his letter to the emperor for their *'stubbornness and unshakable obstinacy.'* He insisted they shouldn't be spared any punishment, for *'a great many individuals of every age and class, both men and women'* were being brought to trial, and it was likely to continue.

In other words, they breed like cockroaches! And the only way to deal with such pests was swiftly and without remorse.

And how did Trajan reply?

With the limp-wristed instruction that Christians *'must not be hunted out'* and anonymous accusations should be ignored.

What a Judas to the Empire! At least he went on to instruct that *'if they are brought before you and the charge against them is proved, they must be punished.'* But still.

Had he continued what Nero unleashed upon the Church, then maybe sanity might have had a fighting chance! As Tacitus the Roman historian wrote: *'Nero fastened the guilt and inflicted the most exquisite tortures on a class hated for their abominations, called Christians by the popular.'*

And inflicted he did.

Borg padded over to a shelf next to the fireplace, the smell of escaping smoke and the intense heat delighting his senses as he searched for the right tome.

"Ahh...there it is."

He snatched a raggedy, fraying gray cloth hardback from the shelf. *Annals*, by the great historian Tacitus, with all of his musings on the Empire.

He flipped the pages to a dog-eared one he had book-marked for those moments when he wanted to fantasize about the Church's destruction and learn about how early Christians suffered. He ran his finger down the page, then stopped short at a section he had underlined previously. The corner of his mouth turned upward, and that tingling sensation returned. He read:

Mockery of every sort was added to their deaths. Covered with the skins of beasts, they were torn by dogs and perished, or were nailed to crosses, or were doomed to the flames and burnt, to serve as a nightly illumination, when daylight had expired. Nero offered his gardens for the spectacle, and was exhibiting a show in the circus, while he mingled with the people in the dress of a charioteer.

With every word his breath picked up pace; his heart quickened along with it. He licked his lips with arousal, then closed the book with a thud and placed it back on the shelf.

Tomorrow, Nero rises again to smite the vermin once and for all!

A soft knocking at the door startled him. He twisted toward the sound, then smiled at the sight.

Sebastian Grey. In all of this tall, blond, brother-of-SEPIO-operative-Silas-Grey glory.

"Seba..." he said, opening his arms to greet the man who was the brother of his new enemy.

They embraced, the man smelling of lemon and spice. A heavenly combo if there ever was one.

"Are you ready?" Sebastian said with fidgety impatience. "Are *we* ready?"

Borg smiled, then motioned toward the cloth chair in front of his large walnut desk. "Sit. Let's have ourselves a chat. Anything to drink? Whisky, bourbon, wine?"

"Yes, please."

He chuckled. He remembered when he himself was first introduced into the upper echelons of Nous and launched some of his first missions against the Church. He was as fidgety, as impatient. Every fiber of his being cried out for the sweet, calming relief of libation. What a lightweight he was back then.

Borg opened the door to a small wooden bar cabinet and withdrew a bottle of Catena Zapata Argentino he had been saving for such occasions. He knew Sebastian was ever the sommelier, and he salivated over Malbecs in particular. So he promptly uncorked the bottle and poured him a generous glass, as well as one for himself.

He walked them over to Sebastian, and announced, "To celebrate the occasion of the Church's imminent demise, a Catena Zapata Nicasia Vineyard Malbec, 2012."

Sebastian gasped with excitement. "A Catena Zapata? For real?"

"In all of its black-and-red currant, raspberries, and touch of French-oak glory. *Prost,*" he cheered.

"Cheers," Sebastian echoed, clinking glasses before they each took a sip.

Borg smacked his lips and hummed with pleasure, then took his seat and said, "Now, in a few hours I'll be leaving for Rome—"

"What do you mean *I'll* be leaving?" Sebastian interrupted.

"Not *we?*" His face had fallen slack with confused disappointment.

Borg smiled again at the cute display of pout. He leaned back and nodded.

"But I don't want to stay behind. I want to join you, Rudolph," Sebastian whined. "I want to be there when my brother prances to the rescue and tries to stop you—only to realize that there is no going back. That you have built a failsafe into the plan that no one can thwart."

He swallowed, then added, "I want to see him rise toward his god in heaven on a chariot of fire and smoke and ash, exploding in a wild mushroom cloud of marble and stone!"

Borg couldn't help but let a giggle slip through his mouth at the pure hatred, grinning wide with pleasure from realizing that Sebastian Grey's transformation was complete.

He was Cain, ready to see his Abel fall into the abyss.

"No, no, no, my precious," he purred. "You mustn't concern yourself with the finale. For you have your own project to worry your pretty little head about."

Sebastian went to continue his protest when Borg put a finger up to his lips to silence him. The man rolled his eyes and huffed, then took a long drink of his Malbec.

A clock chimed above his fireplace, indicating the hour for the ceremony had arrived.

Borg stood and carefully took the bowl of his life force from his desk. He issued a final word of instruction to his protege, then left his study.

He padded down the cold stone stairs of the massive turret anchoring the southern portion of the castle. As he descended lower and lower, he could feel the rhythmic beat within the destination chamber pulsating, its cadence beckoning him onward where the universe awaited him to offer up his sacrifice.

He reached the bottom, confronted by a statue of the ancient Egyptian god Thoth. He smiled at the pagan deity as he passed it on the way toward the gathering hall of the Thirteen, and for some reason a quotation from an early Church father surfaced.

The blood of the martyrs is the seed of the Church.

We shall see about that, brother Tertullian. For tomorrow the Eternal City will run red.

And then we'll witness what grows in its place.

CHAPTER 34

ROME, ITALY.

By the time Silas, Gapinski, and Farhad made it to SEPIO's Rome operational center, Celeste and Torres had been long asleep. There was no sign of the nine Templars either, so the three had retired for the evening.

The smell of blessed black coffee and the warmth of sunlight woke Silas up the next morning. As did his stiff wounded arm and a crick in his neck and lower back from the single bed and lumpy pillow. SEPIO may have been the cutting-edge clandestine operation of the Order of Thaddeus, but they still suffered with monastic accommodations. He was all for the vow of poverty, but couldn't they at least get a full-size mattress with decent support?

He stood and stretched, catching a glimpse of the dome crowning St. Peter's Basilica through the tiny window. The sky was a hopeful blue bearing a reassuring sun, with lazy clouds drifting across the expanse without a care. But he knew better.

Tens of thousands of Christians had made the pilgrimage to the Eternal City to celebrate Jesus' death for the forgiveness of sins and his resurrection for the gift of eternal life. Nous would love nothing more than to see them burned and buried in a fantasmic show of fire and fury.

How fitting that they were attacking the Church commemorating the day Jesus laid buried in the tomb—his flesh very much dead, having been butchered beyond all recognition from the scourging and the cross and suffering decay; but his spirit very much alive, having descended to the dead to proclaim good news to the spirits of the dead. This actual death and later triumph over death is what has given Christians so much hope for two millennia, knowing that our last enemy has been defeated and the way has been open to new, everlasting life—a belief Nous would like to put to the test with the deaths of 15,000 believers that evening.

Not if SEPIO has anything to say about it...

Before leaving, the scent of coffee beckoning him onward now joined by the smell of frying bacon, Silas crouched next to his bed. He stared up at a tiny, unassuming crucifix hanging from a wall of peeling white paint, thanking Christ for enduring the shame and suffering of the cross for even one such as him.

He crossed himself, then prayed the Holy Saturday prayer he had memorized as a child, praying to be joined in Christ's death.

> *O Lord, Your sorrowing Mother stood by Your Cross;*
> *help us in our sorrows to share Your sufferings.*
> *Like the seed buried in the ground, You have*
> *produced the harvest of eternal life for us; make*
> *us always dead to sin and alive to God. Shepard*
> *of all, in death you remained hidden from the*
> *world; teach us to love our hidden spiritual life*
> *with You and the Father. In Your role as the new*
> *Adam, You went down among the dead to release*
> *all the just there since the beginning; grant that*
> *all who are dead in sin may hear Your voice and*
> *rise to new life. Son of the living God, You have*

*allowed us through baptism to be buried with
You; grant that we may also rise with You in
baptism and walk in newness of life.*

"Amen," he said softly. He went to stand, but added: "And
Lord, make speed to save your Church this day, make haste to
help your servants of justice. Celeste and Torres, Gapinski and
me...and Farhad."

Silas nodded and said *Amen* again. Then he crossed himself
and stood, and he left to find that coffee and bacon.

His nose brought him through a series of corridors of brick
and stone painted beige, and down a winding staircase several
stories below. It was his first time inside the SEPIO's Rome
operation, and he had to ask for directions to the central hub
twice from confused agents who hadn't a clue who he was.

Eventually, he arrived at a set of heavy steel doors with a
keypad. He pressed his hand against the plate of glass, as he
had seen Celeste do back in DC. It pulsed blue before turning
green. He smiled as the doors unlocked.

Guess that means I'm a bonafide SEPIO operative.

He pushed through. He was greeted by warm air, laden
heavy with that coffee and bacon he had smelled earlier,
chased by cheesy eggs and berry bread. His stomach rumbled
in eager expectation.

Seated around a large horseshoe table in a vast space ringed
by workstations and monitoring screens were the ones who
had become his family. One in particular sent his pulse soaring.

Seeing Celeste made him lose his breath. He grinned; he
couldn't help it.

"Nice of you to join us, Mr. Sleepyhead," Gapinski said.

"Hey, Silas," Torres said.

"Good morning, everyone," Silas said, walking toward the
group who were already halfway through their breakfast.
"Sorry I'm late. Rough night."

He stopped short at a workstation, surprised to see his favorite Italian techie joined by an Indian man, Abraham if he remembered right.

"Zoe!" he said, grinning and reaching in for an embrace. "I didn't know you were joining us."

She stood and leaned in, stiffly and hesitantly. She retreated and pushed her blue glasses up to her nose, and said, "Yeah, well, Radcliffe thought you might need a helping hand to keep the Church from no uncertain doom."

"And quite the hand it is. You're like Mozart with a computer keyboard. Glad you're with us on this."

She blushed, offering an embarrassed smile before turning back to her workstation.

Silas grabbed a mug and filled it with coffee from a carafe at the start of a table filled with fried and baked breakfast goodies. He loaded up and sat down next to Farhad on one side of the horseshoe table, who was wearing a clean white shirt and slacks. The man nodded a greeting to him; he nodded back.

"Good morning, Dr. Grey," Celeste said with a wink from the center of the table. "How's your arm faring?"

"Ms. Bourne," he said, winking back. "I'll live. I've been dealt worse. So where are your new friends? We look about nine short."

"On their way. Flew in separate from us, although I had expected them by now." She took a sip of her tea, then started the morning briefing. "Right. Shall we get on with it? We've got quite the road ahead of us today. And I'd like it if we were all up to speed on the latest developments and working off the same script."

Silas stuffed his mouth with a forkful of cheesy eggs and crunched into a piece of well-salted bacon. He washed it down with the black coffee and thought he'd died and gone to Heaven. Nothing in the world like a good old-fashioned American breakfast to get the day going.

"I assume you all have been brought up to speed on the latest developments around the world?"

He took another swig of coffee, and said, "What's happened now?"

Gapinski said, "Didn't you read the memo your lady friend sent out this morning?"

"I was too busy saying my morning prayers."

"Well aren't you Mr. Holy."

"More attacks, heavily concentrated in Sub-Saharan Africa, the Middle East, and Asia," Celeste offered.

Silas said, "Let me guess, each one was accompanied by *'Allahu akbar'*?"

Celeste nodded. "A slew of videos broadcasting the mayhem have also been popping up across the Internet as well, propaganda meant to encourage the continued slaughter of Christians and showcase the success of the resurgent jihadi terror, no doubt."

"That isn't all of it, Celeste," Zoe said from her workstation.

"More attacks?"

"Unfortunately, yes. Several prominent megachurches in America were the targets of violent rampages during Good Friday services. Apparently, bands of jihadis bearing automatic weapons stormed the churches and began mowing down the worshippers. It's all over the wires this morning. Even though the Western news agencies are loath to ID the perpetrators as Muslims, SEPIO operatives are reporting back that the attacks have all the hallmarks of what's been happening around the world this week."

Silas glanced at Farhad. He looked sullen at the news, regretful even.

The room went quiet with the revelations. He shoved his plate to the side, looking like he lost his appetite at the news that more of Christ's saints had been martyred.

"The interesting thing, though," Zoe added, "is that the attacks have stopped."

"What do you mean, they stopped?" Silas asked.

"I've been monitoring the wires all morning, as well as the dispatches coming in from SEPIO agents in the field, and there haven't been any more vids on the interwebs or news reports or agented communiques since yesterday."

"Like they're waiting for something bigger to commence?" Celeste said.

Zoe shrugged. "All I know is that it seems like midnight was some sort of cutoff."

The director of operations turned to Farhad. "What do you make of this? Was this part of your operational planning?"

The man stirred, sitting up straighter. "It was. The plan had always been to make St. Peter's Basilica the culmination to the week's events along with several smaller eruptions around the globe in coordination."

"Like a grand Fourth of July celebration, huh, Farhad?" Gapinski asked. "The big show of explosions and Star-Spangled Banner along with some sparklers waving from the stands?"

The man took a breath and frowned. "Something like that."

"So what the heck are we going to do about it?"

Before Celeste could respond, there was a loud thud at the door, then a rattling of the handle.

"Looks like our guests of honor decided to show up after all," Gapinski said.

She said, "Naomi, would you be a good dear and let in the —well, the Templars, or whoever the bloody hell they are."

Torres nodded. She went to the door and opened it.

In strode the mysterious men in white. Well, the men and *women*, given the egalitarian makeup of the resurgent monastic-military order. Silas and Gapinski were finally getting a look at them in person.

They were unmasked but wearing the white tight-fitting outfits emblazoned with red crosses they had seen from earlier videos. They were also missing limbs; a few of them were missing eyes. Radcliffe had shared this bit of intel with them the day before, but seeing them in person in that way drove home the point even further that these men and women were indeed seeking justice—for thousands of other black and brown Christians who had endured similar fates because of their faithful allegiance to Jesus Christ, to the point of paying for it with their lives.

One of the African men was unlike the others, having not appeared to have been abused. He was leading the group inside, looking ever the leader of the risen Templars. Silas stood to greet him.

"Silas Grey," he said, extending his hand.

The man took it, offering a grin of white teeth. "Mukasa Mwonyonyi..." he said before trailing off.

His eyes were dead set against the man behind him sitting next to Gapinski

Marwan Farhad.

"What is *he* doing here!" Mukasa roared, pointing a boney, shaking finger at the man. "Seize him!"

The room seemed to collectively spring into action: the Templars withdrew weapons and stood ready to pounce; Silas took a protective step backward and put both palms up in caution, while both Gapinski and Torres leaped up from their seats ready for a confrontation.

"What is the meaning of this?" Celeste yelled, rising and pointing a questioning finger of her own.

"The man is a murderer!" Mukasa shouted, continuing to point at Farhad who had lowered his head. The other Templars echoed with agreement.

"Back off, Templar Dude!" Gapinski growled, stepping up to the African man and pressing his hand into his chest.

Mukasa narrowed his eyes and lowered his head, taking a restrained step backward. He said lowly, "Why is he here? I demand to know."

"Isa, Jesus, visited him in a dream," Silas said. He turned toward the former Nous leader. "Farhad has decided to follow Jesus, putting his faith in him as Savior."

"So there you go. That's why he's here," Gapinski said, folding his arms.

This revelation seemed to give the Templar pause. He took in a long, contemplative breath through his nose, then said softly, "That man is singularly responsible for the most reprehensible violence and oppression of Christians across the majority world in recent memory."

"Yeah, and so was the apostle Paul," Gapinski said in defense, "but that didn't stop Jesus from dropping into his life and inviting him into the family of God, open armed. So I'll say it again: back off."

Mukasa looked at Farhad, face softening and recognition registering. He slowly walked over to the man, then extended his hand and said, "If Jesus has visited you and beckoned you into his eternal life, then far be it for me to deny you a proper welcome into his family. So, brother, I welcome you; in the name of the Father, and of the Son, and of the Holy Ghost."

Farhad chanced a grin and took his hand. The African pulled him in suddenly, then embraced him, one brother in Christ to another.

Silas and Gapinski sighed at the deflating tension.

So did Celeste. She said, "Now that we've gotten the introductions out of the way, how about we start discussing how the bloody hell we're going to get the Church out of this mess. We haven't much time before the queue begins for the evening vigil, and I'd love to have a plan in place."

Mukasa stepped back to his fellow Templars. Farhad sat down.

"Farhad," she continued, "were you privy to the day's final events?"

"Privy?" Farhad said, "I helped plan the blasted finale."

"Which is?"

"As I said, the use of suicide vests on the most devoted of the ISIS jihadis, coordinated to explode with maximum impact and damage."

"But surely they would be detectable by the security in place," Silas said.

The man shook his head. "Not these. Nous developed a special alloy circuitry and wire set that is undetectable. And the explosives used in the vest is a proprietary compound as well. So, no, I'm afraid they will be very much undetectable to the Swiss Guards."

"Always something," Gapinski complained.

"But surely Vatican security could simply be on the lookout for Arab men," Torres said.

"Not the most PC of suggestions, but I'll take it."

Torres hit him in the shoulder. "I'm not in the racial profiling business, Hoss, but let's face it: the threat against the Church ain't Anglos, but Arabs."

"That's not entirely accurate," Farhad corrected. "Yes, the Nous-ISIS partnership was a marriage of convenience. And yes, we utilized Arab men to carry out our attacks. But Westerners were also involved."

Silas added, "And besides, there's no way the Pope and his administration is going to authorize such profiling, with his recent courtship of the Islamic world and all."

"I do have a suggestion that may very well be the answer to our problem, the Church's problem."

He smiled at the way Farhad talked about the Church as *ours*. He was as much apart of it now as the rest of them, a family bound not by the blood of lineage but the blood of Christ.

"All ears, Farhad," Celeste said.

The man sat forward. "Unbeknownst to the jihadis who have volunteered for the task, the actual detonation of the bomb is triggered remotely. The will of the volunteer has been taken entirely out of the equation by a guarantor."

"Come again?"

"Let's just say that ISIS and those jihadis who have joined their cause from elsewhere have perfected the art of suicide bombs, especially the final leg of the mission after having witnessed several volunteers getting...how shall I say? Cold feet."

She said, "You're saying that when push comes to shove, many can't deliver. Can't go through with triggering the bomb."

"Exactly."

"Well there go their forty virgins," Gapinski said.

"Seventy-two virgins," Farhad corrected.

"Even better."

Torres hit him again.

"So what you're saying," Silas intervened, "is that the only way those bombs will explode in St. Peter's Basilica is if the signal gets through from some outside source, rather than from the jihadis themselves triggering the device."

"Correct."

"Which means if we were to jam the transmission, we could make the bombs inert."

Farhad nodded as the rest of the room understood the implications.

Silas turned toward their resident operational support techie. He called across the room, "Zoe, can we do this? Can we jam their transmission?"

She swiveled around and leaned back in her chair, pushing her bright blue glasses against her nose and crossing her arms. "Theoretically, yes—"

"But?" Celeste interrupted.

"But we would need to know what that signal is and be in range of it. The thickness of the marble and stone of the basilica itself could be a factor. And that's not even factoring in the mad hustle I'd need to pull off getting the right equipment and transmitters and coding in the next few hours to have even a snowball's chance in Hades to make it happen in the first place."

"Those are a helluva lot of variables," Silas mumbled, leaning forward.

"But can it be done?" Celeste pressed again.

Zoe sighed, undoing her arms and adjusting her glasses again. "I can try."

"There is no try, Zoe, only do. The Church depends on it."

"Thanks, Yoda," Gapinski mumbled, letting a giggle slip at his funny.

Torres hit him again.

"And what if that doesn't work?" a voice bellowed from the back of the room. It was Mukasa.

Celeste leaned back in her chair and folded her arms. "Then what do you suggest?"

"We join the throngs of pilgrims, secreting ourselves inside, and take them out. Kill shot to the head, right here." He pointed at his forehead, his hand in the shape of a gun.

"More violence, that's your answer?" Silas said.

Mukasa said nothing.

"I'll just say that's going to be a big fat negatory on that one. Not only would that put 15,000 civilians in harm's way. But the idea that we would be able to find the jihadi needles in the basilica haystack is ludicrous. And that's not even addressing the unholy idea of killing people inside St. Peter's Basilica during the Easter Vigil Mass!"

The African went to offer a retort when Farhad cleared his throat. "There was one other thing, however. Something I'm now remembering from the desert that Borg mentioned just before you two unceremoniously ended our meeting."

"You're welcome, by the way," Gapinski said.

The room collectively turned toward the man, waiting for him to continue.

He rubbed his temple, as if searching for the memory inside. "Borg wanted a contingency."

"A contingency," Celeste said, glancing at Silas. He returned her glance, brow furrowed with worry.

Contingencies meant back-up plans, unknown variables. Which never bode well.

"What contingencies?" Silas asked.

Farhad shook his head. "We never got around to discussing it, because, well...You happened." He nodded toward Gapinski.

"My bad," the man mumbled, shifting in his chair. "But I'm not the only one on the hook for that."

"And you haven't a clue what it could be, none whatsoever?" Celeste pressed.

"I am sorry. I've been wracking my brain and I have no idea."

"What about the sewers?" Silas said. "Men with vests down below would sure make things difficult and cause a heck of a lot of damage."

"Perhaps," she said. "But then why even enter the basilica to begin with?"

"What about rocket launchers?" Gapinski said.

"Surely security measures within Vatican City would have cleared the rooftops within a radius preventing such an attack."

The Templars began stirring in the back. Mukasa began walking toward the door, taking the rest of his brothers and sisters with him.

"Wait a minute, where are you going?" Silas asked.

The Templar spun around and drilled him with irritated eyes. "To finish what we started."

He didn't wait for a reply of protest. He wrenched the door open with purpose and strode out, the other men and women leaving with him, the metal doors clanging behind them.

Silas looked at Celeste. "They're going to be trouble."

She sighed. "Don't I know it."

"I much prefer the Knights Who Say Ni than those blokes," Gapinski said.

Celeste shook her head and stood. "No matter. We've got our plan of action. Zoe, you and Abraham get to work putting together the signal-jamming apparatus we need for the Easter Vigil. Silas and I will coordinate with Vatican security. We may not be able to convince the Swiss Guards of the threat against the vigil, but we can at least elbow our way into its security."

Silas nodded and stood as well. "Let's do this, folks. Tonight is our last stand against Christian persecution."

"No, it's our stand *for* the Church."

CHAPTER 35

The clear blue morning sky gave way to an evening set on fire by burnt-orange ribbons of clouds, bathing the world below in a soft glow as the Church prepared to stand vigil and remember Christ's death.

After the morning planning session, SEPIO got to work. Abraham and Zoe put together the electronics package in an outfitted mobile command center that would service their signal-jamming operation in St. Peter's Square. Silas and Celeste got to work trying to talk some sense into the Vatican gendarmerie.

Which didn't go very well.

The commander of the Swiss Guard was alarmed about the possible terror threat, but adamant the vigil would go forward. He insisted the security measures were more than adequate.

When that didn't work, the two coordinated with Radcliffe to send the threat and request for canceling the vigil up the food chain to the highest levels within the pontificate. The one ranking member of the corp responsible for papal ceremonies refused to give consideration to their pleadings. The man only relented to allowing the Order to have access to the plaza for coordinating with the Swiss Guard for security protection. The

SEPIO operatives were also allowed inside to give aid to the security measures already in place.

Silas was still hot under the collar about it, but he understood why: the show must go on. He even respected the pontiff and his administration for refusing to bend in the face of evil and persecution. The Eternal City of all places should stand as a beacon of hopeful solidarity with the worldwide Church.

Even if a band of explosive-laden jihadi whack jobs were threatening to take down St. Peter's Basilica and everyone inside.

Silas and Gapinski were helping with security, while Celeste, Torres, Zoe, and Abraham were stationed outside in the mobile command center anchored in the plaza. For hours, they helped scan thousands of Christians who wanted to take part in the holy ceremony, eyeing everyone who entered as a possible terrorist.

Several made the mental list Silas was tracking, but they were powerless to do anything about it. He said a prayer—said *prayers*, plural—throughout the afternoon and early evening for the team outside, trusting the good Lord above would ultimately keep them safe.

By the eight o'clock hour, the Renaissance church was humming with excitement and expectation. Only thirty minutes to go and His Holiness himself would take the stage, so to speak, and lead the gathered believers through the liturgy standing vigil for Christ's death, all the while anticipating his resurrection the following day.

Soon the moment arrived: the Pope himself stepped forward, joined by an attendant bearing a large open book, steadying it in front of the pontiff for his readings, an organ and bells and male choir announcing the services commencement.

The Pope raised his arms high above his head, as if summoning the Holy Ghost himself to meet with his people. A holy hush settled across the nave, the people of God preparing themselves to keep watch this night of death on the way toward the glorious morning of resurrection.

In a sturdy, solemn voice, he said, "Dear friends in Christ, on this most holy night when our Savior Jesus Christ passed from death to life, we gather with all the Church throughout the world in vigil and prayer. This is the Passover of Jesus Christ. Through light and word, through water, bread and wine we celebrate the new life that Christ shares with us. On this holy night, the Church keeps watch, celebrating the resurrection of Christ in the sacraments and awaiting his return in glory."

The Great Vigil of Easter had commenced. Which meant it was only a matter of time before the jihadi whack jobs launched their attack against the Church.

Lord Jesus Christ, Son of God, be close to your holy people this night. And help Zoe work her magic!

"How are we cracking along, Zoe?" Celeste asked, pacing inside the mobile command center anchored in the plaza outside the basilica.

Zoe ignored her, pushing her glasses back up to her face and continuing to type, working her keyboard like a baby grand piano. She whispered every so often to Abraham, consulting his expertise in the electronics side of things. He was the Yin to her Yang of coding superpower.

Celeste grabbed for a lock of hair and began twisting it with impatience, her gut twisting in sync with anxiety at the clock ticking toward no uncertain doom. The service had begun, and there was no telling how much time they had if the jihadis had indeed infiltrated the basilica.

Come on, Zoe...

She let a few more minutes tick by. But the silence was too much to bear.

Rolling her eyes and sighing at the silence, she leaned over Zoe's shoulder, asking her again: "Zoe, dear, a progress report, if you would."

The Italian held up a finger, continuing to type one-handed, leaning closer to her monitor.

Celeste took the cue. She leaned back and folded her arms, glancing at Torres who offered only a shrug.

The woman continued, stopping briefly only to huddle with Abraham and consult on whatever it was she was coding.

She returned to her keyboard. A few more minutes of *clickity-clack* silence ticked by.

Then all at once, with a final flourish of typing, Zoe lifted her hands and leaned back, a grin of satisfaction splaying across her face.

"Score," she simply said.

Celeste let her arms drop and chanced a hopeful grin, cautiously optimistic that they were in the clear.

She said, "So it's done, then. You sure, 100 percent positive?"

"Should be. I mean, yes. We're good to go. Abraham offered a gold-star workaround that got us out of quite the pickle."

"What pickle?" Torres wondered.

"Well, the signal from the devices was strong, but damn-near tightly barricaded behind a mess of code that—"

"What do you mean by '*the signal*'?" Celeste interrupted.

Zoe motioned toward the basilica standing outside the command center.

At first it didn't register. Then she startled and glanced at the sacred structure gleaming through a narrow window. "You mean, inside St. Peter's Basilica? The jihadis managed to penetrate the Catholic structure, then?"

She nodded slowly, but quickly added: "But not to worry. All should be well. The jamming signal is steady and strong, and the code is sure and sturdy."

And yet, there was that damn word again.

Should.

But Celeste offered a cautious sigh of relief, then squeezed Zoe's shoulders with congratulations. "Jolly good show, Zoe. I trust your work will prove itself true."

Rubbing her head blossoming with ache, she walked over to the narrow window facing the basilica, Michelangelo's dome glowing white from the spotlights under the darkened sky, praying to God that Zoe had delivered.

Because if she hadn't, the epicenter of Christianity would burn.

So far, so good.

No jihadi whack jobs had showed themselves yet. Silas prayed it stayed that way.

The service began after the lighting of the Paschal candle from the Easter fire that had been set ablaze outside earlier, symbolizing the light of Christ that came into the darkened world to offer it the light of salvation. It had been carried by a deacon through the nave, itself darkened but for a few lights shining from the side. He had stopped three times to chant the *Lumen Christi*, the acclamation *'Light of Christ,'* to which the assembly responded: *'Thanks be to God!'*

When he had proceeded on through to the Papal Altar, several readings of Scripture were offered for the second part of the vigil, The Ministry of the Word: from reading the Creation Narrative of Genesis 1 reminding the congregants of God's creative enterprise and the restoration of human nature through Christ assuming the flesh and blood of humanity; to the reminder that salvation is freely offered with a reading of Isaiah 55, proclaiming that by the power of his Word God creates all things, and by his Spirit he renews the Earth.

After the Old Testament readings, His Holiness read a New

Testament reminder of our new life in Jesus Christ, from the book of Romans, chapter 6:

> *Do you not know that all of us who have been*
> *baptized into Christ Jesus were baptized into his*
> *death? Therefore we have been buried with him*
> *by baptism into death, so that, just as Christ was*
> *raised from the dead by the glory of the Father, so*
> *we too might walk in newness of life.*

The Pope offered a final reading, from the Gospel of Matthew chapter 28, the resurrection of Jesus Christ. He followed by offering a short homily on the significance of this monumental event, a small taste of what he would bring the following day in the plaza outside.

If it lasted that long, that is.

Although, Silas was encouraged the service was nearly half over with and still nothing—giving him a degree of hope that the terrorist event was a false flag or the jihadis were scared off with the security measures.

He paced at the back of the nave, eyeing everyone within his vision in the darkened space as the Pope's sermon continued to ring throughout the high-vaulted space of chocolate and dark brown tile floor and massive Corinthian columns rising toward a gilded ceiling of intricate design, the famous Michelangelo dome hovering over Bernini's baldachin canopy at the end, itself hovering over the Papal Altar.

The sight was much to behold, and he allowed himself a moment to breathe it all in, the majesty of it all directing the soul heavenward with all of its earthly beauty—a pale comparison to what the throne of Christ himself must be like.

The papal sermon wound to a close, and the 15,000-strong congregation of Christians from around the world offered a hearty *Amen* at the end of his remarks.

A number of men and women in white began making their way toward the front for the Liturgy of Baptism. The Vatican had chosen a handful of representative catechumens from around the world, people who had been working through the teachings of the Church and ready to commit their lives in faith to Jesus Christ. Euros and Americans, Africans and Arabs, Asians and Latinos all congregated near the Papal Altar to be baptized into the faith.

The memory of Silas's own baptism still burned within his bosom as they each received the sacrament, the public act of confession an act of defiance now in the face of persecution and terror.

This went on for several long minutes until the token catechumens had been baptized into the faith with the holy water. Afterward, the Pope invited everyone to stand and affirm their commitment to Christ and their rejection of all that is evil.

"Do you believe in God the Father?" he asked.

They all affirmed: *I believe in God the Father almighty, creator of heaven and earth.*

"Do you believe in Jesus Christ, the Son of God?"

They continued reciting from one of the Church's central creeds, the Apostles' Creed:

> *I believe in Jesus Christ, God's only Son, our Lord,*
> *who was conceived by the Holy Spirit, born of the*
>   *Virgin Mary,*
> *suffered under Pontius Pilate, was crucified, died, and*
>   *was buried; he descended to the dead.*
> *On the third day he rose again;*
> *he ascended into heaven, is seated at the right hand*
>   *of the Father,*
> *and will come again to judge the living and the dead.*

He asked, "Do you believe in God the Holy Spirit?"

They responded:

> *I believe in the Holy Spirit,*
> *the holy catholic Church, the communion of saints,*
> *the forgiveness of sins, the resurrection of the body,*
> *and the life everlasting.*

"Amen," he closed.

The congregants dutifully echoed him: *Amen*

His Holiness then posed a series of questions, about one's commitment to faith in Jesus and to the Christian life, to loving God and neighbor, to following Jesus at all costs.

The sacred space responded in the affirmative: *I will, with God's help.*

The Pope raised his arms and motioned for the congregants to sit. When they did, a number of attendants began to set into motion the final act of the evening: the Ministry of the Sacrament, the Eucharist.

After arranging all of the elements, the bread and cup, the Pope raised the Host up toward the heavens, blessing it and consecrating it for consumption. When he did a shrilling voice sliced through the silent chamber, followed by a smattering of echoing voices throughout the vast space.

"Allahu akbar!"

And then more chants of response: "Allahu akbar!" "Allahu akbar!" "Allahu akbar!"

Silas's guts seized with fear, shot through with activating adrenaline that actually had the complete opposite effect in the face of the reality facing him across the room.

Like everyone else, he froze.

But brain switched into high gear, quickly counting at least thirteen men, maybe more, all ranging in varying ethnicities and nationalities, all standing tall and proud and arms wide open, ready to offer themselves as sacrifices to their god.

It's happening...My God it's really happening!

But then it didn't.

The chamber had been seized by a collective breath-holding, all time ceasing for an eternal second and all motion draining from the sacred space as the gathered Christians waited for the expected, for the inevitable.

But the coordinated series of explosions never came.

St. Peter's Basilica still stood and the 15,000 believers were safe.

Silas closed his eyes and eased his held breath out of his mouth with a weak sigh, feeling like his body was about to collapse onto the ceramic tile floor from the tenuous weight of the moment.

It worked!

Zoe had jammed the bombs' signals.

Then everyone else sighed with relief—unsure what had just happened, but completely certain an Easter Vigil miracle had just been wrought in their midst, having escaped the terrifying, terrorizing persecution other churches and other believers had witnessed first hand throughout the week. Even His Holiness himself seemed to feel relief, having set the Host on the table and slumped into his chair.

Then the jihadi whack jobs themselves registered their failure, all at once ripping their shirts open to inspect their hardware, then furiously pressing what they thought were the detonation devices.

Nada.

The room began to ripple with shouts and screams of protest and terror.

Security guards, festooned with all the ceremonial trappings of the holy basilica, began to arrive in forceful groups, wading through the crowds of people to apprehend the terrorists.

A shot rang out. A Swiss Guard dropped to the floor.

One of the terrorists was somehow armed and trying to flee.

But he was dropped by another series of shots, ringing out from the other side

Trailing the sound of gunfire was the unmistakable, all-too-familiar Latin.

Voices shouting *"Non nobis, Domine, non nobis, sed Nomini tuo da gloriam!"* echoed around the basilica nave as African, Arab, and Asian Templars stepped out from the shadows, robed in their scaly-white garb emblazoned with the recognizable crimson cross of the ancient monastic-military order, faces masked by grey helmets and white capes billowing behind them. They were all armed, some with polished steel swords, some with charcoal weapons outstretched and read to answer the call of duty.

Their presence set off another series of screams and shouts of protest, followed by many fleeing toward safer ground.

There was pandemonium now with the mixture of the jihadis trying to escape, the pontificate guards pouring into the chamber to apprehend the terrorists and restore order, and the added element of the Templars rising to once again avenge the Church and protect her people.

The worst case scenario ever.

Chaos began to swell within the nave as the forces began to collide.

Several of the jihadis had been tackled to the ground; others were fleeing down the center aisle toward the doors at the back and off toward the side.

But the Templars wouldn't let them.

They took off after the men, shouting at the civilian bystanders to clear the way as they tore through the nave across the polished brown floor.

"It's go time, partner!" Silas shouted to Gapinski.

His partner chambered a round in his SIG Sauer and nodded, his face set as flint. "Locked and loaded."

Silas nodded back, Beretta pulled and ready for business. *Time for SEPIO to end this.*

At LEAST HALF of the jihadi terrorists had made it out alive and were fleeing through the entrance that had remained open through the evening, dashing out into the plaza and pounding across its stone pavement in all directions.

Close on their tails were the Templars, weapons unsheathed and drawn for battle. Cries of vengeance rang out from them as they themselves pounded after the men.

Following them were Silas and Gapinski, who didn't know whether to keep after the terrorists or let the Templars fulfill their sworn mission to defend the city of God and protect Christian pilgrims.

Gapinski led the way, even as sirens sliced through the evening air in the background, broadcasting that help was close at hand.

"Hold up a second," he said, stopping suddenly and turning around toward the basilica. He stood still, his arms held out as if steadying himself with concentration.

Silas came up next to him. "What is it?"

"Shh..."

The two stood still, people were fleeing the basilica now, beginning to stream around them throughout the piazza of St. Peter.

Gapinski turned to him and pointed a finger into the air, brow furrowed with a mixture of confusion and concern. "Do you hear that?"

Silas strained his head toward the sky—listening, discerning, divining—his eyes going wide with instant recognition.

Yes. He definitely heard it. A buzzing, high and dreadful.

And he knew exactly what it meant.

Drones!

CHAPTER 36

Silas threw open the door to the mobile command center, startling the occupants inside.

"We've got company," he said as he climbed inside, Gapinski following close behind.

"Why? What's the matter?" Celeste asked.

"One word, sister," Gapinski answered, pausing a beat before saying: "Drones."

"What's he playing at?" she asked Silas.

He pointed toward the roof of the van. "Outside, in the sky. Not sure how many of them, but I can hear their whine fast approaching."

"The contingency plan."

Silas nodded, saying nothing.

He remembered reading reports in recent months about the increasingly alarmed military and foreign policy experts at the possible threat of terrorists using the devices now readily available to any consumer to wreak havoc and mayhem. They had already disrupted air traffic and travel at London's Heathrow and Gatwick airports. Those episodes were simply stupid citizens out joyriding with their toys, but still—the chaos had offered a glimpse into how easy a terrorist cell could act against civilian targets, arming such devices with explosives. Frankly, he was surprised hostile actors hadn't added such devices to their arsenal of terror.

Until now.

Celeste turned to Zoe. "Can't we just jam them, like we did with the explosive devices inside the basilica?"

"Negatory," Zoe answered, shaking her head while her fingers furiously worked her keyboard. "Before, we had hours to lock into the devices' signals. This is..."

She trailed off without completing her thought, but telling the van all they needed to know.

"Bloody hell..." Celeste raked a hand through her hair, then began pacing the length of the van.

"Don't worry, all is not lost. It might take some finger grease, but we're on it."

"How long until they reach the basilica, do you think?"

Gapinski chuckled. "Sister, I'm pretty sure they're nearly at St. Pete's door!"

Celeste cursed again. "So minutes, is what you're saying, until all is lost."

Silas said nothing. Neither did Gapinski.

"Got it!" Zoe shouted.

Silas and Celeste crowded around her, bending low to look at her monitor.

"Got what?" she asked.

"A lock on the coordinating signal sending those buzzards on a mission to kill."

Celeste sighed with relief. "Jolly good, Zoe."

"I wouldn't *'Jolly good, Zoe,'* me just yet," she mumbled. "We're definitely not out the coding woods."

Her fingers were flying across the keyboard, joined by Abraham who was providing crucial back up—doing something God only knew. And something Silas hoped God would use to offer one more Easter Vigil miracle for his people.

And quickly.

"Why don't we just shoot 'em down?" Gapinski asked. "Should make for easy target practice."

"And send high explosives raining down upon the basilica and the civilian Christians below?" Silas said.

He frowned. "You do have a point. Then what's the plan?"

"This..." Zoe said, pointing at her monitor.

"Did you break through?" Celeste said crouching toward the monitor.

"Way more than that. We've commandeered the buzzards, using a triangulated—"

"Got it, my dear. And bloody good work!"

She leaned back and pushed her glasses up her nose with pride, grinning at their accomplishment.

A flashing indicator light drew her face back toward her monitor.

"Uhh-oh..." Abraham said, leaning forward as well with a huff.

"What happened?" Celeste said.

"Someone's hacked my hack!" Zoe said with disbelief.

Silas ran his hand through his hair, anxiety over the loss of control over the situation beginning to grip him. His hand moved for his pocket, finger twitching for nicotine relief.

An explosion outside snapped him back to the moment.

The group collectively moved to one of the two windows of the large van facing the basilica.

Pluming orange light from the residual exploding drone cast down from above, and stoney debris rained down to the ground below.

But not St. Peter's Basilica.

Another of the pontificate properties was burning. The Palazzo Apostolico, if Silas placed it right.

Better than the basilica. But still not good.

"What the hell happened?" he demanded.

Zoe answered, "They're regaining control of the units, but only barely. We've got a tug-of-war on our hands here!"

More *clickity-clacking* of the keyboard sounded forth the truth of what she was saying.

Another explosion rocked the plaza, sending jolting vibrations through the van itself.

That was much closer!

They shifted to the other window to steal another glance outside.

This time the plaza itself was on fire.

A large hole several yards east toward the entrance to St. Peter's Square was belching smoke and soot, flaming fingers reaching high into the sky with malicious intent. Several bodies lay still around the ground of the blast site, others were limping away clutching maimed or missing limbs.

More martyrs of the faith added to the pile of the week's dead.

"Alright, we've got control again," Zoe said, trading a high-five victory with Abraham.

Which was short lived.

Frustrated moans returned again as the hackers on the other end of the drones wrested back control.

Zoe was right: it was a tug-of-war.

Good versus evil. SEPIO versus Nous.

And so far Nous had the edge.

"Wait a minute," Silas said, spinning from the window with an idea. "If you've got a lock on the signal, then you've got a lock on the *location* of that signal, right?"

"What are you thinking?" Celeste asked.

"What I'm thinking is, these drones don't have the same kind of reach as their military-grade older brothers. The controlling signal has a limited reach."

"Which means the blokes must be nearby..."

"And within striking distance. If we can locate them."

"And before they blow us all up to kingdom come," Gapinski added.

The two turned to him and frowned.

"What? It's true."

"Hold a second. I think I have something," Abraham said. His keyboard clacked away for several more seconds. "Got it! They're eight blocks east of here. By the looks of it, chilling along the Piazza Adrianna."

Silas knew right where that was, just outside Vatican City near the front door to Castle Sant'Angelo.

Score one for SEPIO!

He climbed through the van's compact space and up to the driver's seat. Gapinski followed him, squeezing into the co-pilot's seat as Silas took the controls.

"Hold on…"

Silas threw the van into gear and floored it, spinning it around the plaza toward the direction of the hostiles, tires squealing and Christian pilgrims screaming from the sudden act.

"Don't worry," Gapinski yelled out his window. "We're the good guys!"

He navigated around the hole still flaming hot, racing onto a vacant road that had been closed for the vigil. It was a blessedly clear path that gave Silas the ground he needed to make up precious seconds before—

Another explosion lit up the night, its flames reflecting off a building in the rear mirrors.

Dear God, let it not be the basilica…

"Zoe!"

"We're working on it!" she yelled.

"Please tell me that wasn't St. Peter's Basilica."

"Negatory. We've got GPS coordinates now on all of the drones. Just another of the pontificate buildings."

"All the drones?" Celeste said. "How many are left?"

"Eleven or twelve, by the looks of it."

"Eleven or twelve?" The SEPIO operatives said in unison.

"Jeez Louise, sister!" Gapinski said. "You weren't lying when you said we've got a war on our hands."

Silas threw the van into higher gear, pressing the accelerator and pushing the beast for its rendezvous with Nous.

Up ahead, the circular, second-century castle of brown brick rose into view. He hung a left to navigate around the star-shaped property lined with aged cypress and sycamore trees.

"We're here!" Silas shouted. "Now where the hell is that van?"

"Other side of the plaza," Abraham shouted back.

He sped underneath an ancient Roman aqueduct left behind from ages past and slung the van right around the first point of the star.

Nothing yet...

He sped through the vacant streets and rounded the highest point of the star-shaped grounds.

A white-panel delivery van sped from the other direction and slammed on its brakes as Silas rounded the bend, its horn screaming in protest as he sharply turned his wheel to avoid the collision.

"Apparently, someone didn't get the memo that the Church is under attack!" Gapinski shouted out his window.

The truck blared an angry curse again; Gapinski returned the favor.

Then all at once, there it was.

Black and paneled and burly, a small satellite on top indicating they had definitely found their target.

Bingo!

Silas floored it and shouted for everyone to brace themselves.

Three...two...one...

Impact.

The vans collided with a deafening, jarring crunch—the front windshield spider-webbing from the collision and the side windows shattering completely.

Nous's ride didn't fare much better. The back popped open upon impact. Two men fell overboard to the cobblestone road as the van bounced onward, the men rattling and shouting in pain underneath SEPIO's mobile command center continued its pursuit.

Nous's van slid into the intersection of three adjoining streets, getting smacked around by a rust-bucket Peugeot and a high-class Beamer, limping to a stop near the stairs of a courthouse.

Silas brought their van to a halt.

"You all OK?" Silas said, twisting back to assess the damage even as he felt blood on his own forehead.

"We're alive!" Celeste shouted.

"What about the drones?"

Zoe said, "We've got control again."

"For now," Abraham added. "There are some damn-fine coders in that van."

"Leave that to me..." Farhad growled.

Suddenly he was out the door, running toward the moored vehicle.

"No, wait!" Silas shouted.

He stumbled out of the truck and fell to the ground from disorientation. Gapinski did the same, landing hard with similar disorientation from the crash.

Farhad was already at the van by the time they recovered.

The two agents withdrew their handguns and slowly padded forward as the former Nousati operative yelled at the driver's side window, hands held high and waving wildly.

They couldn't understand all of what he said, but it sounded like he was pleading with them to stop the violent terror.

And for Isa's sake.

A single *pop* sliced through the deadened streets, just before Farhad's chest plumed in a spray of crimson—ending his plea and sending him recoiling backward to the pavement in a crumpled heap.

"No!" Gapinski screamed.

He hustled past Silas over to Farhad's fallen body, stooping down and cradling his head as he coughed up bouts of blood.

Silas quickly followed him, weapon raised and pointing at the man seated in the driver's seat.

Borg...

Farhad wasn't going to last much longer. Gapinski started whispering the Lord's Prayer, the coughing becoming less and the man's color draining fast.

Another believer in Christ martyred during the deadliest week of persecution in the Church's history.

"It's over, Borg!" Silas yelled.

The man was grinning, his mouth wide with polished white teeth and face framed by that wretched, greasy black hair. He held up both his hands, weapon swinging from a thumb.

"You bastard," Gapinski growled. "Why'd you shoot him?"

The window cracked slightly. The man shrugged. "He betrayed his brothers. Betrayed all that Nous had planned—for him, for the organization, for the Church. And then there was that matter of ultimate betrayal. The nonsense about him following that wretched Christ figure."

"He told you that?" Silas asked.

"His last words before I popped that pathetic, pleading look off the face of that weak-willed Judas," Borg sneered. "He had to go, simple as that. Although, I guess now he won't get his hands on those seventy virgins since he converted to Christianity. Poor thing..."

Silas narrowed his eyes and set his jaw tight. He gripped his weapon tighter.

"Out!" he yelled.

The man offered no reply, made no movement.

Then Borg pointed toward the sky with a hand shaped like a gun. He pressed his thumb forward like a trigger and started laughing, a shrill cackle that raised the hair on Silas's neck.

He tore his gaze from Borg and looked high and around.

And then he heard it.

That familiar whine, distant but closing in.

And fast.

"Gapinski! Take cover..."

The two men hustled toward a grouping of several parked cars along the road and dove for cover.

Just before the sky erupted in fire and fury a few stories above as a drone slammed into the high-rise, chunks of stone and twisted metal and flaming plastic falling with complete disregard for the human casualties below.

The two crawled farther under the vehicles as the chaos continued to fall.

Squealing tires brought them back out, the fallout settling and Borg's van making a hail Mary getaway.

"Like hell you are..." Silas said, standing and whipping out his Beretta.

Gapinski pushed himself off the pavement and joined him.

The agents opened fire on the fleeing vehicle, but it kept going.

A tire shredded under the assault, then another, but it continued its desperate retreat on sparking rims toward a bridge crossing the Tiber.

"Come on!" Silas yelled, ceasing fire and turning back toward their own vehicle.

The agents ran back to the van and climbed inside.

"How are we with the drones," he yelled behind him as he brought the beast back to life.

"We have command of all the drones, but they're still putting up a fight."

"Let's see if we can't bring this whole damn thing to an end."

He lurched their own van forward, which was faring better than the competition. But not by much.

It hissed a complaint and grumbled loudly as he pushed the accelerator, the Nous van dead ahead and crawling on all fours across the stone bridge.

Silas narrowed his eyes and clenched his jaw, then floored it —not giving two rats patooties what the beast thought about it all.

He came up on them fast. But instead of smacking them in the rear again, he veered slightly to the right before aiming for the right rear wheel. It was one of those classic alley-oops from COPS, that television show he had seen a bazillion times growing up as a kid when the police were trying to bring a high-speed chase to a dramatic halt.

He'd always wanted to give it a whirl. He was not a little thankful Nous had given him the opportunity.

The maneuver did the trick.

The Nous van moaned as it twirled before smacking into the bridge's stone side, sparks flying everywhere and nearly sending it overboard right then and there.

Apparently Borg and his lackeys inside didn't take a liking to the maneuver, either.

Their own van started sparking with bullets pinging off the metal sides and rear as they sped past.

Time to end this.

Just one more time...

Silas spun the wheel, the van banking left from the centripetal force of it all before they faced the final showdown. Like one of those OK Corral western moments when the Hero and the Villain face off with six-shooters, flexing their fingers like cowboy pros.

Except SEPIO held all the bullets.

He floored it, dead center mass before yanking the wheel again at just the right moment.

They slammed into the side of the beast with a deafening crunch.

Silas held firm, not letting go, shoving Nous's van riding on four sparking rims.

The van slammed into the wall again—this time crashing through the stone barrier and sailing overboard.

It plummeted face-first down into the icy spring waters of the Tiber and plunged into its depths with a fantastic splash.

Silas slid the van to a halt. He threw open his door and ran to the edge of the bridge. Gapinski followed, as did Celeste and Torres out the back.

They watched as the Roman river enveloped the van, sucking it down fast and disappearing it with nothing but a foamy residue marking its point of entry. A sudden release of bubbly air indicated complete success.

A shout of *woo-hoo* from Zoe and Abraham inside the van confirmed it.

Woo-hoo, indeed.

Within minutes the two had regained control over the remaining drones. This time it held, the equipment in the van completely fried and the Nousati hackers presumably dead.

And Borg?

The four SEPIO operatives held their positions along the bridge's edge a good ten minutes, silently scoping the dark waters below.

No movement, no bodies, no nothing—the length of the river and from bank to bank.

But there was no doubt they would see that greasy-haired menace again.

The sound of sudden gunfire erupting on the other side of the bridge drew their attention.

Then shouts of protest and return fire.

And the all too familiar Latin battlecry they had come to know and love.

The terrorists, chased by the Templars.

Time to end this.

CHAPTER 37

"Come on!" Silas urged, motioning for his fellow SEPIO operatives to follow as he ran toward the sound of melee across the Tiber.

Gapinski, Celeste, and Torres followed close behind.

No one else was visible in the darkened streets beyond a row of swaying trees anchoring the other side of the bridge. But the disturbance was echoing toward them, and it was growing.

A shout of protest and a clang of swords, then more gunfire confirmed the battle was drawing close.

Two men in desert fatigues, faces masked by black ran across the street dead ahead, disappearing past a nightclub that was completely oblivious to the drama unfolding outside their doors of alcohol- and drug-fueled dance.

"If that doesn't scream jihadi whack job, I don't know what does," Silas said.

"Don't look so tough without their swords and guns, now do they?" Gapinski added.

Two more men in the same getup ran into view, now less than a block away. They stopped and turned around, then opened fire back where they came.

"Guess I spoke too soon..."

The four SEPIO operatives slowed their pace on instinct, fanning to the edges of the bridge in caution and drawing their own weapons in response.

They continued padding forward in pairs—Silas and Gapinski on the right, Celeste and Torres on the left. Their weapons were outstretched and ready for business, but they hoped to bring the men to justice so they held off firing.

The weapon fire died suddenly. Both hostiles looked at their pistols, then they threw them to the side, apparently spent.

They went to take off running when Silas shouted, "On your knees!"

The men looked at each other, backing up and speaking rapidly. The operatives ran to apprehend them in the midst of their indecision before they could make a move.

Two terrorists brought to justice was better than none, Silas figured.

"Hands in the air, jihadi whack jobs," Gapinski commanded.

Celeste and Torres met them in the middle as the four crossed the bridge.

"On your knees!" Silas said again, holding his weapon forward with his one good arm and motioning for them to the ground with his still-aching one.

The two men continued jabbering away, but slowly started kneeling in surrender.

Silas sighed with relief, thankful—

A sudden crack echoed from the right and one of the men fell over.

The other man recoiled in fear at the sudden burst of gunfire, joining his comrade cowering on the cobblestone street who was screaming in pain.

The four SEPIO agents ran toward the men, pivoting to the

right in time to see a wave of white cresting toward them and yelling with bloodlust.

The Knights Templar. Men and women in white bearing swords and pistols with their remaining limbs and a burning passion for vengeance in their hardened hearts.

"Hold your fire!" Silas ordered, standing with his back to the terrorists and weapon trained on the monastic-military order rushing them in the dark.

"Back off, Templar Dudes and Dudettes!" Gapinski echoed, coming up fast to Silas's side.

Celeste and Torres were close behind, weapons drawn and pointing at their Templar brothers and sisters.

All in defense of two men who had helped persecute the Church and were lying on the street behind them, one with a gunshot wound in his leg and a shaky future.

The wave of white slowed to a sudden halt several yards from crashing into their intended targets, weapons of war still at the ready for instant use.

"Step aside!" Mukasa demanded.

He lowered his sword but strode toward the SEPIO operatives with vengeful purpose, his eight companions arrayed around him with swords and guns still drawn in agreement and crimson crosses announcing the righteousness of their intent.

He announced, "We are here to avenge our fallen brothers and sisters of the faith. This is none of your concern."

"Like hell you are..." Silas growled.

"Time for you folks to be on your merry way," Celeste added. "These men surrendered and are prisoners of the Order of Thaddeus. We're taking them in for proper justice."

The African man scoffed and spat to the side, then he began to raise his sword.

Which SEPIO didn't like one bit.

Each of the four chambered a round with intent and took a step forward.

This show of force seemed to give the man pause.

He lowered his weapon and tossed his head back with a chuckle.

"You people make me laugh. You and your Western Christendom privilege. You who can exercise your faith without a care in the world for any sort of consequence. You who have never tasted the bitter injustice of losing limb and life for claiming the name of Christ!"

"Which is the whole point, Templar Dude!" Gapinski said, waving his SIG Sauer around in exasperation.

The man recoiled at the outburst. "What are you saying, Westerner?"

"Umm, hello? You seem to forget Jesus calling each of us to follow him by bearing our crosses—however that might look. *'For those who want to save their life will lose it, and those who lose their life for my sake will find it.'* You didn't think he meant giving up smoking and the Beatles and *Game of Thrones*, now did you?"

Mukasa scowled and shook his head, saying nothing but searching for a reply.

"The Christian life is a cross-shaped life, my man," he continued. "Literally! Jesus expected all of us who declare our allegiance to him to be hated for it, even facing the very likely prospect of persecuting death, just as he faced. Yet Jesus calls us to follow him anyway. Even into death, and death by the same cross he himself bore. Which the earliest Christians literally faced for decades!"

"I will not let you lecture me, Westerner, on the merits of Christian discipleship when we and our families and friends face the prospect of terrifying, terrorizing persecution every day we still hold breath in our lungs! The Templars of old offered us a righteous example when they sought to right the injustices of those wicked, bloodthirsty radicals who terrorized Christian pilgrims and laid siege to Christian cities."

"Even at the end of a sword?" Torres asked.

"If need be, yes!"

"*Beloved, never avenge yourselves, but leave room for the wrath of God,*" Gapinski said, "*for it is written, "Vengeance is mine, I will repay, says the Lord." Do not be overcome by evil, but overcome evil with good.*"

"What in God's name are you—"

"That's Scripture, Templar Dude!" Gapinski interrupted. "My martyred grandpappy taught me that. Made me memorize it forward and backward. And there's no way in hot Hades that you're going to spit on that memory by doing what God himself forbids to these here jihadi whack jobs. Your eyes and hearts might be so blind that you can't see the truth of it, but God loves them. He died for them. So I'll say it again: Back off."

Mukasa huffed, tightening his grip and inching forward. "I'm warning—"

"*Bless those who persecute you; bless and do not curse them,*' Paul continues in Romans 12. Oh, and you gotta give the guy credit for having the balls to quote this crazy Jewish Proverb: '*if your enemies are hungry, feed them; if they are thirsty, give them something to drink; for by doing this you will heap burning coals on their heads.*'"

"I swear to you, I will slay you without a care and without mercy if you do not step aside!"

Gapinski threw his weapon to the ground and took a step forward, his face set as flint.

He stretched his arms out wide and smiled. "Then do it, Templar Dude."

The man recoiled in surprise, his face twisting with a mix of confusion and appall.

"You would lay down your life for these...these *locusts*?"

"You bet your sweet bippy!"

"*Why?!*"

"Because that's what Jesus himself did!" Gapinski shouted,

his voice ricocheting around the street with holy truth. "He died for these two men, as much as he died for you and me, bro. Think about the cross, dude. On either side of Jesus hung two criminals, who were basically insurrectionists. And the one man he invited into Paradise because he recognized the truth of who Jesus was! So if the Son of God could love a Roman terrorist, then why can't we love jihadi ones?"

The man paused and offered a chuckle, then continued, "And frankly, deep down I ain't no better than them, and you ain't either. Enemies of God, the whole lot of us, that is what we were until Jesus' crazy love reached into our lives and brought us into his family. That's what he did for me, for you, for Farhad—"

He looked down at the Muslim terrorists who had gone still behind him on the street, the one man losing blood and needing a doctor soon.

"Jesus laid down his life for them as well." He looked back up to Mukasa, and said, "It's also what Grandpappy would have done, lay down his life for one who would take his own life. So yeah, you'll have to shoot me yourself if you want at 'em."

Mukasa said nothing, did nothing.

Silas couldn't help but smile at the courage and conviction of his partner. He hoped it worked.

He joined him, and said, "Me too."

"And me," Torres offered, stepping next to Gapinski.

"Likewise," Celeste added, coming to Silas's side.

The African lowered his gaze to the men on the ground behind the SEPIO operatives, then slowly lowered his weapon.

His companions didn't, the Templars continuing to keep the SEPIO operatives in their sights even as they lowered their weapons.

"But what about my daughter..." he said softly, his lips trembling with the revelation he voiced to Celeste and Torres. "What about her?"

Gapinski glanced at the ladies standing on either side.

Celeste offered, "We understand your need to avenge your daughter's death at the hands of the wicked. But the Lord assures us he will deal a final blow of justice in the end. Repaying with affliction those who afflict us is his job, not ours."

The African man closed his eyes and sighed, head dipping and eyes beginning to leak, as if the weight of his vengeance, and his failure at exacting it, had become too much to bear.

A silent stalemate grew between the two forces, each side waiting for the other to make a move.

"This isn't over, Westerners," Mukasa finally spat, raising his head and taking angry, plodding steps backward with narrowed eyes, his companions matching his indignation step for step.

Then the man spun around; so did the others. And they fled through the streets back the way they came.

Silas stepped forward; his three companions followed, Gapinski dragging both jihadi hostiles along with him by their collars.

They watched them slip around a corner down an abandoned street, sirens and lights screaming toward them from behind. Apparently the Swiss Guards decided all the hubbub was now worth their time and attention.

Gapinski said, "What are the chances that our zombie superhero dudes and dudettes sporting those thermal whitey tighties emblazoned with a red cross on the front like the Church's ill-forgotten guardians of yore will make a come back anytime soon."

Silas paused a beat, contemplating the craziness of it all—the week's events, the fact of the Templars rising to new life.

He put his hands on his hips and grunted a sigh. "I'd say better than Vegas odds."

His partner shook his head. "That's what I was afraid of."

"Always something," Torres huffed.

Celeste threw her a glance, stifling a smile. "Come on. We best get back to Zoe and Abraham before the authorities think they themselves were the jihadi whack jobs."

"What a day," Silas complained as they hobbled toward the show of lights swarming their van.

"Yeah, but just wait until tomorrow," Gapinski encouraged.

"Why?"

"Because it's Easter, man! Which means Jesus lives. And because he lives, I can face tomorrow. No matter what." He paused, then added: "Even knowing Grandpappy is dead in this life, because I know he lives with Christ in the next."

Couldn't argue with that; the man had a point.

Because Jesus lives, life is worth living.

Even when that means staring down a gun's barrel or a sword's blade for our faithful allegiance to him as Lord and Savior.

CHAPTER 38

VATICAN CITY. EASTER SUNDAY.

"Christ has risen," His Holiness bellowed from the balcony overlooking *Piazza San Pietro*, lifting his arms as if asking for a reply.

"Christ has risen, indeed!" his audience of parishioners down below bellowed back, echoing the affirmation the Church has been confessing for millennia.

St. Peter's Square was filled to the brim with 80,000 Christian pilgrims from around the world who had made the defiant trek in the face of global Christian persecution to celebrate Mass on the day climaxing the Church calendar: the resurrection of Jesus Christ, Easter Sunday.

"Indeed, he is. Jesus has risen from the dead. And this is not a fantasy," the Pope continued. "And the fact of it was one of the reasons why the Church flourished so, given the monumental violence waged against her despite Christianity's unwavering belief that the man from Nazareth had not only died for the sins for the world, the Lamb of God, slaughtered to pay our price in our place, as John the Baptist called him. But had also come back from the dead to new life, paving the way for our own eternal life.

"Because if it was a fantasy and not a fact, then why die for a lie? Why would early Christians pay the ultimate price of being boiled in vats of oil, or being subjugated to the same death-by-crucifixion as our Lord, or being torn asunder by man and beast in the amphitheaters of Rome? The persecution of the Church, and the Church's *willingness* to be persecuted, makes no sense unless the good news she preaches is the truth.

"And the truth of the matter is that humanity is gravely ill, perpetuating the most atrocious of deeds. We need a heart transplant, one that only a surgeon of the highest caliber could orchestrate, the Creator of that heart himself. And that is what we believe, we who have gathered here today in defiance of terrorizing persecution. As the foundational creed of our faith professes:

> *I believe in one Lord Jesus Christ, the Only Begotten*
> *   Son of God,*
> *born of the Father before all ages.*
> *God from God, Light from Light, true God from*
> *   true God,*
> *begotten, not made, consubstantial with the Father;*
> *through him all things were made.*
> *For us men and for our salvation he came down from*
> *   heaven,*
> *and by the Holy Spirit was incarnate of the Virgin*
> *   Mary, and became man.*
> *For our sake he was crucified under Pontius Pilate,*
> *he suffered death and was buried,*
> *and rose again on the third day in accordance with*
> *   the Scriptures.*
> *He ascended into heaven and is seated at the right*
> *   hand of the Father.*
> *He will come again in glory to judge the living and*
> *   the dead*
> *and his kingdom will have no end.*

"Amen," His Holiness voiced after reciting part of the Nicene Creed.

Silas considered the history surrounding that creed, and all of the men who showed up at Nicaea in AD 325 at the First Council. Contrary to what Western detractors would like people to think, Christianity was not written by dead white guys. Rather, it was forged in the blood of Africans, Palestinians, and Asians from the center of the Roman Empire. And much of them came to that first council bearing all the marks of Roman persecution, missing eyes and limbs—all in order to faithfully obey the Word of God's instructions to the Church outlined in Saint Jude Thaddeus's exhortation in his letter to early Christians:

'contend for the faith that was once for all entrusted to the saints.'

Contend for, preserve, protect, guard what followers of Jesus Christ have always believed.

That was the central mission of the Order of Thaddeus as well. One Silas himself had devoted his life to living out. And he was beyond thankful the Order had invited him to help execute that mission. Especially with the people standing beside him in the Square of St. Peter.

Gapinski and Torres, Zoe and Abraham.

And Celeste.

He only wished that Farhad could have been standing next to them, arm in arm as new siblings in the family of Christ, experiencing his first encounter with the memory markers of Christ's broken Body and shed Blood as a Christian brother—rather than on the other side as a Christian persecutor.

The Pope continued, "It is the mystery of the thrown-away stone, that ends up being the cornerstone of our existence. Christ has risen from the dead. In this throwaway culture, where that which is not useful takes the path of the use-and-throw, where that which is not useful is discarded, Jesus Christ, that stone that was discarded, is the fountain of life."

"And even us, little pebbles," he continued, "who have been thrown into an Earth full of suffering and tragedy, into a world of hateful persecution and the threat of terror for our allegiance to the King of Kings and Lord of Lords, with faith in the risen Christ each of us have a reason for being amidst so much calamity and persecution. We have no need to look around us at the darkness, but only need to look beyond toward the light of Christ. For there is not a wall of wickedness, but a horizon of hope for those who are in him."

As far as Catholic homilies go, Silas thought the Pope was bringing it. His childhood priest, Father Rafferty, from his hometown in Falls Church, Virginia, had a golden tongue himself. Although, young Silas was too busy throwing spit wads during Mass to have paid much attention or received its benefits. It was his brother who had been the more spiritually sensitive and interested one of the Grey twin boys.

Oh, Sebastian...Where are you? What are you doing?

He clenched his fist at the thought of all that his twin had done to betray him the last year.

All that he had done to betray his faith, the one he himself had once been so utterly devoted to as a young man.

But Silas knew at one level it made entire sense, given how the stewards of that faith had abandoned him through years of abuse. Another statistic in the litany of names and faces that had been victims of the Church's ever-increasing list from across the Christian spectrum—from Catholic to Southern Baptist.

Then of course there was the man who had groomed his brother to join the ranks of the Church's archenemy.

Rudolph Borg.

The SEPIO operatives had all witnessed the van with him driving it plunge into the dark, icy waters of the Tiber, sinking fast and with completion to the bottom. Yet he couldn't trust his eyes; he needed proof.

SEPIO agents later confirmed what his gut had told him: there wasn't a body to be found inside when divers searched it in the dawning hours.

Borg apparently lived on, and so did Nous.

Which meant that the Order's mission to surround the Church—her faith and the memory of her faith—with a protective hedge was more vital than ever, given the violent stakes the week proved.

"Today the Church continues to say, '*Stop, Jesus is risen!*'" the Pope continued. "And because he lives, you can face tomorrow. You, little pebble, have a reason in life. Because you're a pebble holding on to the cornerstone, the Chief Cornerstone of Christ —that stone that wickedness had discarded but the Father raised to new life is your sure footing."

A few of the bystanders packed into St. Peter's Square offered hearty *Amens!* of agreement.

"What does the Church say amidst so much tragedy, amidst the terrorizing violence of the past week and the ongoing persecution of Christ's little lambs around the world? The Church says the stone that was discarded, much like the little stones of God's adoptive children, truly wasn't! From within her heart, the Church says Jesus is risen! And so will we, one day, in the twinkling of an eye be changed into the likeness of our Savior, bodily raised to new life and fully restored. And that means the eyes and arms, the legs and, yes, even heads of those maimed and slain for the faith will be restored, as well. That is their hope, and it is our hope, we who have stood face to face with terrorizing persecution this Holy Week."

Silas cringed slightly inside at that bald-faced honesty of His Holiness's words referencing the gory reality of Christian persecution. But he also appreciated it, confronting the truth of it in all its vividness.

He also thought about the Templars, the men and women from Africa and Arabia and Asia who had themselves lost eyes and limbs for their faith, only to escape and seek to avenge and protect their fellow brothers and sisters—to seek justice for those who've suffered at the hands of a great evil menace. He wondered what had happened to them, where they had run off to.

And whether they would resurface again.

Radcliffe said they would continue to search known locales and tap SEPIO intelligence operatives in the field for a read on the Templar's whereabouts, but Silas figured they would come up empty handed.

He did not, however, believe it would be the last the Order or the Church would hear from them. In their minds, their cause was too righteous, their mission too relevant to fade back into the memory of history.

No, the Templars seemed to have risen back for good.

Which could make life interesting for SEPIO in the coming months and years.

Thankfully the other part of their mission had found surer resolution: the terrorizing persecution of the Church.

Farhad had provided vital counterintelligence in his debrief before the group huddle in the Rome operations center, which SEPIO used to coordinate with national intelligence and law enforcement services across the Western and majority world to halt the terror. Between that disruption and Borg back on the run, the partnership between Nous and ISIS had dissolved and the persecution that had burned white hot across the Church had been doused.

Yes, the world was back to normal. At least for now.

His Holiness ended his homily with the words of Paul in his second letter to the Church of Thessalonica, another group of Christians who had been hard pressed under the weight of State-sponsored persecution. He read:

For it is indeed just of God to repay with affliction those who afflict you, and to give relief to the afflicted as well as to us, when the Lord Jesus is revealed from heaven with his mighty angels in flaming fire, inflicting vengeance on those who do not know God and on those who do not obey the gospel of our Lord Jesus....To this end we always pray for you, asking that our God will make you worthy of his call and will fulfill by his power every good resolve and work of faith, so that the name of our Lord Jesus may be glorified in you, and you in him, according to the grace of our God and the Lord Jesus Christ.

"These words of Paul remind us that one day the persecutor will receive his just rewards. But it equally reminds us to continue living our life of faith in faithful devotion to our Savior and allegiance to him as Lord. For one day he will come again to resurrect his saints and call them to himself."

Then he added with a shout: "Christ is risen!"

Everyone shouted back: "Christ is risen, indeed!"

"Let us pray."

When they did, Celeste grabbed his hand.

Silas caught his breath and allowed himself a smile, feeling the gesture was bold but all at once right.

After he was finished, thanking Christ for his sacrifice and praying for the persecuted, the Pope ended with an "Amen." The gathered Church echoed him.

Silas leaned over and whispered in her ear, "That was nice."

Celeste whispered back, "Which part?"

"All of it." Then he held up their still-holding hands, and added, "But especially this."

"Seemed appropriate, given the circumstances of the week."

"Yeah, but it's more than that."

She turned toward him as the Pope continued his priestly duties. "Do tell, Dr. Grey."

He took a breath and grinned boyishly. "I know I've been a jerk about us and our status and all the past few months. Being all coy about it and noncommittal. And taking you out to dinner one day, then playing like we're just friends the next."

Silas was reddening, his tongue feeling like it was stumbling over itself.

Not at all what he had planned for in the middle of Easter Mass in St. Peter's Square!

Celeste tilted her head slightly, her lips playing with a smile that signaled amusement. "Why, Dr. Grey, are we having our first DTR?"

Silas felt his face flush. "I guess we are, Ms. Bourne. So what do you say? Shall we…" He cleared his throat, feeling himself redden even more. Then he took a breath and stiffened, and said, "Let's date. Just you and me."

"Like boyfriend and girlfriend?"

Now he tilted his head and smiled himself. "Yes, like boyfriend and girlfriend."

"I do believe I fancy the sound of that."

She smiled and slipped her arm inside his as the Pope began his remarks to consecrate the elements that would provoke the believers gathered together to remember the sacrifice their Lord and Savior offered for them, for the world. Nourishing their faith, solidifying their faith, provoking faith in and through Christ's broken Body and shed Blood.

There they were, two agents of the Church sent to help preserve and contend for that faith, to surround its memory with a hedge of protection. And they would be doing it together, side-by-side.

Just as Silas wanted it to be.

ENJOY TEMPLARS RISING?

A big thanks for joining Silas Grey and the rest of SEPIO on their adventure saving the Church!

Enjoy the story? Here's what you can do next:

If you loved the book and have a moment to spare, **a short review is much appreciated.** Nothing fancy, just your honest take. Spreading the word is probably the #1 way you can help independent authors like me and help others enjoy the story.

If you're ready for another adventure, you can get a full-length novel in the series for free! All you have to do is join the insider's group to be notified of specials and new releases by going to this link:
www.jabouma.com/free

AUTHOR'S NOTE
THE HISTORY BEHIND THE STORY

Like many, a few years ago I was horrified to see images of men in orange jumpsuits kneeling in the hot sands of Libya awaiting their execution by black-masked Islamic jihadis. These graphic images of the mass beheadings of twenty-one men in a video ISIS released and paraded online stirred within me deep questions about my own commitment to Christ, even unto death. It also forced me to consider what it means to take Jesus' words seriously to not only consider such persecution a blessing, but to love our enemies, blessing and praying for those who curse us.

So I thought it would be interesting to explore these themes in a griping thriller that takes an honest, frank look at the situation facing Christian brothers and sisters throughout the majority world on a daily basis. As in all of my books, this one is more than a story about "some zombie superhero dudes (and dudettes) sporting thermal whitey tighties emblazoned with a red cross on the front like the Church's ill-forgotten guardians of yore," as Gapinski so eloquently put it, rising from the shadows of history once again to avenge and protect the Church, and all of their remarkable history. It's a story of faith and persecution, vengeance and martyrdom for believers and non-believers alike about the nature of faith and ones unashamed commitment to it—even unto death.

As with all of my books, I like to add a note at the end with some of the thoughts and research that went into the story. So, if you care to learn more about the foundation of this episode in the Order of Thaddeus, here is some of what I discovered that made its way into SEPIO's latest adventure.

The Rise and Fall of the Templars

Although this book is at its heart about the persecuted Church, it is equally about an unlikely group of monastic warriors who rose to life amidst similar persecution at the hands of Muslim hordes during a tenuous period of Church history known as the Crusades. Popularly, they were the Knights Templar, or simply the Templars, but their full designation is instructive: The Poor Fellow-Soldiers of Christ and of the Temple of Solomon.

The Templars were indeed a monastic order first and foremost, as Radcliffe corrected Celeste in chapter 8, although there was certainly a militancy about them and their core mission given they were the product of the Crusades and they were called to '*the defense of Jerusalem and the protection of pilgrims,*' in the words of their charter. But everything about their dress and order of life, their vows and conduct was chiefly monastic, not military as with the knighthood of the day.

But who were the Templars exactly, this band of monastic warriors who rose and fell in such a dramatic fashion over a storied three centuries? Perhaps Dan Jones frames the question best in his book *The Templars:*

It is sometimes hard to tell. Featured in numerous works of fiction, television shows and films, the Templars have been presented variously as heroes, martyrs, thugs, bullies, victims, criminals, perverts, heretics, depraved subversives, guardians of the Holy Grail, protectors of Christ's secret bloodline and time-traveling agents of global conspiracy. Within the field of "popular" history, a cottage industry exists in exposing "the mysteries of the Templars"—suggesting their role in some timeless plot to conceal Christianity's dirty secrets and hinting that the medieval order is still out there, manipulating the world from the shadows. Occasionally this is very entertaining. None of it has very much to do with the Templars themselves. (2-3)

He's right, which is why I abandoned Hollywood-style Templar conspiracies for the remarkable historical truth behind the ancient religious order—which Radcliffe basically retells in chapters 8 and 11, and Celeste and Torres research in chapters 13 and 22. The Easter massacre at the Jordan River 900 years ago to the date by Muslims stationed in two surrounding cities is historically accurate, and it was in many ways the straw that broke the camel's back in the formation of what became the Templars at the end of the year. I thought reenacting it as a way to open the main storyline with Grandpappy Gapinski was a perfect way to frame the historical and modern-day reality of Christian persecution and terror—for the modern-day manifestation was resurrected for the same reason the original one was formed: in response to violent persecution and in protection of defenseless Christians.

For centuries, the Muslim hordes had waged a brutal religious-political war of colonialist occupation and forced conversion throughout the Middle East, stretching through North Africa and Central Asia, and marching through the Iberian Peninsula and Ottoman Empire on toward Europe. Although there has been tremendous historical revisionism and mistruths about it all since September 2001, this is the history of Muslim occupation of former supermajority Christian lands. In many ways, the reason why Christianity became a so-called European religion is because two-thirds of the Church was decimated at the hand of militant Muslims by the First Crusade. So the idea those early wars launched by European nations and spurred by the sermon of Pope Urban II recounted in chapter 10 were entirely defensive is far closer to the mark than the prevailing modern notion they were seeking colonialist expansion, looting, and religious conversion. A splendid book on the subject is Rodney Stark's *God's Battalions*.

However, this isn't a book on the Crusades but one aspect of that era, the Templars—including what may have become of them. The prologue is a fictionalization of the historical account given by one priest named Ludolph of Sudheim. When I read about it in Jones's and Michael Haag's *The Templars* books, I thought it was the perfect opening that could offer a plausible "remnant" who survived the fall of Acre, arguably the beginning of the end of the Templars, along with the subsequent arrests and trials of the brotherhood by King Philip IV (which I referenced in *Holy Shroud*). Apparently, the two remnant Templars were repatriated to their homelands of Burgundy and Toulouse, and were allowed to live out the remainder of their lives with their families. The story ends there, but I took it a step further by suggesting they carried the mission and calling of the original Templars to the Order of Christ, one of several iterations of the monastic order that lived on—a connection that was a creation of my own, but I thought plausible; why couldn't they have been biding their time in wait, readying to show themselves once more when the time was right?

Such as during another time when the persecution of the

Church raged hot across the globe, ravaging not only the West but especially the majority world.

Ancient and Modern Martyrs of the Church

Yes, this book is about the Templars, rising from the shadows of history to once again heed the call of defending the cities of God and believers in Christ. It's also about the unreported headlines chronicling the horrifying persecution of the worldwide Church that has been raging in recent years—yes, mostly by militant Muslims. There has been a sharp rise in persecution throughout Africa, Arabia, and Asia—which is why I chose the Templars to be representative of those regions, instead of Europe like one might have expected. Because as Mukasa says: "Persecution in the West isn't persecution. It's an inconvenience." It is far different across the non-Western world for people who claim allegiance to Jesus Christ, and refuse to recant and voice the *shahada*, the central creed of Islam.

A spokesperson for an international persecution watch group described a potent cocktail ravaging the worldwide Church: the militant Islam in Nigeria; the statism of China's communism; the militant Hinduism in India; the North Korean combination of communism and emperor worship. In all of these countries and more, intolerance toward Christian worship and even personal confession has ratcheted up remarkably, played out in violence and oppression. The report of jihadi militants in Nigeria slaughtering 120 Christians and reports in India pegging an increase of persecution at 57 percent both reflect recent news reports. And the pleading from the archbishop of Canterbury is also accurate: Christian communities that were the foundation of the universal Church now face the threat of "imminent extinction." I understand some readers may not have appreciated the level of violence I chose to incorporate in the story, but I felt it important to capture the depth of what actual men, women, and children have endured and are enduring for the name of Christ. The two live-stream video beheadings and executions in the story reflect real ones that were posted to the Internet in recent years—including most of Farhad's monologue in each of them, which I borrowed from an actual transcript of one ISIS video posted in 2015.

Each of the nine Templars Celeste and Torres meet in chapter 30 are fictionalizations of real martyrs of the faith from their given homelands. It bears repeating their names for the sake of their martyr memory:

Wang Yi, China
Andrew Kim Taegon, Korea
Yu Cidu, Korea
Abednego Solomon, Nigeria
Mukasa Kiriwawanvu, Uganda
Gonzaga Gonza, Uganda
Malak Abram (Sinweet), Egypt
Sufia, Somalia
Esther, Pakistan

The causes of persecution and martyrdom over the last two millennia are varied. Early, it was the Roman Empire that brought the sword down upon the necks of brothers and sisters in the faith. All of the history and quotations from Rudolph Borg in chapter 33 are accurate and describe the early decades of the Church. It is safe to say the birth and growth and flourishing of the Church was a miraculous intervention of the Spirit of God. It still is, for as Tertullian said: *"The blood of the martyrs is the seed of the Church."*

During the decades leading up to the Crusades beginning in the seventh century, Muhammad and the Caliph generals led battalions of Arabs out of the Arabian Peninsula and on toward Europe, slaughtering, raping and ravaging, and enslaving the Church along the way. The uncomfortable truth Silas outlines in chapter 32 is accurate as far as the Quran teaches. And although more secular-minded Islamic teachers have moderated the hard edges of jihad, the late Nabeel Qureshi who converted from Islam to Christianity states the reality plainly:

> "violent and offensive jihad is commanded in the Quran and we find corroborating traditions in the life of Muhammad. The foundations of Islam command Muslims to engage in holy war, offering them salvation if they die while fighting. It took Muslims 1,300 years to depart from the foundations of Islam so radically as to insist that Islam is a religion of peace." (*Answering Jihad*, 137)

Let me be clear: not all Muslims are "jihadi whack jobs" as I sought to frame those who were terrorizing the Church in my fictional story. Not at all! Most live good, quiet lives who want what everyone else wants: the freedoms to live and raise a family and find meaningful work, and live in devotion to their god. And yes, Christianity certainly has its own violence to answer for, from aspects of the Crusades to the Inquisition to the witch trials. But as Qureshi also writes, "I am thankful it took a millennium for Christians to distort Jesus' teachings to support holy war....Jesus did not commission any concept of holy war, and it took Christians a thousand years to depart from the foundations of Christianity radically enough to engage in it."

However, thousands of believers are now being murdered, raped, and enslaved across Africa and the Middle East and parts of Asia by militant Muslims, whether so-called radical jihadis or not. That's in addition to state-sponsored terrorism in such countries as China and North Korea. And that's the story I hoped to confront in this one. Last year, Church leaders in Nigeria reported that Christians were experiencing "pure genocide" as 6,000 mostly women and children were slaughtered—believers in Jesus who were deliberately targeted for their faith. Recent reports out of China show a crackdown by the Communist government on churches and pastors, burning buildings and imprisoning believers under harsh conditions for their faith. The same is going on all across the world.

The story Mukasa recounts of his daughter in chapter 31 actually reflects an ancient one by a Christian martyr, Perpetua, a twenty-two-year-old mother who was put to death in AD 203 along with others in the Roman province of Carthage in Africa with exterminating brutality for their faithful witness to Jesus. I thought the story would provide an important motivation for why the African from Guinea would want to see the Templars rise again—because who wouldn't want to avenge their daughter's death? I also hope I captured that visceral impulse in the drama that unfolded around Grandpappy Gapinski as well, who I referenced in *Hidden Covenant* and *Grail of Power*. Of course, Mukasa and Gapinski each offered two different responses to Christian persecution.

Which leads to an all-important question...

How Should Christians Respond to Persecution?

There is no easy answer to this question, and I hope you felt the tension in this story between the Westerners and non-Westerners who have endured radical hostility to their faith, even bearing the scars and burdens of that witness still in their bodies with missing eyes and limbs—not to mention missing loved ones who were killed or enslaved.

The history behind the Templars is true: they were formed to protect the innocent from murderous violence. Yes, they bore the sword to defend Christian pilgrims from attack, but one could make the case their cause was just. Much of the foundation to just war doctrine theorized by the early Church fathers Augustine and Ambrose that led to the Crusades is biblical and theologically defendable; Christians still use it to argue the same justice with regards to war.

And yet, all of the biblical quotations from Jesus and Paul voiced by Celeste, Torres, and Gapinski state the obvious: violence and vengeance have no place in the Christian life. Even in the face of violent persecution.

As a Westerner, this is easy for me to write; I face zero violence for my faith in Jesus. And living in one of the most Christian pockets of the world, Grand Rapids, Michigan, America, I don't even face non-violent persecution for my faith, the sort mocked by the majority-world Templars. I'm certainly conflicted when it comes to questions of pacifism and just war, but I can't shake the example Jesus Christ himself gave us on the cross, dying the death he died in all of its pornographic violence for not only you and me, but also those who nailed him to the cross. He didn't utter a word of rebuke, he didn't strike back, and the Gospels record him saying that he could have appealed to his Father to dispatch legions of angels to fight for him, but he didn't. Instead he came to serve those who persecuted him, die for them, and ultimately love them through his sacrifice.

This example combined with Jesus' non-violent teachings, especially those concerning persecution—to love and pray for our persecutors, to self-sacrificially serve them—seems to leave little doubt as to the kind of response he would want me to have if I were ever to stare down the barrel of a gun or the blade of a sword.

Besides, avenging those martyred for their faith would leave little opportunity for the persecutor to become what Marwan Farhad himself became: a brother in Christ. This story reflects actual stories coming out of the Middle East of ISIS fighters having visions and dreams of Isa, Jesus Christ, and then repenting of their sinful violence and coming to faith in him as his follower. In fact, one recent account tells the story of a so-called "Prince of ISIS" coming to faith in Christ through the kind of ecstatic vision I told in chapters 16 and 21. Astute observers will note the similarities between some of the elements in chapter 21 as Isaiah 6 and Revelation 4, but I hope it created a meaningful encounter for Farhad, and you.

In chapter 11, Radcliffe notes that early in the life of the church pagans came to the Christian faith in droves as the result of Christians being flayed alive and covered with salt, slowly roasted over open spits normally kept for fattened hogs, fed to lions and bears only to be sliced to ribbons and mauled to death. They were dumbfounded that people would willingly go to their death rather than simply recant their beliefs to save their life. Pliny the Younger's observation of Christians' "stubbornness and unshakable obstinacy" from "a great many individuals of every age and class, both men and women" speaks the truth of their diverse resolve. So does Ignatius of Antioch, who wrote: "I am truly earnest about dying for God...pray leave me to be a meal for the beasts, for it is they who can provide my way to God. I am His wheat, ground fine by the lions' teeth to be made purest bread for Christ." It was this unwavering, public allegiance to Christ that truly was the seedbed of the early Church blossoming in all of its fullness, as Tertullian insisted; it still is.

May our own unfailing, faithful witness to Jesus Christ as singular King of Kings, Lord of Lords, and Savior of the world draw untold men and women into the loving arms of God amidst the rising tide of terrorizing, exterminating persecution —whether in the Western or majority world.

Research is an important part of my process for creating compelling stories that entertain, inform, and inspire. Here are a few resources I used to research the history behind the Templars:

- Barber, Malcom. *The New Knighthood: A History of the Order of the Temple*. NY: Cambridge University Press. Prologue story. www.bouma.us/templars1
- Hagg, Michael. *The Templars: The History and the Myth*. New York: HarperCollins, 2009. www.bouma.us/templars2
- Jones, Dan. *The Templars: The Rise and Spectacular Fall of God's Holy Warriors*. New York: Viking, 2017. www.bouma.us/templars3
- Stark, Rodney. *God's Battalions*. New York: HarperOne, 2009. www.bouma.us/templars4
- ————— . *The Triumph of Christianity*. New York: HarperOne, 2011. www.bouma.us/templars5

GET YOUR FREE THRILLER

Building a relationship with my readers is one of my all-time favorite joys of writing! Once in a while I like to send out a newsletter with giveaways, free stories, pre-release content, updates on new books, and other bits on my stories.

Join my insider's group for updates, giveaways, and your free novel—a full-length action-adventure story in my *Order of Thaddeus* thriller series. Just tell me where to send it.

Follow this link to subscribe:
www.jabouma.com/free

ALSO BY J. A. BOUMA

Nobody should have to read bad religious fiction—whether it's cheesy plots with pat answers or misrepresentations of the Christian faith and the Bible. So J. A. Bouma tells compelling, propulsive stories that thrill as much as inspire, offering a dose of insight along the way.

Order of Thaddeus Action-Adventure Thriller Series

Holy Shroud • Book 1

The Thirteenth Apostle • Book 2

Hidden Covenant • Book 3

American God • Book 4

Grail of Power • Book 5

Templars Rising • Book 6

Rite of Darkness • Book 7

Gospel Zero • Book 8

The Emperor's Code • Book 9

Deadly Hope • Book 10

Fallen Ones • Book 11

Silas Grey Collection 1 (Books 1-3)

Silas Grey Collection 2 (Books 4-6)

Silas Grey Collection 3 (Books 7-9)

Backstories: Short Story Collection 1

Martyrs Bones: Short Story Collection 2

Group X Cases **Supernatural Suspense Series**

Not of This World • Book 1

The Darkest Valley • Book 2

Deliver Us from Evil • Book 3

Ichthus Chronicles **Sci-Fi Apocalyptic Series**

Apostasy Rising / Season 1, Episode 1

Apostasy Rising / Season 1, Episode 2

Apostasy Rising / Season 1, Episode 3

Apostasy Rising / Season 1, Episode 4

Apostasy Rising / Full Season 1 (Episodes 1 to 4)

Apocalypse Rising / Season 2, Episode 1

Apocalypse Rising / Season 2, Episode 2

Apocalypse Rising / Season 2, Episode 3

Apocalypse Rising / Season 2, Episode 4

Apocalypse Rising / Full Season 2 (Episodes 1 to 4)

Faith Reimagined **Spiritual Coming-of-Age Series**

A Reimagined Faith • Book 1

A Rediscovered Faith • Book 2

Mill Creek Junction **Short Story Series**

The New Normal • Collection 1

My Name's Johnny Pope • Collection 2

Joy to the Junction! • Collection 3

The Ties that Bind Us • Collection 4

A Matter of Justice • Collection 5

Get all the latest short stories at: www.millcreekjunction.com

Find all of my latest book releases at: www.jabouma.com

ABOUT THE AUTHOR

J. A. Bouma believes nobody should have to read bad religious fiction—whether it's cheesy plots with pat answers or misrepresentations of the Christian faith and the Bible. So he wants to do something about it by telling compelling, propulsive stories that thrill as much as inspire, while offering a dose of insight along the way.

As a former congressional staffer and pastor, and best-selling author of over thirty religious fiction and nonfiction books, he blends a love for ideas and adventure, exploration and discovery, thrill and thought. With graduate degrees in Christian thought and the Bible, and armed with a voracious appetite for most mainstream genres, he tells stories you'll read with abandon and recommend with pride -- exploring the tension of faith and doubt, spirituality and culture, belief and practice, and the gritty drama that is our pilgrim story.

When not putting fingers to keyboard, he loves vintage jazz vinyl, a glass of Malbec, and an epic read -- preferably together. He lives in Grand Rapids with his wife, two kiddos, and rambunctious boxer-pug-terrier.

www.jabouma.com • jeremy@jabouma.com

facebook.com/jaboumabooks
twitter.com/bouma
amazon.com/author/jabouma

Printed in Great Britain
by Amazon

83503681R00231